MW01132946

VERACITY

Douglas E. Richards

Paragon Press

This book is a work of fiction. The characters, incidents, and dialogues are products of the author's imagination and are not to be construed as real. Any resemblance to actual events or persons, living or dead, is entirely coincidental.

Copyright © 2019 by Douglas E. Richards
Published by Paragon Press, 2019

Email the author at douglaserichards1@gmail.com

Friend him on Facebook at Douglas E. Richards Author

Visit the author's website at www.douglaserichards.com

All rights reserved. With the exception of excerpts for review purposes, no part of this book may be reproduced or transmitted in any form or by any means, electronic or mechanical, including photocopying, recording, or by any information storage and retrieval system.

First Edition

PART 1

Veracity (noun)

<u>Synonyms</u>: truth, honesty, integrity, trustworthiness, reliability.

1. Conformity to Facts; Accuracy. "Officials expressed doubts concerning the veracity of the story."
2. Habitual Truthfulness. "Voters should be concerned about his veracity and character."

1

Jared Sprouse was smart, ruthless, and ethically challenged.

Combine these traits with innate athleticism, the best military training Delta Force could provide, and more than a decade of becoming so acclimated to violence and death in hellholes around the world that civilian life bored him out of his mind, and you ended up with the perfect soldier of fortune.

After he left the military, Captain Sprouse had quickly signed on with one of the many Private Military Corporations, or PMCs, that were quietly coming to dominate operations in conflict zones and reconstruction environments in scores of war-torn countries. As the name implied, PMCs were nothing more than private armies, collections of seasoned ex-soldiers who provided security, protection, and armed combat to the highest bidders.

While these companies referred to their people as "contractors," they were mercenaries, plain and simple. And while they worked for both private citizens and major corporations, their number one client, by far, was the US military itself.

Remarkably, although the occasional scandal did pop up and put these PMCs in the news, they did a brilliant job of flying under the radar, of existing in plain sight but not attracting the media coverage one might expect of vast private armies headquartered in major cities throughout America.

Sprouse was as effective as they came, but three years earlier, when he had developed a reputation for being a bit too loose with ethics, he had eventually been fired and blackballed from the PMC community.

He remained unemployed for just over a month.

And then he got a call from Darth Vader.

The caller didn't introduce himself this way, of course. The man had arranged for a one-way holographic video call, where he could see Sprouse, but Sprouse couldn't see him, and introduced himself only as *Jake.*

But he had insisted on speaking into a microphone, into an electronic voice changer, so that his words came out in the exact dulcet tones of James Earl Jones, the voice of the original Darth Vader. Since the man continued using this voice changer for every call, Sprouse and his colleagues couldn't help but call him Vader behind his back.

Sprouse had access to the services of some of the best electronics and communications experts on the planet, but Vader's calls were untraceable, showing an impressive level of sophistication. For all Sprouse knew, the man was calling from a Death Star parked somewhere beyond the orbit of Mars. But absent any advanced *Star Wars* communication technology, the lack of any time lag in the conversation made it clear that the call was coming from the continental United States.

This Jake/Vader had proceeded to probe the limits of Sprouse's ethical and moral standards over several one-way video calls, and had finally been satisfied that they were as loose as he wanted. Less than a month later, Sprouse became the CEO of his own PMC, funded by Vader, with instructions to hire handfuls of like-minded contractors, who shared Sprouse's flexible definition of right and wrong.

Just like that, Caliber Security was born.

Vader allowed Sprouse to run Caliber without interference, but whenever Vader needed a job done, this took full priority, no matter what else was going on. If they lost business, so be it. Vader had provided the seed money for the firm, after all, and continued to be extremely generous, so Sprouse was happy to drop everything whenever it was necessary to attend to the man's needs.

Apparently, Vader had some pressing needs now, as evidenced by a call that he had hastily arranged that morning, and which was now less than two minutes away.

The man never called without giving Caliber an assignment, and never wasted time on idle chatter. And he was nothing if not punctual.

Sure enough, at three o'clock on the nose, Darth Vader's theme song, *The Imperial March*, issued from Sprouse's cell phone, as majestic and foreboding as ever.

Dum, dum, dum—dum de dum—dum de dum.

This ring-tone had announced a call from Vader dozens of times now, but it never failed to bring a smile to Sprouse's face.

"Sprouse here," he said unnecessarily, annoyed, as always, that Vader insisted on a one-way video call, so he was forced to control his expressions, while Vader retained full anonymity. "What can I do for you, Jake?" he added immediately, knowing that Vader never wasted time on small talk.

"I have an assignment for you, Captain," said the booming voice of James Earl Jones. "One that's a bit more . . . delicate than usual." During each communication, Sprouse half-expected him to say something like, "Join me, and together we can rule the galaxy as father and son," but that day had never come.

"Go on," said Sprouse.

"I need you and two of your men to kill someone. A man in his fifties."

Sprouse's eyes widened. He and his men had broken the law any number of times for their benefactor, often completing assignments involving complex corporate espionage and theft. Vader also frequently provided nearly flawless intel to guide them to collect proof of sexual indiscretions or confirm the existence of skeletons in the closets of powerful people, including a number of high-ranking politicians and government officials.

But he had never requested a *murder*. This was crossing a line, even for Caliber Security. "Look . . . Jake," he began, "you know how much I value our relationship. And I've never questioned the . . . legality of my assignments. But murder? That's another story."

When there was no immediate answer, he continued. "Is the target at least outside of the US?"

"No. He's in California."

Damn, thought Sprouse. He might have considered sending his men to kill someone on foreign soil, especially in a Second or Third World country, but *definitely* not in the US. "Is he a crime lord, or a mass murderer himself?" he asked.

"I'm afraid not," came the deep bass reply. "As far as I know, he's as pure as the driven snow. Zero military training. Doesn't own a single gun. And if he were Catholic, he'd probably be put up for Sainthood."

Sprouse blew out a long breath. He had to hand it to Vader. He didn't sugarcoat it. He knew Sprouse was looking for a justification to kill this target, and Vader refused to help him in the slightest.

Sprouse considered this request for several long seconds. He and his people had killed any number of men before, after all. But these were all snuffed out in the throes of combat. Kill or be killed. Even he wasn't comfortable taking the life of an innocent civilian.

"You've done a lot for me in the last three years, Jake," he said finally. "And I'm grateful. But while Caliber has crossed many lines, we aren't assassins. I'm afraid that killing a non-combatant on American soil is a bridge too far. I'm really sorry, but I can't help you."

"No need to be sorry, Captain," replied Vader pleasantly. "Because I know you're going to do this for me."

"You did hear what I just said, right?"

"Loud and clear. But you're about to change your mind. Because I'm going to give you a carrot, a stick, *and* a way for you to justify the necessity of it to yourself. First, the justification. This man *will* be killed. And soon. I have vast resources. If I want him dead, he *will be* dead. Whether your team takes care of it or not."

Vader paused to let this sink in. "So refusing this assignment won't change this man's fate in the slightest," he continued, "but it will change *yours*. Do this, and you and your two underlings each get a million-dollar bonus. Refuse to do this, and the men I *do* get to kill the current target will also be assigned to do the same to you."

"What men?"

"Do you think you're the only group I employ, Captain? You're my first choice for this mission, because it's about time you got your hands a little bloodier. But I have any number of other groups that make you and your men look like a bunch of choir boys."

Sprouse inhaled sharply. Could it be? It had never occurred to him that Vader would have other groups doing his bidding. But why not? He could spread his assignments out, and pit one group against another, as he was threatening now.

"You're very good at what you do, Captain," continued Vader. "So you might kill them instead of the other way around. But then again," he added pointedly, "you might not."

Sprouse's eyes narrowed. He had known this Jake was bad news, but he was beginning to think he might put the *real* Darth Vader to shame.

"So what's it going to be?" continued Vader. "A million dollars each to kill a man who's already as good as dead anyway? Or wondering when you'll be getting a bullet in the back of your head?"

Sprouse shook his head in disbelief. "You'd really send hitters after me?" he asked. "Just for refusing one assignment?"

"I really would. I'd hate to lose you, but it's your choice. And the good news is that I'd manage to get over it."

"Tell me this," said Sprouse. "If this target of yours is so helpless, if he's such an innocent, why do you need three of us?"

"For good measure," said Vader simply. "Better safe than sorry," he added, finding yet another platitude. "Now I need a decision. Yes, or no?"

Sprouse weighed his options for several more seconds. Despite having successfully completed numerous assignments for this man for almost three years, he knew almost nothing about him. But for some chilling reason, he was convinced that Vader wasn't bluffing. The target would die anyway, and Vader would mark Sprouse for elimination if he refused.

Finally, Sprouse shook his head in disgust. "Okay, I'm in," he spat icily, not bothering to hide his growing rage. "But this is the last time I do something like this. And threaten me again, I don't care how good you are, I'll learn who you are. And then we'll see who can take out who."

"Agreed," said Vader. "I wouldn't have it any other way." He paused. "But I believe it's, 'who can take out *whom*.'"

"Kiss my ass!" snapped Sprouse. "Are you really going to quibble about grammar, or do you want your target dead?"

"You're right, of course," boomed the amused, synthesized voice of a man known only as Jake. "So on that note, let me tell you the specifics of your assignment."

"I'm all ears," said Sprouse.

2

Connor Gibson clenched his teeth and fantasized about hurling his desktop computer through his second-story window and watching it explode into shrapnel on the ground below. Only the issuance of a primal scream and the use of every last shred of his willpower prevented him from turning this vivid imagery into reality.

His first attempt at writing a blockbuster tech thriller was looking to be forever stillborn, despite well over a month of preparation and thought.

How could writing a novel be this *hard*? Thousands upon thousands of people were doing it nowadays, so why couldn't *he*?

He had all the advantages, at least on paper. He was a brilliant science geek, and one of the few who could find ways to make highly complex subjects understandable to the masses, something that both tech startups and established corporations desperately needed in this day of high-tech *everything*.

Turned out a lot of math and science whizzes weren't that great at writing. But Connor Gibson was a double threat, capable of understanding complex science and technology and finding the words to make it digestible to just about anyone. In addition to earning a good living as a technical writer for an ever-growing number of corporations, he also contributed articles to popular science magazines.

At the relatively tender age of twenty-eight, Connor Gibson could hardly complain.

And yet complaining was *all* that he'd been doing recently. For well over a month now.

All because he was determined to stop playing it safe, to stop being a coward. He was determined to step out of his comfort zone and parlay his talents into fame and fortune as a technothriller novelist.

This career path seemed to be a perfect fit for him. He was well versed in science and futurism, and could write a half-decent sentence. Equally important, he loved thrillers of all kinds—especially technothrillers—and had immersed himself in these fictional rushes of adrenaline since he had begun reading adult fare.

When he wasn't learning about tech, or writing, or climbing towering walls at a rock climbing gym, he was either reading near-future science-fiction thrillers—another name for the technothriller—or viewing such offerings at the movies or on television.

Technothrillers had been all the rage for many years now, and the reason for this was obvious. Technology was playing an increasingly central role in human life, and was advancing at a blistering pace. Technological capabilities that a generation before had seemed impossible, *unthinkable*, were now taken for granted, and even more magical capabilities were just around the corner.

What wonders would the tech giants think of next? How would these advances affect society? Would a certain technology dramatically improve the human condition, or were there hidden aspects to the tech that were dangerous or chilling?

Science fiction thrillers were once considered wild flights of impossible fancy. Not anymore. Now they were widely seen as detailed road maps to possible futures that were bearing down on the world at an ever-accelerating pace.

Connor Gibson had read so many gripping thrillers in his time, he had been confident that he'd be able to write one. But now he wasn't so sure. Knowing what beats he needed to hit in his novel was one thing.

Plotting it was another thing entirely. This seemed nearly impossible—at least for him.

Connor decided that he needed a time machine. If he had one of these, he could travel years ahead to when he had finally finished the novel and bring it back to the present. If he stole from his future self, it really wasn't theft—or even plagiarism. And his present self would reap the benefits of his talent without having to do any of the actual work. Sounded like heaven.

Perhaps he could write a novel about *that*.

As he thought about this more, he realized that even time travel wouldn't help him. Because if he didn't commit himself to do the work in the present, his future self wouldn't have a completed novel lying around for him to take. Instead, the timeline would be packed with nothing but a series of lazy Connor Gibsons, each waiting for a future Connor Gibson to finally get off his ass and write something.

So much for that idea.

Mercifully, the familiar tone of his phone cried out in the stillness, interrupting his self-imposed misery. Never had he been so happy to hear a phone ring. It was his father, Elias Gibson, with the call coming in audio-only, as usual. The elder Gibson could have transmitted his holographic image so that it appeared in the room beside Connor, like in a *Star Wars* movie, but rarely chose to do so. Few people did. It was easier just to talk, without worrying about your appearance, or having to keep your eyes trained on the person to whom you were speaking.

"Dad!" said Connor happily as he answered the call. "What's new?"

"Good question," said his father. "A lot, as it turns out. But before I tell you, how's the novel coming?"

"I'll let you know when I start it."

"I thought you started over a month ago."

"So did I," said the younger Gibson miserably. "Instead of writing, I'm doing a lot of wallowing in frustration. Not to mention self-doubt. But on the plus side, I am finding ever more creative excuses for not committing to an opening."

"Way to find the silver lining," said his dad in amusement.

Connor couldn't help but smile. "Yeah, I'm a glass half-full kind of guy," he said wryly. "So more good news, I've also discovered the ultimate torture—being alone with nothing but my thoughts, hour after hour, with mounting pressure for these thoughts to congeal into something meaningful."

"Wow, *congeal into something meaningful*. Who says that, Con? You were obviously born to write."

"I thought so too," said Connor miserably.

"Sorry to hear it's been so much of a struggle."

"Maybe I'm overreacting, you know, just a bit. Probably wouldn't get a lot of sympathy from coal miners and sewage workers."

"Probably not," said Elias Gibson, and despite this being an audio call, Connor knew his father was grinning. "Normally you'd get some sympathy from me, but I need to make this short, and there's something big I want to tell you about."

"How big?"

His father blew out a long breath. "Enormous," he said earnestly. "Nothing short of earth-shattering."

The younger Gibson paused, replaying these words in his mind to be sure his father wasn't just putting him on. But he detected no sarcasm in his father's tone. Besides, Elias Gibson was brilliant, thoughtful, and sober, not a man given to hyperbole.

"*Earth-shattering?*" Connor repeated, needing one more confirmation.

"I know it sounds like an exaggeration, but it isn't. If anything, it's an understatement. I've come up with something that will change humanity forever. Something that will have an unprecedented, transformative impact on society—the likes of which the world has never seen."

"You've cured male pattern baldness?" said Connor wryly.

"Nothing *that* momentous," said his father, playing along.

The younger Gibson laughed. They had mused years earlier about this subject as it applied to the *Star Trek* universe, which they both loved. In the twenty-fourth century, mankind had conquered the stars, had solved teleportation, and had made mind-blowing medical breakthroughs. But, apparently—as evidenced by Jean-Luc Picard's shiny dome—mankind had made no progress, whatsoever, in conquering male pattern *baldness,* the *real* final frontier.

Connor's smile vanished and he braced himself. "Okay, Dad," he said. "I'm ready. Tell me what's going on."

"I will," said his father. "But this is too big to tell you over the phone. I need for you to come out to San Diego to see me. And Paige also," he added, referring to his son's wife of just over a year. Connor was an only child, and his father treated Paige as if she were truly his daughter. Having lost Connor's mom in a car accident four years before the wedding, his father had been thrilled to welcome such an impressive addition to the family.

"I can book the two of you on a flight for tomorrow morning. I know this is last minute, and that Paige will have to arrange for a substitute teacher, but I'd really appreciate it if you could both find a way to make it."

"Actually, Paige is at a teachers conference in LA. But it ends tonight, and I'm guessing her sub would be willing to stay a few more days."

"Great. Assuming this works out, does that mean you're in?"

"Absolutely," said Connor. His curiosity had never been more piqued, exactly what his father was counting on. "I'll fly out, and Paige can drive down to meet us."

A smile crept over Connor's face. "Despite all the fun I'm having staring at a blank computer screen for hours on end," he added, "I wouldn't miss it for the world."

3

The early-morning flight from Denver to San Diego was a breeze, just over two hours of calm before the . . . what? The storm?

Connor Gibson wasn't sure. Certainly before the revelation that, from his father's description, was the most consequential since Moses received the Ten Commandments on Mt. Sinai.

He called his father to let him know he had landed, and soon he was in the passenger's seat of the elder Gibson's white Mercedes SUV, the largest model they offered. They headed northeast to Elias's new home in San Marcos, a city in San Diego County whose magnificent hills provided glorious views of mountains as far as the eye could see.

After their initial greeting they drove in silence until the SUV had raced up a highway on-ramp. "Can you at least give me a hint as to what this breakthrough of yours is all about?" said Connor. "I mean, it's obviously something in the realm of virtual reality."

Elias Gibson laughed. "And yet it's not."

"What else could it be?"

"I will reveal all," said his father in amusement. "I promise. But let's wait for your wife."

"You can't just drop a bombshell like this and expect me to be patient," complained Connor.

"Sorry. But it won't be long now. And this way I don't have to repeat myself. Didn't you say Paige will be arriving just a few minutes after us?"

"I did," replied Connor miserably. "But what if she's late?"

"I'm pretty sure you'll live," said his father dryly.

"Okay then," said Connor, "let me ask you this: how did you even manage it? Whatever *it* is. I thought you were supposed to be retired."

"I was supposed to be," said his father with a grin. "But I was actually completing a stealth project of my own."

"I knew it!" said Connor.

He had never fully believed that a man like his father would really retire in his late fifties. Not a man this brilliant, with this much vitality, and with this much to offer.

Elias Gibson's career had been remarkable by any measure. He had graduated at the top of his class from MIT with a degree in computer science, one of the more brilliant alumni this storied university had ever produced, and certainly one of the most idealistic. Instead of going directly into industry and making ridiculous amounts of money, he had been one of the first participants in a bold new program that was just getting off the ground, called *Teach For America*, or TFA. This non-profit organization recruited the best recent graduates from around the country to make a difference in the lives of underprivileged kids.

Even though Elias hadn't taken a single course in teaching at MIT, this wasn't critical to Teach For America. Anyone deemed impressive enough to make the severe cut imposed by the organization, regardless of major, was welcomed. True, those who entered the program had to attend a summer boot camp, and pass tests to get the proper certifications, but for the brilliant graduates TFA recruited, passing these tests was never in doubt.

Later, after Elias had finished a two-year stint teaching third-graders in Dayton, Ohio, he had reluctantly decided not to re-enlist. He realized during his two years of teaching that he could use his computer skills to help more than just the underprivileged. He could use them to help *all* students, not just classes of twenty to thirty at a time. His teaching experience had made it clear to him that he could improve how knowledge was presented and absorbed. He could make learning more user-friendly, both at home and in the classroom.

Every day he taught, he thought of better ways to reach the kids, better teaching methods that computers made possible. He began at an education start-up company and achieved great initial success. Over several decades, as both computers and his skills improved, he continued to be at the forefront of the education market, achieving substantial wealth and acclaim, not that either one of these had been his motivation.

Then, four years earlier, he had joined the most powerful of the emerging virtual reality players, Total Immersion Systems, hired to build the company's education and training division. Total Immersion Systems had considered him the ideal recruit for this critical position, as he was a man whose passion for education, and whose AI and machine learning expertise, were second to none.

As virtual reality became better and better, and the technology more and more affordable, breathtaking applications became possible. Mankind could finally go where science fiction had been for decades, and not just for third-graders, but for anyone who wanted to learn.

Although gaming was the primary thrust of Total Immersion Systems, the opportunities to use VR to enhance knowledge and skill-set acquisition were endless.

The day wasn't far off when medical students would take virtual journeys through the human body, like the inhabitants of the microscopic submarine in the classic movie *Fantastic Voyage*—without the need for miniaturization. And additional possibilities abounded. Students often found history dry and boring, but VR could change this in dramatic fashion. High school students could be immersed in historical simulations, actual participants in famous battles, flawless and interactive reenactments that would do more to bring history to life than a time machine.

VR would soon bring about the most historic transformation of human learning since the invention of the written word, across all fields and all walks of life.

While the technology was still being perfected, the day would soon come when computer renderings of people and scenes within simulations became flawless. When simulations could engage all five senses, making the virtual world truly indistinguishable from reality. On that day, a perfect simulation, like that depicted in the movie *The Matrix*, would become possible. But unlike the movie, these simulations would be used by humanity for its own training and edification, rather than controlled by AI overlords.

Elias had built Total Immersion Systems' education and training department, had made significant advances, and then, just like that, had taken early retirement, leaving the company just over two years after he had joined it. He had cashed in his stock, donated twenty-five of the thirty-two million in proceeds to charitable causes, and left his division in the hands of the brilliant younger AI and VR superstars he had recruited.

Connor had been shocked. While giving away most of his fortune was entirely within his father's character, leaving his job was not. So a retirement that really wasn't a retirement made perfect sense.

"So how's Paige doing?" asked Elias, breaking a long silence and making an obvious attempt to avoid talking about his breakthrough. "I can't wait to see her."

"She's fine," said Connor.

His father adored his new wife. She was a grade school teacher like Elias had been, teaching fifth grade rather than third, and she was kind and full of life, with an insatiable intellectual curiosity. And while Connor was very bright, maybe even brilliant, Paige was likely even brighter, although she was so unassuming that few would ever guess it. But Elias certainly recognized her gifts. He was convinced that if she hadn't selflessly elected to teach, her innate talents could have lifted her to rarified heights in many other fields.

"That's it?" said Elias. "No specifics?"

"I'll let her tell you what's she's been up to herself."

"You're just trying to get back at me for not giving you any hints about my work, aren't you?"

Connor laughed. "Maybe."

His father smiled. "Fair enough," he said. "In any case, we'll be there soon. I can't wait for you and Paige to see the place."

Elias had recently moved from a small condo on the ocean to a much larger, more isolated home in nearby San Marcos. The estate was over six thousand square feet, and had been built a decade earlier on top of a small mountain by a wealthy recluse, including the private corkscrew road that reached it from the canyons below.

"We're looking forward to it," said Connor, feeling a little guilty that they hadn't visited before now.

"The view is breathtaking," continued Elias. "And it's surrounded by wilderness. Hills, mountains, and canyons covered by dense brush.

And every day I get to see hawks, lizards, rabbits, deer, and coyotes. Even the occasional scorpion and rattlesnake."

Connor made a face. "These last don't sound like too much fun."

Elias smiled. "You just have to keep your eyes open," he said. "But I did purposely leave off the one animal that's quickly become my favorite." He paused for effect. "The roadrunner."

Connor wasn't sure what he had expected, but it wasn't this. "Like the old cartoon?" he said in disbelief. "The bird that races around and says, *meep meep*?"

"Exactly! Didn't know your generation was familiar with the classics. The roadrunner and its arch nemesis, Wile E. Coyote. Although it turns out the cartoon bird in question actually says *beep beep*. I looked it up because I wasn't sure. The cartoon's creators, however, will accept both meep meep *and* beep beep."

"Good to know," said Connor, rolling his eyes. "I can't believe you've done something that will change the world, and this is the discussion we're having. Beep beep or meep meep."

His father laughed. "You have to see one of these things run. They're so cool. And I've actually seen a coyote chasing one of them."

"Was the coyote strapped to a rocket?" said Connor, trying to keep a straight face. "And did it fall off a cliff, and then have an anvil land on its head?"

"Of course. But before it attacked, it waited until the roadrunner had stopped to peck at a pile of birdseed."

Connor laughed. "But in all seriousness," he added, "I'm not sure I even knew this was a real bird."

"I think a lot of people probably don't. The greater roadrunner is about a foot tall and two feet long. And it looks a lot like the cartoon. Big plume on its head, like a reverse Mohawk haircut, big feet, and a long, thin tail, pointing skyward. So even its appearance is interesting. But then you see one of them run. Wow! They can streak across the ground at twenty miles an hour. It's a riot to see a bird this small run as fast as an Olympic sprinter."

"Do they leave a trail of dust behind them?"

Elias grinned. "Just a bit, yeah. And if they aren't already cool enough, they're known to eat scorpions and tarantulas. *Really*. But it gets even better. They're also one of the few species fast enough to prey on rattlesnakes. They can grab the snake's head with their bill, somehow avoiding the fangs, and smash it on the ground repeatedly until it's dead."

Elias changed lanes to avoid a sea of eighteen-wheelers ahead of him and glanced over at his son. "I don't know if these guys evolved from velociraptors, but it wouldn't surprise me."

"Who knew?" said Connor. "You have me fascinated. I'm not leaving until I see one of these guys run."

"It's a deal," said his father.

Okay, then," said Connor. "Two things to look forward to. Spotting a sprinting bird. And learning what you think is the break-through of the century."

Elias Gibson smiled. "The breakthrough of the century?" he re-peated, feigning indignation. "I guess you weren't paying attention. What I'll be sharing with you is much bigger than that."

4

Ernesto Navarro craned his neck to see a lone home set on a series of plateaus far above him, but the home was set too far from the edge for him to see in the distance.

Navarro lowered his head and gestured at the steep slope in front of him, covered in thick vegetation. "Is this considered a large hill, or a small mountain?" he whispered to the two men beside him. "Or is it a canyon?"

Jared Sprouse shot him a look of contempt. "How the hell should I know?" he whispered back. "Do I look like Dictionary.com?"

He regretted this response immediately, but he couldn't help it. He was in a decidedly bad mood. He didn't want any part of killing a Boy Scout.

After Vader had given him the particulars, he had researched the target and confirmed what Vader had said. The guy didn't have as much as an outstanding parking ticket against him, and seemed devoted to charitable causes and to improving humanity's lot. For the life of him, Sprouse couldn't begin to fathom why the owner of Caliber Protection wanted this middle-aged guy dead so badly.

Having to scale a steep, chaparral-covered hillside to kill a harmless do-gooder would put anyone in a bad mood. But being forced into it against his will pissed Sprouse off more than the actual murder itself. When this was over, he would assign two men to drop everything and work full time on discovering Vader's identity, something he should have done long ago.

But not the two men he had standing beside him now, former master sergeant Ernesto Navarro and former lieutenant Shane Hayden. These two weren't his best men, but they were certainly his most bloodthirsty. Like him, they were wearing green and brown camouflage and were heavily armed.

Navarro and Hayden, who had agreed to this mission, as expected, were much younger than Sprouse—and hungrier. The million dollars he had promised them would change their lives forever, and while they were troubled by the necessity of ending an innocent life to earn it, they weren't *that* troubled. Especially because the op was sure to be a walk in the park.

They couldn't have asked for a more ideal scenario. Three trained commandos, armed to the teeth, against an upper middle-aged civilian who didn't own a gun, and didn't even have the most rudimentary of security systems protecting his home. And the biggest bonus of all, his home just happened to be among the most isolated in the entire area.

If they had allowed themselves to drive up the winding private road to the residence, instead of climbing up a steep incline through a thicket of brown and green vegetation—some of which had thorns—this would be the easiest op in history. But why risk being seen?

The road was private, and any vehicle on it stood out like a neon sign, easily visible to anyone at the top for most of the trip. It probably wouldn't matter if their target *did* see them, but why take any chances? Vader was paying a massive sum of money to snuff this man out, after all. In Sprouse's experience, anyone who had done something to warrant this kind of reaction had to suspect something like this might be coming. The man could well be on his guard, despite all appearances to the contrary.

While their target wouldn't be able to call for help, as they had killed cell phone reception in the area, he *could* try to escape by car. He would still surely die, but why chance the op becoming more complicated than necessary?

So instead of driving up the hill, they would climb up. They would treat the target with at least some respect. A little strenuous activity wouldn't hurt them, after all.

And for a million dollars each, he and his two comrades would get over it.

5

Paige Estrella Gibson arrived at her San Marcos destination only ten minutes behind her husband and father-in-law, and greeted them both warmly. The elder Gibson gave them a quick tour of the residence, which could have comfortably housed a family of eight. He was clearly embarrassed by the grandiosity of the place, but he had moved there for the view and privacy, and had joked when he was buying it that he would cordon off most of the home with "do-not-cross" police tape and pretend these rooms didn't exist.

In a way, this is exactly what he had done, only furnishing the great room, master bedroom, and two of the guest rooms. Still, the home was even more impressive than Connor had expected. The back of the home and the backyard were magnificent. A long sliding glass door led out to the yard, which was mostly hardscaped with silver travertine.

Just beyond the slider, a room-sized section of the patio was covered by a stuccoed ceiling, which itself was the floor of a spacious balcony extending out from the master bedroom above. A sparkling blue pool with a vanishing edge sat at one end of the property, creating the illusion that the water was forever flowing into an abyss.

Elias had taken great care to furnish the backyard so he could take advantage of the view, and suggested that they take the conversation out to a large glass patio table and wicker chairs near one edge of the property, opposite the pool. He set a tray with assorted drinks down on the table next to a pair of high-powered binoculars that seemed to be a permanent mainstay there.

Connor smiled upon seeing them. Apparently, his father was an even bigger fan of the natural reality show taking place around the property than he had let on.

A cool breeze kicked up from the hillside, making the setting even *more* idyllic. After just a few more minutes of catching up with Paige, Elias Gibson indicated he was ready to tell them why they were there.

"Thanks for coming on short notice," he said. "And for being patient. If you could just indulge me for a little bit longer, I'd like to bring you up to speed in my own way. Hopefully, I won't be *too* meandering."

Connor and his wife exchanged glances and then nodded their assent. It wasn't as if he had given them a choice.

Elias Gibson cleared his throat to begin, and a wave of emotion swept over his face. Connor knew this was a big moment for him, and it showed.

"It probably isn't a mystery to either of you that everything seems to be going to hell," he said. "Humanity seems to be constantly on the brink of disaster, with our security, prosperity, and hopes for the future looking worse than ever. There seems to be a growing hopelessness in our society. Everywhere we turn we see drug cartels and wars. We see terrorism, poverty, and social unrest. Perhaps even more alarming, ever more powerful weapons of mass destruction are being developed by ever more unstable dictators. School shootings are out of control. Riots seem to be breaking out every day. Massive unemployment in the near future seems assured as automation continues to advance. New, incurable diseases are cropping up. Famine in Third World countries. Xenophobia seems to be on the rise, and race relations seem to be getting worse and worse."

Elias paused to catch his breath. "I could go on and on," he continued, "but I assume you're getting the gist."

Paige swallowed hard. "*More* than getting it," she said miserably.

Connor winced. His father should stop if he didn't want them jumping off the edge of his property. "We already know the world is going to hell," said the younger Gibson grimly. "But we really do appreciate the reminder," he added, rolling his eyes.

"Any time," replied his father with a wistful smile. "The point I'm trying to make," he continued, "is that human misery seems to be rising. Human happiness plummeting. Prospects for the future survival of the species seem as bleak as they ever have. Our species is more stressed out than ever."

"And now," mumbled Connor, "so am I."

"I could talk about this in a global context," continued Elias, ignoring his son's attempt at humor, "as a global phenomenon. But to simplify things, let me talk about the US for a while. In addition to the concerns I've just listed, our country is more divided than ever. More pessimistic. The rhetoric in our culture ever more divisive. I've seen this get worse and worse over the course of my lifetime. People used to be able to engage in civil discourse. Now, everyone seems so polarized, so certain of the infallibility of their positions, so emotional and passionate about their beliefs, that many refuse to even *listen* to opposing points of view."

Connor's eyes narrowed. He was confused, and a glance at Paige showed that she was the same. Where was his father going with this? He had expected to celebrate a major breakthrough, not to be driven into depression.

"Don't worry," said Elias, as if reading his son's mind, "I promise you that this really is leading somewhere."

"Of course," mumbled Connor. "Never doubted it for a second."

The corners of Elias's mouth turned up into the hint of a smile. "As you know," he continued, "I was involved in virtual reality research for many years before I joined Total Immersion Systems. And while the potential of virtual reality to revolutionize education and training has always been obvious, I'm also well aware of the medium's appeal as an entertainment vehicle. And not just for gaming applications. Perfect virtual reality could offer a far superior way to experience fiction—an immersive television if you will. It could produce video conferences that would seem to all involved to be actual, physical meetings. I could go on, but once again, I think you get the gist."

Elias Gibson unscrewed the cap from the plastic bottle of water in front of him and took a long drink. "So about nine years ago," he continued, "as I was becoming ever more keenly aware of the divisiveness all around me, of the pessimism and unhappiness, I decided to take stock of what I was attempting to do. I had always been so certain VR would dramatically improve human happiness and well-being. But a number of recent tech advances that I thought would dramatically improve our well-being seemed to be backfiring. So I decided I needed to engage in further analysis and self-reflection, just to be sure. To take a long, sober look at possible negative consequences that virtual reality might bring about."

"Like what?" asked Paige.

"My biggest concern was addiction. One of humanity's most insidious and growing problems, but one that I left off the list I just cited."

"Because you knew you would be addressing it now," guessed Paige.

"You caught me," said Elias in amusement. "It's possible that I rehearsed the flow of this a few times before you got here."

"Go on," said Connor.

"People are wired for addiction, plain and simple. I'll spare you the biochemistry lesson, and the explanation of how this biochemistry actually helped our species survive in primitive times. The important point is that addiction is an enormous problem, and getting worse in a hurry. It's hard to find someone who isn't addicted to *something*. Millions of us in this country are alcoholics. Millions more are addicted to opioids and other drugs. We're addicted to sex, gambling, nicotine, and caffeine. And now to our phones, to the Internet, and to video games and social media."

Elias paused to let this sink in. "Not only does human brain chemistry make us highly susceptible to addiction," he continued, "but our technology and our lifestyles are taking us further and further away from our basic natures. Evolution perfected our wiring to allow us to survive and reproduce in a simpler, less distracting world. But our brains are poorly suited to modern society. There are so many people now. So much is happening so fast, and there is so much information to absorb, coming from all directions. There are so many distractions. Endless temptations being pedaled to us everywhere we look. Our outmoded wiring now ensures that we're stressed out much of the time, in a constant addictive frenzy, rarely able to fully relax."

A hawk began circling the skies just a hair above them, scanning for rodents and reptiles in the canyon below, its aerodynamic grace on full display. Elias paused so that he and his guests could admire the magnificent bird of prey and then continued. "Being addicted makes us feel anxious," he said. "But, often, *succumbing* to our addiction makes us feel even *more* anxious."

"I thought giving in to the addiction was supposed to relieve the anxiety," said Connor. "At least temporarily."

"In many cases it does. But in many others it doesn't. You may be addicted to checking incoming emails on your phone, for instance, but these can often be stressful. You may be addicted to checking your Facebook account. Sometimes doing so results in a positive experience. But for many, the opposite is often true. You see political stories on your newsfeed that enrage you, opinions that make you crazy. You're jealous that everyone posting seems to have a better life than you. Better vacations, cars, significant others, or families. Or you're concerned about your place in the social pecking order. Concerned that so many others have more friends than you. Or that the photo of your new coffee mug isn't getting enough 'likes.' This is especially true among adolescents." Elias shook his head. "But despite making you feel worse, your addiction to Facebook keeps you coming back for more."

Connor nodded. His father made some good points.

"I'm not saying that social media hasn't had a very positive impact in some ways," Elias continued. "But there's a growing realization that instead of uniting people, it often makes people feel more isolated, more depressed."

"And you were worried that virtual reality might have the same effect," said Connor.

"That's right. My hope was that it would help reduce stress rather than increase it. And there are plenty of reasons to believe this might be true. Our wiring and physiology cause us to require certain things for our well-being. Sunlight, for instance. Human touch and affection. Human intimacy. Our brains require these things for smooth functioning. Our *souls* require it. But I would argue that we have a need to spend more time in the natural world, the world in which we originally evolved."

"Which virtual reality can assist us in doing," said Paige.

"Exactly!" said her father-in-law, quite pleased. "Perfect, immersive VR would mean that we're no longer trapped within cities. If we wanted to, we could spend an hour a day immersed in the Amazon rainforest, away from our daily grind, letting nature soothe our souls. Even better, we could experience it with all of our senses, really *be* there, but dial down the heat, humidity, and danger. The rainforest without the rain. We could go on tranquil hikes without the bug bites, sauna-like conditions, and poisonous snakes. We could take micro-vacations to set our heads right without leaving home."

"Sounds amazing," said Paige.

"The question is," said Connor, "does *amazing* also mean *addictive?*"

"That's certainly the key question," agreed Elias. "Will this technology restore sanity to a world spiraling out of control? Or will it make things even worse? Will it calm us and make us happier? Or, in the end, will it addict us and make us even more miserable?"

The elder Gibson sighed. "Which brings me to the next link in my chain of meandering," he said with the hint of a smile. "And that is happiness itself. How could I determine if perfect VR would make us happy or not without understanding what this means? We all know the US Constitution gives us the inalienable right to life, liberty, and the pursuit of happiness. But what is this *happiness* that we're pursuing, exactly? And how do we know when we've caught it? It became clear to me that I needed to come up to speed on the science of happiness, familiarize myself with the latest research."

"I had no idea this *was* a science," said Paige.

Elias nodded. "It has been for some time now. I could spend many hours on the subject, but I'll just give you a quick take-home. First, people are born to worry. That's how we made it to the top of the food chain. Constant anxiety is the curse that comes with consciousness, with sentience. We're the only species smart enough to fear not only actual, present threats, but also a myriad of *imagined* threats. Worse, we're the only species burdened with the knowledge of our own mortality. And this makes us the most neurotic animal on Earth."

Connor nodded thoughtfully. He had never considered the human condition in just this way before.

"All other apex predators are completely content when not facing an imminent threat. Not a care in the world. This is rarely true of the human species. Because there are an infinite number of *possible* threats to worry about. We worry about issues that are decades off, like our retirements. We worry about finances, and what people think of us, and our salt intake, and everything else under the sun. Our jobs, and our kids, and legislation being passed in Washington, even if it won't impact our lives in the slightest. Our imaginations are so great, in fact, that fear of a pending public speaking engagement, trepidation over next month's family reunion, or anxiety over an upcoming performance review can engage our *fight-or-flight* response just as surely as can a dangerous predator."

Elias paused. "So we're often in a state of high anxiety over endless possibilities that never even come to pass," he continued. "We're constantly tilting at phantoms. If I drive to the store now, will there be bad traffic? I worry about it. I'm anxious about it. Even if my worry turns out to be completely unfounded. This ability to foresee possible dangers has helped us to survive, to dominate the planet, but at a great cost to our psychological well-being."

Connor considered this in the context of his own life. He had a beautiful, caring wife who loved him, good friends, a sport he loved, and enough money to live in comfort, and yet he had been highly stressed by his inability to begin a novel. His father was absolutely right.

"Not only is worry innate," continued Elias Gibson, "it's also one reason we gravitate to drugs and alcohol in the first place. To help us forget our worries, however temporarily. To reduce anxiety. To take the edge off.

"Regardless," he continued, "you can't be happy when you're overcome with worry. So a key ingredient to achieving happiness is to become engaged in activities that consume our concentration, that don't give our imaginations room to find new things to worry about. If we're totally focused on something we enjoy, living in the moment, like every other animal in the animal kingdom, we're alive, electric— and happy. Especially if we're challenging ourselves, overcoming obstacles, improving, achieving."

"I've learned that on my own," said Paige. "I used to think that endless leisure would lead to happiness, but it doesn't. It leads to boredom. And loss of purpose." She paused. "What about money? How big of a role does it play?"

"Surprisingly little," said Elias. "Rich men and women are just as likely to be depressed, and commit suicide, as anyone else. But I'll tell you the most important factor of all when it comes to being happy. Having strong relationships. With friends, or neighbors, or lovers, or spouses, or family. Maintaining a strong social network."

"Which social media, ironically enough, seems to be weakening," said Connor. "We used to spend quality time with a few people. Actually *with* them—physically. For hours on end. Now we spend time interacting with *hundreds* of people, but on our phones, or sitting in a chair all alone facing a computer screen."

"Exactly right," said Elias. "Another reason to fear the unintended consequence of perfect virtual reality. On the plus side, it has the potential to be engaging and allow us to soothe our souls on mini-vacations. Allow us to learn and explore our world like never before. But if we aren't careful, it also has the potential of being the ultimate in addictive media. Of trapping us inside so that we lose touch with reality and real human interaction."

Connor nodded thoughtfully. "This is all truly fascinating, Dad," he said. "It really is. But you told me in the car that your discovery has nothing to do with VR."

Elias smiled. "I did at that. So let me continue. Once I brought myself up to speed on what is known about human happiness, and analyzed VR in this context, I decided to take the next step, to try to understand why our species seems to be going off the rails. To gain a deeper understanding of why our future seems so bleak."

He paused and nodded at his son. "Do you remember what you said, Con, after I went through my litany of world problems?"

"Not exactly."

"You told me that you appreciated the reminder that the world is going to hell, but that this was something you already knew."

"Right," said Connor.

"Well, that's just it," said his father. "Because you might *know* it, but it isn't true. On almost every dimension I listed, things are *better* than they've ever been, not worse."

Connor and his wife both shook their heads as if they hadn't heard correctly. "What?" said Paige for the both of them.

"You heard me. Turns out the world isn't going to hell at all. Turns out I was just horribly, tragically, misinformed. Almost all of us are. In fact, the world is doing so much better on so many key facets that it's *ridiculous*. Every trend line indicates the same thing. We aren't headed off a cliff. Instead, we're headed toward a glorious future."

He frowned grimly. "And yet we're convinced it's just the opposite."

6

Captain Jared Sprouse checked the time once again and cursed inwardly. They had been milling around at the bottom of a canyon now for well over an hour. Their clothing and gear were getting hot, and they were beginning to sweat under their bulletproof vests, despite these vests being state-of-the art technology, making use of a lightweight gel that became harder than diamond, but only when hit with great force.

The vests were almost certainly unnecessary, but Sprouse was thorough, by nature. As an additional precaution, he had made sure that he and his men carried fake FBI credentials, in the extremely unlikely event someone discovered them while they were staging their attack.

God damn you, Jake! Sprouse said to himself. Why was Vader so insistent that the job be completed today? Not yesterday. Not tomorrow. *Today.*

Sprouse and his men had surveilled the property for almost a week now, and their target had been a sitting duck the entire time. But on this day of days, when the mission *had* to be completed for some reason, the man they were after, a man named Elias Gibson, had left his residence. When he had returned he had a guest in tow—with another joining the party minutes later. Worse, Sprouse had researched the man, and knew that these two visitors were Connor Gibson and Paige Estrella Gibson, Elias's son and daughter-in-law, who would almost certainly be staying overnight.

Sprouse had waited over an hour now in the hope that Connor and his wife would drive down the hillside on an outing, leaving Elias to himself for a while. But this hadn't happened, and Sprouse had to face the fact that this was little more than wishful thinking.

It was more likely that all three of them would go on an outing, making the operation far more problematic. It was time to strike, visitors or no visitors. He didn't really have a choice.

Vader was making the mission much harder than it needed to be. Not only had he insisted that the mission be carried out today, but also that if Elias Gibson wasn't alone when they struck, no one else was to be harmed under any circumstances. If this were to happen, even if by accident, they wouldn't get paid a single cent.

Sprouse was irate. Given that he couldn't risk injury to Gibson's two guests, he was forced to change tactics in mid-operation. While they were climbing and getting into position, the road leading down from the residence would be out of view for about twenty minutes. He had originally planned to leave Navarro hidden near the bottom of the road as an insurance policy, in case Elias Gibson just happened to descend while they were climbing to greet him. But Sprouse could no longer afford this luxury. Not when he had to take out one target while babying two others.

So now, if Elias chose to leave within this small window, there was little they could do about it. Unlikely this would happen, but it was sloppy and unprofessional. They would still have other options for taking him out later in the day, but things would become more complicated than necessary.

Sprouse checked his phone, studying the footage from a tiny drone he had sent up before they arrived, with a telescopic video camera that allowed it to fly far enough away to evade any possible detection. His three targets hadn't moved since they had arrived, apparently engaged in vigorous conversation around a glass patio table in Gibson's backyard. If they stayed put, Sprouse and his men would have no trouble getting quite close to them before needing to take any shots.

Sprouse cursed at his employer one last time, blew out a long breath, and motioned to his two comrades. "Time to move," he announced. He pulled down his ski mask and gestured for them to do the same.

"Stay hidden within the ground cover," he whispered, "just in case. When we're in place, remember to wait for my mark. I want to take all three of them out at once."

"Roger that," said Ernesto Navarro in low tones.

"Remember," whispered Sprouse, "I'll be taking out the old man. Navarro, you've got the son. And Hayden, you're on the daughter-in-law. But you both had better be damn sure you're only using tranquilizing darts. And also that neither target is near the pool when you knock them out. Can't have them drowning. Got it?"

"Loud and clear," replied Hayden for them both, rolling his eyes, which, along with his mouth, could be seen through the ski mask. It was the third time Sprouse had given the same instructions. Not that Hayden blamed him. He had made it clear what was at stake if someone other than Elias Gibson became collateral damage.

"Why take *any* chance of losing our payday?" complained Navarro. "No matter how careful we are, if one of these two smashes their head on the ground after we tranq them, we're screwed. It would be a lot smarter to come back here in a few days when this guy is alone again."

"*No shit*," growled Sprouse. "But if Vader wants this done now, we're doing it now."

He took his first step up the steep slope and turned to the two men behind him. "We don't want him to have to use the dark side of the force against us, do we?" he finished wryly.

But as he thought about it further, he wasn't entirely sure he was joking.

7

Connor studied his father carefully, looking for signs of dementia, and noticed his wife seemed to be doing the same. But if Elias Gibson's faculties had become any less sharp, Connor wouldn't know it based on the current discussion. His father was being as lucid as ever.

An enormous crow soared nearby, and Connor was surprised to note that its flight was nearly as elegant as the hawk's.

Connor's eyes returned to his father. "So after beginning this conversation explaining why things are worse than ever," he said, "now you're saying it's just the opposite? Are you kidding me?"

"Sorry. I did it this way for dramatic effect. And because I knew that when I went through a litany of problems, you'd agree that the world was going to hell. Like you did," he reminded his son.

"So we shouldn't believe what you said thirty minutes ago?" said Connor.

"No, believe what I'm saying now."

Paige tilted her head in thought. "If things really are looking rosier than ever," she said, "then it's the best-kept secret in history."

"This is unfortunately true," said Elias. "Not only is our future brighter than ever, at the same time, we're more pessimistic about it than we've ever been. Surveys show this in dramatic fashion, across the globe. For example, ninety percent of Swedes think the world is getting worse, rather than better. But it's even bleaker here. Ninety-four percent of Americans think things are getting worse. *Ninety-four percent*. You can't even get ninety-four percent of Americans to agree that we actually landed on the moon."

Connor and Paige both grinned, despite themselves.

"So the two of you aren't alone in your misguided beliefs," continued Elias. "And, as I said, I was right there with you not too long ago."

"If so many people share these beliefs," said Connor skeptically, "what makes you so sure they're misguided?"

"Copious research," replied his father. "Finding the actual data to compare the world today with the world of the fairly recent past. It's out there. A number of writers and researchers have even compiled these data into bestselling books. Take poverty, for example. In 1950, seventy-five percent of the world's population lived in extreme poverty. Thirty years ago, it was down to about forty percent. Today, it's fewer than *ten* percent."

"Hard to believe that's true," said Paige.

"I know. And yet it is. What's even harder to believe is that we've seen this kind of immense improvement, and yet most believe that poverty is *worse* than it's ever been."

He paused a few seconds to let this sink in and then continued. "Thirty years ago, there were twenty-three wars being waged worldwide. Today there are only eleven. This is still eleven wars too many," he added soberly, "but we're going in the right direction. Today, there are ten thousand nuclear weapons in existence. Which sounds terrifying and untenable. And it *is*. But just thirty years ago there were six times as many."

Connor and Paige said nothing, but continued to listen, spellbound.

"Pick any important metric you can think of. Racism? If you really think America is more racist than ever, you don't have any idea what things were like thirty years ago. Or fifty years ago. In your generation, sixty-six million Americans voted for a black president. Do you think that would have happened fifty years ago?

"Back then, minorities routinely faced open, unabashed discrimination. Discrimination about what jobs they could have, schools they could attend, country clubs they could join, or neighborhoods they could move into. This affected blacks, Italians, Asians, Irish, Jews, women, gays, and so many other groups. I'll bet you had no idea that interracial marriage was once illegal in a number of states. Believe it or not, until 1967. Fifty years ago only three percent of newlyweds were interracial. Today it's close to eighteen percent, almost a six-fold increase."

"But you aren't saying that there are no longer any bigots, are you?" said Paige.

"Of course not. And *any* racism is unacceptable. I'm also not saying that there can't be a temporary increase for short periods, or that we still don't have a long way to go. But over time, every metric shows that the long-term trend line is moving in a positive direction. Racism, sexism, and intolerance have been in decline in America and around the world for decades."

"But we hear about racism in the US constantly," said Paige.

"We do. Because it still exists. But also because we're far more conscious of it than we used to be. More ready than ever to call it out. More determined that it be completely eradicated. Which adds to the perception that the problem is worse than ever, and also, unfortunately, makes false allegations of racism more powerful than ever. But if you take a look from thirty thousand feet, racism is declining, and movements dedicated to making sure it continues to decline are thriving."

Elias took another long drink of water, finishing the bottle. "Let me give you a list of other examples of how the world is improving," he said. "Take health and longevity. We're now living far longer, and in far better health, than at any time. Freedom? A far greater percentage of the world's population live in free societies than ever before. Literacy? A few hundred years ago, only a small minority could read and write. Now, ninety percent of young people around the world are literate. Safety? We're safer than ever before in countless ways. Just to choose one metric, we're more than ninety percent less likely to be killed in a car accident than we were in the fifties or sixties."

"Well, yeah," said Paige. "Back then they didn't do crash testing to make cars safer. And hardly anyone even wore a seat belt."

"Not only that," added Connor, "but there were no airbags, blind spot indicators, or cameras for backing up."

"I'm not saying any of this should come as a revelation," replied Elias. "I'm just saying that, collectively, people's perception of today versus yesterday doesn't match the reality."

"Go on," urged Connor, fascinated.

"Today, we have access to more entertainment than even the most farsighted visionary could even dream of in centuries past. Imagine how limited your entertainment choices were before the invention of radio and television. Even fifty years ago, you had three or four television channels to choose from. There was no cable, no streaming, no Internet. If you missed part of a program, there was no rewinding, you just missed it. If you wanted to read a book, your choices were limited to what was in the local bookstore or library. Now you have instant access to *millions* of titles, to books that have been out of print for decades and more."

Elias paused. "I could go on forever. But our wealth and quality of life is substantially better now than it has ever been. In eighteen hundred, forty percent of children died before the age of five. Forty percent. We've invented indoor plumbing and created sewer systems. We have instant access to unlimited clean water. Instead of spending months crossing our country in covered wagons—a dangerous journey—we fly across in hours. We have tiny cell phones that take the place of an array of hardware that was required decades earlier. A handheld device that's an all-in-one computer, camera, camcorder, gaming system, telephone, and Internet-access-system that blows away each of the individual devices it replaces.

"And these examples are just off the top of my head," he said. "Countless goods and services that used to be scarce are now abundant. We have better clothing, better housing, and better living conditions. Imagine summers before the invention of air-conditioning," he added with a horrified look on his face.

"In the seventeenth century, mirrors were so expensive that only a king could afford what we can now buy at Walmart for ten dollars. And this *more-for-less* trend can be seen everywhere. Every decade the cost of computing power, electricity, transportation, long-distance communication, and countless other goods and services has plummeted."

"What about violence?" said Connor. "The rise of terrorism?"

"Still bad, and still troubling. But we're now instantly aware of mass killings anywhere in the world, amplifying our perception of the prevalence of violence. And we don't often put raw numbers into the proper perspective. As our population has skyrocketed, *of course* the raw number of violent deaths has risen as well. But if you calculate the number of violent deaths as a *percentage* of the population, this percentage has fallen dramatically, and is now the lowest in history. The murder rate in medieval Europe was more than *thirty times* what it is today. Wars between First World countries have all but vanished, and those that are being waged kill only a fraction of what they did before."

"Okay," said Paige. "Let's say the world *is* better than ever before. And I have to admit, you've made a good case for it. So why do most of us believe the opposite?"

Connor's eyes were glued to his father. He was eager to hear his reply. But at the same time, he was wondering if his dad would ever get around to disclosing what he considered to be his major breakthrough.

Connor jerked to his left, startled, as the sliding glass door entrance into his father's backyard burst open. His father and wife were just as shocked, as a woman in her mid-thirties exploded through the opening. She was attractive, raven-haired, but with a wild look in her piercing blue eyes.

Was this some berserker escapee from a psychiatric ward? Connor braced himself as the woman rushed toward them.

"Get down!" she demanded as she continued moving toward the glass patio table. "All of you. On your stomachs. Hurry!"

8

Jared Sprouse was relieved to be on level ground as he and his two comrades carefully made their way through the thick, hard scrub, just enough over their heads to conceal them entirely. The chaparral didn't limit itself to the steep incline, but also covered ninety percent of the mesa Gibson's residence was on. The other ten percent of the mesa, at least two acres in extent, had been cleared by whoever had originally built the home.

They crept toward the clearing as stealthily as possible. Sprouse had checked his phone just a few minutes earlier, confirming that the trio they were after were still locked in place around a glass table in the backyard. He took several more steps and then absently checked the drone footage once again.

His eyes widened and he stopped in his tracks. He held up a fist, a signal for his two comrades to halt behind him, and then turned toward them, holding out his phone so they could see it.

Yet another visitor was joining the party.

"I don't believe it!" whispered Sprouse in dismay. Elias Gibson hadn't hosted a single guest until the day they needed to take him out, and suddenly he was the most popular guy in the city.

The newcomer was a woman, one who had apparently driven up the winding road while it was out of their view. She was entering the front door of Gibson's home like she owned it. She looked fit and self-assured, and she was moving in a hurry.

Sprouse shook his head in disgust. He should never have accepted Vader's *no-collateral-damage* restriction—not when the timing of the op was also constrained. He had done so because he agreed with the wisdom of not hurting additional innocents, and had failed to consider the possibility of overnight guests.

But these constraints were turning the simplest of operations into a tactical nightmare. Not to mention necessitating the use of ski masks to be sure a survivor couldn't describe their faces later on—masks that had become hot, itchy, and a general pain in the ass.

Moments later the drone's camera picked up the newcomer again as she emerged from under the covered section of patio in the backyard, moving quickly toward the glass table. Despite telephoto lenses, the image of the woman was tiny, but even so, she seemed to be quite agitated, perhaps even panicked.

Was she tipping them off that they were being stalked? Impossible. How could she know?

As they continued watching, Elias Gibson rose, put a pair of binoculars to his eyes, and began a two-hundred-seventy-degree sweep of his surroundings.

They were fortunate to still be within the chaparral, or Elias's search would have picked them up. "I have no idea who this woman is," whispered Sprouse, "but she seems to have them spooked."

He gestured toward the lieutenant. "Hayden," he said hurriedly, "work your way around the property until you have a good vantage point on the driveway. If you don't hear from me that we took them out when you get there, make your presence known. Make sure it's clear to them that they can't leave by car. Remember, no one gets hurt other than the senior Gibson, no matter what."

He turned to the master sergeant. "Navarro, you're with me," he whispered. "We need to get into position to take them out before they bolt. Let's move with a purpose!" he added, setting off at a fast trot.

* * *

Connor Gibson had no idea what to make of this trespasser, but he wasn't about to dive to the ground, and Paige and his father weren't moving either.

"What the hell kind of entrance is this, Kayla?" said Elias Gibson. "And why are you so early?"

Connor traded glances with Paige. His father *knew* this crazed woman? He wasn't sure if he should be relieved, or even *more* worried.

The woman—apparently named Kayla—didn't respond. Instead, she rushed past them and scanned the landscape around them in all directions like she had seen a ghost.

When she finally finished she turned back toward the table. "Thank God, Elias!" she said in relief. "It looks like you aren't in immediate danger, but we aren't out of the woods yet. And next time, when I tell you to get down, how about *listening*."

"What are you talking about?" he said. "Why would I be in danger?"

The woman's stoic resolve suddenly began to melt away before their eyes. "Someone just tried to *kill me*," she said, almost hysterically, looking like she might burst into tears. "While I was at home," she continued, visibly trying to pull herself back together, "waiting for your call to come meet your family."

She shook her head, and her features hardened. "Come on, Elias!" she demanded, the fire returning to her eyes. "We have to get out of here!"

"Slow down," said Elias. "Someone tried to kill you? How?"

"By shooting at me!" whispered Kayla in horror. "From a distance. I think it must have been a sniper. A sniper!" she repeated, as if she still couldn't believe it. "I'm lucky to be alive. I must have moved just as he was shooting, so the bullet only grazed my arm."

As she said this, Connor noticed for the first time that her right arm was bandaged.

"I'm not even sure I heard the first shot," she continued. "All I know is that I felt a sharp pain, felt blood running down my arm, and heard the glass trophy case behind me shatter at the same instant. I was so startled by the glass I spun around, just as several more shots came in. Then I saw several holes in my window and got the hell out of there."

Elias rose from his chair as she was speaking and put the binoculars to his eyes, scanning his surroundings as if his life depended on it. "And you think this is related to our project?" he asked.

"What else?"

"No one else knows about it," he said. "And even if they did, why would they want us dead?"

"The question goes beyond how they know about it. How did they know where to find *me*? You know how low of a profile I've been keeping."

"None of this makes sense," said Elias. "But I'm not seeing anything out of the ordinary out there," he added, lowering the binoculars.

"Let's get inside, anyway!" she insisted. "I tried to warn you by phone, but cell reception is out. It's been out up here before, so maybe it's just a coincidence." She shook her head worriedly. "But maybe it's not."

Elias turned toward his son and daughter-in-law. "She's right," he said, and this time he had a little of Kayla's panic in his eyes. The lack of cell phone coverage, combined with the threat on her life, was finally lighting a fire under him. "Let's get inside. I'll make introductions later."

Connor and Paige rose from the table and followed Elias and the newcomer as they strode to the back of the house. As they neared the covered part of the patio and the now half-open sliding glass door, a gunshot rang out in the distance. Kayla shrieked in terror as one pane of the slider shattered into thousands of diamond-sized pieces.

And Paige Estrella Gibson crumpled to the hard travertine surface like a puppet whose strings had been cut.

* * *

"Shit!" whispered Jared Sprouse to himself as they continued to near the proper vantage point he had chosen for the op. Glancing at the drone's images on his phone, he could see that Elias and his guests were agitated in the extreme, and he knew in his heart they would be rushing back inside in a matter of seconds. It was a wonder they hadn't done so already.

He and Navarro had made it to the clearing, but were still too far away to be sure of an accurate shot. But they had no other choice. Elias Gibson would know soon enough they were after him, so no use waiting any longer. If their target made it inside, things would get more difficult.

Sprouse called a halt and barked instructions to Navarro, just as the party of four began moving rapidly toward the house, entirely as expected.

Sprouse was vaguely aware that Navarro was lifting his dart rifle to his shoulder, as ordered, but he had his own business to attend to. Elias would be out of sight under the covered part of the patio in seconds.

Sprouse squeezed the trigger of his assault rifle, set on single shot, but missed his target by several inches. He heard the sound of shattering glass in the distance, followed immediately by a shriek of surprise. He was about to pull the trigger a second time, but Elias had moved closer to the woman who had just arrived, making additional shots too risky.

Damn! Navarro must have missed with his dart rifle as well, as none of the four were visible any longer. Failure wasn't surprising at this range, but he was still disappointed.

Even so, with Hayden in place to discourage any of them from leaving by car, and cell phones suppressed, Sprouse had more than enough time to search every square inch of the house until he completed his mission.

* * *

"Nooo!" whispered Connor Gibson hysterically, so horrified that the word was barely able to escape his mouth.

He dropped to the pavement beside his wife, while his father and the mystery woman—who were ahead of them and wisely hadn't looked back after the shot—raced through the opening and into the house, ignoring the glass shards that had sprayed everywhere.

Connor lifted his wife as if she were weightless, his strength boosted to superhero levels by the adrenaline now surging through his body. He felt sure that her momentum had taken her just out of sight of whoever was doing the shooting. But if he was wrong, the back of his head might explode into a bloody pulp at any moment. He rushed Paige across the threshold of the slider and into the house, relieved to still be alive.

His father and the woman named Kayla were taking cover in a room behind a large brick fireplace in the great room, and Connor joined them, depositing his wife gently on the hardwood floor.

"What happened?" whispered Elias in horror, not having seen her go down. "How bad is it?"

"She's still breathing," replied Connor, blinking back tears. "I'm not sure where she was hit," he added, frantically inspecting every inch of her body.

Where was the gunshot wound? He couldn't even seem to find any blood.

"I don't think she was shot," said Kayla excitedly. "Look," she added, reaching forward and carefully removing a small dart that had pierced Paige's shirt and was embedded in her side. "I think she was tranquilized."

Connor inhaled sharply and closed his eyes, basking in newfound hope. But he allowed himself only a second of silent thanks to a higher power before bending down to quickly check her pulse and breathing.

It remained strong. Kayla was right! She hadn't been shot after all. She was going to survive.

His elation vanished as he realized that *none of them* were likely to survive for much longer, regardless of their present condition. The fact that Paige had only been hit with a dart might indicate that the shooters wanted them alive for some reason, but he had to assume the worst. After all, the slider hadn't shattered the way it had from a *dart*. Someone out there was firing more lethal ammunition. And someone had just tried to kill this Kayla in her home, as well.

Elias dashed out from the room behind the fireplace, rushed to a nearby table, and returned moments later with a small remote. He pressed one of the buttons and expensive blackout blinds began to lower themselves over every window on the floor, including over the entire expanse of the slider, ensuring that they couldn't be seen from anywhere outside, and darkening the first floor to a surprising degree.

"Let's get to my car!" said Elias, leaving the remote on the floor. "Do you need help with Paige?" he asked his son.

Connor didn't waste breath on an answer, lifting Paige into his arms once again and following his father toward the door to the garage, just as a lengthy barrage of machine gun fire tore across the driveway outside, shredding plants and stucco and ripping through Kayla's car, putting it out of commission in seconds.

Connor lowered Paige to the floor once again. "Looks like they don't want us driving," he said grimly. "And I'm betting there's more than one of them out there."

"So now what?" said Elias, his voice now taking on notes of panic. "I don't have a single weapon. How do we get out of this?"

Kayla shook her head, and once again looked to be on the verge of bursting into tears.

Elias turned toward his son and his features hardened. "It's up to you, Connor," he said. "You've read hundreds of thrillers. You know more about these types of situations than any of us. There has to be a way for us to survive this. Find it!" he demanded.

His father's words were like a brisk slap in the face, waking him up, reminding him that in this situation, he couldn't rely on anyone but himself. He didn't have combat training of any kind, but the best thriller heroes relied on brains as much as brawn to get out of tight spots. There must be something he had learned from all of his reading that would somehow save the day.

He turned to Kayla. "I don't suppose you're armed," he said.

She shook her head.

"No, I didn't think so," he said with a frown. "Dad, do you have any security you can activate on the doors? Any alarms?"

"None," said Elias.

"Motion sensors?"

His father shook his head. "Not if you don't count a few motion-activated nightlights plugged into a few bathrooms."

Connor rolled his eyes. "I don't."

It was becoming clear to Connor that he had absolutely nothing to work with. Which meant he needed to get out of his comfort zone, be as creative as he had ever been. His mind raced, considering and rejecting possibilities at a blistering pace.

Connor's eyes widened as a plan began to take shape. He turned to his father. "Please tell me that you still keep a box of emergency flares in your car," he pleaded, and then held his breath as he awaited the answer.

Elias nodded. "I do."

Connor blew out a long, relieved breath. In the days of cell phones, emergency flares had largely become obsolete, but Elias was a creature of habit, and had kept a box since he had first learned to drive. Perhaps they still had a chance. "Get them!" he barked. "Hurry!"

Elias returned from the garage only twenty seconds later with a box of four red flares and handed them to his son.

Connor was painfully aware that they had already been inside for almost two minutes, and that whoever was out there would be joining them soon. The only reason the attackers had yet to enter was that they had started a considerable distance away, and would be moving slowly, carefully.

And why not? They knew they held all the cards. No one inside the house could phone out or use a car. So the attackers could hunt them down at their leisure, or burn the place down and flush them out that way.

Still, even if those who were after them were taking their time tightening the noose, Connor didn't want to risk loitering here even a moment longer.

He gestured to his father and Kayla. "Follow me," he said. "Stay close. We're leaving through the side door to the south."

"Wait!" said Elias, taking off at a run. "I have to get something. I'll meet you at the side door."

Connor opened his mouth to tell him that this wasn't necessary, but his father was already racing up the stairs. It was a stupid, reckless move, and Connor was furious with him. With their lives at stake, nothing material could possibly be worth the additional risk.

Connor turned to Kayla. "Come on!" he said, already beginning to move toward their destination.

"What about Paige?"

"We have to risk leaving her here for a short time," he said, feeling sick to his stomach from this necessity. If he had miscalculated, he would never forgive himself. At least in the few minutes he would have left to live.

They made it to the side door and Connor opened it a crack. As he had recalled from his father's brief tour, the side yard in this direction was virtually non-existent, nothing more than ten feet of level ground that gave way immediately to a steep downward slope into yet another sunken, wild canyon. It was also the farthest exit away from where the shots had been fired at both the backyard and driveway.

As expected, the coast appeared to be clear.

Connor hastily skimmed the instructions on the box of handheld emergency flares he now carried. Flares had been used to good effect in a novel he had once read, but he had never used one himself. These were self-lighting, containing an internal flint/steel striking mechanism. Pulling a tab, hard, to yank off the cap at one end would ignite them immediately.

Elias joined them seconds later, out of breath, carrying a small hard-sided briefcase. "Lead on," he whispered to Connor, ignoring the cross look on his son's face.

Connor wanted to chew him out, but there was no time. He handed Kayla and his father a flare, took two for himself, and hastily issued instructions, including explaining why the briefcase that his father had just retrieved would be staying behind.

He still couldn't believe this was happening. How had it come to this? His life had been as exciting as watching paint dry. The greatest danger he ever faced was the prospect of getting a *paper cut*.

But in just a matter of minutes, everything had changed. Not only was he now fighting for his life, he was expected to outthink trained assassins to save the lives of the two people he loved most in all the world, along with a woman he had never met.

Connor took a deep breath, nodded at Kayla and his father, and yanked the caps off both of his flares, knowing that they would be doing the same with theirs.

The moment all four flares ignited they rushed outside, crouching low, holding the flares at knee level and fanning out, creating a wall of thick, billowing red smoke twenty feet wide. The smoke swallowed them inside, advertising their presence but totally masking them from any gunmen, no matter how close.

They arrived at the edge of the property in seconds and began a swift descent, as smoke continued to gush from the flares. Connor had been concerned about his father and the newcomer being able to navigate the steep decline without plummeting to their deaths at the bottom, but each made the fifteen feet he had asked for in one piece, even carrying a flare in one hand. Despite being beside them within the wall of smoke, visibility was so poor that Connor could only make them out when they moved, and then just barely.

"Stay concealed inside the scrub!" he shouted. "The flares won't last long. When we make it to the bottom, I'll give you further instructions."

Upon hearing this pre-arranged signal, Elias and Kayla scrambled back up to the top of the property and back into the house, the flares they were carrying further reinforcing the still-thick smoke near the side door.

Connor had chosen his signal carefully, hoping that if the men after them heard what he had said, this would sell his bluff all the more.

He now held two flares in one hand, but years of rock climbing had increased his strength, agility, and balance so much that he had no problem scrambling another twenty feet down the steep, scrub-filled slope. He paused there for just a moment, tossed both flares a further fifteen feet down, and then scrambled back up and into the house, the smoke continuing to provide more than enough cover to mask his retreat.

He soon joined his father and Kayla behind the fireplace once again. He blew out a long, relieved breath upon seeing that Paige hadn't been disturbed in the brief time they were away. "*Thank God,*" he whispered to himself. She was still unconscious, but her pulse and breathing remained strong.

Connor vaguely realized that he and his two companions were now bleeding fairly extensively. The blood loss was nothing to worry about, but they had collected a wide variety of minor cuts and abrasions during their headlong climb down, and then back up, the steep incline. Of course they had. The terrain was strewn with sharp rocks, and the thick vegetation was about as soft and forgiving as steel wool.

Connor would have loved to rest for a few seconds and appreciate how well his deception seemed to have gone. But he knew he couldn't.

They weren't out of this yet, and he would likely need to conjure up a few more clever ideas before it was over.

9

Sprouse and Navarro worked their way toward the back of the house, slowly but surely, aware that they had all the time they needed. Given that Hayden had a clear line of sight to the driveway, their targets weren't going *anywhere*. Which was a good thing, since the need to ensure that only Elias was harmed was continuing to make their lives miserable, slowing them down and removing easy options.

Still, they were lucky the estate was so isolated, allowing them to proceed carefully, by the numbers, secure in the knowledge that the only living things that could help their quarry now were rabbits and coyotes.

Sprouse stopped in mid-stride as a thick cloud of red smoke billowed up from the far side of the house. His eyes narrowed in confusion, but only for a moment. It was a flare. Had to be. And not just one, he now realized, but *many*.

He had to hand it to this group. They were clearly trying to be proactive.

Not that it would do them any good.

"Lieutenant!" he said into his comm. "We can see smoke, but other than that our view is blocked by the house. Can you make out what's happening?"

"Can't see anyone through the smoke," replied Hayden, "but I'd guess from the extent of it that all four of them are holding flares. And the smoke is descending. They're trying to escape down the slope, carrying the flares with them for cover."

Sprouse heard shouted words coming from the direction of the smoke. He eyed Navarro questioningly, but the master sergeant shrugged, indicating that he hadn't caught the content, either.

"Lieutenant," said Sprouse into his comm, knowing that Hayden not only had a better vantage point on the side yard, but was considerably closer, "we just heard shouting. Were you able to make out any of the words?"

"Yes, I'm pretty sure it was the son. He was telling the others to stay hidden in the scrub all the way down, since their flares wouldn't last long."

Sprouse considered. Surely this escape attempt was as straightforward as it seemed. Impressive, actually, for a bunch of civilians. Using handheld flares to provide cover for a hasty escape was brilliant, and might even be effective if they could beat Sprouse and his men down the canyon.

And the son's instructions to the others demonstrated just how smart and clearheaded he was being.

But something didn't feel right. The younger Gibson's shouted command was just a little *too* loud. Maybe he was flush with adrenaline and scared out of his mind, which accounted for the amped-up volume.

But maybe that wasn't it at all. Maybe he had *wanted* to be heard. In which case, he was being too clever by half.

Were the four civilians really headed down the slope? Or, was this simply a bluff, intended to bait Sprouse and his men into scurrying down after them while they remained in the house, preparing to drive to safety?

Elias's son was only a technical writer, not a commando. While doing his usual thorough research, Sprouse had learned that Connor Gibson, like his father, had never owned a gun, and had about as much experience in combat tactics and strategy as a newborn baby.

So perhaps Sprouse's imagination was running wild. The younger Gibson couldn't be *that* good.

He sighed. Either way, it paid for him to cover all the bases.

"Master Sergeant Navarro," he said, "Lieutenant Hayden, you two go after them. I'll stay up top and search the house to make sure they didn't double back."

Before they even replied, he thought better of it. "Cancel that," he said. "Hayden, don't move. We're coming to you."

Hayden still had to cover the driveway, Sprouse realized, at least until he determined if the targets *had* doubled back. And he would need Navarro's lock-picking skills. "You and Navarro can follow them down the slope once I'm inside the house."

"It'd be faster if the two of you pursued them," Hayden pointed out. "I can go in through the front door and make sure they aren't inside."

"Negative," said Sprouse.

Hayden was right. Having him scour the house would save time, but the man was too reckless for Sprouse to allow it. Conducting a room-to-room search required patience and delicacy, and Sprouse wasn't about to delegate.

"I won't delay you by more than a few minutes," added the captain. "They don't have proper clothing, so that vegetation will tear them to shreds. You and Navarro will catch up to them in no time."

Navarro caught his commander's eye and frowned. "So you really think they might have doubled back?" he said skeptically. "That would be some advanced and ballsy tactics for a bunch of panicked civilians."

"Yes, it would be," agreed Sprouse. "But if I'm wrong, I know you and Hayden can handle them without me."

"Just wouldn't want you missing out on all the fun."

"Very thoughtful," said the captain. "And speaking of fun, you won't be having any. Too risky for you to tranq any of Elias's visitors while they're clinging to steep terrain. So you'll have to be patient, and completing the mission will be a giant pain in the ass."

Navarro frowned. "Yeah, tell me about it," he said unhappily.

10

"That was brilliant, Con," said Elias, seconds after his son had rejoined them inside the house. "Well done."

"Maybe," said Connor cautiously, "but maybe not. Let's be sure they took the bait." He paused. "Dad, do you still use a doorbell camera in the front entryway?"

His father nodded.

"Open the app and keep an eye on the front, so we know if someone's trying to approach."

"Got it," said Elias.

Connor lifted his wife into his arms. Given his exertions and the weakening of his initial adrenaline boost, he now felt her full weight. Even so, she was relatively light, and rock climbers' muscles were lean and steel-cable strong. "Let's take this to your bedroom, Dad," he said, moving toward the staircase.

When they arrived in the master bedroom upstairs, Connor set his wife down gently on the bed. He turned to his father. "I need you to go out on your balcony," he said, "and see if you can spot anyone below. But be careful," he implored. "Inch the slider open and crawl out on your stomach. But only as far as you need to go to get a wide view down below. "

"Understood," said Elias.

"Good. I'll be right back."

"Where are you going?"

"I'll be doing the same as you on the front side," he replied, already moving. One of the second-floor rooms at the front of the house had a small balcony as well, which he remembered from his father's recent tour. "The doorbell camera is a help, but its view is pretty limited."

Connor returned to the master bedroom less than a minute later, joining Elias, who had just reentered the room from his balcony. "I didn't see anyone," he told his son.

"I didn't, either," said Connor.

"It looks like your plan worked," said Elias.

Connor didn't look convinced. "I'd like to think we fooled them," he said, "and all of them are now racing down the canyon after us." He shook his head. "But we can't afford to make that assumption. Just because we didn't spot anyone, doesn't mean they aren't out there. If they're smart, one of them will stay up here, just to be sure."

Connor paused, analyzing their situation at a furious pace, aware that he was thinking faster, and more clearly, than ever before. Perhaps his father had a point. Life-and-death stakes did seem to focus the mind.

He surveyed the room, looking for anything that could be used as a weapon, anything that could help them.

Bingo, he thought, as he spied a set of iron fireplace tools sitting on a rectangular array of marble between the fireplace and carpeting. The set contained a poker, broom, log lifter, and shovel—all of which had never been used. The fireplace in the master bedroom was gas-powered, and contained nothing but fake logs, so the tools were there for decoration only.

But maybe not today.

Connor frowned. Even so, as lethal as the small iron shovel could be, using one to go up against a gun wasn't much of a contest. He wouldn't stand a chance.

It was then he spied a small black object on his father's end-table, about the size and shape of a soda can, and his eyes widened.

Perhaps there was a way to even the odds after all.

11

Captain Jared Sprouse accompanied Ernesto Navarro to the side yard, avoiding the doorbell camera he knew was installed on the front door. Navarro had never met a lock he couldn't pick, and the one on the side door was as easy as they came. For an estate of this size, the lack of anything even approaching security was remarkable.

Hayden was continuing to watch the driveway, but once he heard Navarro's voice in his ear, confirming that Sprouse had made it inside, he double-timed it to the side yard so they could begin their pursuit down the slope.

Inside the house, Sprouse kept his back to one wall and his dart gun facing forward, trying not to feel like an idiot for wielding such a relatively impotent weapon. He had left his assault rifle outside, along with a tranquilizer rifle. Now he only had two handguns, one that fired darts, and one that fired bullets.

The safest way to proceed, if anyone *was* in the house, was to tranquilize first and worry about identity later. Once they were all unconscious he could introduce Elias Gibson to more lethal weaponry.

He crept silently through the first floor, opening every door and closet with extreme caution. The home was surprisingly dark, and he was just able to see without additional illumination. Despite the blazing sun outside, the residents had turned off every light in the house and drawn remarkably opaque blinds over every last window.

Another smart move. If Sprouse had flipped on a light switch without thinking, he would have given away his presence within the house.

Sprouse could have proceeded much more rapidly, but he couldn't be sure the woman who had tipped Elias off wasn't armed. He knew the other three weren't, but this newcomer was a mystery in every way.

Sprouse entered the great room, strewn with shattered glass, and noted several small drops of blood, already dry, on the hardwood floor. Elias or one of his three guests could have been cut when the slider had shattered.

But it was also possible this was an indication that they *had* doubled back, as he suspected, and the hard scrub and sharp rocks on the slope had chewed them up.

He bent closer to the floor to search for any additional traces of blood, when he spied a tranquilizer dart lying on its side. He inspected the tip carefully. It was blood red, indicating it had found a human target.

Navarro's shot *had* hit someone, after all, he realized, and the dart had been pulled out by the others after this person had been pulled inside. Which made it far more likely that the group's descent into the canyon was a deception, after all. He doubted they had the intestinal fortitude to leave an unconscious member of their party behind, even though it would have been the smart thing to do.

Sprouse continued to search the floor for blood and after only fifteen seconds or so, even in the near darkness, he became convinced there was a directionality to the tiny red spots. They led to the stairs, and then up to the second floor, leaving a faint, but still discernible, breadcrumb trail.

As he mounted the first stair, a small but powerful light sprang to life at his feet, startling him.

Shit! he cursed silently, bending down to inspect the source of this unexpected and unwanted brightness. It was a goddamned plug-in nightlight, firmly inserted into a wall outlet near the stairs. Motion-activated, like a kid might have in his room, or in a dark hallway.

What a joke.

Or maybe not, Sprouse realized.

Maybe this wasn't here because Elias Gibson was a light sleeper who wanted illumination as he made his way to the kitchen for a midnight snack. Maybe it had been placed here, *recently*, as a warning. Maybe someone was camped out near the top stair, waiting for this makeshift signal. The house was dark enough for the small plug-in device to throw just enough light to be used for this purpose.

So be it, thought Sprouse. Even if this was designed to be a trap, it wouldn't work. Even if the woman who had warned his quarry off did have a gun—which he continued to think was unlikely—and even if she managed to get the drop on him—even more unlikely—she would shoot him center mass, hitting nothing but his protective vest.

Still, why take any more chances than necessary? He crouched low and worked his way up the stairs on his elbows and stomach. When he neared a sharp turn in the long staircase, he removed a dollar-bill-sized steel mirror from a compartment of his combat jacket and extended it around the turn, just enough for the reflection to reveal if anyone was waiting for him there.

The stairs were empty.

He used the mirror again to get a view of the hallway before he entered. It, too, was uninhabited.

Sprouse continued following the blood trail, which, sparse though it had become, led down a hallway, past a linen closet, and to a closed door that he guessed opened into the master bedroom.

He eyed the linen closet as he approached. It was possible the breadcrumb trail was a deliberate lure, and someone was waiting inside the closet to ambush him from behind when he passed it.

But as he crept closer, he heard voices behind the bedroom door. He listened for almost a full minute, until he was sure that all four of his quarry were in the room. He heard three voices, not four, but they were discussing the vital signs of the fourth, Paige Gibson—whom Navarro's dart must have hit. Her heart and respiration rate were apparently still strong and steady.

"Any guesses as to how long she'll be out?" Connor Gibson was saying. "She doesn't look like she's about to awaken."

"No way to know," came an older male voice, no doubt belonging to Elias Gibson. "Depends on the drug, the dart, Paige's weight, and any number of other factors."

"Just be happy she's alive," said a woman's voice, the one who had joined them last. "But let's get the hell out of here already!" she said impatiently.

"Just a few minutes longer," said Connor. "Give them more time to get farther down the canyon," he added.

A smile slowly spread across Sprouse's face, the first positive emotion he had shown since the op had begun.

He had them. No need to check the linen closet, or anywhere else, after all.

It was about damn time.

He thought through various ways to play this, before choosing a strategy he thought would achieve his goals, with the least risk that someone other than Elias Gibson would end up as collateral damage.

He walked silently up to the door, making sure his mask was still hiding every inch of his face. "This is Special Agent Mike Foley of the FBI," he announced loudly. "You can come out now. The danger has passed."

The conversation inside stopped dead.

"I can explain everything," he continued. "The two men who were after you are now climbing down the canyon. Sorry I arrived late, but you've done brilliantly for yourselves. I'm here to help. Come out and I'll show you my badge."

He paused for several seconds, but there was no reply.

"Look, the two hostiles won't be fooled for long, and I've learned that more are on the way. So we have to go. Now!"

After yet another pause he added, "I'm going to shoot the lock and come in. I just want to be sure you're all okay. Stand away from the door! I don't want anyone hurt."

He transferred his tranquilizer gun to his left hand and drew his Sig Sauer P226, loaded with armor-piercing rounds, illegal in the US.

"I'll be firing at the door in five seconds," he announced, "so you'd better stand clear. Four. Three. Two. One!" he finished, pumping three rounds into the door handle and lock, which obliterated both and pushed the door wide open.

Even though Sprouse couldn't hear anything behind him while he was shooting, he suddenly had a strange sixth sense that someone was there.

He wheeled around, but it was too late. Before he completed his turn, a small iron shovel slammed into his upper forehead with tremendous force. He went down, dazed, falling against the now-open bedroom door. He stumbled through the threshold and crashed to the carpeted floor, losing his grip on both guns as he struggled to retain consciousness.

Sprouse rolled onto his back just in time to see Connor Gibson entering the room from behind him, an iron shovel still in his hand. In the hallway a few feet away, the door to the linen closet was now open as well.

The younger Gibson had been inside after all, preparing an ambush.

But how? It wasn't possible. He had heard Connor's voice in the bedroom. He had heard *all* of their voices.

And then Sprouse's eyes fell on a small black cylinder resting on the bedroom carpeting only a few feet away from where he had landed. A black cylinder with an Amazon logo near the bottom. He vaguely realized what it was, a fifth-generation Echo device. A smart speaker powered by the ever-improving AI capabilities of an electronic assistant named Alexa.

But what was it doing on the floor in the center of the room?

As Sprouse clung to consciousness, he had a sudden flash of insight, and all became clear to him in a single instant.

Connor Gibson had used his phone to pre-record the conversation Sprouse had just heard. He and the others had put on the briefest of stage plays, performed for an audience of one, and then Connor had paired his phone to the Echo device. He had waited near the top stair until he had seen the nightlight activate, and then had hidden inside the linen closet.

When Sprouse had crept toward the bedroom door, the younger Gibson had simply pressed the "play" button on his phone's touch screen, having already set up the recording to be played through the Echo speaker in the bedroom.

The *voices* of those Sprouse was hunting may have been inside the master bedroom, but the *owners* of these voices were not. They were all hiding out somewhere else upstairs, knowing he would follow the blood trail they had laid down to exactly where they wanted him.

Their strategy was nothing short of inspired.

But as he strained to consider his situation further, his addled mind could hold on no longer, and his tenuous grip on consciousness finally slipped away.

12

Connor Gibson saw the light go out in the assailant's eyes through the holes in the man's ski mask, and felt mixed emotions. Elated that they had stopped a man who was trying to kill them, but horrified at having to commit such a primal act of violence to do it.

And disturbed by how triumphant he had felt when the shovel had connected.

Two different guns were on the floor, and he picked up the one that had just been used, lowering the small iron shovel as he did so. Given what had happened to his wife, he guessed the other gun fired tranquilizer darts.

He quickly confirmed that the man was still breathing, however shallowly, and blew out a sigh of relief, backing up and pointing the gun at the fallen assailant.

"Dad, pull off his mask and frisk him," he said. "If he wakes up, I've got him covered."

Elias shook his head as if he wasn't seeing right. "You know how to shoot a gun?" he asked in disbelief.

"Just barely," replied Connor. He had gone to a shooting range with a gun-owning friend just the month before, having decided that a thriller writer should have experience with a gun. Paige had come also, but was an even worse shot than him. "Dad, hurry!" he added, since his father was making no move to follow his instructions.

"We don't have time for this!" said Kayla. "We need to go. What if they're on their way back to us right now?" she asked.

"Then we're screwed," said Connor simply. "I'm all out of deceptions."

While his son was speaking, Elias removed the man's ski mask to reveal a deep purple welt on the upper right side of his forehead. The mask had protected his skin from tearing, preventing the lacerations and bleeding he otherwise would have received from the blow.

Connor studied the man carefully, reaching down and removing a tiny microphone that was velcroed to his lapel, along with a receiver embedded in his ear. He showed them both to his father and Kayla and then crushed them beneath his shoe.

"Either of you recognize this guy?" asked Connor.

They both quickly shook their heads no.

Elias's fingers danced over every inch of the man's assault jacket and black, military-issue assault clothing, and into what seemed to be an unlimited number of pockets and special compartments.

"Could he really be with the FBI?" asked Kayla.

"Sure," said Connor sarcastically, "if FBI agents have begun wearing ski masks and trying to kill innocent people."

Just as these words left his mouth, his father removed a thin leather wallet from the man's front pocket, which opened to reveal a badge on the top half, and a photo ID on the bottom. Both indicated that the man was FBI Special Agent Michael Foley. Elias held it up for his son and Kayla to see. "Does this look legit?"

"Legit enough," said Connor. "But like I was saying, given the circumstances, it has to be a fake."

"Or else it's real, and this guy is doing some freelancing on the side," noted Elias.

"That's a possibility also," admitted Connor, annoyed that this hadn't occurred to him. In his mind, FBI agents were white knights, not the kind of scum who would willingly commit murder for money. But no organization on Earth could avoid corruption, could avoid the occasional poisonous apple within its ranks.

Elias continued his search and discovered a whole host of items, which he removed and placed on the carpet nearby. These included a small steel mirror, two combat knives—one that had been inside an ankle holster—and a first-aid kit. There were also three small grenades, which Connor recognized from having read so many thrillers as being flash-bangs, and dozens of long plastic zip-ties, which could be used to instantly bind wrists and ankles.

Connor decided the zip-ties were particularly useful. He picked up several off the floor. "I'm going to immobilize him," he announced. "Then we'll drive out of here in your SUV," he said to his father, handing him the iron shovel. "If he wakes up before I've finished, clock him in the head again."

Elias swallowed hard, but nodded his assent.

Connor went to work ratcheting one zip-tie tight around the assailant's ankles, and one around his wrists, rolling him over first so that his hands were tied behind his back.

"You should also anchor him to the bed," suggested Elias. "To make sure he's still here when the authorities arrive."

"We aren't leaving him for the authorities," said Connor. "We're taking him with us."

"Are you out of your mind?" said Kayla. "This guy could probably kill us with his *pinky*."

Connor couldn't help but smile. "Then it's a good thing his pinky is bound behind his back, isn't it?" he said.

"Very funny," said Kayla.

"Look," said Connor with a grim expression, "I get how dangerous this guy is. Even bound. But we have to take the risk. We're civilians, with no experience, no training, and no skills. So our first instinct is to run. Leave the bad guys behind and count our blessings. I get that. But this could be our only chance to learn what we're up against. I don't have to remind you that they tried to kill you, also, do I?"

Kayla paled and shook her head.

"If we don't figure this out," said Connor, "get proactive, we may win this battle, but we'll lose the war."

"I agree," said Elias, staring at Kayla as he did.

She didn't look happy, but she finally nodded her agreement. "Okay, we'll take him with us. But don't take your eyes off of him. Assume he's still very dangerous."

No kidding, thought Connor. "Of course," he said, as reasonably as possible.

"Then it's settled," said Elias. "Let's get out of here." He caught his son's eye. "I can get Paige, but you'll have to carry the, uh . . . you know, the prisoner."

Elias reached under his bed, removed the briefcase he had retrieved earlier, and asked Kayla to carry it for him.

"Wait a minute, Dad," said Connor. "I get that you want to bring the briefcase with us, but I want to bring the shovel also. And everything else that was in this guy's pockets, including both guns. Do you have something big enough to carry it all?"

Elias disappeared into his cavernous walk-in closet and came out seconds later with a large blue duffel bag, made from ballistic nylon.

"Perfect," said Connor when he saw it.

Kayla quickly loaded the bag while Connor lifted Paige off the bed and passed her to his father. Elias wasn't nearly as strong as his son, but Paige was relatively light, and he could manage over a short distance, even given stairs. Especially after Connor demonstrated how to perform a fireman's carry. Connor lifted the unconscious assailant to his shoulders and the group made their way to Elias's SUV.

When they arrived, Connor laid the prisoner on his back on the floor, in front of the third row of beige leather seats, and sat in this row, facing the front of the car. He then traded the gun for the iron fireplace shovel—a weapon he was more comfortable with—and held it at the ready, in the off chance that the prisoner awakened and tried to cause trouble, despite now lying on his bound hands.

Elias Gibson laid Paige carefully across the second row of seats and sat on the edge, ensuring his daughter-in-law wouldn't roll off, which necessitated having his back to his son and their prisoner.

Kayla took the wheel, driving as fast as she could without screeching the tires, unsure if the men now descending into the canyon could see their escape, but trusting they'd be unable to hit them with any gunfire, regardless. Still, the conscious inhabitants of the spacious SUV practically held their breaths until they had made it safely down the hill and onto a main road, and confirmed that no one seemed to be following.

Connor pulled his phone from his pocket. "I'm calling the cops," he announced after confirming that the device was now getting reception.

"Wait!" said Elias from the row in front of him. "Are we sure that's wise?"

"You were the one who wanted to call the authorities," said Connor, "and leave this guy behind for them."

"I know. But I'm having second thoughts. These attacks were professional—and coordinated. A sniper tried to kill Kayla, so chances are these guys have military backgrounds. And she's kept such a low profile, the fact that they even *found* her suggests they might have government resources at their disposal."

"So you aren't in a trusting mood," guessed Connor.

"Not so much. Whoever they are, they're sophisticated, and probably have some serious money behind them. And if they really have infiltrated the FBI, they could have tentacles everywhere. Including other law enforcement agencies."

"You make some good points," said Connor, slipping his phone back into his pocket. "No cops—for now." A call to the police was probably safe, but without knowing what they were dealing with, it could also backfire, leading additional assassins directly to them.

"Wait!" said Connor, as he was struck by the obvious. "We need to get rid of our phones. Right now! They're the ultimate homing beacons."

Kayla cursed from the driver's seat. "That sucks," she said miserably, not arguing the point but clearly not thrilled to have to jettison a device that had come to be so essential to her daily life.

Elias accepted his son's decree with equanimity and appeared to be deep in thought. "If someone is using our phones to track us," he said finally, "we can't just toss them on the side of the road. Whoever is after us might find them, hack them, and get more information to use against us."

"So let's smash them on the ground first," suggested Connor.

"Will that be enough?" said Elias. "Aren't there experts who can still extract the data?"

"I'm not sure," replied Connor. "Maybe." He paused in thought. "Any bodies of water nearby?"

Elias studied the SUV's surroundings for several seconds to get his bearings. "There's a small man-made lake about three miles from here."

"Perfect. We'll drown our phones there. A burial at sea."

"I'll direct Kayla," said Elias.

Connor nodded, realizing that he still knew almost nothing about the woman who was driving. She and his father were obviously working on the same project together, but as much as he wanted to learn how she fit in, his curiosity would have to wait. "So after we ditch the phones," he said, "then what? We need a destination. And we need a plan."

He paused. "Any ideas?"

"Yes," said Kayla immediately. "Borrego Springs. I had a safe house built there. Just in case things ever got rough."

"You *expected* something like this to happen?" said Elias in disbelief.

"Not at this point, I didn't. But yes. Eventually. We're about to usher in the greatest transformation of society the world has ever seen. The consequences will be profound and, in many ways, unpredictable. We're kicking all kinds of powerful hornets' nests. And the most powerful, most ruthless people on Earth are bound to be the angriest hornets."

She shrugged. "So I took precautions."

Connor shook his head in dismay. This was getting crazier by the second—and given what had come before, that was really saying something. "Where's Borrego Springs?" he said. He had heard the name, but knew little else about it.

"It's about ninety minutes away, almost directly due— "

"Take this exit," interrupted Elias, "and turn right. The lake will be on the left."

Kayla nodded, guided the large SUV onto the approaching off-ramp, and then continued. "Borrego Springs is almost directly due east of us, in the Sonoran Desert. The safe house is secluded, but near enough the town for grocery and supply runs. No way the people after us know about it. And even if anyone recognized it for what it was, there's no way it could ever be connected to me."

"What do you mean, recognized it for what it was?" said Connor. "It's just a house off the grid, right?"

Kayla shook her head. "It's a lot more than that. It's like a house-sized panic room. State of the art. There's no way anyone sneaks up on it. It has concentric rings of sensors, beginning miles away, as good as those at the most secure military installations. The photonic sensors are especially sensitive since Borrego Springs is designated an International Dark-Sky Community by the International Dark-Sky Association."

"I have no idea what that means," said Connor.

"It's a haven for public astronomy," replied Kayla. "So there are no traffic lights in all of Borrego Springs, and nighttime lighting is substantially reduced. An ideal place to live if you want great views of the night sky." She paused. "Or, if you want to place security sensors around your safe house that monitor for external light."

Connor was stunned. Who *was* this woman? A woman who not only knew there was such a thing as an International Dark-Sky Community, but recognized the advantages of setting up a safe house near one.

"If anyone did find a way to sneak up on us there and attack," she continued, "they'd find it impregnable. Automatic armaments outside. A separate, self-contained air supply. Steel that can automatically slide down over windows and inner doors." A smile slowly made its way across her face. "It's like something from a science fiction movie."

"Okay," said Connor, as they arrived at the lake, "I'm sold. My idea was to stay at a cheap motel under assumed names. But I guess staying at a secret, impenetrable lair would work too," he added wryly.

Kayla drove as close to the lake as she could, keeping the engine running. Connor collected all phones, including those belonging to Paige and their prisoner, exited the car, made sure no one was looking, and flung them as hard as he could into the deepest part of the lake.

Moments later they were back on the road.

"Now that that's been settled, Con," said Elias as they headed back toward the highway, "let me tell you about Kayla. And just so you aren't totally taken aback when you learn who she is, I can warn you that she's a bit . . . infamous, you might say. But I can tell you why she's not what people think she is. And why I know you can trust her."

Connor sighed. Of course this woman's background wouldn't be straightforward. At this point, he'd be disappointed if it were.

13

Kayla objected immediately. "I'm not sure now is a great time for lengthy backgrounders, Elias," she said as she accelerated up an on-ramp, returning to the two-lane highway they had just left. "We should wait until Paige awakens, at minimum."

"Hold up!" said Connor, having detected movement below him. The prisoner—who was probably named anything but the Mike Foley that was printed on his FBI identification—was beginning to stir. "This guy is coming to," he told his fellow passengers, and then readied the shovel he was holding, shifting to a sideways position on the seat so his legs were no longer on the ground near the man.

His father stood, turned around, and extended his body over Paige and the seat backs in the second row, so he was now facing Connor and looking down on the prisoner's face.

Sprouse moaned for several seconds and then opened his eyes, blinking rapidly as if to clear blurred, groggy vision. He tilted his head toward Connor. "Who are you?" he whispered. "Where am I?"

"Do you really think you've earned the right to ask questions?" snapped Connor.

The man's face reflected nothing but pain. No wonder. A blow to the forehead with an iron shovel couldn't have felt good. "It doesn't matter," he said, his voice weak but quickly gaining strength. "It's all coming back to me."

"What's your name?" demanded Connor.

The man looked at him and blinked for several seconds, as if still coming to his senses. Or perhaps he was trying to decide which name he wanted to give. "I told you," he said finally. "I'm Special Agent Mike Foley."

"Sure you are, *Mike*," said Connor dismissively.

"I don't expect you to believe me. Not yet. But it's true. I assume you've had a look at my credentials by now."

"So is the FBI now in the business of assassination?"

"No. But we do go undercover. There's someone we've nicknamed Darth Vader who we've been after for years. He uses a network of—"

"So what's his real name?" interrupted Connor.

"We have no idea. He goes by Jake. We call him Vader because he uses a voice changer that makes him sound like James Earl Jones. Whoever he is, he uses a network of mercenaries around the country to do his bidding, but we know almost nothing about him. I went undercover, using the little we *do* know to get on his radar."

Connor shot him a look of disgust. "Do I really look *that* stupid?" he said. "No agent working undercover would have his badge on him."

"I didn't assume a fake identity," replied Sprouse smoothly. "I went undercover as *myself*. I simply portrayed myself as an FBI agent willing to do wetwork on the side for extra income. And it worked. I succeeded in getting Vader's attention."

"So he's behind this, is that what you're saying?"

"Yes."

"Is that supposed to let you off the *hook*?" said Connor in disbelief. "So it wasn't your idea to kill us, you just *needed* to kill us. To solidify your cover so you could get cozier with Vader and eventually get your man. Well, in *that* case," he added in disgust, "I guess you're a saint. Should we be apologizing for not letting you succeed?"

"I was never going to kill anyone. And if I hadn't taken the job, he'd have given it to someone else. Someone else who would have tried to *actually* kill you. Vader wanted Elias dead, but I insisted that we spare any innocent who was with him. Which is why Paige is unconscious right now, and not dead."

Connor had to admit that the man made some good points.

"I had a plan to get the other two men Vader assigned out of the way for a while," continued Sprouse. "So they weren't around when I found Elias. But I never had to carry this plan out. Your ploy with the flares was inspired. I knew it was a ploy, but it gave me the perfect excuse to send the other men off on a wild goose chase."

"How did you see through it?"

"Because you shouted at the others about making it to the bottom of the canyon. Seemed like you *wanted* us to hear you. So I figured it was a deception."

Connor scowled. This mistake seemed obvious once the prisoner had pointed it out, but hindsight was twenty-twenty, and he had no time to dwell on it. "So if you *had* managed to get to my father," he said, "then what?"

"My plan was to tell him he was a target and get his cooperation. Then I'd tranq him and make it look like he was dead."

"How? The two men with you would want to verify his death, wouldn't they?"

The prisoner paused, and Connor had the feeling that this question had caught him off guard, and he was racking his brain to come up with a convincing answer.

"Did you not hear the question?" snapped Connor. "If you really are an undercover FBI agent who planned to fake a hit, you would have a plan to, you know, fake a hit."

"I did!" insisted Sprouse. "I also have a splitting headache—I wonder why? It's a miracle I can even speak." He paused. "To answer your question, I had a vial of blood with me that could make his fake death look plenty convincing. And a drug that would make his heartbeat undetectable."

Connor shook his head. "Wow," he said. "Very creative. You almost had me. Problem is," he continued, "we searched every square inch of you and didn't find any vials of fake blood, or any drugs."

"I loaded the drug in a tranquilizer dart. It would have put him out and kept his heartbeat faint at the same time."

"Good try," said Connor. "But what about the vial of blood?"

"I had it in my left hand," insisted Sprouse, "with the tranq gun. Maybe I dropped it and it rolled under the bed. You know," he snapped heatedly, "when you were cracking my goddamned skull!" He paused and shook his head. "I know I had it. I have no idea why you didn't find it."

"I do," said Connor. "Because your story is bullshit."

"Then why do I have FBI credentials? Why is Paige still alive?"

"I thought you were with the FBI," said Elias in contempt. "So it's hard to understand why you'd be worried about blowing your criminal street cred."

The prisoner remained silent.

"So once you find dirt on this guy's enemies," said Elias, "do you know what he does with it?"

"I have no idea. That's his business."

"Maybe so," said Elias, "but you do have an idea, at least in general."

"Of course I do. And so do you. Dumbest question ever. It's like I stole diamonds for the guy, and now you're asking me what he does with the diamonds. I don't know for sure, but it's obvious, isn't it? He fences them. In this guy's case, I assume he uses the evidence we bring him for blackmail. What else would you do with this kind of dirt?"

"Provide it to the authorities," said Elias. "Or, like you said, leverage it to find dirt on even more people. It could be that he's a vigilante, and eventually plans to use what he has to take all of these powerful people down."

Sprouse laughed. "That's *so* cute," he said sarcastically. "So you think this guy—who just hired me to *kill* you, by the way—might be Robin Hood? Might be breaking the law to get dirt on lawbreakers so he can put them away? I can assure you, it's the opposite. He puts them in his pocket. He began this expedition incredibly powerful, and as he gathers more and more dirt on other powerful people, his reach only increases."

"Do you think he has high-ranking law enforcement officials in his pocket?" asked Elias.

"I think he owns whoever he wants to own," said the prisoner.

"You have to know more about this Vader than you're letting on," said Elias.

"I wish I did," said Sprouse. "All I know is that you did something to piss him off. And he's the wrong guy to make an enemy of. As far as I can tell, he's amassed more power than God. And he wants you dead."

Elias swallowed hard. He studied the prisoner for an extended period, considering additional possible questions to ask.

Finally, he lifted his eyes to meet Connor's. "That's all we're going to get from him," he said.

"How can you be so sure?"

"Just trust that I am," said Elias.

"Kayla," added the elder Gibson, still facing the back of the SUV, "find somewhere private and pull over. We need to dump this guy. We've gotten what we're going to get from him. And like you said, he's too dangerous to keep around, even bound."

"Will do," said Kayla.

"What's going on?" mumbled Paige faintly from the seats below Elias. "Where am I?"

"Paige, *thank God*," said Connor, unaware of just how worried he had been about his wife until that moment. He was desperate to see her, to hold her, but couldn't risk climbing over the prisoner to get to the second row of seats. "We'll explain everything, sweetie. Just rest for a few more minutes, okay?"

"Okay," she said sleepily, sounding so happy to oblige that it was clear the drug wasn't completely out of her system.

Elias put his hand reassuringly on his daughter-in-law's shoulder. "We just need to drop something off," he added softly, "and we'll be right with you."

"Okay," said Paige serenely, closing her eyes.

Connor wanted badly to focus on Paige, but he forced himself to push her from his thoughts. "One problem, Dad," he said. "We have no choice but to keep the prisoner with us. He woke up just after we picked a destination. But what if he was playing possum, and just *pretended* to be unconscious? If he knows where we're headed, we can't let him go."

"Great point," acknowledged Elias. He looked down at Sprouse. "Well, do you?" he asked.

"Do I what?"

"Do you know where we're going? Did you overhear our conversation?"

"Of course I didn't," he said emphatically.

Elias turned to his son. "We're good, Con. We can drop him off. He doesn't know."

"You're just going to take his word on that? *Are you out of your mind?*"

Elias sighed. "We can talk about this in a minute, Con. First, let's tranquilize him, so we can have a private conversation. I mean, we need to put him out either way, right? Whether we're leaving him in a field, or taking him with us, it's a lot safer if he's unconscious."

"Agreed," said Connor.

Elias pulled a tranquilizer gun from the ballistic nylon duffel bag on the floor beside him and studied it uncertainly. "Does this have any kind of safety I should know about?" he asked the prisoner.

"You think I'm going to help you drug me?" said Sprouse.

Connor shot the prisoner a look of contempt. "It's either the tranq gun," he said icily, "or another shovel to the head. Your choice."

Sprouse's eyes burned with rage, but just for a moment. "The safety is off," he told Elias, not wanting to go another round with the iron fireplace tool.

"Great," said Elias. "So I just push down on the trigger, and I'm good, right? How about recoil?"

"Some, but not nearly as much as an actual gun."

"If I shoot at your thigh, will the dart be able to penetrate your clothing?"

"Yes!" barked Sprouse in frustration. "But look, I have no idea where you're planning to go. So there's no need to put me out. Dump me off somewhere a few miles from any road, without a phone. You'll have all the head start you need."

"Do you think we're crazy enough to move you while you're awake?" said Connor. "Or cut you loose from your restraints?"

"Not to mention that you tried to *assassinate* me," growled Elias. "You're lucky you're only getting a few darts."

"A *few?*" said Sprouse in surprise. "What are you talking about? One dart will do the job just fine."

"Maybe, but I'll be using an extra for good measure," said Elias, aiming the gun at Sprouse's thigh from three feet away.

"How do you know that two darts won't kill me?" asked the prisoner.

Elias pulled the trigger twice, nodding in satisfaction as both darts found their mark. "I don't," he replied simply.

14

Even though the prisoner was now unconscious once again, Connor Gibson held his shovel at the ready, just in case, for ten more seconds. Finally, he lowered it to the floor and closed his eyes, reveling in the knowledge that he was safe for the first time in what seemed like forever.

Connor then had Kayla pull over, and quickly changed places with his father, so he was now in the same row as his sleeping wife.

He gazed at her lovingly, and his eyes moistened as he relived the moment when he had thought she'd been shot, and probably killed. He couldn't even imagine life without her. After his father's discussion, and now this, he vowed to never take the good things in his life for granted again, and to strive to keep his decidedly First World problems in the proper perspective.

Provided they survived this. Whatever *this* was.

Paige appeared to be sleeping peacefully, too addled upon first awakening to have become alarmed at surroundings that should have sent her into a minor panic.

Connor kissed her gently on the forehead and then turned back toward his father. "Okay, Dad," he said, "you wanted to have a private conversation. Now we can have one. It's likely that this guy *wasn't* playing possum, and *didn't* hear about Borrego Springs. But we can't take that chance. And just because he says he didn't hear us means nothing. If you're willing to trust this guy for a *second*, then you've totally lost it."

Elias blew out a long, weary breath. "Normally, you'd be right," he said. "And I wanted to reveal this to you in my own way. But that's not possible now. So I'll just come out with it already. I *know* he's telling the truth about this," he insisted. "Because he *can't* lie to me, Con. He *cannot* lie to me. About *anything*."

"What does that even mean?"

"It means that this is the breakthrough I've been building to. Perfect lie detection. A hundred percent accurate. With a polygraph, you need a willing subject. And an expert to hook them up to all kinds of sensors. Pressure cuffs, fingerplates, rubber tubes to measure respiration rates, and so on. You have wires everywhere. You need a computer and expensive equipment. Then the expert has to take careful baseline readings. And after all of that, the results are often inaccurate or inconclusive."

Elias Gibson raised his eyebrows. "But I've developed a technology that allows *anyone* to separate truth from lies," he said triumphantly. "Every time. Instantly. *Perfectly*. No expert needed. No preparation needed. No willing subject needed. No need to cover anyone in sensors."

"*This* is your once-in-a-millennium breakthrough?" said Connor in disbelief. "That's what you were building up to at the house?"

"Not impressed?" said Elias.

"Assuming you've really done this, it's undeniably impressive. But after all of your build-up . . . " He stopped there, leaving the thought hanging.

"It's a bit of a letdown, right?" finished his father.

"Well, yeah."

Elias seemed more amused than insulted. "So it's not as momentous a breakthrough as you were expecting," he said.

"Not at all."

"So what *were* you expecting?"

"I don't know. Antigravity. *Matrix*-like VR. Teleportation. Room temperature superconductivity. But not *this*. Lie detection? Really?"

"You just haven't had the time to think it through, Con. When you do, you'll get just how transformative this really is. Since man first crawled out of the primordial ooze, lying has been part of our natures. And it's getting worse. Truth is rarer than it's ever been."

Elias paused and his eyes lit up. "But imagine a world where lies are no longer possible," he continued. "Well, I should say where lies are still possible, but *getting away* with them isn't. But, anyway, imagine a world where no lie goes undetected."

Connor thought about this for a few seconds and realized that if such a thing *were* possible, it would be a lot more disruptive, a lot more transformative, than he had first thought.

"And yes," continued Elias, "I'm aware that this isn't as sexy as the breakthroughs you just listed. But when it comes to having an impact on the fabric of human society—on the very future and survival of our species—there's little doubt that this new technology will be even more consequential than these others."

"If this could really be done," said Connor, "you might have a point. I'm not doubting your brilliance, Dad," he hastened to add, "or your word. It's just that I don't see how this could ever be possible."

"*Ever?*" said Elias. "Really, Con? You're the futurist in the family. The one able to envision fantastic, impossible technologies that others can't. And *ever* is an awfully long time." He smiled. "Besides, if you aren't doubting my brilliance, *or* my word, then the only way you can still be skeptical is if you're doubting my *sanity*. Are you?"

Connor winced. "No, of course not," he said, but he wasn't all that convincing.

"No matter," said his father. "I don't blame you for being skeptical. Anyone would be. My plan was to reveal the technical details of my invention back at the house, and then give you and Paige a demonstration. Instead, I'll provide the demonstration now."

He paused and leaned closer to his son. "Stare into my eyes."

"Are you trying to hypnotize me, Dad?"

Elias laughed again. "No! I'm wearing contact lenses. If you look very, very closely, you should be able to make them out."

"Ohhh," said Connor, bending forward to study his father's eyes. He was able to identify the lenses swimming on his father's corneas in short order. "Okay—so you're wearing contacts."

"They're experimental prototypes. A number of high-tech companies view contact lenses as the next big platform for their tech, eventually replacing phones and more. They hope to embed them with advanced computer and sensor technologies, micro-antennae capable of streaming Internet content, virtual reality capabilities, and so on. It's a brave new world."

Connor nodded. "I wrote an article about smart lenses for an online science magazine," he said.

"Right," said his father, suddenly recalling his son's article. "You've written so many great pieces, Con, that it's hard for me to keep them all straight. In any event," he added, "I co-opted this technology for one purpose only, to turn contact lenses into perfect lie detectors. Not that this was necessary. I can turn *anything* able to collect visual and audio data into a lie detector. A pair of glasses. A phone. A computer or television. Or a tiny camera you can wear on your lapel."

"It's true," said Kayla, who had already pulled off the main highway and was looking for stretch of road off the beaten path on which to jettison the prisoner. "All of it. Which is how your father knew if our guest was lying or not."

Connor didn't respond to this. He found Kayla's reassurances interesting, but far from conclusive. After all, this might only indicate that she and his father were *both* out of their minds.

"Okay, Con," said Elias, "let's begin the demonstration. What did you have for dinner last night? Lie to me, tell the truth, either way, I'll know. When you lie, the contacts shoot a brief flash of light into my retinas, too faint and fast for you to detect."

"Dad, this is ridiculous."

"Humor me."

"Okay," said Connor after a brief pause. "I had an omelet. For some reason, I was in the mood to have breakfast for dinner."

"No you didn't. Try again."

Connor shrugged. "Okay," he said, "the truth is that Paige was out of town at her conference, so I ordered a pizza."

"Try again," said Elias immediately.

Connor's eyes narrowed. He had thought he had been convincing. Still, the fact that his father had been correct, twice, meant very little. The elder Gibson had a one in four chance of being right, even if he had been guessing.

"I warmed up something in the microwave," said Connor. "A pasta dish."

"You did warm something in the microwave," said his father. "But it wasn't pasta."

Connor nodded slowly. He was impressed, but still a far cry from being convinced. "You're right," he said. "In every case."

"You don't need to tell me that. I know I am."

Connor spent the next five minutes trying to stump his father, putting on the perfect poker face. When he lied, he tried to convince even *himself* that his lies were true, to eliminate any possible tells that his father might be using. But after stating dozens of truths, and dozens of lies, his father was right in every case. The odds of this being luck had gone from one in four, to more than one in a billion.

"We can stop now," said Connor finally. He broke out into a broad grin. "Maybe you aren't so crazy, after all. I'm beginning to think the implications of this are as staggering as you suggest."

"Thanks, Connor," said Elias. "That's very kind of you to say." He smiled. "Especially since I know you really mean it."

Connor nodded at the unconscious prisoner. "So I guess this guy really *didn't* overhear us," he said. "Good to know. So he has no idea where we're going."

"That's right," said Elias. "And he isn't with the FBI. But he *is* working for a mystery man named Vader."

"Right," said Connor. "And he really *doesn't* know why Vader wants you dead."

"As I said, he has nothing more to tell us."

"Then what are we waiting for?" said Connor with a twinkle in his eye. "Let's dump this pile of human garbage and get our asses to Borrego Springs."

15

Connor was eager to learn how his father could have possibly perfected a technology that, like Arthur C. Clarke's famous quote, was so advanced it was indistinguishable from magic, but knew this would have to wait.

He reached out and gently shook his wife. "Paige," he said softly, "it's time to wake up now."

This time, when she opened her eyes, she no longer looked high, and regained her full faculties quickly as adrenaline took hold. "Where am I?" she said in alarm, bringing herself to an upright position so she could look through the window.

Connor threw his arms around her and hugged her tight, despite the cramped quarters. "Welcome back," he said, his joy and relief unmistakable, which only served to further intensify the look of confusion on her face. He pulled himself away. "Do you remember waking up in this car once before?" he added softly.

She shook her head no.

"Do you remember the woman who stormed into my father's backyard and told us we might be in danger?"

There was a brief pause and then her eyes began to widen. "Yes," she replied enthusiastically, "I do. We were heading toward the slider to get inside." She searched her memory further, and her expression darkened. "But after that, I don't remember anything. All I know is that I woke up here."

"You were hit with a tranquilizer dart," explained Connor. "You lost consciousness almost immediately. But you're going to be fine now. I promise."

He went on to explain the events that had transpired since she had been put to sleep, with his father and Kayla also chiming in on occasion.

While they brought Paige up to speed, Kayla pulled off the highway, found a fairly flat and extended piece of land, and off-roaded for about a mile. She finally stopped near a wall of cacti, composed of a number of different species that had probably been growing there for hundreds of years.

Connor lugged Sprouse's dead weight from the SUV, deposited him behind the prickly wall, and then cut him loose. When he eventually awoke, the man would have something of a short hike to get back to civilization, but that was his problem, not theirs.

Paige continued to gain strength and mental clarity as Connor described how they had escaped from Elias's home. "Sounds like you were amazing, Connor," she said in admiration. "I had no idea I married Jason Bourne."

"Well, yeah," said Connor with a grin, "Jason Bourne without any of his marksmanship, speed, or hand-to-hand fighting skills." He paused. "But I do have to admit, I surprised myself."

"I've never seen this side of you," she said.

Connor shook his head. "And you still haven't," he said with a smile. "I finally do something heroic, and you decide to take a nap the whole time."

Paige laughed.

They went on to describe the interrogation of their prisoner and Kayla's Borrego Springs safe house, which led to the true nature of her father-in-law's breakthrough.

Paige had the same reactions to Elias's claim of perfect lie detection as her husband. She was initially underwhelmed. Then, she was disbelieving. And, finally—after a thorough demonstration—impressed beyond words, and able to begin to appreciate the immensity of the breakthrough.

"I did the technical work," explained Elias, "which I'll tell you about later. And Kayla provided financial and logistical support."

"So who is she?" said Paige, and then, addressing Kayla, added, "Who are you?"

"I'd love for you to know," replied Kayla. "Elias has raved about you and Connor. But he was supposed to have laid some groundwork in preparation for my visit later today."

She stared into the rearview mirror until she caught Elias's eye. "So can we wait on this, Elias?" she asked. "I'd still prefer if you laid the groundwork first."

"I understand," said Elias.

"Thank you," said Kayla. "Once we get to the safe house, I can give you some privacy. That way you can discuss me at length without it getting awkward."

"Of course," replied Elias. "On that note, how much longer until we're there?"

"Maybe fifty minutes."

"In that case," said Elias, turning to his son and daughter-in-law, "why don't I pick up my narrative where I left off. We can't begin to get to the bottom of this without access to phones and computers, so now's a good time. I can disclose my breakthrough the way I had originally intended. Well, sort of."

Connor's lips curled up into the hint of a smile. "You mean despite the fact that you've already, you know . . . *disclosed* your breakthrough?"

Elias sighed. "Yeah, I do seem to have blown the big reveal," he replied, returning his son's shallow smile. "But I'm prepared to pretend this didn't happen."

"I'm game," said Paige.

"And I'll stay out of the conversation completely," said Kayla. "I'll just drive and monitor the road behind us, just in case. Just pretend I'm not even here."

Connor nodded. "Okay," he said. "Why not? I'm not sure what the big deal is about meeting you, but okay." He gestured toward his father. "So where were we before your mysterious colleague interrupted?"

"It wasn't really Kayla who interrupted us," corrected Elias. "I mean, *technically* it was. But the men trying to kill me were the cause. I'm pretty sure she saved my life." He paused. "Speaking of which, Kayla, I never did thank you. Let me correct that now. *Thank you*," he said emphatically.

"You're very welcome," she replied. "I'm just glad I made it in time. And it was your son who saved your life." She smiled. "Just promise me that you won't let my contribution become public," she added. "Might ruin my villainous reputation."

"Then I'll make sure it does," said Elias. "Not that you'll need it, but it'll be icing on the cake."

He turned back to Connor and Paige, who were now sitting sideways at opposite ends of the row of seats, facing each other, so they could also see Elias behind them. "Are you ready to resume?"

"Absolutely," said Paige. "Where were we?"

16

"If I'm remembering right," said Elias, "I was about to tell you why, if the world is getting so much better, we all think it's getting so much worse."

"That's my recollection, also," said Connor, feeling as if Paige had asked this question a lifetime ago.

Elias took a deep breath and gathered his thoughts. "The question is, why are so many of us feeling so much unnecessary despair?" he began. "And why are so many of us so pessimistic about our future? *Especially* since this pessimism is almost entirely unwarranted."

He paused. "First, and perhaps most importantly, despair and pessimism are in our very natures. We're wired to seek out bad news over good, and to always fear the worst. So bad news seizes our attention, while good news is often ignored. "

"Why would that be?" said Paige.

"Evolution," said Elias simply. "These are indispensable behaviors for surviving in a harsh environment. Say you were walking along the savanna, tens of thousands of years ago, and heard a rustle in the grass. This rustle may have been caused by the wind. Then again, it may have been caused by a lion that was stalking you. If you assumed this was *bad* news—a lion—and you were wrong, what would be the consequences?"

He paused. "Well, you'd have wasted your time coming to attention and preparing your spear for action. And you might feel a little silly. But so what?"

"But if you assumed it was the wind," said Connor, having guessed where his father was headed, "and it was actually the *lion* . . . " He cringed. "Not so great."

"Exactly," said his father. "Then you'd be dead. So which is the better mistake to make?"

"Makes sense," said Paige.

"We tend to think of evolution as only shaping us physically," said Elias, "but much of our psychology and our behaviors have also been shaped by this force. We evolved to pay attention to bad news over good, and to always fear the worst—for good reason. Good news is nice. Bad news can threaten our lives."

He paused. "So we tend to freak ourselves out on a regular basis. I'll give you a few examples. In 1798, Thomas Malthus published an essay describing how population growth is exponential, but the growth of the food supply is linear. If the population kept growing, he insisted, mass starvation was inevitable. But as I told you at my house, poverty and starvation are at lower levels than ever before, and the population is more than seven-fold higher than it was in Malthus's time. Turns out he couldn't have been more wrong.

"Why? Because we developed ever more efficient methods of food production and farming. We automated what had been the most labor-intensive process on Earth. We dramatically improved the yields of our plants and animals, found better ways to protect crops from bugs and blight, invented better irrigation methods, and so on. The bottom line is that we found ways to grow our food supply even faster than our population."

"I've heard of Malthus," said Paige. "He was wrong, but he did get a lot of people stressed out about the future."

"Exactly. He was just one in an endless line of doomsayers. Yet our species is still here, thriving like never before. Not that you would know it."

"Because disaster sells," said Connor.

"Not only sells, but seizes our attention and imagination. Feeds our neurotic natures. There were other scholars at the time of Malthus who predicted that we'd be fine, that we'd find better ways to produce food. Malthus was dead wrong, and they were absolutely right. But *they* died as unknowns, while Malthus became famous.

"Throughout history, pessimistic books warning of a coming Armageddon have outsold optimistic books a hundred to one. Pessimists win fame and adoration. Those who attempt to refute a doomsday thesis are called naïve, or simpletons, and are often attacked as incompetent. And this, despite the fact that the dooms-day criers have always been wrong, and those who refute them have always been right. But no one ever goes back to check the record, to realize that humanity has been panicked into believing the sky is falling every year for many hundreds of years, and yet it has never once fallen."

"Yet the next time we hear that it's falling," said Connor, "we, um . . . *fall* for it yet again."

"Over and over and over again," said Elias, ignoring his son's play on words. "Because, as a species wired to attend to possible danger, we never learn. I'm not saying we shouldn't worry about the future of our species. There are plenty of legitimate causes for alarm. But we need to keep them all in the proper perspective. We need to understand that we tend to overestimate risks and dangers, and keep our heads about us."

Elias paused. "The more research I did, the more I came to truly appreciate how deeply this tendency is embedded in our natures. I'll give you just a few more examples. In 1880, leading experts confidently predicted that because Manhattan was growing so fast, in the decades to come, the city would be knee-deep in horse manure. Knee-deep. In horse manure. This was inevitable, according to them."

Paige made a face. "Glad we dodged *that* bullet," she said in disgust.

Elias smiled. "In 1968," he continued, "Stanford University biologist Paul Ehrlich echoed Malthus in many ways in a wildly influential book entitled *The Population Bomb*, again predicting an inevitable disaster that never came. He later declared with conviction that four billion people worldwide, and sixty-five million Americans, would die of starvation by the year 1990.

"In the seventies, many scientists became convinced that the globe was *cooling*, and raised alarms that a new ice age was just around the corner." Elias shook his head. "I could provide endless examples of other coming disasters and doomsday scenarios that evoked widespread anxiety, but that were grossly exaggerated. Acid rain and low sperm counts. Y2K, AIDS, Ebola, mad-cow disease, and killer bees. The bird flu and the reversal of Earth's magnetic poles. Severe shortages of everything under the sun, from oil, to food, to zinc. Black holes created by the Large Hadron Collider, and unstoppable genetically engineered organisms breaking free of the lab. Famine, nuclear war, and asteroid collisions. Oh, yeah, and predictions of the near extinction of all species on Earth, which was supposed to have already occurred. And on and on and on. Esteemed scientists or government experts convinced us to fear all of these coming catastrophes. Most never happened at all. Those that did wreaked only a tiny fraction of the havoc that we were assured was coming."

Connor was fascinated, despite the surreal nature of their circumstances. His father was fleeing from an unknown enemy trying to kill him, but he was still able to engage their minds in a thirty-thousand-foot contemplation of nothing less than the nature of humanity, and the history of human society.

"You pointed out earlier that we're the only species smart enough to fear future threats," said Connor. "*Imagined* threats. So as *individuals*, we're cursed with worrying about anything and everything, from public speaking to salt intake. So aren't these just examples of the same thing at the species level? Of our species using our powerful imaginations, and knowledge of human mortality, to find endless things to worry about?"

Elias nodded grimly. "That's right. Which is why humanity as a whole has always been a sucker for a good crisis, for a good doomsday scenario."

"But you're suggesting that it's much worse now than it's ever been," said Paige.

"Yes. Because we're inundated with one crisis after another, nonstop. And in addition to global famine and the like, these alarms are now being sounded much closer to home, largely within the political realm. We have 24/7 news channels, thousands of news websites, and social media, which all deliver an endless stream of pessimism and alarm. Because the people who deliver the news know that the more overblown and dramatic the headline, the more alarming or contentious, the more clicks and eyeballs it will attract. I'm sure you've heard the expression, 'if it bleeds—it leads.' The news now provides a nonstop barrage of fear, despair, and distrust of other groups. And while these headlines are all irresistible to our primitive psyches, they steadily eat away at our souls, promoting divisiveness and pessimism."

"You make it sound like an evil conspiracy by the news providers," said Paige.

"It isn't. They didn't get together and say, 'wouldn't it be great if we could collectively whip the world into a frenzy of despair by making every story seem cataclysmic.' They just do it. Because they know that panic sells far better than sobriety. But now we can't get away from it. Any media outlet that focuses on more boring, less apocalyptic news—dare I say *optimistic* news—risks going out of business. Especially in the current climate.

"Causes don't attract followers by publicizing how much *better* things are getting. A news story about the gradual increase in our per-capita wealth over a fifty-year period will never make the front page. Good news doesn't sell, so the media go to great lengths to find kernels of despair, of alarm, in the most optimistic of results."

Elias frowned deeply. "So the newsmakers and pundit class manipulate us emotionally, exaggerate every danger, and spend endless hours speculating about future fears. And as Connor just pointed out, it isn't as if we don't already do this enough in our personal lives. But in modern times, we don't hear that the sky is falling every year, we hear it every *hour*. The sky is in a *perpetual* state of falling. And add politicians into the mix, who *do* collectively desire to whip their followers into a frenzy, and you land where we are now."

"More pessimistic and more polarized than ever before," whispered Connor.

"Yes. Led by our media and our politicians, who couldn't be more divisive, more vitriolic. Who couldn't create a more toxic climate. Friends and families have been torn apart over politics, over apocalyptic fears that are constantly fanned on both sides."

Elias paused, almost as if remembering where he was for just a moment, and scanned his surroundings through the window. "You'd tell us if you noticed anyone following, right Kayla?"

"No, I'd keep that to myself," she replied sarcastically. "Elias, that may be the dumbest question you've ever asked. Don't worry, I'm paying attention. Go on with your chat. I'll let you know if I have even the slightest concern."

"Thanks," he said, and then turned his attention to the conversation once more. "Politics has always been a blood sport," he continued, "ever since the beginning of our country. Rivalries and animosities among our politicians today are no worse than those among Jefferson, Hamilton, Washington, and Adams. Newspapers called George Washington's farewell address the 'loathings of a sick mind,' and accused him of being traitorous, like Benedict Arnold. We're talking *George Washington*, the guy whose picture is on the dollar bill."

"Good to know his reputation has been rehabilitated," said Connor wryly.

Elias smiled. "Adams was called a worthless public figure," he continued, "who needed to be cast out the back door 'like polluted water.' Hamilton referred to Jefferson and Madison as ruthless purveyors of people's rights who would bring a reign of terror to America."

Paige shook her head in wonder. "When you research a topic," she said to Elias, "you really research a topic."

"I had no idea America's founders were so venomous," added Connor.

"They were. That's nothing new. What *is* new is that now it's impossible to get away from the venom, the hostility, the *hysteria* on both sides. Politicians delight in using the sky-is-falling theme every day, which is amplified by the media. If you want to get your base out to vote, rage and fear are great motivators. When Reagan was elected, certain Democratic pundits took to the airwaves declaring that this was basically the end of the world, or at least the end of America. He was unfit for office, stupid, and a war monger who would surely cause a nuclear holocaust.

"When Obama was elected, certain Republican pundits saw *this* as the end of the world. Saw him as being a closet socialist, biased in favor of Muslims, and a terrorist sympathizer, who would purposely weaken America and bring the country to its knees."

Elias paused. "These are just two examples of doomsday prophecies that come with every new president," he noted. "You're old enough to remember the almost nonstop end-of-the-world prophecies that came with more recent presidents. God only knows I don't have to list these. And since President Jameson only has about three years left in his second term, we'll see this yet again when the next president comes to power."

He shook his head. "Every single time we elect a president, the out party does everything possible to convince its followers that this means the end of the world. Or at least the end of America. Granted, this is more intense for some presidents than for others. But it happens to even the most polished and outwardly benign of them."

Elias blew out a long breath. "When Jameson was elected, I was *sure* the divisiveness would improve—dramatically. He's as boring and non-confrontational as any president we've ever had. But, astonishingly, while it did improve—it almost had to—it improved far less than you'd have thought. Over the past few decades it seems like we can only move in one direction politically. Toward more polarization—more *demonization*—rather than less. If a resident of the White House is caught torturing babies, his own side gives him a pass. But, conversely, if a resident of the White House walks on water, the out-party scorns him for not knowing how to *swim*."

He frowned. "Or worse, claims that walking on water defies the laws of physics, which will probably kill us all.

"But no matter how much the politicians sow divisiveness," continued Elias, "and the media report breathlessly on the crises of the day, on the imminent destruction of America, the country continues to thrive. Through Democratic and Republican administrations alike."

Paige nodded thoughtfully. "But the fiftieth time a president does something the opposition is convinced will destroy democracy as we know it," said Paige, "no one recalls that they've cried wolf forty-nine other times."

"Unfortunately, no. The rhetoric whips people into a frenzy every time. And if people are reminded of this, or reminded that we have a centuries-old political tradition of crying wolf, they don't care. They insist that *this* time it's different. That the current president, whoever he or she is, finally *will* spell the end."

17

Elias paused for an extended period to let Connor and Paige digest all that he had said, while the scenery continued to race by outside the SUV's window.

Finally, Elias reached into his pocket and removed a tightly folded sheet of laser printer paper, which he carefully unfolded. "I prepared this just for fun," he said. "Although it would have been *more* fun if I had read it in my backyard, as planned," he added, rolling his eyes, "instead of while fleeing from hired killers."

"What is it?" asked Paige.

"It's an excerpt from a speech given in 2017, almost a year after Donald Trump had become president. I know that this was a number of years ago now, but my question for you is this: who said it?" Elias paused. "Are you ready?"

Connor and Paige both nodded.

The elder Gibson cleared his throat and began reading:

"By just about every measure, America is better, and the world is better, than it was fifty years ago, thirty years ago, or even ten years ago.

"I know that statement doesn't jibe with the steady stream of bad news and cynicism that we're fed through television and Twitter. But I was born at a time when women and people of color were systematically, routinely excluded from enormous portions of American life. Today, women and minorities have risen up the ranks in business, and politics, and everywhere else. The shift is . . . astonishing, remarkable, and it's happened, when you measure it against the scope of human history, in an instant.

"If you had to choose any moment in history in which to be born, and you didn't know in advance whether you were going to be male or female, what country you were going to be from, what your status was . . . you'd choose right now. Because the world has never been healthier or wealthier. Or better educated. Or, in many ways, more tolerant. Or less violent than it is today."

Elias lifted his eyes from the printed quote and turned to his son and daughter-in-law. "Any guesses?" he asked. "Who said in 2017 that the world has never been healthier, wealthier, more tolerant, and less violent?"

Connor shrugged. "Donald Trump?"

Elias grinned. "No," he said with obvious satisfaction. "Paige, do you have a guess?"

"Not really. Whoever was the head of the Republican National Committee at the time?"

"No," said Elias, still smiling, "but these are good guesses. This is a supremely optimistic statement, and Republicans were as optimistic as ever at the time, at least when it came to the direction in which the country was heading. Democrats were reeling at the time, in many ways as *pessimistic* as ever. So it might surprise you that these sober, optimistic words were delivered by Barack Obama."

Paige's eyes widened and she glanced at Connor, who also seemed shocked. "You're right," she said for them both. "Didn't see that coming."

"That's not to say he wasn't a fierce critic of his successor, or wasn't worried about the direction of the country. And he did sound alarms. But, with these words, at least, he made a case that if you allow yourself to rise above a short-term perspective and super-charged rhetoric, the big picture is still looking better than ever before."

Elias re-folded the laser paper and returned it to his pocket. "When it came to his praise of America in 2017, it was one of the rare times that he and Republicans agreed about anything."

Elias paused to let his audience digest the many points he had been trying to make.

"But to move on," he said finally, "another problem is that many of us are *addicted* to news itself. And this is a drug that can eat away at rationality and happiness both. No matter how much the news alarms someone with this addiction, or depresses them, or makes them absolutely miserable with the unfairness of the world, or puts them in a state of perpetual rage, they can't help but seek out even *more* news. And this news stokes even *more* outrage, and exposes them to even *more* dire warnings of coming catastrophes."

Connor knew exactly what his father meant. There were a few times when he had become so agitated by the news that he had forced himself to ignore it completely for long stretches of time. And it had worked. His stress had declined dramatically, and he had found that, in the case of purposely divisive news, ignorance really was bliss.

Once, he had ignored the news for *six months*. And underscoring the points his father was making, when he returned to the news, America was still standing strong, having avoided all of the dire predictions made six months earlier, but with an entirely new list having been generated.

"What makes all of this worse, of course," continued Elias, "is that along with being wired to be sucked in by bad news, we're also actually wired to be partisan and polarized. We hear the word *tribalism* tossed about all the time nowadays, but most people think it's just an evil tendency of the group they *oppose*. They don't understand how deeply it's embedded into the DNA of our entire species."

"How so?" asked Connor.

"People have an innate tendency to almost instantly form discrete groups. And almost instantly become biased against anyone in a different group."

Paige looked pained. "That's horrible," she said. "Why would we be designed this way? Evolution again?"

Elias nodded. "Given limited food, and limited physical gifts, our species had to work in close-knit groups, and become territorial, to stay alive. Tribalism is one result of this. We largely define ourselves by asserting our loyalty to the groups that we're in. A psychologist in the seventies named Henri Tajfel showed that humans can enter into *us-versus-them* thinking in seconds, over just about anything. He showed that as conflict grows between groups, it becomes more difficult to think about those you're competing against as individuals, with positive qualities, making it easier to discount their feelings, arguments, needs, and so on."

"You said he *showed* these things," said Connor. "How?"

"Lots of groundbreaking experiments," replied Elias. "He sorted volunteers into groups based on major differences between them, and then conducted studies. I won't get into the experimental design, but basically he found that if you identify with a group, you'll exhibit favoritism toward your group, and bias toward the other.

"But then he continued these experiments, sorting people into groups based on ever more trivial differences. What shocked him in the end was that it didn't really matter *why* the groups had formed, how trivial the rationale. He could separate people into groups based on their preferences for the paintings of abstract artist A, or abstract artist B, for example. And if they were in the A group, they treated other As better, and those in the B group worse.

"But what was really wild was that even if he *randomly* assigned people into two groups—and they *knew* they had been randomly assigned—they still exhibited favoritism toward their group, and bias toward the other."

"Incredible," mumbled Connor.

"Other social scientists built upon Tajfel's work," continued Elias, "and basically found there is no distinction around which opposing groups won't form, no matter how meaningless. And once they do, individuals in these groups immediately begin exhibiting favoritism and bias."

Paige nodded thoughtfully. "You can see some of this behavior even in fifth-graders," she noted.

"The worst part about it," said Elias, "is that this tendency causes us to impugn the motives of the other side. We know *we're* acting in good faith, but assume the other side is acting in bad faith. We know that our motivations are noble and pure, but suspect those of the other side are dubious, corrupt, or self-interested. Makes it impossible to have a reasoned discussion."

"Seems so incredibly bleak," said Connor. "I know your point is that things *aren't* bleak. But human nature itself seems to be our worst enemy."

Elias sighed. "Sadly, this is true. Any number of behaviors that once helped us survive are now working against us. I'll just throw out one more. Confirmation bias. This is our tendency to seek out information that supports and reinforces our beliefs, and ignore or discount any information that is contrary to them. So we stick to our guns, even against overwhelming evidence that we're wrong."

"Perfect," said Connor unhappily. "We're tribal, stubborn, and stupid."

"Not stupid," said Elias. "Just wired in these unfortunate ways. But there you have it. We always look on the dark side, are suckers for the crisis of the day, and quickly separate into groups. But it's gotten even worse lately."

"This has been super uplifting, Dad," said Connor sarcastically. "Glad you're able to spread such optimism and good cheer."

"I'll get to that part soon," said Elias. "And our species can, and will, overcome all of this. But the nonstop barrage of partisan alarmism and fear mongering is taking a huge toll. And if this isn't bad enough, we now have so *much* news that we effectively have *none*. Not news we can trust to be accurate. Because the media are comprised of human beings, with the same tribalism in their genes that we all have. They take sides and choose what to report. And now they each have their camps, and their followers, which all exist in separate universes. There's an old saying, 'the man with two watches never knows what time it is.' Well, now we have a thousand different watches, all reading a different time."

He shook his head in disgust. "So the old saying now becomes, 'the man with a thousand media outlets, each providing its own, differing spin on the news, never knows what's true.'"

Connor nodded thoughtfully. "And the ability to choose our own news plays into our tribalism and confirmation bias."

"Absolutely right. You can pick your side, and pick which facts you want to cling to. Pick your news channels and newsfeeds. So you have ever more reason to identify with your side, and be biased against the other side. And an ever greater tendency to stop seeing those on the other side as being like you, with hopes and dreams and virtuous motivations of their own."

"And social media makes this worse, doesn't it?" said Paige.

"*Much* worse. Because it provides a bubble, an echo chamber. And it provides distance and anonymity, so people can be as vicious as they want, and never have to look their opponent in the eye. They never see them as loving parents or thoughtful neighbors, just as unseen members of a nebulous *other*."

Elias frowned deeply. "I don't attack people on social media," he added, "but I'm not immune from tribalism and confirmation bias either. No one is. But when I'm really riled up about a political point, I remind myself that at least some of the people on the other side are kind and well-meaning people—even if, in my opinion, they're woefully misguided. And at least some of the people on my side are total assholes. Men and women who agree with me on the issue, but who beat their wives, or bilk charities, or engage in other despicable behaviors. My side isn't filled only with the virtuous, and theirs only with the corrupt and immoral."

Paige nodded appreciatively. "Well said."

"That's a nice perspective, Dad," said Connor, "but most people aren't so open-minded. And each side uses the most extreme, least flattering examples of behavior from the other side and tries to paint them all with this same brush. They ascribe horrible motives to the other side, like you said, and won't even listen to the arguments they're making."

"Right," said Elias. "And if you really believe that the other side is evil, or dangerous, then what *wouldn't* you do to stop them? What lies *wouldn't* you tell? What underhanded actions, what smears, *wouldn't* you engage in?"

He shook his head. "So we have to try to fight this instinct. If you paint the other side as evil, or dangerous, you stop listening to anything they say. But every once in a while, the other side can make a good argument. One we may not have considered.

"The problem is that it's getting harder than ever to even listen to each other," continued Elias. "Because as difficult as it is to overcome tribalism and confirmation bias, as hard as it is to meet the other group halfway—or *any* of the way—politicians and members of the media have made an art form out of *lying*.

"Not all of them," he added, "and not all of the time. But enough to make a bad situation much worse. Enough to make it impossible for us to agree on the simplest facts. Divisive and apocalyptic rhetoric are the lifeblood of both groups. And they're using this rhetoric to manipulate, exaggerate, and distort—or just outright lie—to whip the public into a frenzy. All in pursuit of ratings or political power. Knowing that their lies will go undetected—or, if detected, ignored."

"Ah," said Conner with a smile. "We get to the punchline at last. Let me guess, you finished this analysis, and you thought to yourself, 'if only there were a technology that could make lying impossible. A technology that could help reverse this poisonous spiral.'"

"Wow, Connor, good guess," said Elias, rolling his eyes. "Way to pretend I didn't already spoil the ending for you."

18

The white SUV drove on in silence for several long seconds, racing ever closer to Borrego Springs and absolute safety. To a place where they could roll up their sleeves and try to piece together just what they were up against, determine whom they could trust, and plan next steps.

"Just one more point before I discuss lying," said Elias Gibson, "a small silver lining in the current acrimony. The fact that it's so vigorous and public shows just how free our society really is. In dictatorships, disagreeing publicly with the government can get you swiftly killed. And some of the causes that are driving wedges between us are indicative of the affluence and leisure time we have. If you're starving to death and struggling to find your next meal, you don't have time to protest over the plight of a salamander in Ecuador. This is an exaggeration, but I think you'll agree that those struggling to meet basic needs aren't paying attention to the manufactured crises of the day. Members of societies that are thriving, on the other hand, like ours, now have the luxury of performing a thorough self-examination to identify every possible fault. And they tend to amplify any deficiencies they find to scare up support."

"But isn't being hard on ourselves a good thing?" asked Paige.

"In many ways, a very good thing. Affluent nations *should* be striving for perfection. And we have a long way to go. Worse, large swaths of poverty still exist around the world, so we can't rest on our laurels."

Elias frowned. "But at the same time, we need to keep the doomsaying in perspective. And to recognize just how much progress we've made. We need to recognize the positive course that we've been on now for hundreds of years."

He paused for several seconds. "Which brings me full circle," he continued. "We're living in the best of times. But if we allow our perception of humanity to be shaped by the news, it's easy to believe that we're living in the worst of times."

"And you think identifying all lies is the answer," said Connor.

"No, there isn't a single answer. But if politicians and those behind the never-ending stream of news can't lie, *ever*, this will go a long way toward calming things down."

Connor thought about this, but didn't reply.

"It's human nature to lie," said Elias. "We all know that. Some of us can exhibit deceptive behavior as early as six months old. Even our primate ancestors can lie. Koko, the famous signing gorilla, once blamed her pet kitten for ripping a sink out of the wall."

"Wow," said Paige in amusement, "that is one powerful kitty."

"Exactly," said Elias with a grin. "We lie *so* much," he continued, "that we're often barely aware that we're doing it. Meet someone for the first time and chat for ten minutes. If someone secretly recorded the meeting, and you had a chance to study the video—and were scrupulously honest with yourself—you'd be stunned by how many lies you told in this short period."

"Sounds like something scientists have actually done," said Connor.

"They have, and the results are astonishing. We exaggerate, say things to make ourselves look better. Pretend to have seen a popular movie so we don't feel left out. Tell lies to spare the feelings of others. And lie because it greases the skids of social interaction. If you've had a horrible day, for example, and someone you've just met asks you how your day is going, it rarely even *occurs* to you to answer honestly."

Elias raised his eyebrows. "And then there are lies of a more malicious variety. Those intended to manipulate, or that have real negative impact. And the number and audacity of *these* lies have been increasing every century since primitive times."

"Why is that?" asked Connor.

"In prehistoric times, we lived in small clans. Every member of the clan knew every other member. And everyone had to pull their own weight, or the clan wouldn't survive. Teamwork was paramount, and lies were almost non-existent. No quarterback lies to his team in the huddle about what he intends to do with the ball."

"Right," said Connor. "Everyone had to be on pretty much the same page to survive."

"Yes," said his father. "And if anyone was caught being deceitful, there was nowhere to hide. He or she was marked as a liar forever."

Elias frowned. "But now there are many billions of us. In our day, lying has become an art form, and liars are flourishing like never before. In the early days of our ascent, being a prolific liar would have gotten you shunned from the tribe. Now, it's almost a prerequisite for fame and fortune. And especially political power. Each side has no trouble believing that every single politician on the other side lies every time they speak, while believing their side says nothing but the truth."

"I assume you believe that the lying is equal on *both* sides," said Connor.

"I do," said Elias. "Tragically, politicians these days almost *have* to lie. It's nearly impossible to win office if you don't. If your opponent is lying about his positions, and telling voters what they want to hear, and you insist on strict honesty, you don't stand a chance. It'd be like trying to win the Tour de France as the only rider who isn't doping."

"But your technology will change this," said Connor.

"Yes. The key is to make the detection automatic, and almost *unavoidable* for the public to absorb. Because we often resist the truth, hide from it. We don't want to acknowledge that our guy is lying as much as his competitor. Confirmation bias prevents us from checking the record, even when it's dead easy to do. Let's face it, political lies and distortions are often simple to uncover. A few minutes of online research will usually do the trick. But how many go to the trouble? Politicians couldn't be more brazen. A candidate swears that he never said X, knowing full well that he said *exactly* X just the day before, *on video*, but knowing that few will go back and check."

"Because people don't want to have their bubbles burst, do they?" said Paige. "Most of us would rather cling to our illusions rather than face harsh truths. I have to say that I get that. If someone doesn't like me, for example, I'd prefer not to know it. I'll take socially polite deception every time."

"That's an argument against putting my new technology out there," said Elias. "Because it might be too much of an assault on the glue that holds society together. No way to know for sure. But it will definitely be a huge change."

"When do you plan to launch?" asked Connor.

"Kayla and I are still discussing that," said Elias. "I'm for getting this out very soon. She wants to be much more patient. Make sure we have all of our ducks in a row. I'm just about done perfecting some of the key implementations. And I'm finishing up a handful of key patents. The heart and soul of the tech I'm keeping as a trade secret, as I'll explain later, but the user interfaces can be patented. Someone is going to make a fortune on this, and who better than me?" he said. "Especially since I plan to give a hundred percent of the proceeds to charity."

Connor nodded. This last didn't surprise him at all. "So getting back to how easily politicians and the media get away with lying," he said, returning to the central theme of the discussion, "your technology would end this, wouldn't it? Lies would be instantly and effortlessly called out. We couldn't be fooled. Even if we were *desperate* to be."

"I couldn't have said it better," replied his father. "That's exactly the idea. We'll still have massive bias in how stories are reported, but at least we'll know truth from fiction."

"Won't we also detect the bias?" asked Paige.

"Indirectly," said Elias. "It will be clear if we look for it. But a story can take the same facts and present them in very different ways. I watch a lot of tennis. Several years ago, Novak Djokovic won Wimbledon and the US Open back to back. Afterward, Roger Federer commented that as great as his rival was playing, Novak was capable of playing even *better*. The next day I saw two headlines in two different media outlets. The first was something like, 'Federer says that the incredible Djokovic has yet to reach his peak.' The second headline read, 'Federer critical of rival.'"

Connor nodded. "And reporters on the political beat take this to the next level, don't they?"

"You can say that again," replied Elias. "So my technology won't completely eradicate bias, but it will be a great start. And it will be part of a two-pronged approach to get humanity's head right. First, prevent the powerful from manipulating us like so many puppets. Eliminate deception. Then, with so much noise removed from the equation, with politicians unable to use gross exaggerations and apocalyptic rhetoric to freak us out, spread the gospel of optimism. Correct our misguided perceptions of our present and our future. Educate."

"Talk about Teach for America," said Paige, nodding. "More like Teach for the World."

"It's the part I'm looking forward to the most," said Elias. "I'll devote myself to building an army of writers, speakers, politicians, and news people to help us realize that we live in the best of times—and getting better—while reminding us that there is still much we have left to do. An army of town criers who will help people understand why we're obsessed with doomsday predictions, and why they often feed our worst natures. Who can convince people to take a step back from the brink of despair and take a breath. Live our lives. Love the people who are important to us. Fight the good fight, but realize that the species continues to move in the right direction. Even if there are minor blips and setbacks along the way. Even if your guy or gal isn't currently in the White House. Convince people that the sky always seems to be falling, but it never really falls, and that your favorite candidate will be in charge soon enough."

"A worthy goal," said Paige. "And with your anti-lying technology, it seems like you're halfway home."

Elias frowned. "Sure, if you forget that there's a man named Vader who won't rest until Kayla and I are dead. If she hadn't moved right when a sniper was shooting at her, we'd both be dead already."

Paige swallowed hard. "Yeah, there is that," she said. She tilted her head in thought. "So who would benefit if you were prevented from releasing your technology?"

"Offhand," replied Elias, "I'd say just about *everyone*."

"Way to narrow it down," said Connor.

"Okay," amended Elias, "not everyone. Just any powerful person in the world who's lied to get where they are. Or who intends to do so going forward."

"Now we're talking," said Connor wryly. "Can't be more than a few hundred million people who match *that* description," he added, rolling his eyes. "We should be able to figure out who this Vader is by nightfall."

PART 2

Excerpt from a Louis CK comedy routine (*Everything's Amazing, and Nobody's Happy*).

Everything's amazing right now and nobody is happy. In my lifetime the changes in the world have been incredible. We now live in an amazing, amazing world, and it's wasted on a generation of spoiled idiots who don't care.

I was on an airplane and there was internet—high-speed internet—on the airplane. It is fast and I am watching YouTube clips. I mean I am in the airplane! And then it breaks down. And the guy next to me goes, "This is total bullshit." Like how quickly the world owes him something he knew existed only ten seconds ago.

People come back from flights and they tell you their story. And it's like a horror story. It was the worst day of my life! We had to sit on the runway for forty minutes!

Oh, really? What happened next? Did you fly through the air? Incredibly—like a bird? Did you soar into the clouds, *impossibly*? Did you partake in the miracle of human flight? You are flying! It's amazing. You're sitting in a *chair* in the *sky*! You're like a Greek myth right now.

People say there are delays in flights. Delays? Really? New York to California in five hours! That used to take thirty years. And a bunch of you would die on the way there, and you'd get shot in the neck with an arrow, and the other passengers would just bury you and keep walking.

19

Kayla's safe house looked like just about any other southwestern-style desert home—at least outwardly. Beige stucco, low-pitched tile roof, large and surprisingly colorful cacti planted symmetrically in the crushed-rock front yard and along the oversized brick driveway and garage, and a few strategic patches of artificial grass to soften the yard and complete the landscaping.

But the thick stucco concealed equally thick steel within, and while the home looked to be one story tall, and only a thousand or so square feet in area, another thousand square feet was buried firmly beneath the ground, a reinforced bunker that a survivalist would drool over. No handheld weapons could breach this bunker, and this was also true for a wide variety of munitions that might be launched from the air above.

If the US Air Force wanted to reduce the inhabitants of the facility to bloody corpses, of course, they could readily do so. It wasn't *that* good. But those within were well protected from any kind of strike a conventional enemy might attempt.

What really drew attention to the home was that it was the only one for almost a mile, and only accessible after almost a half mile of off-road driving across hard, level desert. The cost to plumb the home for sewage and utilities must have been enormous, but Kayla had somehow managed it.

The inside was comfortably furnished, and its two kitchens were both well stocked, although not with anything fresh. The kitchen in the bunker also contained a massive pantry with supplies and rations that could last for months without restocking.

Large monitors were hung in every room, including the bathrooms, and could display anything the AI who controlled the system decided was worthy of attention outside, where it constantly monitored sensors and concentric rings of video surveillance.

At any sign of trouble, windows and doors could be covered with steel, and every room had its own oxygen supply, if needed, and could be hermetically sealed.

Kayla showed them around, and also produced a metal first aid box, the size of a large briefcase, so they could all attend to a host of minor cuts and bruises. She then left them to their privacy, descending into the lower level for a quick shower and to change the bandage on her arm.

Elias led his son and daughter-in-law back into the relatively spacious first-floor kitchen and motioned for them to take a seat around a tiled table. "Are you hungry?" he asked, opening the stainless steel refrigerator/freezer and studying the contents.

"Very," said Paige, and Connor nodded his agreement.

Elias sighed. "Looks like Kayla hasn't been to a grocery for a while," he said. "Even the long-lasting items in here look like they're past the expiration date." He threw open a small pantry near the refrigerator to discover a giant jar of unopened peanut butter, canned meats, and vegetables of every kind, and box after box of protein bars.

He removed an assortment of differently flavored bars from several of the boxes and placed them on the kitchen table. "Okay then," he said, making a face, "lunch is served. Not exactly the lunch I had planned for you back at my house," he added apologetically. "But you know the old saying about protein bars. The perfect food for after you've foiled an assassination attempt."

Paige laughed. "Who hasn't heard *that* old adage," she said wryly. "Chicken soup for a cold, protein bars after an attempt on your life."

She and Connor selected a few bars and began to dine while Elias opened the light blue nylon duffel bag he had brought from the car, removing his hard-sided briefcase.

"Paige, have you ever worn contact lenses?" he asked, dialing in a seven-digit combination and opening the case.

She told him she hadn't, so he handed her a pair of tortoiseshell glasses that had been inside the case. "Put these on when I tell you to," he instructed, first pressing a tiny indentation on the frame with this thumb, activating a battery and booting up the sophisticated computer chip inside. "The lenses aren't prescription, so they won't affect your vision."

He then handed his son a small plastic container.

"Contact lenses?" guessed Connor, who had worn a pair for several years until he had finally worked up the courage for corrective vision surgery.

Elias nodded. "Put them in. These and the glasses are both prototypes of my technology. I call the system *Veracity,* by the way. And the company that will release it will be called *Ufree Technologies,*" he added, and then quickly spelled the name for them. "U-f-r-e-e."

Elias arched an eyebrow, and Connor got the distinct impression that his father wanted him to figure out the significance of the company's name. Veracity was a good choice, meaning, as it did, not only truth and accuracy, but also *truthfulness.* It might have been a bit *too* on the nose, in Connor's opinion, but it was still a good choice.

But Ufree? What could Ufree mean?

Elias continued to pause, seemingly willing to wait until his son put it together.

"Really, Dad?" said Connor when it finally came to him, unable to suppress a groan. "Ufree? The words *you* and *free* smashed together. Are you really getting biblical?"

"And you shall know the truth," recited Elias by way of an answer. "And the truth shall set you free."

"Talk about a company name that suffers from a Jesus complex," said Paige in amusement.

"Maybe so," replied Elias with a twinkle in his eye, "but are the two of you ready to be set free? Put on your Veracity interfaces now, and you'll experience the system firsthand. You can begin getting used to it while I tell you about Kayla."

Paige slid the glasses on her face and waited for Connor to insert the contacts, which he did expertly, without even needing a mirror.

Connor had studied contact lenses as a technology platform, and knew that these not only had a microcomputer on board, but were likely Wi-Fi enabled, all the while needing such a tiny trickle of power that they could stay charged using the electricity generated by tears and blinks alone.

Elias remained standing, but leaned against a small granite island facing his audience at the table. "The system is as simple as I could make it," he said when they were ready. He paused. "I assume you both just saw a momentary flash of green in your retinas when I made this statement, correct?"

Connor and Paige exchanged glances, and both nodded.

"That's because what I just said is true," he explained. "And because I'm actually a visitor from the planet Rigel Five."

He smiled. "Now you should have seen the briefest flash of green after my first sentence, and then the briefest flash of *red* after my second. That's because my second sentence was a lie. I'm really *not* a visitor from the planet Rigel Five."

"Thank God for Veracity, then," said Connor with a grin. "Because I was pretty sure that the Rigel Five thing was true."

Elias laughed.

"But the answer is yes," continued Connor. "I did see the red flash, and this was followed by green again for your last several statements, because they're true again."

"Exactly. Green for truth. Red for lies. Yellow for not entirely clear. Some statements contain both truth and lies simultaneously. Yellow indicates the strong possibility of deception, which encourages follow-up questions to tease out what is true and what isn't."

"Fascinating," said Connor. "But that's a lot of flashes. Pretty much a flash for every statement."

"You'll get used to it. The flashes are so brief and so minute that they're very close to being subliminal. Even if someone is staring into your eyes, they won't detect them."

Connor nodded, being able to attest to this himself. He hadn't detected any flashes in his father's eyes, and the elder Gibson had obviously been wearing his lenses since he picked Connor up at the airport that morning.

"They're so brief and unobtrusive," continued Elias, "that it's a wonder the flashes even register with those *wearing* the interfaces. Before you know it, you won't even realize they're happening. Your brain will train itself, and you'll just know what is true or not, forget-ting that you're even being prompted. The Veracity interface can use different readouts, of course. You can set different indicator colors, or have the glasses vibrate, or use any other system you can come up with. I could have also set your interfaces to ignore truth, and only indicate lies, which is how mine is set up. In that case, unless you see red or yellow, you know you're hearing the truth."

"So if you were talking with someone with no reason to lie to you," said Paige, "you might not see a single flash during the entire conversation."

"The flashes would be dramatically reduced," said Elias, "but you'd still probably see a few. Like when your best friend tells you that she loves your new shoes."

"Which is what makes someone a best friend in the first place," said Paige, fighting to keep a straight face. "Willingness to lie about your hideous shoes."

Elias smiled. "I chose not to put the system in this mode for you," he continued, "because you're new at this. It's better if you continue to see green for truth, just so you know that Veracity is always paying attention, and not just taking a few statements off."

"That makes sense," said Connor.

"How does it work?" asked Paige.

"I'll give you the short version. The tech doesn't reside in the glasses, or contacts, or phone, or screen. All are programmed to have a constant Wi-Fi connection with a master supercomputer. This com-puter is the heart and brains of Veracity. The peripheral devices are merely user interfaces, transmitting both video and audio. And the Veracity computer is absolutely unhackable. I can tell you later how this was managed at great length, but just trust me for now."

"Well, you are reading green," said Connor, "so at least *you* think it's unhackable."

"Ensuring the sanctity of the system was as important to me as perfecting Veracity itself," said Elias.

"Because it has to be foolproof," guessed Connor, "beyond re-proach. It has to work a hundred percent of the time. Ninety-nine isn't good enough. Not if you want the tech to be truly transformative.

Everyone has to be certain that its verdicts are absolutely reliable, and tamper-proof."

"That's exactly right," said Elias, biting off a piece of a peanut butter flavored protein bar. "And they are," he continued after chewing and swallowing. "The supercomputer that houses Veracity is an advanced prototype with some very special features. One-of-a-kind features. Paige's glasses and your contacts are linked to its brain. So it sees what you see, and hears what you hear. It's able to diagnose a statement in an instant and send you the result."

"On what basis?" asked Connor.

"The highly abbreviated explanation is that it studies a subject's voice, face, and more at the rate of many thousands of frames per second, and analyzes this data using a proprietary algorithm."

"And you developed the algorithm?" asked Connor.

"No. *Veracity* did. I set the initial conditions and forced it to rapidly evolve through many millions of generations, to select the best lie detector in each generation to produce additional . . . well, the equivalent of offspring. At the end, I had evolved a lie detector beyond my greatest hopes. But I can't even *locate* the algorithm it uses, let alone decipher it."

Connor's eyes widened. *Of course.* His father had used a variation of something called *reinforcement learning.* Connor had written an article on the subject for an online magazine. Google's AI subsidiary *DeepMind* had been one of the first to wow the world with this approach, but his father had taken it into an unexpected arena.

In 2015, DeepMind's AlphaGo stunned computer experts around the world by becoming the first program to ever beat the world's best players in the Chinese game of Go, which had fifty-four orders of magnitude more possible configurations than chess.

But this was only the beginning.

Only two years later, a descendant of this program, AlphaZero, taught itself to play three games of nearly infinite complexity—all with superhuman skill—in less than a *day.* Programmers simply input the rules of the games and set it the goal of winning, without any further strategy, tactics, or instruction on how to play.

And then it did play—against itself. Many millions and billions of games.

After only eight hours of self-play, this new program was able to beat its talented predecessor, AlphaGo. Then, after four hours of teaching itself the game of chess—four hours!—it destroyed the world's best computer chess program, Stockfish, which had long been capable of destroying the best humans. AlphaZero *annihilated* Stockfish, using a style of play that experts described as totally alien—not human, not computer, but a style that had never been seen before in the history of chess.

Then, almost as an afterthought, after two additional hours of self-play, AlphaZero became the world's best program in the game of shogi, a Japanese version of chess.

These performances were as alarming as they were stunning, especially since the programmers had *no idea* how AlphaZero was choosing its moves. It had grown far beyond its creators' ability to fathom.

And now Elias Gibson had applied this process to human lie detection.

20

Connor asked his father to pause for just a moment so he could quickly provide Paige with the briefest of backgrounders on machine learning, evolvable computing, and reinforcement learning, and describe systems like AlphaZero that had achieved superhuman abilities.

"Sorry to interrupt your flow," said Connor when he had finished.

"Not at all," replied Elias. "I'm glad you did. This will help Paige understand the daunting power of these approaches."

"Getting back to what you've accomplished," said Connor, "what data did you input at the start?"

"I began with as many books on the subject of lying and human nature as I could. Including what scientists have discovered about lying that has nothing to do with the sorts of physiologic responses a polygraph might examine. Or even facial expressions or body language."

"Like what?" asked Paige.

"For example, one good sign of a possible deception is a story *too* well told. Too clean. Too chronological."

"Why?" asked Paige. "Because it seems rehearsed?"

"Very good," said Elias. "That's it, exactly. When people tell complex stories, they don't usually tell them in a perfect progression from start to finish."

"Can you give us a few more examples?" asked Paige.

"Sure," said her father-in-law amiably. "Another tell is when someone gives a thirty-word answer when 'absolutely not!' would suffice.

"Pauses in answering can be important too. If I asked you where you were on May 7th, 2008, you'd have to pause and think, probably for a long time, to have any chance of giving an answer. But if I asked you if you had *murdered* someone on that date, you could answer 'no' immediately. Why? Because you know that you've *never* murdered anyone. On *any* date."

"Unless you did," said Paige. "Then your denial might take a moment longer."

"Exactly," said Elias. "There are many other examples, but this gives you a sense of what I'm talking about. So I fed the supercomputer this information, along with numerous textbooks on human physiology, facial expressions, body language, psychology, behavior, and medicine. And scores of other relevant books, as well. In addition, I allowed it to draw on any of the trillions of pages of Internet information as it saw fit. I also included many thousands of video clips of people telling the truth, or lying. Some I proactively filmed for this purpose, instructing subjects to tell lies or truths. Many other clips were of men and women in the public eye whose videoed words were later shown to be lies. I told Veracity which were true, and which were lies, and tasked it with finding a way to come to these exact conclusions without having been told beforehand."

"Outstanding," said Connor in awe.

"Thanks," said his father awkwardly, allowing himself a proud smile for just a moment. "In the end, as I've said, Veracity taught itself how to be a flawless lie detector. I was hoping for ninety-five-percent accuracy, but didn't think the system could get there. I was convinced that a hundred percent accuracy wasn't even *theoretically* possible, like exceeding the speed of light. But I was wrong. The results blew me away. Veracity somehow found a way," he added, gushing as if speaking about a living being. "One much too complex for a human to comprehend. Which is what I wanted, actually. If no one knows how it works, it can't be circumvented."

"But there's a flaw in your methodology," said Connor. "You tasked the system with finding a way to get to answers you had already provided to it. Can I assume you went on to verify it was just as accurate for *new* statements? Ones for which it *didn't* know the answers ahead of time?"

Elias smiled. "Good catch, Con," he said proudly. "I was concerned about this as well. But further experiments showed this wasn't a problem. But before I get into that, I should tell you that I had

Veracity evolve its own security at the same time as it was evolving its lie-detecting abilities. A novel idea also. I fed it everything I could about the art and science of hacking and gave it the goal of being absolutely impregnable. Afterwards, I confirmed it was successful by offering a million-dollar reward to eight of the best hackers in the world if they could find a way inside. None collected the reward."

Connor considered. "But *you* can still get inside, right?"

"Not anymore. Once I verified the system was a perfect lie catcher, I locked up my own programming conduit and threw away the key. Yes, I can tweak the user interface and some of its functionality, but its lie-detector function is absolutely tamper-proof. But just in case someone does find a way in someday, the program is self-policing. If it detects a single change in its programming, no matter how minute, it will instantly alert all of its myriad interfaces in use around the world, so users all know that the system is no longer reliable."

"Truly brilliant," said Connor.

Elias nodded his thanks. "I assume you're both still getting the appropriate flashes while we've been talking."

"Absolutely," said Paige. "Veracity reports that everything you've been saying is true. And you're right, the flashes get less noticeable all the time. In a day or two, I'm sure I won't even realize I'm seeing them."

"I agree," said Connor. "But please go on, Dad," he added, eager to learn more. "How did you confirm that Veracity was working?"

"I paid thousands of people, over many months, to tell truths and lies under the guise of a psychology study. I offered them additional money every time they could lie convincingly enough to fool other volunteers I had hired."

Elias paused. "These other volunteers were often fooled," he continued proudly. "But Veracity never was. Not a single time. I even carried these experiments a step further," he added, "but I'll save that for another time."

"You have to have some idea how the system is working," said Paige.

"I do. The interfaces, like your glasses and contacts, capture fish-eye views of the entire face you're watching. So, yes, you do have to be looking at the person who is speaking. Or facing the person if you're wearing a lapel camera. Unless that person is being televised, which would be the case for politicians and other power brokers. If on television, or YouTube, or Twitter, for example, the version of Veracity that is loaded onto your TV, computer monitor, or cell phone can analyze this feed."

He paused to let this sink in. "Veracity analyzes a subject's word choices, story coherence, voice, and facial expressions—slicing audio and video into many thousands of discrete units each second."

"Looking for what?" asked Connor.

"It's not entirely clear," replied Elias. "But earlier studies lead me to believe that facial expressions are the most telling, followed by voice analysis. A human face has forty-three independent muscles," he explained. "Working in concert, these facial muscles can create nearly an unlimited number of expressions. Have either of you heard the term, *microexpression?*"

Both Connor and Paige indicated they had not.

"These are expressions below the surface, which flash across a face in one twenty-fifth of a second. Too quickly for humans to process. But they can be very telling. For example, those recovering from failed suicide attempts often try to fool doctors about their state of mind. A patient might *claim* to be upbeat and optimistic, so he or she can be released from the hospital—only to then commit suicide."

"That's awful," said Paige.

"It truly is," said Elias. "Imagine how guilty you'd feel if you were the doctor who was fooled?

"Anyway," he continued after a brief pause, "in the late sixties, a clinical psychologist named Paul Ekman studied these cases, trying to find a way to help doctors determine if such patients were being truthful or not. While watching a taped interview in super slow-motion, over and over again, of a patient who had gone on to commit suicide after her discharge, Ekman made a major breakthrough. Just as the patient was saying she was fine, and *smiling*, for the briefest instant a look of total despair flashed across her face. So briefly, it was only noticeable when a frame was frozen in place."

"A microexpression," said Paige.

"Exactly. The patient's face was revealing how she really felt, just too quickly for the eye to catch."

"But not too quickly for your Veracity to catch," said Connor.

"That's right. One twenty-fifth of a second is an eternity for a supercomputer. Veracity can unerringly catch all of these microexpressions—along with all macro-expressions—and in a fraction of a second, apply complex analysis that might take a human years to complete. But Veracity doesn't just scour subjects for expressions and the movements of facial muscles. It watches blinks—duration, frequency, and pattern. It analyzes movements of the tongue and teeth, and microscopic changes in pupil dilation—movements too fine for human detection. And it studies subtle mouth and nostril movements to detect changes in breathing patterns."

Elias paused. "With respect to the audio side, it listens carefully for pauses in speech and overall cadence. It listens to a subject's voice, including micro-variations in vocal timbre, pitch, tone, syllable stressing, and so on, that no human could possibly detect. It considers word choices. Duration of pauses between words and sentences. And likely other factors humans never would have dreamed would play a role. Somehow, it combines all of this input, and more, and comes to the correct conclusion. Every time."

"You've really outdone yourself, Dad," said Connor.

"Thank you. And I should add that the contact lenses themselves are pretty special. We're hoping to incorporate some of the science-fiction-like features you wrote about in your piece, but we do have a few already present. The one that blows my mind is night vision. You can put the contacts in IR mode. Night-vision goggles without the goggles."

Connor grinned. "Very cool," he said. "Not something most of us need," he added, "since we're rarely really in darkness—but very cool. Does the night-vision feature come on automatically when needed?"

Elias shook his head. "No, the contacts are gas permeable, so you can sleep with them. Don't want IR vision coming alive every time you shut your eyes. You activate this capability by closing your right eye—an extended blink—three times in quick succession. Do this again, and the feature is *deactivated.*"

He paused. "Other features are also activated by blink patterns. Although most of these blink patterns are much more complex. Which actually makes them much less noticeable if done right. This blinking takes a lot of practice to pull off with fluidity, and without having to think about it. Or without looking like you have something in your eye. But the subconscious is remarkable. As long as you're getting feedback from Veracity, indicating if you're doing the pattern correctly or not, your subconscious adds a mental subroutine that lets you do it without even thinking. Well, once you get the hang of it."

Paige looked dubious. "Seems hard to imagine that something as subtle as fast, undetectable eye-blink patterns can be so well controlled," she said.

"Why not?" said Elias. "When you speak, your mouth and tongue and lips are carrying out an insanely complex and intricate chorus of movements to form words. Try to consciously picture all the movements your mouth and tongue have to make to say a word." He shook his head. "You can't do it. Because you have *no idea* how you're forming words. But that doesn't stop you from doing it anyway, effortlessly, without any conscious thought."

"Interesting," said Paige. "I never really thought about that, but it's a great point."

"So what else can these contacts do?" asked Connor.

"I'll tell you later," said Elias. "I think we should stop here for now. I've spent too much time on this already. I just wanted you and Paige to begin getting used to Veracity. But we still have pressing matters to consider. And I need to tell you about Kayla so she can join us."

"I understand," said Connor, realizing that he had temporarily forgotten all about Kayla in his zeal to learn more about his father's breakthrough.

"Let me get right to it, then," said Elias. He took a deep breath and then slowly exhaled. "Kayla's last name is Keller. She's Kayla Anne Keller. Ring a bell?"

He waited patiently for her name and history to register, and was rewarded when his son's mouth dropped open. "Kayla *Keller*?"

repeated Connor incredulously. "Are you kidding? You warned us it wouldn't be pretty. But Kayla *Keller*?"

Connor glanced at his wife, who also now wore a horrified expression. "What's the matter," he added in disgust, "was Satan unavailable when you were looking for a partner?"

21

Elias tore off a piece of a second protein bar and chewed, waiting for the shock on the faces of his son and daughter-in-law to subside before he continued.

"I don't know, Con," he said finally, "you've interacted with this notorious villain for some time now. You've been on the run with her. So did she seem like Satan to *you*?"

"No," admitted Connor. "But even Satan can be charming when he wants to be."

"Her warning also just saved my life," said Elias.

"This is also true," admitted Connor.

"She doesn't look anything like I remember from the news," said Paige.

"She changed her hairstyle, hair color, makeup, and so on. Changed her eye color from brown to piercing blue with contact lenses. Lost a few pounds."

"So she went out of her way to not be recognized," said Connor, "and basically removed herself from the grid," he added, remembering that she had been almost as shocked that someone had managed to *find* her as she was that they had tried to take her life.

"Can you blame her?" said Elias.

"Are you about to tell me she's innocent?" said Connor. "Because that would be the most audacious claim you've made all day—and that is *really* saying something."

"What do you remember about her?" asked Elias.

"It's been at least five years now," replied Connor. "But she's a psychopath who slipped through the system. A scientist who started a VR company. Which is why I followed the case so closely. Because of your involvement in virtual reality, and my love of future tech." He paused. "So you must have known her back then."

"A little. Mostly, I knew *of* her. I did meet her a few times in passing. And the VR company she founded, by the way, was the progenitor of Total Immersion Systems."

Connor's eyes narrowed. "How did I miss that?"

"Because you were *supposed* to. Do you think management wanted to advertise that she was the founder? Total Immersion Systems began life as Keller Virtual Technologies. But after Kayla's name became poison, it was quietly reincorporated under its new name, and her initial involvement was hidden as much as possible. After she was acquitted in court, she had her name legally changed to Karen Preston, and her forty-five percent stock ownership was listed under this name. But trust me, much of the technology I worked with for two years was her doing. She wasn't just the founder of the company, but also its Chief Technology Officer. She's absolutely brilliant technically."

"I remember hearing that," said Paige. "She graduated college at sixteen and set the world on fire."

"Yeah," chimed in Connor, "but in her case, this isn't a figure of speech. She *actually* set the world on fire."

"Come on Connor," said Elias in annoyance, "arson was one of the few things she *wasn't* accused of."

"I know. I was being sarcastic. But she did work secret deals with China to provide technology they weren't supposed to have. Rumor has it that she tortured fluffy animals for kicks when she was a kid. Later, not surprisingly, she was a ruthless boss, berating employees and using physical and psychological violence against them. She stole intellectual property from others, and took credit for work she didn't do. Then, she tortured and murdered an innocent woman who had met with the FBI as a whistleblower. They had her dead to rights on the murder, but the three people whose testimony was the most damning all died in mysterious circumstances before they could testify."

"Which was so suspicious that the authorities climbed up her ass with a microscope," said Elias. "As if they weren't investigating her enough already. Yet, despite the charges you just listed, and many others, she was never convicted of anything. Why do you think that is?"

"I don't know," said Connor. "Maybe because she took a page from the mob. The best witnesses against her were killed, and others were intimidated into changing their stories. And the justice system isn't infallible. How did OJ Simpson win *his* criminal case? Do you really think that means he's innocent?"

Connor shook his head. "From all accounts, Kayla Keller was OJ Simpson and Bernie Madoff combined. Based on a mountain of evidence uncovered by the press, she was *Cruella DeVille*. Except worse. A hundred Dalmatian puppies wouldn't have been cruel *enough* for her."

"I'll ask again," said Elias, "does any of this jibe with the behavior you've observed?"

"No. But people can be easily deceived."

"Veracity can't."

"Even by a psychopath?" said Connor. "I should have raised this earlier, but psychopaths are known to have a genius for deception. Even the ones who aren't *actual* geniuses, like she is. Many of them can beat a polygraph with ease. They're wired differently than normal. They have no compassion, no shame, no fear. MRIs show their brains to be so different from normals that they're almost their own separate species, making no lie detector test reliable."

"Yeah, I read your article on the science of what makes psychopaths tick a long time ago, Con. *Before* I perfected Veracity. I told you earlier that I had conducted additional experiments, ones I wanted to wait to tell you about until we had more time. Well, that's what these experiments were about. Psychopaths. I know they're world-class when it comes to lying. So as part of my studies, I got permission to enter prisons and interview a variety of known psychopaths, from con artists to cold-blooded killers. They can, indeed, fool polygraph tests."

He shook his head. "But they can't fool Veracity. When I said a hundred percent accuracy, I wasn't giving psychopaths a pass. God knows if Veracity couldn't see through psychopaths, it would be useless for keeping *politicians* honest."

Elias flashed a wry smile, but he clearly hadn't said this entirely in jest.

"So your system is foolproof, is that what you're saying?" asked Connor.

"That's exactly what I'm saying. What I've *been* saying."

"And Veracity gives Kayla Keller a clean bill of health?" said Paige. "You have no doubt of that?"

"*No* doubt," replied Elias emphatically.

The elder Gibson paused. "Not that she's been a saint," he added. "She used questionable ethics on a number of occasions, and did work her employees into the ground. But she did this for a cause that she believed in. One I find noble. In that sense, she was no worse than Steve Jobs or Elon Musk. One could argue that a saint would be at an extreme disadvantage in the dog-eat-dog world of high-tech business."

Elias shook his head. "But I can tell you she's anything but a psychopath, and didn't do any of the things she's accused of. I've found her to be nothing but caring, brilliant, and kind. She was framed for all of it."

Connor saw nothing but flashes of green during his father's entire impassioned defense of this woman, so he knew that the elder Gibson believed every word. But based on everything he had read and heard about Kayla Keller, it still wasn't an easy sell, even with Veracity's blessing. He now understood why his father was so reluctant to have this discussion on the fly. If not for Elias's powerful demonstration of the system, and explanation of his breakthrough, Connor would never have believed anything but the worst about Keller, and he never would have agreed to accompany her anywhere.

"So just how was she framed?" asked Connor.

Elias's answer was interrupted by four sharp raps on the kitchen door, just before it flew open. "Sorry to interrupt," said Kayla, ignoring the icy stares she was now receiving from Paige and Connor. "But this is important. You didn't mess with any controls did you, Elias? Or give any orders to the AI controlling the house?"

"Of course not," said Elias. "Would the AI even follow my orders if I did?"

"No," she admitted. "Sorry. I'm clutching at straws here, but the outer perimeter sensors just stopped registering. Which isn't supposed to be possible. Not like this."

She turned to a thirty-inch monitor affixed to one wall of the kitchen. "Harold," she called out, "are the video cameras still running?"

"They are," replied a pleasant male voice from speakers in the ceiling. "I'm working on returning the sensors to full-functionality. It shouldn't be long."

"Do you know of any technology that could have caused this?" she asked the AI.

"Negative," it replied.

"I still can't believe this is a simple malfunction," said Kayla uneasily. "Not after everything that's happened today."

"I should hide the briefcase," said Elias.

"We don't need to be too worried just yet," replied Kayla. "Harold isn't seeing anything worrisome on video. So no one can possibly sneak up on us. Even if they could, they'd have an easier time breaking into Fort Knox."

Elias blew out a long breath. "That may be, but I'm not using the briefcase now anyway. So why not store it someplace more . . . hidden."

Kayla stared at him for several seconds and nodded. "Okay. Why not? There's a secret compartment downstairs. Follow me."

Just after they left the kitchen, Connor opened the blue duffel bag, pocketed the fake FBI agent's two guns—tranquilizer and actual—and removed the three flash-bang grenades inside.

"I'm going to hide these around the house," he told Paige, holding up the small grenades. "Just in case."

"Where did *those* come from?"

"Took them from the guy attacking us at my dad's house. You were unconscious at the time."

"Well, put them away!" demanded Paige. "You can't use hand grenades in here! You're more likely to blow *us* up than an intruder."

"These aren't hand grenades. They're flash-bangs. Stun grenades. They're so bright and loud that they temporarily blind and deafen an enemy. They also cause a temporary loss of balance, since the bang affects the fluid in the inner ear."

"Wow, that sounds pleasant," said Paige wryly.

"A lot more pleasant than an actual grenade."

"I'll have to give you that," she replied with a nod. Then, after blowing out a long breath, she added, "For the first time in my life, I wish I had read more thrillers. Didn't know I'd ever need this particular form of education."

"You never should have," said Connor grimly.

She gestured at the flash-bangs. "I'm glad you know what those things can do, but you still don't need to hide them. Veracity registered everything Kayla just said as being true. So she's certain we're safe here. Do you really think someone could find a way to break in?"

"Hard to imagine," said Connor. "But like my dad said," he added, arching an eyebrow, "I'm not *using* these flash-bangs at the moment, anyway. So why not hide them?"

Paige smiled, despite the increased tension brought on by the sensor malfunction. "Okay, then," she said. "I guess paranoid times call for paranoid measures."

"Exactly," said Connor, moving swiftly through the kitchen door.

22

Connor finished his mission and returned to the kitchen, just as his father and Kayla Keller were doing the same.

"Harold, are the sensors back online?" she asked her AI.

"Not yet," it reported, "but all other systems are working perfectly, and there is no other reason for alarm."

Connor turned to Kayla and shook his head. "You named your AI *Harold*?" he said in disbelief. He had wanted to ask this question when he had first heard this name, but it hadn't been the right time.

Kayla actually smiled. "Let me guess," she said. "Now that your father told you who I am, it's hard for you to believe someone with my notorious reputation would use such a silly name?"

"Pretty much," admitted Connor.

"Well, first of all, with respect to my reputation, don't believe everything you hear. Especially from the media, as your father's been saying. And second, it isn't Harold, the man's name. It's *Herald*," she explained, spelling the word. "H-e-r-a-l-d. Meaning a sign, a portent. That something momentous is about to happen. Or something *bad*."

Connor raised his eyebrows. "I stand corrected," he said. "Not silly at all. Actually, not a bad choice for a security system."

This homophone of Harold would have never occurred to him. And Kayla's innocence wouldn't have either. Perhaps he had been wrong about both.

"I'll go back downstairs now so your father can finish talking about me," said Kayla.

Elias turned to her and sighed. "Sorry about that," he said earnestly. "We won't be much longer."

"Take all the time you need," she replied. "I'm enjoying the alone time," she added good-naturedly, and Connor, Paige, and Elias all received the briefest flash of red in their eyes.

The hint of a smile came over Connor's face. So Kayla wasn't enjoying her excommunication, after all, he realized. She was simply trying to make them feel better about excluding her. Which Connor had to admit was a social nicety he wouldn't expect from Cruella DeVille.

Just as she turned to leave, a loud humming sound came from the walls surrounding the door. Before Connor could wonder what it was, steel panels slid out to cover the wooden door, riding on steel tracks on top and bottom that created a hermetic seal when the panels were fully deployed.

"Herald, what's going on?" shouted Kayla. "Why did you seal the room?"

"I didn't," replied the AI, and if an AI could register dismay and anxiety, this one did now. "I'm attempting an override."

Kayla had a wild, cornered-animal look in her eye. "Hurry!" she barked. "Are your perimeter cameras picking up anything we should know about?"

"Nothing," said the AI. "But the hidden munitions outside are not responding to my *ready* commands."

Just as Kayla was about to respond with another query, the AI's voice came back to life. "All video cameras just went down," it reported. "I repeat, all cameras are down. We are now blind to the outside."

"I thought this place was impregnable!" said Paige.

"Yeah, so did I," said Kayla gravely. "But I was wrong. And if whoever is responsible wants us dead, there's nothing we can do about it."

And this time, Connor didn't need a flash of green to tell him that her last sentence was absolutely true.

23

Connor fought back panic. There were no windows in the small kitchen, and the only exit was now sealed with an impregnable fortification. "Do those steel panels have a manual override?" he asked, gesturing to where the kitchen door had been.

Kayla shook her head no.

"So we're blind and trapped like rats," said Connor.

"That about sums it up," she replied miserably.

"Perfect!" said Connor. "Are the walls about to start closing in like that trash compactor scene from *Star Wars*?"

"I'm not sure that would be any worse," she replied.

Connor's mind raced. "Wait a minute," he said. "It's true that we can't get out of here. But they can't get *in*, either. Not without retracting the panels. Once they do, they'll have to come in through the door to get us. Will we have any warning that the steel panels are about to retract?" he asked Kayla.

"Not much. We'll hear the same sound we heard before the panels deployed, for just a second, and then they'll slide back into the walls."

"No matter," said Connor. "We can wait on either side of the door for this to happen. I won't go down without a fight."

Kayla nodded her agreement, as Connor removed both guns from his pockets, one in each hand.

"Where did *those* come from?" asked Elias.

"When you left to hide the briefcase," said Connor, "I decided to hold on to these until the sensors were back up." He turned to Kayla. "Have you ever shot a gun?" he asked. While he knew that Paige had, he also knew she couldn't hit anything more than fifteen feet away, and certainly nothing on the move.

"A few times," replied Kayla. "But I'm horrible at it. The safest place to be when I'm shooting is where I'm aiming," she added wryly.

Elias reached out toward his son. "Give me the stun gun," he said. "At least I've fired it before. You keep the other one."

Connor handed his father the tranquilizer gun and shifted the real one to his right hand. Could he really bring himself to shoot someone? He cringed at the thought. He had no interest in killing *anyone*.

On the other hand, he decided, he had even *less* interest in anyone killing *him*.

His jaw tightened and a look of resolve came over his face. If he had to kill to protect Paige and his father, so be it.

"What are we *doing*?" said Paige emphatically. "We need to call the police! If you're worried the bad guys will intercept the call and learn where we are, don't be. They already know! So what do we have to lose?"

"You're absolutely right," said Connor.

"*We* don't have anything to lose," said Kayla, "but the cops do. They'll be way out of their league. If we call them here, we'll probably get them killed."

"They *are* trained for this sort of thing," said Paige.

"They're trained to face common criminals," responded Kayla. "Not what *we're* up against. Borrego Springs isn't exactly inner city Chicago. They won't have any experience with armed conflict. They won't stand a chance against whoever is coming for us."

"Maybe," said Connor. "But maybe the people who've disarmed your system are nothing but tech geeks. All we can do is tell the cops that we're surrounded by heavily armed men. If we aren't, so much the better. If we are, at least the cops will come warned and prepared."

Kayla nodded. "Agreed," she said. "Herald, place a call to the closest police station."

"Unable to comply," said the AI almost immediately. "Something is blocking all communications."

"This just keeps on getting better," mumbled Elias, while Paige looked like she was about to throw up.

A hissing sound issued from the ceiling above, followed by what looked like smoke shooting through three small vents in the ceiling.

"Shit!" screamed Kayla in a blind panic. "They're gassing us. Through my own oxygen system. That's impossible!"

All four inhabitants of the small kitchen instinctively lowered themselves to the floor, to remain as far from the cloud of gas as possible.

But it was an exercise in futility.

Connor placed the gun on the floor, since it had now been rendered useless. Apparently, those who were coming for them didn't need to open the door after all.

He took his wife into his arms and held her tight. "I love you," he whispered.

"I love you, too," she replied, tears now streaming down her face.

And as the gas enveloped the entire kitchen and Connor's consciousness slipped away, he knew that these would be the last words he would ever hear.

24

Connor bolted awake and noticed several things at once. First, and most importantly, he wasn't dead. Which he considered exceedingly good news. And he had the feeling that he hadn't been out for long.

They were still in the kitchen, but neither the blue duffel bag nor the two guns were anywhere in sight, and the steel door no longer sealed them inside. His hands were loosely bound with zip-ties, and there were two armed men now in the room with them, one of whom was stabbing a thin syringe into his wife's arm and pressing the plunger all the way down.

Paige flashed awake seconds after whatever was in the syringe entered her bloodstream, as the man produced two additional syringes, which he quickly used to revive Elias and Kayla. Like Connor, the other three newly awakened prisoners also had their hands loosely tied together with plastic zip-ties.

The four prisoners each came to their feet and faced a man standing against the back wall, who continued to hold a gun on them, as he had while his partner had administered the reversal drug. He was fit and handsome, and he emanated an air of both menace and authority. Even so, Kayla's lip curled up into a snarl, and her eyes burned with utter contempt. "What is this all about?" she demanded. "Who are you?"

"I'm John," he replied pleasantly, as his syringe-wielding colleague joined him against the wall, his gun now also extended toward them. "And this is Neil."

Two flashes of red struck at Connor's retinas. These men were too careful to even give their real first names. Even so, they apparently wanted to put the group at ease, or they wouldn't have bothered with fictitious ones. It was a positive sign, indicating they just might be after the prisoners' cooperation.

"Did Jake send you?" asked Kayla.

"I have no idea who you mean," said the man who had claimed his name was John.

"Yes you do," said Kayla confidently, and for the first time Connor realized the obvious. The lenses she was wearing didn't just change her eye-color, they were also Veracity enabled. Of course they were. She was his father's partner, after all.

Kayla raised her eyebrows. "Let me refresh your memory, *John*," she said. "Jake's the one who uses a voice synthesizer to make himself sound like Darth Vader."

"A voice *changer*," he said, correcting her. "So you know our boss. So what? I have my orders, and they don't involve answering questions."

"If you do answer our questions, though," said Connor, "we're prepared to be a lot more cooperative."

This wasn't true, as the three other Veracity-enabled prisoners in the kitchen would know, but it was worth a try. Kayla, Paige, and Elias all nodded their hearty agreement with this statement.

The man considered. "Okay," he said at last, glancing at his watch. "Why not? You have five minutes. After that, I'm afraid I'll need to have a private . . . discussion with each of you. Beginning with Kayla," he added.

Connor's eyes narrowed. These men might be lying about their own names, but they were familiar with the names of their prisoners. "A group tried to kill Kayla earlier," said Connor, not wasting any time. "And a separate one tried to kill my dad. Which one of these groups are you with?"

"Neither," replied John. "This is the first assignment we've been given involving any of you."

Both answers registered as true. Connor found this to be surprising. Just how many groups like this did Vader employ, anyway?

"Why are you here?" asked Connor.

"To have a friendly chat," replied John.

This registered yellow—inconclusive, conflicted—which Connor took to mean they were here to have a chat, but it would be anything but friendly.

"I have a laundry list of information my employer would like me to get from you," continued their captor. "Most importantly, he wants a flash drive with certain information about a prototype super-computer, along with its physical location. I was assured you would all know the supercomputer I'm talking about."

"Does that mean that you don't?" said Elias.

"I don't know why my boss wants any of this information. And I don't want to know."

Both registered as true statements.

"Why interrogate us?" asked Elias. "Earlier today, your boss wanted me dead. Without talking to me at all."

"He must have changed his mind," said John with a shrug.

"Do you plan to let all of us live?" asked Connor. "To let us go?"

John smiled. "Since I need your cooperation," he said smoothly, "it serves me no purpose to answer these questions, one way or another."

Connor frowned. It was a true statement, and sound strategy. If their captor told them he planned to kill them, they would be certain to put up a fight, and would have no reason to be cooperative. On the other hand, he also couldn't entirely remove this threat, which was the ultimate inducement to get them to answer his questions.

"How did you beat my security?" asked Kayla.

"The boss gave us detailed instructions, and we followed them."

Truth.

Connor's eyes narrowed. Perhaps this was a useful clue. Maybe Vader worked for the security company who made these systems. Or else he was so powerful, so well placed, that he could get the most highly classified, highly technical information on a whim. "What did you do with our guns?" he asked.

"I took the Sig Sauer, and Neil here has the tranquilizer gun."

"Do you have any idea who your boss really is?" asked Kayla.

"None," said John simply, an answer that was accompanied by an immediate flash of red into the retinas of all Veracity-enabled prisoners.

They all traded excited glances. The man was lying! *He did know.* Or at least had some idea. This could be huge.

"When he speaks to you," asked Kayla, "does he favor military jargon?"

"No," came the truthful reply.

"If you had to guess," said Kayla, "would you guess he's American?"

"I told you, I have no idea who he is."

"I get that," replied Kayla. "But humor me on this, and I swear that I'll give you my absolute cooperation. If you had to *guess*, would you guess he's American?"

"No," said John, which was a lie.

Kayla was brilliant, thought Connor. If she had asked the man if Vader *was* American, John would have just reiterated that he had no idea. But asking him to *guess*—when she was well aware that he *knew*—was inspired.

"Based on how he operates, would you guess that he's in the mob?" she continued.

"No."

"A businessman?" she pressed.

"No."

"A politician?"

"*No!*" he shouted emphatically. "I told you, I have no idea who he is. And my guesses mean nothing!"

Connor's eyes widened. Two of his three *noes* were truthful, but the third was a lie, as was his continued insistence that he didn't know.

Vader *was* a politician.

Of course he was. And no doubt one who was highly successful. A politician who was orders of magnitude more aggressive even than usual in doing research on his political opposition, judging by what the fake FBI agent had told them about Vader's interests.

It wasn't uncommon for powerful criminals to have politicians in their pockets, but this was a politician who had turned the tables. Vader had kicked up so much dirt on so many powerful criminals, business leaders, media titans, and politicians that he would need city-sized pockets to fit them all inside.

Connor had to hand it to Kayla Keller. She had done a brilliant job of squeezing this information from a hostile witness who unwittingly had no choice but to provide the truth in a surreal game of twenty questions. Unfortunately, there was no doubt that this man had run out of patience.

"Would you guess that he's a senator?" asked Kayla, making a last attempt to gain further information, having also concluded that Vader was a major player.

"Enough!" thundered John, not unexpectedly. "*Are you deaf?* I told you I don't know! And yet you keep shooting inane questions at me. Playtime is over. I've more than held up my part of our bargain."

He glared at Kayla. "You're up first. Since I answered your ridiculous questions, I expect you to make good on your vow of cooperation."

Kayla nodded. "Of course," she replied. "I'll tell you anything you want to know."

She said it with such sincerity that Connor was relieved to receive a simultaneous flash of red in his eyes.

He had to admit, despite having been certain that Kayla Keller was one of the most despicable people on the planet, he was beginning to warm to her.

25

The man who had called himself John led a bound Kayla Keller off at gunpoint, escorting her to a private office in the downstairs bunker, while his partner stayed behind. Just after they left, Neil pressed a tiny electronic device hard against the back wall of the kitchen, so that it faced the three remaining prisoners. He let go and nodded in approval as a heavy duty adhesive held it in place.

"This is what's called a smart video surveillance system," he said. "While Kayla is being interrogated, I'll be in the other room. This device has an AI on board that knows what a kitchen knife is, what scissors are, and so on. If you move out of its sight, I'm alerted. If you try to cut your cuffs, or pick up anything the AI deems could be used as a weapon, I'm alerted. In fact, if you do *anything* it judges to be out of the ordinary, I'm alerted."

He shot the three prisoners a menacing scowl. "And if I *am* alerted," he continued, "trust me, it won't go well for you. There's no rule that says you can't have broken fingers before your interrogation even begins. Remember that."

The three prisoners exchanged troubled glances, each having read that everything the man had just told them was true.

"I know you won't believe it, but this is actually me being compassionate. This way, you'll at least retain some freedom of movement. And you'll have your privacy."

Connor expected a flash of red at this last statement, but received green instead. "So you won't be able to hear *any* of our conversation?" he said skeptically, feeling the need to be sure he hadn't misinterpreted the green signal. "Really?"

"That's right," confirmed Neil, and Connor saw green yet again.

Maybe he had read *too* many thrillers. If it were him, he would have told his prisoners that their conversation was private, but would have secretly listened in using the system on the wall, or some other bug. Veracity continued to earn its pay.

A moment later the man they knew as Neil was gone, and less than a minute after this, the steel panels slid shut over the kitchen door as before, sealing them inside once again.

Connor eyed the electronic device now watching them. He'd had no idea such a thing existed. If he managed to live through this, he'd have to use a similar system in a novel. Because Neil was doing the smart thing.

When Connor read novels or watched movies in which a captor stayed inside an inescapable room to guard a captive, he had always objected. What was the point? The captive wasn't going anywhere.

But if the captor stayed to babysit, anyway, a lot of things could go wrong for the bad guys. The prisoner could be filthy rich and bribe him to switch sides. The prisoner could probe for weaknesses, physical or emotional, and try to exploit them. He could try to pit the captor against his boss. Or perhaps get him to lower his guard, surprise him, and turn the tables. And if this were to happen, not only would the prisoner be free, he would now be armed with the bad guy's weapons.

There was a minute of silence in the kitchen after Neil left, as each prisoner's thoughts turned to escape. Finally, Elias shook his head miserably. "I can't think of any way out of this," he said. He turned to Paige and Connor. "Any ideas?"

Paige sighed. "Only one. A long shot. We could grab some knives and frying pans, and when his AI sentry alerts him and he comes back in, we could attempt an ambush."

"That's all I managed to come up with too, " said Connor. "I'd just add that we could destroy his sentry device first, so he'd be blind when he enters. But even then it would be suicide. He'd be fully prepared for an ambush, and I'm sure he's very good with that gun of his."

Elias blew out a long breath. "So I guess we wait," he said. "Stay alert and look for opportunities. And hope Vader really did change his mind, and decided I'm worth more to him alive than dead."

"It's possible," said Connor. "If he wanted you dead, you'd never have awakened from the gas."

"You always say the most comforting things," said Elias with a wry smile. "But I hope like hell you're right," he added.

For a moment, Connor considered providing a display of false bravado for Paige and his father, a rousing insistence that he was sure they'd prevail—somehow—but he decided against it.

Veracity would only shoot flashes of red into their eyes, and call him out for the liar he was being.

26

Kayla Keller sat on a heavy chair in front of a Cherrywood desk. Her legs had been tied to the chair with plastic strips, and her hands tied to the desk the same way, with her arms extended. John remained standing across from her, eyeing her with great interest. "Ready to cooperate?" he asked.

"Ready."

"You'd better be," he said sternly. "If not, you'll regret it much sooner than you think."

With this said, his tone became conversational once again. "So let me start with the most important question first." He leaned in toward her. "Where is this supercomputer located? If you answer this honestly—and after I've confirmed it, of course—I wouldn't feel the need to ask any additional questions. We can be done here. Just like that."

"I really wish I had an answer for you," she replied. "But I don't."

"My boss is convinced you do."

"I'm afraid he's misinformed."

John digested this and considered what to say next. "I'll level with you, the boss tells me that Connor and Paige are basically along for the ride on this deal. You and Elias are supposed to be the ones with all the information. So if you make this easy, everyone wins, including you."

He shook his head. 'But if you make this hard, then I have to work on Elias. And from what I've been told, he has nothing but weak spots. You're one of them. But then we have Connor and Paige, his beloved son and daughter-in-law. With this kind of leverage, he's going to tell me what I want to know. So let's save everyone the trouble now.'

Kayla swallowed hard. "As much as I would love to do that," she said, "I can't tell you what I don't know. I do know what supercomputer you mean, but I don't know its location. And I know nothing about this flash drive you're talking about."

"So you're saying that only Elias knows?"

Kayla hesitated. "I'm not sure. You'd have to ask him."

"Is this what you call cooperation?" said John angrily.

"Yes! I've answered all of your questions truthfully."

"Why don't I believe you?" barked John.

His demeanor darkened. "You should know that my boss authorized the use of torture. Encouraged it, actually. Although he insisted that I keep it all below the neck. I'm guessing he's beaten a lot of women in his day, and knows that it's easier for them to cover up the, ah . . . crime scene, if their faces haven't been touched."

"Very thoughtful of him," mumbled Kayla.

"Or it may just be that he's attracted to you," said John. "I can't blame him for that," he added with a creepy smile.

Kayla ignored this last. "He wouldn't worry about my appearance if he planned to have you kill me," she said. "So does that mean you'll be letting me go when we're through?"

"Let's just say that, worst case, you'll be the last to die. But even though I have to keep any torture below the neck, this still gives me a wide latitude. Especially since this territory includes below the *waist*," he added suggestively, raising his eyebrows.

"So if I don't cooperate you'll rape me, is that it?"

"I'm not saying that. But I'm not ruling it out, either."

Kayla shot him a look so cold it could freeze lava. "If you want to have a working dick when this is all over," she hissed through clenched teeth, "I'd recommend against it."

John shrank back without even knowing it, but quickly recovered his composure. "Be careful what you wish for," he responded with a sneer. "There are tortures a lot worse than rape."

"Torture won't work, anyway," she insisted. "Because I don't have the information you need."

John shrugged. "Even if this is the case, it will have a cumulative impact. If you go back upstairs bloodied and bruised, it might make Elias think twice about keeping secrets. And if we're forced to give him a similar treatment, he'll be certain we'll do this and worse to his son and daughter-in-law. So maybe torture won't work—on *you*. But if you don't tell me what I want to know right now, we're about to find out."

Kayla just stared at him stoically. "I can't tell you what I don't know," she repeated.

John lunged at her with magician-like fluidity, slashing her arm with a razor-edged knife so quickly that she felt searing pain before she even knew that he had moved. She screamed in surprise and agony as a one-inch incision appeared just above her elbow and leaked blood down her arm.

"You goddamned prick!" she shouted. "I'd tell you if I knew! This is Elias's secret, not mine."

Her captor raised his eyebrows. "See, now we're getting somewhere. So Elias does know, after all. What did I tell you? That wasn't so hard."

He repeated the slashing move and another incision blossomed into blood four inches higher, near her shoulder, turning her into the beginnings of a living Jackson Pollock painting. She screamed once again. "What was that for?" she demanded.

"Now that you've started down the right path, I wanted to give you a quick reminder of what awaits you down the *wrong* path."

"No you didn't!" she shouted. "I get it now. You plan to get me good and bloodied no matter what I do, don't you? So you can use me as a cautionary tale for Elias. Or else you're just a raging sadist."

He ignored her outburst, seemingly mesmerized by the blood that was soaking into her clothing. "I'm not sure anyone has told you this," he said conversationally, "but *red* is definitely your color."

27

Connor took a seat around the kitchen table and motioned for his father and wife to join him. A small pile of protein bars were still present at the center of the table, oblivious to the changing fate of the humans around them.

They continued to consider ideas for escape, and the identity of the man behind it all, but this conversation stopped abruptly as an extended scream arose from the basement, somehow making it up the stairs and into the hermetically sealed room. It was faint when it arrived, but unmistakably bloodcurdling.

Elias shrank back as if he'd been hit in the gut with a battering ram, and closed his eyes in horror, and there was no doubt that he cared for this woman a great deal.

"We need to get our minds off of what might be happening downstairs," said Connor.

His father didn't reply.

"Tell us more about Veracity," said Paige. "How did it start? When did Kayla come on the scene?"

Elias remained unresponsive.

"Come on, Dad!" said Connor. "Snap out of it. Making yourself sick with worry won't help her. There's nothing we can do right now. So tell us more about Veracity until that changes."

Elias glanced at his son and nodded woodenly. "You're right," he said with a sigh. He straightened his back in an attempt to regain some of his usual vigor.

He gathered himself for several more seconds and then began. "I completed my analysis on the state of America, and the world, about nine years ago. Shortly after this time, I left my job for a company called Virtuality. But between these two jobs, I took three months off, to think harder about what I'd uncovered about our pessimistic and tribal natures. To try to make sense of it all. It was during this time that I came up with the concept for Veracity."

"You've been working on this for almost nine years?" said Connor in disbelief.

Elias shook his head. "No. I made an attempt back then, but it failed. I filed patents on the project while I was between jobs, as it turns out, so the intellectual property belonged to me. After I joined Virtuality, I pitched the project to the CEO. I was a valuable hire, and couldn't have been more passionate. Besides, he couldn't argue that nerves weren't as raw as ever, and it was clear that this had the potential to be revolutionary."

He sighed. "To the CEO's credit, he finally did give me the green light, and funding, to attempt a skunk works program within the company. I was given a budget of five million, and I agreed to sign over my patent rights to the company if I was successful. I was asked to keep the project top secret, as it was high risk, outside of Virtuality's core business, and highly unusual."

Another scream invaded the peace of the kitchen and Elias stopped, squeezed his eyes shut, and looked to be in total anguish. Connor and Paige felt anguish at Kayla's suffering as well, but not nearly at the intensity level of Elias, whose reaction made it clear that Kayla meant the world to him.

After almost a minute passed, Elias managed to find his voice again. "I studied relevant science for months," he continued, pained and reluctant, but doing his best to move forward. "Then I flew around the world and interviewed experts in lying, facial expressions, polygraph testing, evolvable programming, and reinforcement learning. I read all available scientific literature on how DeepMind did what it did, and then interviewed several of the scientists behind it."

"But you just said your project was top secret," said Paige.

"I didn't tell any of them my *real* objective. They all thought I was trying to improve the facial expressions, body language, and general authenticity of characters in virtual reality simulations."

"So you lied," said Connor dryly. "You lied about a project designed to end all lying."

"I'm aware of the irony," said his father. "But to go on, I programmed the most advanced supercomputer available, and used the best optics, the best data on microexpressions, and so on." He shook his head. "But as I said, it ended in failure."

"Total failure?" asked Connor.

"Almost. It was right about sixty-two percent of the time. Better than guessing, but not by that much. And not as good as a polygraph, although, admittedly, without the pesky wires and fuss."

"What went wrong?" asked Paige.

"It was unclear at the time. Either what I was attempting just wasn't possible, or else the tech wasn't ready. Maybe I needed higher resolution optics, better initial data inputs, or a better supercomputer. And I knew for certain the 5G Wi-Fi network wasn't sufficient for my needs. The user interface has to be fast enough to flash a signal after every statement, no matter how rapid-fire the conversation or speech. If the flashes lag, so they get out of sync with the statements being made, you have a disaster on your hands."

He shrugged. "The bottom line is that I wasted considerable effort and money on something that wasn't viable. So I abandoned the project, and Virtuality gave up on any residual rights to my patents. "

"That had to be depressing," said Connor.

"Enormously. But there was nothing I could do but move on. My first shot at Veracity gathered cobwebs, and I forced myself to forget about it. I watched in horror as the world kept getting better and we all kept thinking it was getting worse. I watched as social media made us more connected than ever—but also more tribal than ever—and saw political parties continue to go at each other's throats like never before. I watched as the anger and hysteria grew, stoked by politicians looking to push their followers to the polls."

Elias shook his head. "Then, just a few years later, Jameson was elected president. Almost everyone thought that the arrival of this new administration would change the dynamic. That the malice between the parties would lessen considerably. Based on my research, I knew better. But I allowed myself to hope."

"But like you said earlier, not as much changed as everyone thought it would," said Connor.

"No. The environment wasn't nearly as toxic for maybe nine months or so. But then the honeymoon was over, and things became pretty bad again. Not as bad as before, but pretty bad."

Elias sighed. "When I worked on Veracity the first time, Kayla Keller was also at Virtuality. She was the company's youngest ever executive—head of global R & D—and had been informed of the project. I had met her a few times, but only in passing. It was a huge company, and she was several levels above me. Turns out she left to found Keller Virtual Technologies shortly after I had abandoned my dream of creating the perfect lie catcher. Then she tangled with a psychopath named Derek Manning who ruined her life. I'll let her tell you the details," he said as another shriek made its way into the room.

Elias looked ready to vomit, but gritted his teeth and continued.

"The psychopath in question pinned a lot of really horrible crimes on her, and then started a feeding frenzy in the press to destroy her reputation. A self-sustaining chain reaction that mushroomed out of control. She became a ratings darling, the tech CEO that every-one loved to loathe. You remember. Anyone with a negative story to tell about her could get an instant nationwide audience. If someone claimed to have seen her put babies in a blender, and then drink them for breakfast, the press would take this as gospel, never considering if the accusers had mental health issues of their own. Accusers came out of the woodwork to get their fifteen minutes of fame, and each added to her growing infamy. At some point, even those who had originally believed her claims of being framed began to see her as evil. After all, there were so many accusations, how could all of them be false?

"After the dust cleared and Kayla was acquitted, she dropped out of society. Who could possibly blame her? But she remembered my project and thought it was well worth reviving. If I could perfect Veracity, it could clear her name for good, and ensure that something like this never happened to another innocent again. That no one else's reputation could ever be destroyed by packs of media wolves, always looking for the next story, regardless of proof or validity."

Connor nodded thoughtfully. "So she came to you to ask you to try again," he said.

"She didn't just ask," said Elias, "she pleaded. This was a little over two years ago."

"Just before you left Total Immersion Systems," said Connor.

Elias nodded. "Even though she had changed her appearance enough that I didn't recognize her," he continued, "she told me right away who she really was. She explained what had happened to her and that she was innocent. She didn't expect me to believe her, but she asked for the chance to *earn* my belief. She may have been the most infamous woman in America, but she was also worth almost two billion dollars from Total Immersion Systems' stock. Which has since grown to almost five. But trust me, I was just as horrified and repulsed by her as you are. I wanted nothing to do with her. But she was persistent. This was her chance to clear her name and help change the world, and she was determined."

Elias paused and tilted his head, remembering. "And technology had improved considerably," he continued, "even in the short time since I had last tried. The 6G Wi-Fi network had come online that year, and was finally fast and reliable enough for my needs. She had also become aware of a company, Darwin Computing, with an experimental computer whose *hardware* was reconfigurable—evolvable—along with its software. Which increased its potential for machine learning and evolution to undreamed of levels. She offered to buy Darwin, at an asking price of almost nine hundred million dollars, just so I could have access to their prototype. And she offered to triple my salary if I would leave the company she had founded to work on this full time."

"Why have I never heard of this Darwin Computing?" asked Connor.

"She shuttered it right after the purchase. We were both worried that in five to ten years, when the tech was fully developed, the resulting computer could well evolve into artificial superintelligence, obsoleting mankind. We decided to use the prototype for Veracity, and then kill the technology. Not an easy decision, but a discussion for another time."

"I look forward to that time," said Connor.

"She bought the company under her new legal name, Karen Preston, and deposited three times my annual salary into my account, just to show her good faith."

"And because she knew you couldn't possibly trust her at that point," said Paige.

"That's right. And even though she acknowledged that Veracity was a long shot, she thought it was worth it. She was prepared to spend her entire fortune to try to perfect the technology. She saw it as her chance to clear her name and change the future forever."

"But your goal was for *everyone* to use this tech," said Connor. "To have the truth set our society free, so to speak. And almost all of us *would* use it. If you chose not to, when others were, you'd find yourself at a big disadvantage."

"I'm not sure I see your point," said Elias.

"My point is that Ufree Technologies will end up being one of the most valuable companies in the world. So Kayla wasn't spending her fortune on a *charity*. She expected her investment to earn a massive return."

"Not true," said Elias, "for two very important reasons. First, as I just said, Veracity was an extreme long shot. Yes, a miracle happened and the long shot came in. But based on what we knew at the time, this was a terrible investment. She might as well have set her money on fire."

"And the second reason?" asked Connor.

"She originally asked for a forty percent ownership in Ufree. Based on the size of her investment, she deserved ninety-five, so I was happy to give it to her. But before we completed the contract, she came to realize what would happen when we finally made this public. A game-changer like this would quickly capture imaginations, from day one. It would be catnip to the media, bringing immediate celebrity to us both. They'd dig into our pasts with great zeal, and her Karen Preston name would be punctured almost immediately. She worried that if Kayla Keller's fingerprints were found in the same *hemisphere* as Veracity, it would get ugly quick. That we'd be instantly distrusted and maligned. That the first impression of the company and what we were trying to do would be tainted, poisoned."

"She might have had a point," said Connor.

"She *did* have a point," said Elias. "And that's what I told her. Not that I could have lied to her at that time to sugarcoat it if I wanted to," he added with the hint of a smile. "So she insisted I not give her a single share of the company. She had bought Darwin, and was then prepared to fund Ufree, without getting anything in return. She argued that it didn't matter, that she was already more than wealthy enough. And Total Immersion Systems' stock was making her wealthier by the day."

"So she doesn't own any of your company?" said Paige.

"No. She owns forty percent. I couldn't let her do it. And it would have been futile anyway. Even if she didn't have ownership, it would come out that I used a Darwin computer, and they'd learn she had purchased the company. And if the media asked me if I had help, and who helped me, I wouldn't be able to lie. Not the man who had released Veracity into the world. The days of keeping secrets would be over—which is one of the points to this."

"Her involvement will make this more difficult," said Connor.

Elias sighed. "I *know*. But it is what it is. And even though it will muddy up the launch, the technology will ultimately speak for itself. And when people learn that she was innocent, we'll get through this. *Ufree* will get through this."

Connor tilted his head in thought. "Still," he said, "if it were me, her offer not to take any ownership—and all the rest of her story, for that matter—would have seemed *too* good to be true. I may be cynical, but given her reputation, I wouldn't have believed her for a minute. I would have figured she was planning a con that I just couldn't see."

Elias nodded. "Exactly my thinking at the time. Believe me, I wasn't ready to believe a word she said, nor turn my back on her for a moment. But she had bought Darwin, and I did have the money in my account. So even though I thought it was probably all a sham, I agreed to work on it full time. I began by touring the world to once again meet with experts to be sure I was up to speed on all of the latest research about lying. And then I went to work again to incorporate this, and much more, into my system. Kayla promised to be there when I needed money or resources, but to stay completely out of my hair otherwise. And she lived up to that promise."

Elias paused. "I, on the other hand, lied to her at every turn. The day before I pulled the trigger on my software program, and Veracity came into being, I told her it was six months away. Then, when we next met, I had her walk through her history yet again. But this time I secretly videoed the conversation. Then I had Veracity watch it, when she didn't even know there *was* a Veracity."

"And that's when you finally decided you could trust her," said Connor.

"Yes, after the system was perfected and tamperproof. This was about fifteen months ago. Veracity confirmed she was telling the truth. Only then did I finally let my guard down."

"Did you tell her that you had lied to her?" asked Paige.

"Eventually, but not then. I told her that it was vital the system be made tamperproof—not telling her it already *had been*—and she understood the importance of this right away. She told me to spare no expense, buy any necessary technology, and hire any expert I needed, regardless of cost. And because she knew I couldn't really trust her, to keep the security to myself. To not even tell *her*."

Paige smiled. "Too late, anyway, right?" she said. "You'd already taken that advice."

Elias nodded, and then paused in thought. "I think that's basically it," he said. "I think you're finally up to speed. I've spent the last year perfecting the user interfaces, be they contacts, or glasses, or lapel cameras, or a host of others. Which hasn't always been as easy as you might expect."

"I don't doubt it," said Paige.

"Can I assume you also patented them all?" asked Connor.

"I did," he confirmed. "But that's not all I've been doing. I've been wearing these contacts while I watch the news and politicians. It's even more sickening than you could guess. If you thought that there was little truth being told on either side, you don't know the half of it. I'm thinking of changing Veracity's default when I'm watching politicians to only indicate when they're telling the truth. Otherwise, I run the risk of being blinded by red."

He shook his head in disgust. "Anyway, to bring you to where this began for you and Paige, now that the tech has advanced to where it has, I asked Kayla if she'd be okay if I shared it with the two of you. She would have preferred that we continue to keep it just between us until launch. She didn't want to take any chance of it leaking, but knew this was important to me. So she agreed. And she was eager to meet you."

"But first she wanted you to brief us on Veracity," said Connor. "*And* the infamous Kayla Keller. So we wouldn't see her as the devil when we met."

"She also wanted you to be wearing a Veracity interface when you first spoke with her, so you could tell if she was lying."

"Have you ever caught her in a lie?" asked Paige.

"Of course," said Elias. "No human can go for long without one. And I already told you she wasn't a saint. As I said, she told me the truth about a number of questionable activities she'd been involved with. Although none of these were illegal. She also told little white lies, that sort of thing. I'm sure you caught her lie earlier when she said she was enjoying her alone time downstairs. Even if you know others are Veracity enabled, lying to grease the skids of social interaction is an old habit that's hard to break."

"Like her saying that she was eager to meet us," said Connor, the corners of his mouth turning up into the hint of a smile, "after you forced the issue on her."

His father laughed. "No, she really was eager to meet you. I was with her when she said it, wearing my trusty contact lenses. She just didn't want anyone else to know about Veracity. But I had talked about you two a lot over the months," he added. "And I had laid on the praise pretty thick."

Connor nodded. "So now all she wants is to get her ducks in a row and get back her reputation," said Connor.

"And bring the true psychopath who began this avalanche to justice. But these motives make her sound entirely selfish. And she's not. While her reputation, and justice, are vitally important to her, bringing Veracity to the world is even more important. She's ecstatic about the chances of helping our species get our collective heads on straight."

Elias's feelings for this woman had become more and more obvious as time passed. Connor took a deep breath and stared intently at his father. "Are you in love with her, Dad?" he asked simply.

Elias was taken aback by the question, and didn't respond right away. "No one can ever replace your mother, Con," he finally said softly.

Veracity indicated this was true, and Connor fought off a smile. A true statement, but it also didn't answer his question. Lying might not be possible in a Veracity-enabled world, but artful evasion of the truth apparently still was.

"But are you in love with her?" he asked again.

"She's much too young for me," replied Elias, which again registered as true, but which again didn't answer Connor's question.

"You *are* in love with her, aren't you?"

"I never said that," replied Elias. For a third time, his statement registered as true. He had never said he was in love. But he had never said that he wasn't, either.

Connor decided it was time to leave it alone. If his father was this intent on evading the question, he would let him. And it suddenly occurred to Connor that his father was *afraid* to answer. Because if he did, Veracity might detect a truth that he was trying hard not to admit—even to himself.

28

The steel panels over the kitchen door began to retract, and the original entrance became visible yet again.

Neil entered first, leading with his gun, and then John followed, pushing a bloodied and bruised Kayla Keller ahead of him.

Elias gasped upon seeing her, and he looked to be overcome with emotion.

She was leaking blood from any number of small slashes on her arms and legs, and Connor thought it was a wonder she was even conscious. Surprisingly, she appeared to be untouched above the neck, although the agony she had experienced had taken its toll on her face as well, which reflected a horror that no one should ever have to experience. She had truly come from the bowels of hell, and it showed.

John shoved her forward and motioned to Elias. "Your turn," he said ominously.

Kayla grimaced in pain and turned to face her tormentor. "Look," she rasped, her voice weak, "I'm certain you know your boss's identity. We won't ask his name. Just answer a few more questions about him. If you do, Elias will tell you everything."

"A promise *you* already broke," said John.

"A promise I *kept*," whispered Kayla. "I can't tell you what I don't know," she repeated for maybe the tenth time. "Just a few more questions."

"If I don't tell you his name, how will this help you?"

"Let *us* worry about that," said Kayla. "Come on! Elias sees what you've done to me. He doesn't want that. And he has an insatiable curiosity. Satisfy this itch, and it'll be the straw that broke the camel's back. Or in this case, loosened the prisoner's tongue. He'll tell you what he knows."

"She's right," said Elias. "I swear on everything that's holy, do this, and I'll give you what you want."

"You people make no sense," he said. "But all right. Why not? A few more questions. For whatever they're worth, since you'll never get his name from me."

"So you admit that you know who he is," said Elias.

"*Maybe.* Three weeks ago, during a call, he told me he needed to put me on hold for a minute. But he screwed up, and the call was still active. Someone had knocked, and was entering his office. They called him by his real name and . . . title. But I'm still not sure I believe what I heard. And it doesn't matter. If it's true, it just gives me more reason not to cross him. I won't tell you who he is, but I'll tell you this: he's untouchable. *Literally.*"

"Is he in the White House?" said Kayla, the very question that had just sprung to Connor's mind.

"No!" said John emphatically—which registered as a lie. "Are you out of your mind?"

Of course this was a lie, Connor realized. Who was more powerful, more connected, than President Jameson or someone in his administration?

But it couldn't be just anyone in the administration. If a professional killer like John thought that this Vader was untouchable, he would have to be someone with Secret Service protection. But it wasn't likely to be Jameson himself. He was already in his second term, and he couldn't get around the two-term limit no matter what he did. He had reached the summit already, so what would be the point of all of these machinations? It had to be someone who still had more ladder to climb.

Connor opened his mouth to ask the obvious question this line of reasoning evoked, but once again, Kayla beat him to the punch, despite her weakened and battered condition. "Is your boss Bradley Holloway?" she asked bluntly.

"That's *ridiculous,*" said John, with a fake, uncomfortable smile. "Of course not!"

Connor stifled a gasp. This was a lie that anyone could see through, with or without Veracity.

And it made perfect sense once again. *Of course* it was Bradley Holloway. The Vice President of the United States. Not nearly as popular as Jameson, but still the favorite to be his party's nominee when Jameson left office. But not without a fierce battle in the primaries, as any number of prominent candidates would seek to deny him a chance to take this final step.

Holloway was powerful, untouchable, and connected. And his dirt-gathering expeditions made perfect sense. Dirt on the opposition was the currency of the realm in the political arena. And the reason he had been so careful to disguise his voice was now obvious, as well. His was one of the most recognizable voices in the world.

Finally, Holloway's reason for wanting Elias dead was equally clear. Somehow, he had gotten wind of Veracity, a politician's worst nightmare. Especially *this* politician's, since he had more crimes to conceal than a mobster.

Holloway's reach was truly profound. They had been right not to trust anyone. The vice president was sure to have tentacles in the military, and in all facets of law enforcement.

Part of Connor couldn't believe this was true. It was so preposterous. On the other hand, it explained so much that part of Connor couldn't believe that it *wasn't* true.

"I'm done answering questions!" said John, snatching Elias's arm and shoving him toward the kitchen door. "Now it's *your* turn," he said, turning his back on the other prisoners while his partner held them at gunpoint.

"*Hold on!*" shouted Connor.

John swiveled around and looked him in the eye, just as he had hoped.

"If my dad is fully cooperative," said Connor, "you'll let him live, right?

John sneered, as though annoyed by this persistent question. "Of course," he replied finally.

And once again, Connor received a flash of red in both of his retinas.

29

John and Elias Gibson exited through the kitchen door and disappeared from view. After a brief pause, Neil walked backwards, keeping his gun trained on the prisoners, preparing to follow suit. He nodded toward the device he had stuck to the wall. "Remember, Big Brother is watching."

Kayla slid down to the floor and sat there in a heap, spent, her back against the stainless steel refrigerator.

"Wait!" said Connor before Neil could leave. He gestured toward Kayla with his loosely bound hands. "She needs medical attention. Badly."

Neil shrugged. "Sorry, I'm not a doctor."

As this callous response registered, Connor realized that Kayla's condition wasn't as dire as he had first thought. As badly as she was hurt, she would survive, even without a doctor. And while she had lost significant blood, and was no doubt exhausted, her mind remained sharp, as evidenced by her brilliant elicitation of Vader's identity. John's cuts had been expertly placed to make her appear to have lost more blood than she had, and the bruises to make her appear to have been even more savagely beaten.

"Let me at least patch her up," said Connor. "She'll *die* if I don't," he added, glad that Neil wasn't wearing a Veracity interface.

"You're exaggerating. We were given strict instructions not to kill her. Apparently, the boss has further . . . *uses* for her. My partner is very good at what he does. He knows exactly how far he can go without danger of death."

"Not this time!" insisted Connor frantically. "He miscalculated."

"I don't think so."

"Do you really want to take that chance!" barked Connor. "How long do you think *you'll* live if you kill your boss's prize?"

Neil frowned, but didn't reply.

"There's a first aid kit in the family room," said Connor. "Metal. About the size of a carry-on suitcase. I can tell you where it is."

Neil considered. "All right," he said finally. "But you can get it yourself." He waved his gun toward the door, and stepped aside so that Connor could go through first. "Come on."

Before Connor reached the door, Neil turned to Paige. "Start cleaning her up," he said, gesturing to Kayla. "If you try to free your hands—or hers," he added, "or leave this kitchen, I'll shoot your husband in the head. Understood?"

Paige swallowed hard, but managed to nod.

The two men returned shortly, with Connor gripping the handle of the large first aid kit with both cuffed hands.

He moved to where Paige was cleaning Kayla's wounds and sat beside them. His wife had found a bucket under the sink, which she had filled with soapy water, and had collected several rolls of paper towels. Connor set the box down, unhooked two metal clasps, and threw the lid open, making sure it blocked the contents of the kit from Neil's view.

Inside were a host of bandages, scissors, pills, and other medical supplies.

And a single flash-bang grenade that Connor had hidden in the metal kit just before these men had arrived.

Connor desperately wanted Paige to be able to see it, to let her know what was coming, but couldn't risk moving the box or mouthing any warning.

"Let's hurry this up," he said to his wife, giving Kayla a healthy dose of pain pills and helping Paige apply antibiotic ointment, wound-closing nano-mesh spray, and enough bandages to make a mummy proud. Connor was taking a risk not using the grenade immediately, but the moment he did, all hell would break loose, and it was better if Kayla was bandaged when this happened.

He was counting on John taking time to immobilize his father downstairs, and being somewhat patient before he began any torture. Kayla hadn't issued a scream until five or ten minutes into her interrogation. But if he miscalculated, his father would pay dearly.

"Faster," he implored Paige as he continued to apply bandages and gauze at an Olympic pace, despite this task being made more difficult by the loose restraints around his hands.

Only a minute later, Neil grew bored of the proceedings. "That's good enough!" he said impatiently. "She'll live. Put all of the scissors back in the kit and give it to me."

Connor gathered up three now-bloody scissors of various sizes and affixed them inside the metal box, grabbing the flash-bang as he shut the lid and closed the clasps. "Here you go," he said, hurling the bulky first aid kit as hard as he could in their captor's direction.

Neil was taken completely off guard. His first instinct was to catch the flying metal container, but the gun in his hand made this impossible, so he darted to the side and out of harm's way as the metal kit slammed into the wall.

The instant Connor launched the box, he pulled the pin on the flash-bang and threw it at Neil's feet, squeezing his eyes shut and shoving his face against his forearms to block as much light as possible, just as the small device landed.

Boom!

The kitchen rocked as if a sudden earthquake had struck. He was deafened instantly, as if two sticks of dynamite had gone off inside his ear canals. The flash was so bright that it penetrated through his forearms and eyelids as though he were standing on the surface of the sun, although both of these shields, together, were just able to block enough light to prevent temporary blindness.

Neil, on the other hand, wasn't so fortunate. The concussive force at his feet drove him to the floor, rendering him blind, deaf, and dazed at the same moment, as the kitchen filled with smoke.

In Kayla's weakened condition, the force of the blast knocked her nearly unconscious, and Paige was screaming in terror, although Connor wasn't able to hear a single decibel of it.

Connor rushed over to where Neil had fallen and frisked him rapidly, finding and removing the tranquilizer gun just as the man began to regain his senses. Neil grabbed Connor's bound wrists with one hand and searched frantically, blindly, for his fallen gun with the other, but Connor wrestled free and shot a tranquilizer dart into his thigh, just as Neil's other hand was making contact with his gun.

Connor blew out a relieved breath as his captor quickly lost consciousness. The man had been mere seconds away from shooting *him*, rather than the other way around. And not with a dart.

Paige was still in shock, and Connor considered holding her face in front of his and mouthing something like, "*Flash-bang, only temporary,*" to help settle her down, but he remembered that she would be blind for several seconds longer, and wouldn't be able to see his lips any more than she could hear his words.

Instead, he bolted from the kitchen, well aware that John would be rushing up the stairs to investigate at any second.

Connor entered the living room and practically threw himself on the couch, clawing at the space between two cushions where he had hidden a second stun grenade, just as John emerged from the basement chamber, pushing Elias in front of him as a human shield.

"Stand down or I'll kill him!" shouted the mercenary, just before crossing the threshold to the first floor, unaware that the Veracity-enabled prisoners all knew he intended to kill Elias no matter what they did, and forgetting that none of them could hear him.

"Don't shoot!" yelled Connor, having seen John's lips moving and guessing the gist of what he had said. He rose to his feet, not sure that this was what he was going to do until he did it, operating on pure instinct. He extended his arms straight up into the air, his bound hands together, shielding the second flash-bang, whose pin he had already pulled. "I surrender!" he shouted.

John lowered his guard for just a moment and Connor acted, tomahawking the stun grenade at his father's feet, having no other choice of location, and praying that John wouldn't shoot him in the second before it landed.

Boom!

Sound, fury, blazing light, and smoke erupted from the floor. Once again, Connor was prepared enough to save his eyesight, but his hearing took yet another blow, and now wouldn't be coming back for several minutes.

Elias was thrown from his feet, and his head slammed into a marble table, causing him to lose consciousness. But unlike Neil, who had only been briefly dazed, his head was bleeding onto the carpeting and he wouldn't be regaining consciousness any time soon.

Now blind and deaf, John managed to stay on his feet and shoot wildly in Connor's direction, but Connor had crouched down low the moment the flash-bang had detonated and the wild shots all managed to miss him. When John stopped shooting, Connor moved to point-blank range, undetectable by a man whose only remaining senses were touch, smell, and taste, and shot him twice in the leg with the tranquilizer gun.

As John toppled to the ground, Connor slid to where his father had fallen. Had Connor done Vader's job for him? Had his attempt to save his father's life *taken* it instead?

He pressed two fingers into Elias's neck, and was rewarded with a slow but steady pulse, the relief steadying his own runaway heart. He left his father and returned to the kitchen, where Paige was helping Kayla to her feet, both having regained vision, although Kayla was still somewhat stunned.

"*We're clear*," he mouthed to them carefully, and then began rooting through drawer after drawer until he found a pair of poultry shears, which he used to cut himself, and the two women, free of the plastic restraints.

Connor picked Neil's gun up off the floor and removed two more from John's fallen body in the living room, searching for identification on both men, but finding none. He gathered up the blue duffel bag from the corner of the room and put the guns and first aid kit inside, handing it to Paige.

Kayla had made it to the living room, as well, and parked herself on the floor next to Elias, cradling his head in her lap, a tear running down her face.

Connor crouched down so he was at Kayla's eye level. "*He'll be okay*," he mouthed, hoping this was true. "*We need to go. Get the briefcase.*"

Kayla gently returned Elias's head to the carpeted floor and left to retrieve the case from its temporary hiding place, although her condition wouldn't let her move faster than a walk. She emerged after what seemed like ages and deposited the briefcase once again inside the huge duffel bag that Paige was holding.

Connor pulled a shade away from the corner of a window and studied the front of the house. Elias's SUV was parked on one-third of the brick paver driveway, but whatever vehicle their two assailants had used was nowhere in sight.

"*Come on,*" he mouthed, gently draping his father over his shoulders in a fireman's carry, heading to the front door and his father's SUV.

Kayla pulled on Connor's shirt and waited until he swiveled around and was looking at her mouth. "*Elias's car must have been tracked,*" she said, exaggerating the enunciation of each word to help Connor and his wife read her lips. "*We need to use mine. It's in the garage.*"

"*Good idea,*" mouthed Connor.

"*Wait here,*" she mouthed back, exiting the room and returning less than a minute later with a key fob, which she handed to Connor.

Kayla looked to be in worse shape than ever and was fading fast. They may have prevented further blood loss, but she had already lost enough to make anyone weak, and she had been beaten below the neck. Not to mention being at the receiving end of a flash-bang explosion in a small, enclosed space, which had pushed her to the brink.

Connor could tell she was fighting just to stay awake, let alone alert.

"*Hold on just a little longer,*" he mouthed to her. "*You'll be able to rest very soon.*"

PART 3

"**POLITICS** (noun): <u>Poly</u>, meaning "many" plus <u>Tics</u>, meaning "blood-sucking parasites.""

—Larry Hardiman

"I believe that any politician who comes to power, in part, through his skill in debate and public speeches, who is agile in handling questions at news conferences, with a glistening TV or radio image, has the conversational talents to be a natural liar."

—Paul Ekman, *Telling Lies*

30

Connor Gibson drove across the desert and away from Kayla Keller's safe house—which had been an epic failure when it came to living up to its name. As much as his primitive brain screamed at him to floor the accelerator to get away from the danger they had left behind, he forced himself to drive like a grandmother, well aware that he was carrying two wounded passengers with him.

Kayla's "car" had turned out to be a large minivan, with no windows in back, and a giant blue-and-white logo painted on both sides that read, "Magic Carpet Dry Cleaners," with the words, "Free Pickup and Delivery," in smaller lettering below.

Connor was in awe of the vehicle, which was all-electric. It was large enough to comfortably hold twelve passengers, and could double as a sleeper as necessary. And while it looked like a harmless commercial van on the outside, inside it was reinforced with enough armor to satisfy a *warlord*. He had no doubt that it weighed far more than a normal van—probably many times more.

Even given its weight, it had great pick-up, and while electric cars were known for their quiet operation, this was a veritable *tank* that ran more quietly than a bicycle. Most importantly, since they still didn't have cell phones, it had a twenty-seven-inch touch screen mounted on the dash that not only managed navigation and other features, but was a computer as well, capable of surfing the web.

Across the top of the touch screen were five icons that seemed to be permanent, including one that said "Driverless Mode." Apparently the van was fully autonomous, and didn't need pesky organic life-forms inside to direct it to a destination. While car makers had orchestrated an advertising and media blitz in 2023 to increase consumer demand for this technology, adoption remained slow, as purchasers either enjoyed being in control and actually *driving*, or couldn't bring themselves to entirely trust an AI and sensors to get them safely through their morning commute.

Say what you wanted about Kayla Keller, but she certainly knew how to prepare for an emergency. The van had to have cost a million dollars if it had cost a penny. The fact that she could afford to buy a vehicle like this, only to squirrel it away on the off chance that it might get used one day, underscored her enormous wealth.

Elias had been carefully laid across the second row of seats and strapped in, his head now treated with nano-mesh wound-sealing spray and wrapped in bandages. Kayla was lying across the row behind him, sound asleep.

Connor and Paige drove in silence for several minutes as their ears rang and their heads throbbed from the aftermath of the flash-bangs. Finally, when their hearing returned, Connor glanced anxiously at his wife in the passenger's seat beside him, who seemed to be growing ever more despondent. "Are you okay?" he asked.

She nodded, but it was clear that she wasn't.

Connor decided not to press the point. "So what now?" he asked.

Paige didn't respond for several seconds. "I don't know," she replied finally, blinking back tears. "Any way to turn back time and get our old life back?"

For Connor, seeing the impact this ordeal was having on a woman he loved so deeply brought on a powerful emotional response, and a tear came to his eye as well. This was a painful reminder of what she had been forced to endure. Having this happen to him was one thing, but knowing that she had been dragged into it with him was nearly unbearable.

"I'm so sorry, Paige," he said softly. "This is madness. I know that. Like a nightmare we can't awaken from." He paused. "But we have no choice but to gut it out the best we can."

Paige sighed. "You're right, of course," she said, trying to put on a brave face. "And I guess there's a bright side," she added, forcing a tepid smile. "If we do get through this, I'll never complain about parent-teacher conferences again."

"We are *definitely* going to get through this," he said. "And when we do, we're going to appreciate our old lives more than ever before."

She leaned over and kissed him on the cheek. "I do already, Connor," she said, her spirits brightening. "And I appreciate *you* more than ever. You've been amazing."

"Thanks, but I've been lucky," he replied soberly. "And if we can't figure out what to do next, our luck won't hold up for long."

They had left the desert and were now driving on paved roads. Connor spotted an empty Lutheran church, white brick and stucco, and parked in the lot behind it, out of sight, until they could decide on their next move.

They remained in the van, but he could now take his eyes off the road and face his wife, who had removed her tortoiseshell glasses and was examining them carefully. She slid them back onto her face. "I haven't been paying attention," she said, "but have you seen any flashes recently?"

"None that I can remember," he admitted. "But I didn't look at you much while I was driving."

"I got two green flashes just now," she said. "Your statements are true."

"Yep, and so are the ones you just made."

"I guess your father's Veracity interfaces can withstand a flash-bang attack," she noted.

"Great. We'll have to be sure to put that in the advertisements."

Paige grinned, despite herself.

"Even if they had been fried," said Connor, "I'm pretty sure we'd find more interfaces in the briefcase. Among other things," he added.

They sat in silence for several seconds.

"So," said Paige finally, "the Vice President of the United States is trying to kill your father." She allowed herself a wry smile. "Well *that* sucks."

"It could be worse, I suppose."

"How?"

"It could be the *president* trying to kill him. The commander-in-chief of the most powerful army the world has ever seen."

"Way to look on the bright side," said Paige. "Holloway isn't commander-in-chief, but for my money, he's close enough. He's bound to have some higher-ups at the FBI and DOJ in his pocket. By now, they've probably put out bulletins to all law enforcement agencies to notify them if we call."

"I don't think it matters. Whoever we contact won't believe our story, anyway. *I* don't even believe our story, and I'm *living* it. I can imagine the exchange now. 'Yes, Officer, we're a technical writer and fifth-grade teacher. We're calling to report that Vice President Holloway, using the smooth vocal tones of Darth Vader, has ordered just about every assassin in the country to kill a retired virtual reality executive.'" He shook his head. "They'd have straightjackets waiting for us when we showed up."

"So what's the answer?" asked Paige. "We just keep running? We change our identities and spend the rest of our lives looking over our shoulders? We just let this bastard get away with it?"

"We'll think of something," said Connor.

Paige's eyes widened. "Wait a minute," she said excitedly. "We're looking for salvation in the wrong place. Law enforcement is too risky. But what about the media? There are any number of major reporters, or cable show hosts, with huge audiences—who absolutely *despise* the Jameson administration. And since they know Holloway will start his run for the presidency next year, and will be the front-runner, they've been savaging him lately too."

"That's a great thought, Paige. And any reporter who is busy savaging Holloway probably isn't in the man's pocket."

"Right. Some of them would do anything—*risk* anything—to bring him down."

"And in a way," said Connor, "this would protect us. Protect my dad."

"Exactly," said Paige. "We find a media star we know Holloway doesn't control. One who has a huge megaphone. They put it out there that they've heard from unnamed sources that the vice president is trying to have Elias killed, and they're gathering evidence of this and other major claims against him. After that, if Holloway has his people go anywhere *near* Elias, it will just confirm the story is true. He won't be able to risk it."

"I think you're on to something, " said Connor enthusiastically. "But let's discuss this later. Right now we need to figure out where we go from here. And how we can get my father and Kayla medical attention."

There was a long silence in the van as they pondered these questions.

"So you're sure we can't risk a hospital?" said Paige.

"We may be forced to, but it would be a very bad idea."

"Because you think Holloway will have people monitoring hospital admissions?"

Connor nodded. "He could do this through legitimate channels, or through the ones he controls with his Vader persona."

"We could check in under false names," suggested Paige.

"It's a good thought," said Connor, "but I don't think it will matter, even if they aren't monitoring admissions. We might be able to get away with admitting my father, but not Kayla. She has a gunshot wound from earlier today, and was obviously tortured. No way anyone's going to buy an innocent explanation for that."

"But your father could be dying," whispered Paige.

"*Don't you think I know that?*" barked Connor in frustration.

He lowered his eyes. "I'm sorry, Paige. You didn't deserve that."

"It's okay. It's been a long day."

Connor laughed, releasing some of the enormous tension that he had built up. Yes, it had been a long day. A *very* long day. He had awoken well before five that morning in Denver to make the six-thirty flight to San Diego. And now, twenty years' worth of crazy later, he was in Borrego Springs, in the same never-ending day, with several hours left until nightfall.

"We've wasted too much time already," he said in resolve, even though they had left the safe house less than thirty minutes earlier. "We need to get medical help *now*. And desperate times call for desperate measures," he added.

"What is *that* supposed to mean?"

"It means that since we're on the run like violent criminals," he replied, "we need to ask ourselves what a violent criminal might do in this situation."

"Great," said Paige with a heavy sigh, "this just keeps on getting better. Can I assume you've already asked yourself that question?"

"I have."

"And have you come up with an answer?"

"I have," replied Connor again. He blew out a long breath and then winced. "But I don't think you're going to like it."

31

Connor parked the fake dry cleaning van well out of sight of the home, and office, of Dr. Hector Rosado, and he and Paige walked the remaining distance to their destination. The doctor had built a separate office structure—a small reception area and a huge examination area—ten yards to one side of his home. Both structures were nestled at the edge of an oak and pine forest in the small mountain town of Julian, which, although only forty minutes away from Borrego Springs, bore almost no resemblance to this desert retreat.

Connor and Paige had used the touch-screen computer in the van to scout for local doctors, and had eventually found what they were after, but only after searching a number of nearby towns, as well. They needed a clinic that was isolated, and that would be closing soon after they reached it, assuming a physician would remain for a short time after patient visits ended in order to lock up.

Instead, they found a situation even more ideal, a doctor who officed out of his home, so even though Dr. Rosado had stopped seeing patients hours earlier, he was likely to still be available.

And his home was as private as they could have wanted.

Julian was a historic town in the Cuyamaca Mountains, founded in the mid-eighteen hundreds during the California Gold Rush. Now known for its apple orchards and cattle rather than its gold, its sparse population and surrounding wilderness resulted in any number of cabins and homes that, like the good doctor's, were hidden within multiple acres of tranquil private property.

Connor remained out of sight behind a magnificent oak, while Paige peered inside the glass doors of the small clinic, spying nothing but an empty, unlit waiting room and reception desk, confirming that it was, indeed, closed for the day. So far so good.

getting out." He decided not to mention Holloway. The story was preposterous enough without including the vice president.

"Is that who's injured? Your father?"

"Yes, and a woman. A woman who's been tortured, I'm afraid. I know you don't believe me. I wouldn't either. But I'm betting that if I back up my claims about the contact lenses, you will."

"No need," said the doctor. "I do believe you. It's a unique situation, but it makes sense."

Connor actually laughed. "Wow, your acting skills aren't much better than my wife's. I know you're lying, Doctor, but it's good to meet a man who does this so poorly. Makes me think you don't have a lot of practice at it."

The doctor didn't reply.

"Are you alone in the house?" asked Connor.

"Yes."

"This is true. Are you expecting anyone?"

Rosado shook his head. "I'm not."

"This is true also," he said. "Glad to hear it. Now we're going to play a game. I want you to start making statements. Your favorite color. Favorite flavor of ice cream, or sport, or movie. Lie and tell the truth randomly. I'll tell you what is true and what is a lie each time. After a while, you'll have no choice but to believe what I just told you, namely, that I'm wearing contacts that are perfect lie detectors. And if this is true, you'll realize that the rest of my story is probably true, also."

"Okay," said the doctor uncertainly, still looking at Connor like he was either a harmless lunatic or a dangerous psychopath, but having no real choice but to play along.

"I'll start you off," said Connor helpfully. "Are there any vegetables that you really don't like?"

"Ah . . . yes."

"That's true. Name one of them."

"Asparagus."

"That's a lie. Try again."

"Cabbage."

"Another lie. Try again."

"Artichokes."

Connor smiled. "Now *that's* the truth. Good. Now you get how this works. So keep going. Make whatever statements you want, statements that vary in their . . . *veracity*."

He paused for several seconds, but the doctor remained silent. "Quickly, Doctor, please!" he insisted with a frown. "My father's life is at risk, and we can't waste any time."

32

Dr. Rosado was convinced of Connor's claims by the time Paige pulled the van up to his office, and as Connor had hoped, had little choice but to believe the rest. Connor shoved the gun into the waistband of his pants, praying he would never need to raise it again.

They brought Elias in through the reception area and into the single examination room, one that was twenty times larger than those found in commercial office buildings—which were typically no bigger than cramped closets—and closed the wooden door behind them.

Two stainless steel examination tables, topped with thin, blue, upholstered pads, sat in the middle of the room, ten feet apart, and these were surrounded by drawers, cabinets, needle disposal boxes, blood pressure equipment, and the like. Beyond these utilitarian items, Rosado had gone out of his way to make the room comfortable and inviting. Warm paintings adorned the walls, and a soft black leather sectional couch faced the two tables.

Surprisingly, the doctor, now an ally, praised Connor and Paige for the first aid they had administered to Kayla and Elias, deciding not to remove their dressings and reopen wounds that the married couple had closed with nano-mesh spray—at least for the time being. This was only after Connor had assured him that they had cleaned the wounds to the best of their ability and had made liberal use of the antibiotic ointment they had found in the comprehensive first aid kit.

Even so, Dr. Rosado started IVs for both patients and made sure they received an intravenous course of a potent antibiotic cocktail.

For his part, Connor was delighted by how quickly Veracity was able to demonstrate itself and turn his story from preposterous to believable. It was clear they could do the same with the authorities, if they could somehow find someone they could trust, and then convince them to ignore any bulletins about them that Holloway's powerful associates may have forced into the system.

Paige had brought the blue duffel in with Elias, and Kayla removed one of the handguns and slipped it into her waistband for safekeeping. Then, with the help of the doctor, they hid Elias's briefcase in a large cabinet under a pile of gauze bandages, having learned the hard way to always prepare for the worst.

Rosado focused almost exclusively on Elias. Kayla was still weak, but the hour or so of sleep she had managed had been a godsend, and while she could do with a change of bandages and an infusion of blood, she would recover nicely. As Connor had surmised himself, when it came to torture, John was a sadistic, demented genius. His brushstrokes were able to inflict terrible pain and fear, and create the illusion of maximum bruising and gore, while at the same time ensuring that the actual physical damage was far from lethal.

But Elias was another story. His condition was stable, at the moment, but extremely worrisome. The doctor confirmed he was in a deep coma, finding him unresponsive to sound or painful stimuli, and his pupils unresponsive to light—an ominous sign.

Elias was now flat on his back on one of Rosado's examination tables, an IV in his left arm and a breathing tube protruding from his mouth, expertly inserted by the doctor.

Rosado turned to Kayla once he had finished the intubation. "What's your blood type?" he asked.

"B positive."

"Do you know your dad's?" he asked Connor.

Connor shook his head.

Rosado opened a drawer, removed a paper strip, and pricked Elias's lifeless finger, drawing a drop of blood, which he transferred to the paper. "He's A positive," he said seconds later, taking advantage of a recent invention that made blood typing cheap and fast, rather than a ten- to twenty-minute process that required a lab and a technician.

"He's been lucky," continued the doctor, still standing over Elias. "So far. But he should be in an ICU, with around-the-clock vigilance, medical devices that I don't have here, and supportive care."

He frowned. "With surgical suites nearby—just in case. Ideally, we'd want to run a battery of blood tests and a brain CT scan to try to learn what we're up against. But, at minimum, we need to make sure his respiration and circulation aren't interrupted."

"How do we do that?" asked Kayla.

"The intubation tube and IV are helpful, but you could both use some blood. And I'd feel a lot better if we had a computerized mechanical ventilator on hand, in case his breathing deteriorates."

"Look," said Connor, "if you think we need to bring him to a hospital, it's a risk we'll have to take."

The doctor sighed. "No. Not yet. Like you've said, the people wanting to kill him might try to finish the job. Wouldn't take much," he added grimly. "So *I'll* get us what we need."

"How?" asked Connor.

"I used to work at an urgent care facility a few towns over. For almost twenty years. I still volunteer on occasion. I can go there and get blood for your father and Kayla, a ventilator, and some other needed supplies. But I'll have to be gone about ninety minutes, counting round trip time and the time it will take to gather what I need."

Connor nodded. "And no one will question you?" he said.

"No. I've built up a lot of trust over the years. And speaking of trust, you can trust me not to betray you. I won't tell anyone about you, and I'll return as soon as possible." Rosado paused. "I assume your contact lenses are confirming that I'm telling the truth."

"They are," said Connor simply.

"Good," said the doctor. "Continue to monitor your father's vitals. Call me on my cell if he comes out of it." He frowned. "Or if he takes a turn for the worse. I can try to guide you."

"We can't," said Paige. "We don't have a single phone among us."

"Actually, we do," said Kayla. "There's one hidden in the van."

For a moment, Connor wondered why they were only learning of this now, but realized that Kayla had barely made it to the van before passing out, so hadn't exactly given them a tour.

"That's some van, by the way," he said in admiration.

"You have no idea," she replied with a smile. "It cost me twenty million dollars. I'll tell you about it someday."

Connor whistled. "I look forward to that," he replied.

While this brief exchange was taking place, Rosado had fished a business card from his wallet, and now handed it to Kayla. "Here's my number."

"Thanks," she said, slipping the card into her pocket. "I'll get the phone once you've left. Like the van itself, it's untraceable. If anything important comes up at your end, call us at 527-873-7678. No need to remember it. It spells *Last Resort* on your phone's alphanumeric keypad."

"Last Resort?" said Paige.

Kayla nodded. "It's a safe phone, hidden inside a safe van, parked inside a safe house. I never dreamed I'd actually have to use it."

"Good name, then," said Rosado with a wry smile. "I'll leave in just a few minutes. First though," he added, addressing Connor, "in case your father begins to have trouble breathing while I'm gone, I need to teach you how to use a bag valve mask. I doubt it will be necessary, but it *could* be."

"I understand," said Connor. "What's a bag valve mask?"

"It's a manual resuscitator. A handheld, self-inflating ball. I have several on hand. I can show you how to attach it to your father's endotracheal tube and how to set it up. Which you'll only have to do if your father becomes unable to breathe for himself. If this were to happen, after you've attached it, you'd just have to squeeze it every five seconds until I return."

"Got it," said Connor. "Show me."

33

Dr. Hector Rosado finished his lesson on the use of a manual resuscitator, removed the IV line from Kayla's arm at her request, and left the examination room, which Connor locked behind him. Just after the doctor exited, Kayla walked the short distance to Elias's supine form on the examination table, moving gingerly to protect her injured arms and legs, and kissed him gently on the forehead.

She turned away, visibly fighting back tears. "They were going to kill him for sure," she whispered to Connor. "And you saved his life. You saved all of our lives. For a second time. Thank you."

Connor looked anything but gratified by this praise. "I don't know about that," he said. "The jury is still out on my dad. I might have killed him *for* them."

"You did what you had to do," said Kayla softly.

"Maybe," he replied. "But even so, I didn't save *your* life. Veracity verified that they seemed to have other plans for you."

"In which case I owe you even *more* thanks. For saving me from a fate *worse* than death."

Connor nodded. She did have a point. "Any idea what they wanted you for?" he asked.

"None. But I have no doubt it would have been very … unpleasant."

"Speaking of unpleasant," said Paige, "how are you feeling?"

"Pretty weak," said Kayla, "but otherwise okay." She forced a smile. "No doubt due to the miracles of modern painkillers and sedatives."

"Once you get some more blood in you," said Connor, "you'll regain your strength."

Kayla sighed. "I'm surprised that you care," she said. "After all, I am the most evil woman who ever lived, right?"

Connor smiled. "My father doesn't think so. And apparently, neither does Veracity. So it's possible you really aren't the most evil woman who ever lived. Probably only in the top five," he added with a grin.

Kayla laughed. "Okay then. Good to know I'm making progress."

"So what happened to you?" asked Paige. "Elias gave us the gist, but said you could give us more texture. How were you dragged through the mud so profoundly? How did public perception of you go from adoration to contempt? How did you go from being considered a respected, brilliant executive, to a despicable, contemptible monster in human form?"

"Nicely phrased," said Kayla. "I thought Connor was the writer in the family."

"If only," mumbled Connor, too softly to hear, an image of a blank computer screen jumping to his mind's eye, along with a remembered urge to scream at the top of his lungs.

"I'll tell you what happened," continued Kayla. "But I won't go into much more detail than Elias probably did. Not now. It's too painful, even to tell. And I've suffered enough pain already today. Once we get through this crisis, I can give you a detailed blow-by-blow."

She lowered her eyes. "I've been guarded most of my life," she began. "Didn't let anyone in. I was in a race to tame the world, and there wasn't time for relationships. Even if there had been time, I'm not one who trusts easily."

"Which is another benefit Veracity brings to the table," said Paige.

"If only it had been around earlier," said Kayla miserably. "But I guess the point I'm trying to make is that I rarely got close to anyone. Not only was I guarded, I need to respect someone a great deal to even *want* to get close to them. And I don't respect many. I know this sounds harsh, and it is, but I'm smarter than just about everyone, technology-wise. And I often find even those considered to be brilliant to be on the slow and stupid side. Or insufferably incompetent."

"Charming," said Connor dryly.

Kayla smiled. "I said I'm not evil. I didn't say I was Miss Congeniality. I can be arrogant and dismissive. Demanding and unfriendly. Steve Jobs is a classic example of this personality type. He wasn't always a prince, either, but he did great things."

"But you *are* softening," said Paige.

"Thanks for noticing. Getting fed into a media and publicity wood chipper and having your life and reputation utterly destroyed will do that to a girl—even the cockiest among us. Makes you reevaluate a lot about your life."

Kayla paused. "But I'm getting ahead of myself," she said. "After failing to ever have an extended relationship, or even friendship, I finally found a man I thought was perfect for me. A man named Derek Manning. Charming, brilliant, handsome—the whole works. Impressive in every way. So I let down my guard. All the way. For the first time."

"One time too many, according to my dad," said Connor.

"That's for sure. As I'm sure your father told you, Derek Manning turned out to be an absolute textbook psychopath. Not Hannibal Lecter, not bloodthirsty in that way, but just as twisted. And just as brilliant. And his brilliance was channeled to superhuman levels of charisma, charm, and ability to manipulate others. He was a man smooth enough to con a con artist. Not to mention having no conscience, and being fearless, ruthless, and predatory—the whole psychopathic package. When I finally figured it out, I sounded the alarm. I had enough evidence to ruin his career."

She shook her head in disgust. "But I learned a horrible lesson: never battle with a psychopath. Especially not one as brilliant and skilled as Derek Manning. Even after knowing what I was dealing with, knowing that he wouldn't play fair, I thought I could handle the fallout from our ugly . . . separation.

"I've never been more wrong about *anything*," she admitted, looking sick to her stomach. "I was totally unprepared for the extent of his *savagery*. For the lengths he would go to for revenge. For his maniacal determination to destroy me. He spread so many lies about me, and such huge lies, that I never imagined they would actually work. But they did. He could persuade anyone of anything. But he didn't stop there. He planted evidence against me."

Kayla sighed. "And I came to realize that I had made my own bed, too. People tended not to like me. I had alienated many. And, in retrospect, I couldn't blame them. They were all eager to believe every word Manning said, no matter how preposterous."

"I remember when you were in the media spotlight," said Paige. "The coverage was nonstop. And there was an avalanche of allegations, cruelties you were rumored to have inflicted on others, and crimes. An endless parade. One man couldn't have fabricated all of this single-handedly."

"That's what *I* thought," said Kayla. "But he could if he had help. He could if he lined up dozens of rows of dominoes, and then toppled the first one in each row. This was a man who knew how to set off a chain reaction. He and the people he convinced of my crimes had ins with the media. And he paid anyone who could arguably say they had met me to act as an anonymous source for further disparagement. And the media ate it up. They'd print whatever he wanted them to print, mostly citing anonymous sources. It helped that he planted evidence against me for crimes that *he* committed. He was relentless. And once the steamroller got moving it just kept picking up speed. It achieved a life of its own in the press."

Kayla paused to catch her breath. "And the bastard never rested," she added through clenched teeth. "Worse, I had trusted him implicitly before I discovered who he really was. We lived together for months. He was able to steal my computer passwords and search every inch of my office and condo. He knew everything about me, which helped him enormously.

"So he began by fabricating illegal technology transfer agreements I had supposedly forged with Chinese spies, and any number of other felonies. From whole cloth. Planted evidence on my highly secure computer. Then, when I realized what he was doing to me, I confronted him in a blind rage. I shrieked at him, and I threatened to tear him apart, limb from limb. That sort of thing. Turned out he secretly videoed the entire encounter, and played it for the media."

"Nice," said Connor sarcastically. "He shoots you in the kneecap, and when you scream out in agony and try to stop him from taking out the other knee, he gets you for having a bad temper and attempted assault."

"You don't know the *tenth* of it!" spat Kayla.

She paused, remembering, and the longer she did, the more she began to look like a cartoon character just before its head exploded.

"You have to stay calm, Kayla," said Paige worriedly. "Relax. You're weak, and you've been through a lot. Tell us your story, but try not to relive the emotion of it."

Kayla nodded, and her jaw unclenched. "Thanks," she said simply. She took several deep breaths to calm herself, and then continued. "Eventually, I offered him five million dollars to leave me in peace. He happily took the money—and then savaged me worse than ever. It wouldn't have mattered at that point anyway, to be honest. It was too late. My total destruction had already become irreversible, and every media outlet in the country couldn't wait to pile on. If I was a political figure, I'd at least have one party on my side. But this was one of the rare character assassinations that both sides could agree on.

"In the end, I learned that it wasn't about money for Derek Manning, or even about revenge. Maybe it started that way, but once he had fully unleashed his inner psychopath, there was no putting it back in the bottle. He loved the power and influence he could wield. He loved watching his lies, and frames, and ruthless manipulations spread like runaway brushfires, scorching the earth wherever they touched. He was having far too much fun to stop. The media and authorities were like puppets in his hands, and he played both like a maestro to grind my life and reputation to dust."

"And there was nothing you could do at all?" asked Connor, continuing to periodically check on his father's breathing.

"Believe me, I tried to fight back. Like a cornered badger. But I never had a chance. What are you going to believe, planted evidence of multiple crimes, or my insistence that the charming Derek Manning was responsible? Are you going to believe award-winning reporters with multiple unnamed sources saying that I'm pure evil? Or me when I deny it? *Of course* someone who is pure evil is going to deny it," she added. "The media and public took my denials as just further evidence of my evil."

She shook her head and sighed. "And to be fair, as I've said, I wasn't popular. No one was willing to walk into the teeth of the media buzz saw and risk their own necks to defend someone they didn't particularly like, even knowing I was innocent. And I couldn't blame them."

"What about the woman you supposedly murdered?" said Connor. "And the three witnesses against you who turned up dead?"

"All Derek's doing, of course. He had hired them to help frame me, but he must have thought that murdering them, instead, would implicate me even more than their false testimony. He didn't have an insatiable appetite to take life like some psychopaths, but killing didn't trouble him, either. Naturally, he was much too clever to leave his fingerprints on any of it, no matter how much I pointed the authorities his way. Everyone knew that it couldn't just be a coincidence that these three witnesses had died. And of course it *wasn't*. But not because *I* was responsible."

Kayla's story was utterly fantastic, yet Connor found it believable. She was leaving out many important details about how her nemesis had accomplished what he had, but it somehow rang true, even without Veracity to confirm it all.

And Veracity did confirm it. Every word.

And she had been brutally honest, not trying to pretend she was Mother Teresa, but admitting she had been unfriendly and largely unlikable, making Derek Manning's job that much easier.

"Given all of the evidence against you, how were you acquitted?" asked Connor.

She shrugged. "Expensive lawyers and a lot of luck. Did you follow the trial in the news?"

Connor nodded.

"Then you know as much as I do. Derek's frames were works of art. But I think he made a mistake disappearing the witnesses he was paying. Even so, it was a miracle that I walked. My lawyers insisted that *beyond all reasonable doubt* meant ninety-nine percent certainty. Several of the jurors said later they were ninety-five percent sure I was guilty, but this wasn't good enough. Lucky for me, they had really taken *reasonable doubt* to heart."

"Did you do *any* of what he accused you of?" asked Connor.

"No. But, again, that's not to say I was an angel. I made moves I'm not particularly proud of. Moves that skirted ethical lines. But notice I said *skirted*, not demolished. And I said ethical lines, not legal lines. I did things I'm not proud of, but no different than many other successful CEOs." She paused. "Although, at the end, I *was* planning to break the law in a big way."

"How so?" asked Connor.

"I decided to kill the bastard. My initial threats had just been rage-induced fantasies. But at that point, I vowed to make them real. I was going to shoot him in head, and then set him on fire, and then run him over with a car, and then shoot him again. At *minimum*. I convinced myself that I'd be doing the world a favor. He took *everything* from me. He buried me under an avalanche of dirt and dung so deep I couldn't dig my way out if I had a hundred lifetimes. And now that his full psychopath was on the loose, his appetite for cruelty and power would only increase. Besides, at the time, I was sure they'd find me guilty of his frames, anyway. So, if I was already going to jail for murder, I might as well commit one."

Kayla paused and closed her eyes for several seconds, the passion of her tale sapping her limited strength. "So I bought a gun," she continued, her voice now soft, "and shot it a few times, so I was confident I could hit him. At least at point-blank range. And then I went to find him."

She shook her head. "But he had beaten me *again*. He had somehow anticipated this move. I never found him. He chose that moment to disappear from the grid with my millions, and with the satisfaction of ruining my life."

"So he's still out there?" said Paige.

Kayla's face turned into a mask of thrilling hatred. "I'll find him," she hissed. "But I won't kill him. I'll make sure that he rots in jail for the rest of his life. And I'll make sure that everyone knows what he did to me."

"With the help of Veracity," said Paige.

"That's right. I had any number of epiphanies during my ordeal. I became convinced that all lying, everywhere, needed to stop. That the media needed to be held much more accountable for using unnamed sources. For willingly spreading lies. I vowed that no one's character would ever again be assassinated like mine had been."

"And then you remembered my father," said Connor.

"Yes. I had met him a few times at Virtuality, and knew about his Veracity project. But I decided to bide my time until I thought the technology had advanced enough to make success likely."

She paused. "Not that I was entirely passive during those years. I bought two print newspapers, *The New York Gazette* and the *Washington Herald*, and two popular online-only sites."

"You own the *New York Gazette* and *Washington Herald*?" said Connor incredulously.

Kayla smiled. "*Surprise*," she said weakly. "And you're now one of the few people alive who know that. I did it in such a way as to hide my identity. I used a complex array of holding companies, and hired scores of expensive lawyers to keep my identity as silent partner concealed. Set me back over a half billion dollars. But my goal at the time was to begin to build a media empire, and enforce the strictest standards of accuracy the world has ever seen."

"But now that won't be necessary," said Paige.

"No. Now Veracity will enforce these standards on everyone."

"So when did you decide the tech had advanced to the point at which Veracity might be possible?" asked Connor.

"After the 6G Wi-Fi network was in place, and when I discovered a wildly innovative computer design. Elias has probably told you the rest of the story. How, and when, I came to him to convince him to resuscitate his project."

"He has," said Connor.

"Good," she replied. "But you should know this. The Kayla Keller who approached your father was radically different than the one who existed before Derek Manning. After several years in hell, several years out of the limelight as Karen Preston, I became a better person. I did a lot of soul searching. *A lot.* I learned humility, and I improved my . . . people skills. I didn't deserve what had happened to me—believe me, no one deserves *that*—but I had treated people poorly on the whole. If you get savaged the way I did, and your life destroyed, and you don't see that as the mother of all wake-up calls, then you aren't paying attention."

"I think you're being too hard on yourself," said Paige. "You probably weren't as awful as you think you were."

"It means a lot to me to hear you say that. For years you must have thought of me, of the infamous Kayla Keller, as detestable, not worth spitting on if I were on fire. But a few minutes ago you tried to console me. And now you're suggesting I'm being too hard on myself. *Thank* you."

"You're very welcome," said Paige softly. "I'm just sorry that this happened to you."

Connor nodded at Kayla. "You do seem to be winning us over," he said. "At this rate, you might even fall out of the top five most evil women to have ever lived. Maybe all the way down to *sixth*."

"Dare to dream," said Kayla with a grin.

She watched Elias's lifeless form for several seconds and her smile vanished. "You know, your father has really come to mean a lot to me. I had years to begin to heal from the hurt and betrayal I suffered at the hands of Derek Manning. But when I met your father, I was still bitter. I had erected walls around me that were thicker than ever. And while I'll never fully heal from Manning's betrayals, Elias has been a breath of fresh air. One that I desperately needed. He's as brilliant as Manning, but the opposite of him in every way that counts. Not slick and charismatic. But earnest and idealistic. For a while I didn't trust Elias any more than he trusted me. I thought he was too good to be true. Just a better breed of psychopath, even better able to cover it up than Manning."

She lowered her eyes. "But he isn't," she whispered. "He's genuinely sweet, and kind, and well meaning. Instead of stabbing others in the back, he'd take a bullet for his friends. Instead of taking credit for work he didn't do, he gives credit to others. Even when they don't deserve it. If there *are* any saints in the world, Elias is one of them."

Connor studied her for several seconds. "Did you fall in love with him?" he asked.

Kayla shook her head and made a face, as if what Connor had asked was absurd. "Do you really think I could ever fall in love again? After Derek?"

Connor almost smiled. It wasn't an answer. It was the classic evasion technique of answering a question with another question. Just like his father, she had found a way not to give a direct answer when it came to this possibility. "It doesn't matter if I *think* you could fall in love again. I'm asking you if you *did*."

"You do know that your father is decades older than me, right?"

This time Connor did smile. "I'm pretty sure that's not an answer."

"Even if he *were* my age," said Kayla, "and even if Derek Manning had never happened, falling in love with a business partner is a big mistake."

Veracity once again confirmed this statement as true. Kayla truly believed that falling in love with a business partner was a big mistake. But that didn't mean she hadn't.

"Look," he said softly, "it doesn't matter if you're in love with him or not. I shouldn't be prying. If you don't want to answer the question, I totally get it."

"Of course I'll answer. Elias treated me very well. Not like I was an ogre, or a villain. He's the opposite of a psychopath. And he's brilliant, a man responsible for one of the most important breakthroughs of all time."

Kayla shrugged. "So what's not to love?" she said. Then, after just a moment's pause, she hastened to add, "But I love him as a good friend only. Nothing more."

And for the first time since she had begun her story, Connor received two flashes of red in his eyes, making it clear that Kayla Keller, in her heart of hearts, at least, saw Elias Gibson as much more than just a friend.

34

Connor glanced at his wife, and they came to an unspoken understanding to pretend not to notice that Kayla had lied. Kayla was well aware that he and Paige were wearing Veracity interfaces, so she would know that lying about her feelings for Elias was pointless.

Which could only mean one thing: just like Elias before her, she was really lying to *herself*.

"Nice work back at your safe house, by the way," said Connor, changing the subject, and deciding it wasn't his place to tell her that his father was probably in love with her, too. "It was impressive how you managed to learn that Holloway is behind this."

"Thanks," said Kayla, "but I wish it was someone else. *Anyone* else."

"Amen to that," said Connor. "The question is, once my dad comes around," he added, not letting himself consider any other possibility, "what are we going to do about it?"

"Whatever we do, we'd better do it fast," said Kayla. "Before Holloway finds us again. With the resources he has available, as both the vice president and as Vader, it's no wonder he's been a step ahead of us. And it even makes sense that he'd be able to learn how to defeat my safe house security."

"And law enforcement is even more off-limits than we thought," said Paige. "The second we show up in the system, Holloway will make sure we get railroaded and sent off to his people for . . . handling."

"But Paige did come up with a great idea," said Connor, proceeding to explain her strategy of choosing an anti-Holloway media figure, and confiding in him or her.

Kayla's eyes widened as Connor spoke. "I was thinking along the exact same lines," she said excitedly when he finished. "And if a brilliant fifth-grade teacher and a disgraced, evil tech CEO can come to the same conclusion, it has to be right."

Paige laughed. "I thought you didn't respect *anyone*," she said.

"That was the old me," said Kayla. "But the way you and Connor have been handling yourselves today, even the *old* me would have been won over."

Connor was gratified to note that Kayla wasn't just saying this to be nice, but actually meant it.

"I can pull strings to arrange for the two of you to meet with a reporter who fits the bill at the *Washington Herald*," said Kayla, "but I need to stay out of it. After all, no one knows I actually own the paper. And you can't tell a reporter what we really know about Holloway. If you start talking about how the vice president ordered a hit on Elias, posing as Darth Vader, even the most ardent Holloway-hater will find the story too preposterous to run with."

"Unless I give a demonstration of Veracity," said Connor. "Like I just did with Dr. Rosado. That has a way of instantly turning skeptics into believers."

"Are we really ready to demonstrate the wonders of this tech to a *reporter*?" said Kayla. "When we put Veracity out to the public, we need to do it right. But if we awe a reporter with it, nothing on Earth will stop this reporter from breaking the story, one of the biggest of all time. Much bigger in the long run than even the Holloway story."

"So let me get this right," said Paige, "you're saying we can't disclose the truth. Too far-fetched. And we can't use Veracity to convince anyone that it *is* the truth."

"Well, certainly not a media figure," said Kayla. "But I'm sure I can figure something out. An invented story that we can plant, using the two of you as anonymous sources. One that fingers Holloway for some serious wrongdoing. Wrongdoing which, unlike the truth, is actually *believable*. But which Holloway will be confident he can disprove."

Connor raised his eyebrows. "So you want to plant fake information," he said, "using an anonymous source. The very thing that you've vowed to stop."

"Ironic, I know. But just this once. To bring down a man we know needs to be brought down. The ends justify the means. Just this once."

"I'm not saying I have a problem with it," said Connor. "Not in *this* case. But I did want to point that out. And I'm curious about why you want to finger Holloway for a crime that he can easily wriggle out of."

Kayla smiled. "If we're going to beat someone as devious as Holloway, we have to be even *more* devious. Here's what I'm thinking. We plant a story, anonymously sourced, that isn't *too* far out there—so my pull as the owner, silent or not, can ensure it gets run. The paper will make a big deal about it so that Holloway has to sit up and take notice."

"With the help of his political opposition," said Paige, "who will amplify it to sky-is-falling levels."

"Very good," said Kayla warmly. "Although sorry to see a grade-school teacher become this cynical. In any event, we make sure the *Washington Herald* challenges Holloway to let a representative of the paper interview him privately about the matter. To get to the bottom of the allegations. Have the paper insist that the only reason he'd refuse this challenge is if he was guilty of the charges and had something to hide."

"And because you designed the allegations to be easy for him to disprove," said Paige, "he'll take them up on it."

"Right," said Kayla, "he'll not only agree to an interview, he'll welcome it. He'll be relaxed during the interview, cocky. He'll lower his guard."

"Now I know where you're headed," said Connor in admiration. "You really are devious. So you pull strings from offstage at the *Herald*, and get *yourself* assigned to conduct this interview, as Karen Preston. Or whoever."

"I love working with people who are quick on the uptake."

"I'm not as quick as my husband," said Paige, "but now I see it. You'll interview Holloway with your contact lenses in place. And we've seen the kind of information you can extract by questioning a subject who can't lie."

"Exactly. I'll just ask ever more pointed hypotheticals about unlawful activity, and see which of his denials are lies. Once I pinpoint a skeleton in his closet, I press on until I can learn where to find the proof of his involvement. Doesn't have to be proof that he's moonlighting as Darth Vader, or that he's ordering murders. I just need anything that can bring him down."

"The world should know the truth about him," said Paige.

"They *should*," said Kayla. "And, eventually, they will. But for now, whatever stops this bastard is good enough for me. I don't care if we get him on *jaywalking*. Al Capone was responsible for the slaughter of countless men, but he went to jail for tax evasion. It was the only thing they could ever pin on him."

"It's a sound plan," said Connor. "But if the news story never mentions my father, it doesn't protect him. And Holloway is just the first of many who will come after us. Which is why you had the safe house ready. You know the reality. If Veracity is launched, it will put countless bad actors out of business. Bad actors who will go to any lengths to make sure Veracity never sees the light of day."

"You're right," said Kayla. "For the time being, I'll have to go even further off the grid. And you, Paige, and especially Elias will have to join me. I have considerable money and resources. Now that we've been actively attacked, I'll spare no expense to protect us. If we can get Elias back to health and avoid a further attack for just another day or so, I'm confident we can turn the tide here."

"I'm not," said Connor. "Like I said, Holloway is just the beginning. Word of Veracity has somehow gotten out, which means it's bound to spread further. And quickly. Whoever knows about it won't have any trouble recruiting other powerful people—who have a lot to lose—to the cause of stopping it. Even rivals will become allies in this common cause. We might be able to vanish from the grid and protect ourselves if we're only fighting on one or two fronts. But if we find ourselves fighting on as many fronts as I think we will, no amount of resources, or cleverness, will save us."

Connor's eyes widened. "Wait a minute," he said excitedly, as the answer flashed into his mind, an answer that now seemed painfully obvious. "There is a way to survive this." He paused for effect. "We have to move up the Veracity launch. We have to put it out there right away."

He turned to Kayla. "I know you wanted to wait and do this right. But if everyone is trying to kill us to prevent us from releasing the genie, *let's release the damn genie.* Then they'd have no reason to kill us. With the genie out of the bottle, they'd stop focusing on us, and begin to focus on self-preservation in a world without lies."

"Of course," said Paige immediately. "That *is* obvious. And with Veracity out there, Holloway won't become the next president, even if we can't get any crimes to stick to him. He'd have to drop out of the public eye. He couldn't last five minutes in a world with Veracity in it."

Kayla nodded thoughtfully, but didn't respond.

Connor locked his eyes on hers. "You know this is the only answer, Kayla."

"Maybe," she replied. "But maybe not. An immediate launch won't be as easy to accomplish as you might think." She paused, looking uncertain. "And there may be other options you aren't aware of right now," she added.

"Other options?" said Connor in confusion.

Kayla nodded. "Yes. But let's table this for now," she said. "Why don't we wait until Elias is back with us and take this up again."

"Why?" asked Connor.

"I have my reasons," replied Kayla. "Our brainstorming has been very useful. But the doctor should be back in forty-five minutes or so, and I need to rest and gather my strength."

"Okay," said Connor, "I understand. But getting Veracity out there is the only way to take the pressure off. I can't see how anything's going to change that."

"I know you can't, Connor," replied Kayla with a weary sigh. "But let's get your father back to full health. And then we can discuss this further."

35

Kayla Keller sank into the cushioned black leather sectional sofa and closed her eyes. She remained that way, unmoving, for almost ten minutes, while Paige and Connor stood over Elias, watching to be sure that his condition remained stable.

The young married couple spoke very little to each other. Both were exhausted from the wild events of the never-ending day, and amazed that Kayla was doing as well as she was. They felt as if *they* had run physical and emotional marathon races, and neither of them had been repeatedly cut and beaten about the arms and legs.

"Come on, Dad," whispered Connor, squeezing his wife's hand as they stood over Elias. "Hang in there."

Rap rap! Rap rap! Rap rap!

Connor jumped at the sharp sound of knuckles slamming into the locked examination room door, and Paige did also, releasing his hand. Kayla's eyes shot open and she came to attention. Doctor Rosado had a key and wouldn't need to knock, while any of his friends paying an unexpected visit wouldn't be lurking within the clinic after hours.

Connor and Kayla both raised guns and wheeled toward the door, ready to fire.

"Put the guns down," said a deep male voice from behind the door. "I'm friendly. It's Jalen Howard, Kayla. I'm here to help. Let me in."

Kayla let out a short gasp and lowered her gun hand to her side.

"Can you tell your friend to lower his weapon also," said the voice.

Connor blinked in confusion. The door was solid oak and there were no windows. So how did their visitor have such accurate information as to what was transpiring inside?

"It's okay, Connor," said Kayla. "He's a friend."

"A friend?" said Connor in disbelief. "One who just happens to show up *here*? One you haven't said a word about?"

"Give me just a second, Jalen," called out Kayla, rising from the couch, "and I'll let you in."

"Wait," said Connor, still making no move to lower his weapon. "Jalen," he said loudly, "how are you seeing us?"

"Let me in and I'll tell you."

Kayla unlocked the door and threw it open, ignoring Connor's obvious misgivings.

A black man in his early forties, wearing glasses with black plastic frames, entered the room. He was clean-cut, with a gleam of intelligence and intensity in his eyes, and a small tablet computer in his right hand. He looked the heavily bandaged Kayla Keller up and down with a grim expression. "Are you okay?" he asked anxiously.

She nodded.

"Who did this to you?"

"We can discuss it later," said Kayla.

The newcomer walked over to the unconscious figure on the examination table and shook his head in alarm. "What's his prognosis?"

"Uncertain," said Kayla. "He's in a coma, but his vitals seem to be stable."

"How did this happen?" asked Jalen.

"Like I said, we'll discuss it later. First, let me introduce you to my, ah . . . friends."

Connor lowered his weapon at last as the man turned to face him and his wife.

"My people tell me that you're Connor Gibson and Paige Estrella Gibson," he said, extending a hand. "Nice to meet you."

Connor eyed the extended hand as if it were a snake that might strike at any moment, making no move to shake it. "Your people?" he said suspiciously.

Kayla sighed loudly. "Yes, he's what I was going to tell you about once your father regained consciousness," she said. "His timing is *uncanny*," she added, clearly not pleased about it. "This is Jalen Howard, from the Department of Homeland Security. More specifically, Jalen is undersecretary of DHS's Office of Intelligence and Analysis."

"*Undersecretary* means he runs the division, right?" said Paige.

Kayla nodded.

"How is he here?" asked Connor. "How do you know him?"

"I'll answer your first question," said Jalen. "I finally got wind that Elias's home had been breached, but not until almost *four hours* after it happened." He shook his head in disgust and turned to face Kayla. "I knew we should have kept his home under constant surveillance," he said to her. "I agreed not to against my better judgment."

"You can say you told me so later," she responded.

The newcomer pushed on the bridge of his glasses to reposition them closer to his face. "I am so sorry," he said to the entire group. "I dropped the ball, or I would have come to help sooner. Once I learned of the assault on Elias's home, and that you had made it out alive, I put every resource I had into finding you. I tapped into every camera in the area, and diverted an entire satellite to the case. We tracked you to a home in Borrego Springs, one we learned that Kayla owned, under an alias. A sophisticated safe house."

The undersecretary of the Office of Intelligence and Analysis didn't look happy. "You really should have told me about it, Kayla," he said.

"*No one* should know about a safe house," she insisted unapologetically. "That's one of the reasons that it's *safe*."

"In any event," continued Jalen Howard, not interested in arguing the point, "no one was there by the time we arrived. But we found blood in several different rooms. Tranquilizer darts lying on the floor that had clearly found their targets. Cut zip-tie handcuffs. Used flashbangs. It looked like a *war zone*."

He paused. "I'm familiar with the AI security tech you were using there, Kayla," he continued. "Made by Advanced Safety Systems out of Houston. I've never seen it breached before. Not like this. I would have thought such a breach was *impossible*."

"Yeah, tell me about it," said Kayla. "But moving on," she added, "I assume that after your visit to Borrego Springs, you finally tracked us here."

"Correct. Thank God you're all still alive. But I need to understand what happened, and the players involved, to make sure you *stay* that way. So let's move this party to my helicopter outside. I can debrief you after we're airborne. Satellites and traffic cams aren't showing anyone approaching, so you're safe for now. But the sooner we can get you to real safety the better."

"We aren't leaving," said Connor. "Not until the doctor returns with blood and other supplies for my father, and he says it's safe to move him."

Jalen glanced over at Elias and nodded. "Of course," he said. "You're absolutely right. I'll continue to monitor satellites and traffic cams to be sure we're safe until that time. And my men here will continue to stand guard around the perimeter of the property."

"Your *men*?" said Paige. "How many of you are here?"

"Six. I brought five special forces commandos along for the ride. None of them know who you are, or why I'm here, by the way."

Connor found it hard to believe that there were really five commandos just outside, this time keeping them alive instead of trying to kill them. But Veracity had yet to catch the newcomer in a single lie.

"And you all arrived by helicopter?" said Paige in disbelief. "Must be a big helicopter. How is it that we didn't hear it?"

The DHS undersecretary sighed. "I guess it goes without saying," he replied, "that we'll be elevating your security clearances to the highest levels after this. We brought a helo that incorporates recent advances in noise-canceling technology. Advances not commonly known to the general public."

Connor was impressed, despite himself. No doubt a fleet of helicopters that were whisper quiet would confer quite a military advantage on whoever deployed them.

"You were going to tell me how you managed to see through walls," said Connor, as Kayla sat back down on the couch to conserve strength.

"Why not?" said Jalen with a smile. "Might as well reveal *all* the technology we have that's not supposed to exist. The good doctor has a Wi-Fi router in here. And Wi-Fi signals can penetrate walls, as we all know. They'd be useless if they couldn't. But part of the signals are also reflected when they hit walls or other solid objects."

Connor understood the implications immediately. "So you have tech that captures Wi-Fi exiting a building and analyzes it to map the rooms and objects inside."

"Very good," said Jalen.

"Which is why you were carrying a tablet computer when you entered," said Connor in awe. "It was showing you our images."

Given the breadth of future technology he had studied, he couldn't believe he had missed this. It was an obvious application. Radar, X-rays, Sonar, and now Wi-Fi. *Of course* Wi-Fi. All could be used to reveal properties of objects when light alone wouldn't suffice. "How clear is the mapping?" he asked.

"Very," said Jalen. "Like a nearly perfect black-and-white image. Precise enough for me to look through a wall and tell if you're wearing a ring on your finger. And it's getting better all the time. Still better to watch a hidden camera feed," he added, "but the gap is closing. And the doctor didn't seem to have any hidden cameras available."

Kayla shifted on the couch. "I only let you in because I knew you could see us inside," she said. "I knew you could have killed us if you had wanted to, or taken us prisoner, rather than announcing yourself."

"What?" said Jalen in confusion. "Why would I have done either of those things?"

"Because you might have been working for Holloway. Or Vader. Still might be, and this is part of a deception. I need you to assure us that you aren't."

"Holloway?" said Jalen in dismay. "Holloway *who*? *Bradley* Holloway? The *Vice President* of *the United States* Holloway?"

"That's the one."

"He's trying to kill you?"

Kayla smiled. "Pretty much."

Jalen Howard was visibly taken aback. "If I wasn't wearing Veracity-enabled glasses right now," he said, "I'd worry that you had lost your mind." He shook his head. "And I have no idea who you might mean by *Vader*. But I swear to God and country—and more importantly, to your Veracity contact lenses—that I'm not working with either one. I'm on your side all the way. I even brought the newest generation of blocker prototypes with me to show you."

"Thanks," said Kayla. "Nice to know for sure you aren't working against us. And I will tell you everything," she added. "But first,

I need you to give us fifteen or twenty minutes of privacy. I have some awkward explaining to do to my new friends."

"You have some explaining to do to me too," said Jalen.

"Give us some privacy," repeated Kayla, "and I won't keep you waiting for long."

36

Connor couldn't believe it. Just when he thought he had reached his lifetime quota of surprises, another had literally knocked at the door. And *of course* Jalen Howard's glasses were Veracity enabled. How had he not guessed that the second he saw them?

"You're working with *Homeland*?" he said to Kayla the moment the DHS undersecretary closed the door behind him, leaving them alone once again with his father in the examination room. "How did *that* happen?"

"Not Homeland," she corrected. "I'm only working with Jalen. He's agreed to keep it from the rest of the organization. For now."

"Does my father know about this?"

Kayla shook her head. "Not so much," she replied. "It's an . . . arrangement I set up on my own. I really *was* going to tell him about it. And you. As soon as he came to, like I said. Jalen's timing was horrible, as far as that goes."

"But you *betrayed* Elias," said Paige. "How could you?"

"I would *never* betray Elias," insisted Kayla, a statement that registered as true. "Never."

"You have an interesting definition of the word betrayal," said Paige. "What else would you call working with a high-ranking government official behind his back?"

"Given Veracity," said Connor before Kayla could answer, "how is doing something like this behind my father's back even *possible*?"

Kayla sighed. "Because he never asked," she said. "It never came up. Obviously, if it had, I couldn't have misled him about it."

"But why?" said Connor. "Why would you do this? And why would you keep it from my dad?"

"I think the world of Elias. You know that. But that doesn't mean we're always in complete agreement. When he first perfected Veracity, he wanted to get it out as soon as possible. He wanted interfaces everywhere. Cheap apps that you could get for your phone, computer, and television, and inexpensive peripheral devices. His goal was to make the technology so simple and cheap to acquire that everyone would use it."

Kayla paused for several seconds. "But I urged caution," she continued finally. "I worried that if we let this out universally, it would backfire, end up destroying civilization rather than saving it."

"In what way?" said Connor.

"In *every* way. Lying is evil, but lying is also compassionate. And necessary. It's an integral part of the very fabric of our society. If you tear it away completely, society collapses. For any number of reasons. On the first level we have the relatively harmless lies—*relatively* harmless—which are the cement that holds society together. Strip them all away and things get ugly fast. Does your little girl need to know what you *really* think about her artwork? Or that her dog isn't still alive and running free on a farm somewhere? Or the truth about Santa and the Tooth Fairy?"

She paused to let this sink in. "When your wife accuses you of being attracted to her *sister*," she continued, "do you really want her to be able to see through your denials? Do you really want your boss to know that you think he's an incompetent ass? Or have to confess the real reason you broke up with your girlfriend?" She shook her head. "It would be a disaster."

"Yeah, we get it," said Paige. "And we've already talked about it. Lying about hideous shoes to protect feelings. And I know it goes deeper than that."

"Deeper?" said Kayla. "Are you kidding? I could go on for days. And these are just lies to spare feelings or protect the innocent. But what about sales jobs, or any job that requires negotiations? And it goes beyond just these jobs. Someone once said that life is a series of negotiations, and they're right. Negotiations with your husband, or partner, or friend, or children. Negotiations for homes, and cars, and who'll bring the potato salad to the potluck dinner. That's the second level of disaster. Negotiation is a game a lot like poker, where not showing your full hand is part of the game. But what if you could *never* hide your hand?

"And what about in international relations?" continued Kayla. "A seventeenth-century English politician once famously said, 'a diplomat is an honest man sent abroad to lie for the good of his country.'"

Connor had never heard this particular quote, but there was no denying there was much truth to it.

"And there are other levels of disaster, as well," said Kayla. "If you think marriage is hard now, wait until neither partner can lie. Ever. About anything. Wait until every boss in the world finds out what their employees really think of them, and vice versa. Wait until— "

"Like Paige said," interrupted Connor, "we get it."

"That may be so," said Kayla, "but there is one more layer of the onion I should peel away, because you haven't thought it through like I have. Along with the issues I just described, nearly everyone who is *anyone* has something to hide. Something they aren't proud of. Strange sexual appetites, cheating on taxes, lying to business partners, and endless other transgressions and peculiarities. Everyone in a position of power or authority will look to exploit the newly revealed soft spots of everyone else. It will be absolute carnage—a feeding frenzy unlike any the world has ever seen. Mutually assured destruction as everyone tears down everyone else.

"Elias wants Veracity to take down every politician, academic, executive, media figure, and bureaucrat with even a whiff of corruption. But he's too idealistic to see just how wide a net he'll be casting. He's convinced he'll be taking out a few bad, unnecessary pieces in a world-wide game of Jenga, leaving the structure perfectly intact. The truth is that no structure will be able to survive the coming dislocation. People have gotten too used to getting away with things. You raise the curtain all at once, and you take down almost everyone on stage, *including* the understudies. Then who's going to act in your play? Yes, there *are* good people in the world, at the top, who can withstand the scrutiny of having their lives stripped bare. But fewer than you think. Civilization will collapse like a felled skyscraper, from the top down, from its own weight."

"You paint a vivid picture," said Connor. "So how is it that you only urged my father to be cautious, rather than killing the whole thing? Sounds to me like you're dead set against releasing Veracity at all."

"Have you not heard *anything* I've said today?" replied Kayla. "Of course I want to release it. In the worst way. And not *only* to destroy Derek Manning. The difference is, I want to release it in a way that's safe, and measured, and doesn't destroy civilization in the process."

"Yeah," said Connor skeptically, "and how would you do that?"

"By releasing a Veracity-blocking technology at the same time," she replied immediately. "As inexpensive and accessible as Veracity itself. A bracelet, or phone app, or electronics embedded in clothing that would conceal your face from any camera, disrupting Veracity's ability to read you."

"Is that even possible?" asked Paige.

"Very," said Kayla. "Cameras have more sensitive vision than we do, and this superiority can be used against them. Infrared LEDs can already blind a camera, without affecting human vision in any way. We'd need to take this a few steps further. But there is no theoretical reason why we couldn't develop an inexpensive tech to electronically hide facial expressions from cameras, choking off Veracity's data source. The device could also emit high-pitched sounds, undetectable to the human ear, that could prevent Veracity-enabled interfaces from picking up subtle aspects of vocal tone, thwarting it even more."

Connor thought his brain would explode. He had already absorbed ten years' worth of dramatic revelations and mind-expanding concepts in a single day, but Kayla had taken this to another level. The picture she painted was all too plausible. This, and her proposed solution, were too much to absorb without months of careful consideration.

It wasn't like drinking from a fire hose. It was like drinking from *Niagara Falls.*

Connor looked to be in pain. "Wait a minute," he said, squinting. "Any wearable tech that disrupts Veracity will do the same to every camera. It will render all facial recognition useless. Do you know what impact that will have on law enforcement agencies, who rely on facial recognition for security, and to catch bad guys?"

"When the alternative is the collapse of civilization," said Kayla, "it still seems like a good option to me."

"But what's the point?" said Paige. "Why put Veracity out there if you're going to introduce a tech that can defeat it at the same time?"

Kayla smiled. "Great question," she said. "The answer is that it will allow us to have our cake and eat it too. Anyone with a Veracity interface will know when they're being blocked, when Veracity is unable to read someone. But that's okay. Ordinary people, in ordinary circumstances, won't care. Spouses can block each other, and both will be fine with that, understanding the need. If a wife thinks a husband is cheating on her, she can insist that he remove his blocker while she questions him about it. But how this might play out is their business. So in everyday life, by a sort of unspoken social contract, most of us can go about our lying ways."

She shook her head. "But politicians won't be able to get away with wearing a blocker. Or media figures. The public won't stand for it. Those involved in criminal proceedings won't be able to get away with wearing a blocker, either. If you're on trial, you'd better be prepared to tell the whole truth, and nothing but the truth—which you swear an oath to do, anyway—or hide behind the fifth amendment."

Connor's eyes narrowed. Talk about a brave new world. All the rules of social interaction, all the rules of society, in general, would have to be rewritten. And there would be unintended consequence galore. "So the common man would get a pass," he said. "But the powerful, and those in the public eye, would have to be on their best behavior."

"Exactly right," said Kayla. "These people could wear a blocker in their private lives, but not in their public lives. Which will totally suck for them. But there will be one silver lining. Veracity will protect public figures from false accusations. What happened to me can never happen again. If Veracity says your denial of an accusation is the truth, then it's the truth. In these cases, those making *false* accusations will be held accountable. Which will eliminate false accusations overnight. We'll be able to sort it all out with absolute certainty, including sexual misconduct. No more *he said, she said* cases. We'll have *he said, she said*, and *Veracity said* cases, instead."

She paused. "And this will apply to accusations of racism, sexism, homophobia, and so on. Right now, calling an opponent a racist is a powerful tool that can instantly destroy them. Because society abhors racism like never before. And it's something that can't be disproven."

"Until now," said Connor. "Until Veracity."

"Exactly."

"I don't even know where to begin to process this," said Connor. "But I do have to say, a technology that blocks Veracity from working is a fascinating idea."

"More than fascinating," said Kayla. "*Necessary.* Vital to our survival. And you know it as well as I do. Or should I ask you questions in front of Paige, just for fun, since we're all Veracity-enabled? Like have you ever thought about having sex with one of her friends? Wouldn't you rather be in a world with Veracity blockers when you answer?"

"Don't answer, Con," said Paige immediately.

"No, I've never thought about having sex with one of Paige's friends," replied Connor, ignoring his wife, an answer that registered as being true.

"Good for you," said Kayla. "But you've *both* proven my point. Paige didn't *want* to know. She was *afraid* to know. And who could blame her? You'd both soon realize that your marriage would be better served if you both wore blockers. So you could continue to have a normal marriage, while politicians and media types are always held accountable."

"Even if I were to concede your point," said Connor, "the current political class has a history of lies, which will quickly be exposed. They'll be wiped out. Governments will collapse like the skyscraper you described."

"I've considered this, also," said Kayla. "Which is why I'll be recommending the establishment of ground rules for those in the public eye when we launch. Perhaps their pasts can be grandfathered in, for example. By social convention, politicians won't have to answer open-ended questions that might cause them to *out* themselves for previous wrongdoings. But going forward, on the campaign trail and as they govern, they and media types will have to tell the truth."

She paused. "All of this would have to be thought out further, but society would reach a new equilibrium. One that would be short of the total collapse I fear will happen without the widespread availability of Veracity blockers."

Connor found Kayla's arguments chilling, and all too likely. The consequences of unfettered use of Veracity could well be as devastating as she thought. He turned to his wife. "What do you think?" he asked. "Is she right? If Veracity is launched without a technology to block it, can society survive it?"

Paige sighed. "It's impossible to know. But she makes a lot of sense."

Connor nodded and then paused in thought. "So what was my father's side of the argument?" he asked Kayla.

"He agrees with much of what I said, but believes we have to pull the Band-Aid off quickly. He knows it will be utter chaos for a while, impossibly disruptive to society, but that we have to let the chips fall where they may. Even if civilization has to be partially torn down to be built up again the right way, it's a sacrifice we have to make for the long-term good. You can't have a revolution without breaking some dishes. He knows it's risky. But he believes the rewards of transforming our civilization will be immense, and well worth the risk."

Connor and Paige listened in rapt attention, mesmerized by the weight of the concepts being tossed about.

"Elias agrees that the release of Veracity will create more disruptive change than any event in history," continued Kayla. "But he believes humanity is infinitely adaptable, and that we'll find our way through it. Figure it out. Reach a new and better equilibrium before we destroy ourselves."

She paused. "He also worries that my plan is flawed. If Veracity is only used on a subset of the population—no matter how despicable this subset might be revealed to be—he worries it would create an imbalance, an asymmetry. Some would be held to standards that others would not be. He worries that the blocker, itself, would create unintended consequences, creating a society of haves and have-nots.

Or, in this case, liars and forced truth-tellers. Again, he believes that we have to yank the Band-Aid off, getting through the pain as quickly as possible, rather than prolonging it."

"He makes some good points too," said Paige.

"No doubt about it," said Kayla. "But at the end of the day it comes down to this: how do you feel about human nature? If you're optimistic, believe we can adapt, believe there's enough inherent good in all of us for us to get through this shock, then maybe you side with Elias."

She shook her head in disgust. "But I've seen humanity at its worst. Even before Derek Manning set off a chain reaction that destroyed me. I can't share Elias's optimism. I can't help but be more pessimistic about human nature. As I've said, Elias is a great man. More importantly, he's a good man. Practically a saint. And only a saint would believe we can survive a world without lies of any kind."

37

Connor asked for a moment to pull his thoughts together. This was a lot to take in, but he prided himself on being a futurist, after all. He was more aware than just about anyone that no advance in technology or economics, no dramatic change in society or culture, came without a high cost. There were winners and losers, birthing pains. Change had always been disruptive. There was even a term for it, *creative destruction*, and it was as necessary as it was unfortunate.

The great English philosopher Alfred North Whitehead had written, "It is the business of the future to be dangerous. The major advances in civilization are processes that all but wreck the societies in which they occur."

But some changes were more dangerous than others. Connor had spent many hours thinking through the pros and cons of disruptive technologies, but the elimination of all lying was in another category entirely. Technology extended human reach, but it didn't change what it meant to *be human*. The elimination of such an integral part of human nature and society as the lie surely did, and in a profound way.

Kayla was right. It was as scary as it was awesome.

"Okay," said Connor. "So you and my dad disagreed on the launch. And you both seem to have valid points of view. But what does this have to do with going behind his back and approaching the Department of Homeland Security?"

"In the end, I couldn't convince your father I was right. We reached an impasse. But he owns sixty percent of Ufree Technologies. So I backed off. Stopped arguing."

Kayla gritted her teeth in determination. "But if you think I'm going to let a good man like Elias destroy the world in the interest of saving it," she continued, "you're wrong. I vowed to find a way to save him from his own idealism. Even though, ironically, it's the very thing I love most about him."

"And Homeland?" persisted Connor.

"Long story short, I found Jalen. I met with dozens of high-ranking officials inside DHS as Karen Preston, on false pretexts, so I could vet them using Veracity. It took some doing, but I finally found a good man I could trust. When I did, I confided in him. Demonstrated the technology. Eventually told him who I really am. And proposed a deal."

"Which was?" prompted Connor.

"I'd give him a Veracity interface, and he could use it. But *only* him. He had to keep it secret from everyone else in the department. And he has. Like he said, the men with him now have no idea why he's here, or who we are."

"And what did you get in return?" said Paige. "He mentioned blocker prototypes just before he left us alone. This must be part of it."

"It is. He agreed to spearhead a program to improve methods of defeating facial recognition. He already had a team working on this as it was."

"To help protect US intelligence agents in the field?" guessed Connor.

"Exactly," replied Kayla. "But he learned of other efforts throughout the government. Including at a few black sites. And he's managed to unite them all under his auspices. He agreed to share the research with me, so I could have blocking devices ready for the launch."

"Even though my dad is dead set against them?" said Connor.

"I didn't say I'd use them without Elias's consent," replied Kayla. "I just wanted them to be ready if I could get him to change his mind. And I'm close to doing just that. Very close. I continue to try to persuade him of my case, periodically, and he's nearly there. My hope was that the two of you would be my aces in the hole. That once he brought you into the fold, you'd agree with my side of the argument, and could help persuade him."

Connor traded a glance with his wife. He wouldn't have thought Kayla could explain away Jalen Howard, but she had done a masterful job, and he could tell that Paige felt the same.

"I guess I get why you might want to do this," he said to Kayla. "But why would Jalen agree to it?"

"Are you kidding? Veracity is a *game changer*, never more so than within the intelligence community. Jalen has developed a reputation as being the most effective interrogator US intelligence has ever seen. He's become known for his uncanny ability to ferret out intel that no one else could come close to retrieving. And he's never wrong. He now conducts every critical interrogation in the land. The actionable intel he's pried loose is already responsible for saving tens of thousands of lives around the world. He's become legendary, and is thought to be the leading candidate to one day replace Hugh McKnight as DHS secretary."

"Okay," said Connor sheepishly, "I guess he does benefit from your arrangement, at that. Maybe not the most brilliant question I've ever asked."

Kayla smiled. "It's working out very well for Jalen," she said. "But it could work out even better for us. Assuming I can finally convince Elias of my position—with your help—we would get cheap, reliable technology that can block Veracity. But Jalen has also agreed to give Veracity Homeland Security's Good Housekeeping Seal of Approval. Ideally, if Elias were to finally see things my way, I was hoping he'd agree to open this up even further. To allow fifty or sixty additional members of law enforcement, at the highest levels—each carefully vetted—to become Veracity beta testers. For about nine months. Which is something I'd still love to do, provided we can get Holloway out of the picture."

She paused. "Think about what this would do for our country," she continued excitedly. "What kind of inroads we could make into organized crime, and crime in general, in only nine months. What kind of advantages Veracity would give us in international diplomacy and negotiations. Think of the intel we'd be able to gather. What are North Korea and Iran really hiding? What are Russia's and China's true intentions? Where are terror cells still active? Nine months could change the geopolitical landscape completely."

Connor nodded appreciatively. He had gotten enough of a taste of what Veracity could accomplish already to know that this was no exaggeration.

Her reluctance to let Veracity out immediately now made sense. And her insistence that they had other options he didn't know about, as well.

"Not only would this be patriotic," added Kayla, "but it would give our launch a huge boost. My affiliation with the technology—the infamous Kayla Keller's affiliation—would no longer poison the well. Instead, we'd have the highest levels of government raving about the tech, giving it instant credibility."

"And if my father never does come around to your point of view?" asked Connor

"He owns sixty percent of Ufree. He gets the final call. We'll release Veracity right away like he wants, without blocking technology. But I think this would be catastrophic."

Connor nodded, not sure he didn't agree.

"Either way," continued Kayla, "I'll eventually have to tell him about Jalen, and that I went behind his back. I don't know if he'll ever forgive me. That's what I fear most. Ruining my relationship with a man I've come to admire so much."

She shook her head. "But I felt I had to risk it."

There was a long silence in the room as Connor and Paige digested this mountain of new information.

"Why didn't you call Jalen after you were attacked?" said Paige finally. "Or after Elias was attacked? You know Jalen could have protected us. Was it because, even then, even with Elias's life on the line, you couldn't bring yourself to come clean?"

"Not at all!" snapped Kayla. "And I'm not thrilled about what you're implying. It was because we were always on the run, much of the time without a phone. But most importantly, because Jalen was my *chief suspect*. Who else knew about Veracity?"

She paused to let this sink in. "Then, when we learned about Bradley Holloway, I became even more convinced Jalen was involved.

How else would the vice president find out about the tech, if not through Jalen? So not only didn't I call him in, I would have done anything in my power to *prevent* him from finding us. This would be true, even if Elias had already been on board with our arrangement.

"Fortunately," she finished, "my fears were unfounded. Jalen is still on our side. But I couldn't be certain of that until I could use Veracity to confirm it."

"That makes sense," said Connor. "But is that everything? Please tell me you've run out of surprises."

"All out," said Kayla with a grin. "And sorry to hit you with this one."

"So what's with Elias's briefcase?" asked Paige.

"Oh, right. I guess there is one more loose end. He has a number of Veracity interfaces in there. Contacts, glasses, lapel cameras, and so on. And also two encrypted external hard drives. One contains a file with the hardware configuration for the Veracity supercomputer. The other contains the software. I have no doubt that's what John and Neil were sent after."

"I'm not sure I understand," said Connor.

"The Veracity supercomputer is hidden," replied Kayla. "Only your father knows where. And there is only one of them. So what happens if it breaks down? Dies for some reason? In that case, Veracity would disappear forever."

"Wouldn't Elias just recreate it?" asked Paige. "Evolve a second like he did the first?"

"Not possible," said Kayla. "We used Darwin's most advanced prototype and destroyed the rest, along with the recipe for the complex evolvable architecture. Even if not, evolution is partly random. So even if we began with all the same inputs, we might never get a system that works this well. So Elias generated a file containing the final hardware configuration of the Veracity computer when it had finished evolving. To say that it's unique is an understatement. The bottom line is that if you load the correct software onto a standard supercomputer, you won't get Veracity."

"And if you have the right computer," said Connor, "*without* the software, this doesn't help you either."

Kayla nodded. "So Elias recorded the final configurations of both the hardware *and* software," she said. "With the hardware specifications, we can build a computer with standard, non-evolvable hardware that is locked into place in the final configuration of the Veracity computer. *Now* if you add the software, you get a perfect Veracity clone. And we'll definitely need to manufacture a large number of these—and soon. We'll need them to handle the enormous volume of Veracity-enabled devices we expect to be in use once the technology is fully embraced."

"And each Veracity computer will also be just as tamper-proof as the first," said Connor, "since the hardware and software evolved together to accomplish this."

"Exactly."

"Why would Holloway want these files?" asked Paige.

"He doesn't," said Kayla. "He wants to destroy them. He wants to eradicate every last copy. Then he wants to locate the current Veracity supercomputer and destroy *it*. Which would mark the end of the ultimate lie detection system. And the end of his problems."

"At least until someone else finally manages to develop a similar technology," said Connor.

"That's right."

"Talk about your tangled webs," said Paige.

"No doubt," agreed Connor.

There was silence in the examination room for several seconds. Connor checked on his father's status once again and noted that he remained stable.

"I could go on," said Kayla, "but I think it's time to let Jalen back in the room."

Connor and Paige nodded their agreement.

"Before I do," said Kayla, addressing them both, "just out of curiosity, you've heard my arguments for a Veracity-blocking technology. And you've heard Elias's against it. Where do you fall?"

Connor blew out a long breath. "At the moment, I'm more inclined to side with you."

Paige nodded. "Me too."

"I'm glad to hear it," said Kayla. "So maybe things are finally looking up. We were lucky that Jalen crashed the party, so I could use Veracity to clear him of any suspicion. And now we have a powerful ally we can trust. Finally."

"I guess you were right before," said Connor. "I guess we do have other options for staying alive."

"That's right," said Kayla. "And even more importantly, we have other options for taking out Vice President Bradley Holloway. For stopping the most corrupt, despicable politician to have ever lived."

PART 4

"The Father of Lies."

—Another name for Satan, who lied and deceived angels in heaven, and then told the first lies on Earth to Adam and Eve in the Garden of Eden. Satan is also known as *the accuser*, *the slanderer*, and *the deceiver*.

George Washington and the Cherry Tree—Jay Richardson, James Mason University

"The cherry tree myth is the most well-known and longest enduring legend about George Washington. In the original story, when Washington was six, he received a hatchet as a gift and damaged his father's cherry tree. When his father confronted him, George said, 'I cannot tell a lie,' and admitted to what he had done. Washington's father embraced him and rejoiced that his son's honesty was worth more than a thousand trees.

"Ironically, this iconic story about the value of truth and honesty isn't true or honest. It was invented by one of Washington's first biographers, Mason Locke Weems. After Washington's death in 1799, Weems explained to a publisher, 'Millions are excited to read something about him. My plan is to give his history, sufficiently minute, and then go on to show that his unparalleled rise and elevation were due to his great virtues.'

"Weems' biography, *The Life of Washington*, was first published in 1800 and was an instant bestseller. However, the cherry tree myth did not appear until the book's fifth edition was published in 1806."

38

Colonel Ren Ping stood next to three members of his strike team and studied a large tablet computer. Four other members of the team remained seated inside a car behind them. The team had arrived ten minutes earlier in three vehicles, a large van and two four-door sedans. Like many vehicles sold in the 2020s, all three were electric and whisper quiet, and had been parked well out of sight of Doctor Hector Rosado's home and the five members of US special forces now patrolling the premises.

Night had fallen only thirty minutes earlier, and the wooded, secluded area they were in was getting darker by the minute. The four men still seated in the sedan were all lieutenants, highly skilled but little more than muscle for this operation.

The colonel's *core* team, all standing beside him outside of the three vehicles, included his second-in-command, Major Yan Ling, and two captains, Long Lan and Du Song. All four spoke flawless English, but the colonel and Captain Long had been immersed in American English since birth, so unlike the major and Captain Du, they spoke with no accent. They could well have been born in Nebraska for all anyone listening to them might know.

There were well over one billion people in China, and Ren Ping was arguably the most lethal of them all, with twenty years of distinguished service in the South China Sword, China's equivalent of the US Navy SEALs. He was typically sent on high-profile missions, but this was the highest profile mission of all, commissioned by Pan Shen himself.

Pan had succeeded Xi Jinping two years earlier, after the Paramount Leader's suspicious death, and, like his predecessor, had seized the triple crown of titles, President of the People's Republic of

China, Chairman of the Central Military Commission, and General Secretary of the Communist Party.

The most powerful man on Earth.

While the US president was arguably *as* powerful, his power was severely constrained by a constitution and numerous checks and balances. Not so with President Pan.

Not only had Colonel Ren been given this assignment by Pan himself, he had been ordered to keep it a secret from everyone but the Paramount Leader, including anyone else on the Politburo.

Ren could only guess that a messy purge was on its way, and Pan was waiting on the successful completion of the colonel's mission to use a Veracity system to defame and obliterate anyone not completely loyal to him.

But even though Ren reported only to President Pan, the Paramount Leader made sure that the colonel was given no-questions-asked authority to command any asset that China had at its disposal, as if he were the Chairman of the Central Military Commission himself. It was a feeling of power greater than Ren had ever imagined.

And while it was exhilarating to be able to command entire armies, to shift the gaze of satellites on a whim, what was most gratifying was gaining access to the newest tech toys, prototypes fresh out of China's greatest labs, so advanced, or illegal, that they had yet to be used in the field.

These breakthrough technologies and weapons had been held back until their use was absolutely necessary. Why show off advanced technology when conventional technology would suffice? Especially since premature deployment of a technology would reveal its existence to the US, accelerating this country's attempts to match it, or to develop countermeasures.

But Pan had made it clear to the colonel that this mission was so important, Ren was authorized to show China's hand whenever he deemed it necessary.

And the colonel had deemed it necessary now.

So he had used prototype technology to mask their arrival in the area. To shield them from the many spying technologies available to

US Homeland Security, which Jalen Howard was no doubt using to ensure the safety of Elias Gibson and Kayla Keller.

All three of their vehicles were highly specialized, but Ren was annoyed at having to bring a relatively clumsy and low-performance van on the mission. The van was enormous, a fully stocked type II ambulance, although painted white to disguise its true nature. The top of the van had been removed and a cap added to heighten the roof, as was typical for this kind of medical vehicle.

Readying the disguised ambulance had also delayed their arrival by hours, but it appeared to be a necessity. The Chinese satellite the colonel had commandeered had backtracked the group to Kayla Keller's safe house in Borrego Springs, and had shown Elias Gibson to be injured and unconscious. And the state of the elder Gibson's health had been confirmed thirty minutes earlier, when the reconnaissance drone they had sent ahead of their arrival had revealed Dr. Rosado returning with a ventilator and other telltale medical equipment.

"Captain Long, " whispered Ren to his third-in-command in Mandarin Chinese, not needing to use the comm system since they were standing next to each other, "are the micro-drones programmed?"

"Affirmative," replied the captain. "I'll release five on your command. Each has the facial recognition data for the five men patrolling the grounds that we identified earlier. Each has been assigned a separate target. Each will find its target and hover near the ground, in noise-canceling mode, exactly twenty meters away, and await further orders."

Ren nodded. These micro-drones, affectionately named *assassin bugs*, were one of the prototype technologies that had yet to be used in the field. Until now.

The colonel could hardly contain his excitement. These drones were sure to be an absolute game changer, a technology that would revolutionize the nature of warfare. A lethal force nearly impossible to defend against, especially if they were deployed without warning.

Ren checked the signal coming from the drones, and noted with satisfaction that it couldn't be any stronger. "Captain," he whispered, "block any cell calls in or out, as well as texts and emails. But allow the frequencies that *we're* using to continue to operate. Also, allow their Veracity signal to pass unimpeded so they won't become alarmed."

Long Lan issued commands into his tablet computer, which controlled additional prototype technology that magically allowed these orders to be carried out. He nodded at his commander. "Signal coverage has been established as you specified, Colonel," he reported. "All signals will remain viable within a circle of a half-kilometer radius, centered on the house. This way, they won't know there are any issues unless they try to call out. All signals beyond this circle—other than the Veracity frequency and our cell frequency—will be blocked."

"Thank you, Captain," said Ren.

This completed, the colonel opened a stainless steel box, the size of a small suitcase. Inside, fifty micro-drones were nestled within a foam honeycomb of fifty separate cells.

"Deploy now, Captain," he said to Long, and watched in awe as five quad-copter drones, each not much larger than his thumbnail, whisked into the night sky, representing the very apex of human achievement.

The tiny drones had sensors a self-driving car would envy, with vision that was just as acute in the day or night, due to the use of the most advanced infrared and ultraviolet light collection and enhancement technology ever developed. Each had tiny AI computer chips on board, with state-of-the-art facial recognition and decision-making capabilities, enabling them to actively conceal themselves at all times. They also contained state-of-the-art noise canceling tech, along with cameras, lasers, and GPS systems.

And one other item. A small, shaped charge of a potent explosive.

Ren watched the progress of the tiny drones on his tablet computer, each video feed now appearing in one of five separate tiles on the screen. Less than a minute later, a small orange dot appeared at the top of each sector on the screen, indicating that each speedy drone had found its target and was now hovering twenty meters distant from its final destination.

As much as Ren was eager to unleash this new technology in the field, he couldn't help but feel some guilt, as well.

It wouldn't be a fair fight. The commandos Jalen Howard had brought with him were some of the best America had to offer. They possessed almost superhuman reflexes, endurance, and proficiency with multiple weapons, not to mention the most advanced gear and body armor in the world.

Ren would have liked to test the mettle of his team against theirs. He and his men were even more highly trained than the Americans, and would have the benefit of surprise. And even though they would be trying to root out a semi-hidden enemy in entrenched positions, he was confident they would prevail, losing at most one or two of their team.

But this wasn't a video game, and when a life was lost, it *stayed* lost. And he didn't have the luxury of playing fair.

He took a deep breath and studied the five tiles on his monitor one last time. Finally, he glanced at Captain Long beside him and nodded. "Commence the strike," he commanded.

Almost a quarter-mile away, the five drones accelerated to over a hundred miles an hour, unerringly zeroing in on the foreheads of each of their targets. While the rest of the soldiers' bodies were sure to be protected by advanced armor, the area an inch above the bridge of their noses would be totally exposed. The tiny drones arrived at their respective target foreheads at the same instant and triggered their shaped charges, explosive power that burst through thick skulls and turned each brain into a *puree*.

Blood erupted from just above the eyes of all five men, and they collapsed to the ground simultaneously, dancers in a grisly, choreographed ballet of death, not one of them having seen the drones approaching, and only hearing the largely noise-canceled buzz an instant before their deaths. Even the sound of the explosions were eerily muffled by foreheads, brainpans, and gray matter, so much so that no one inside the building heard anything out of the ordinary.

Each drone communicated back the final GPS coordinates of their targets as they struck, and five more of the drones burst from the colonel's still-open steel container like metal shards summoned by an irresistible magnet. They streaked toward the five sights of carnage, attaining speeds of almost two hundred miles an hour to reach their destinations in seconds.

Each drone shined a bright light on a different fallen soldier and sent back video footage of their bodies and caved-in foreheads to the colonel and major, who couldn't help but cringe upon seeing it. The expressions of the fallen were largely tranquil, since they had been oblivious to the death that had raced toward them, not to be denied.

The technology had worked as flawlessly as expected, as hundreds of simulated tests had long demonstrated, but Ren was sickened by the sight. Perhaps it was better for civilians to be unable to see death coming, but *warriors* would want to know. Would want a chance to fight, regardless of the odds against them. And these men had been allowed neither opportunity.

Ren and his second-in-command, Major Yan Ling, jumped into the empty sedan, while the two captains manned the disguised ambulance. "Move out!" the colonel ordered through the comm system. "Quickly and quietly!" he added.

39

Connor Gibson sat with his wife and Kayla Keller on the large sectional sofa, sinking into the leather cushion like it was a life preserver, exhausted. He felt wildly apprehensive, as though ants were scurrying haphazardly under his skin—and this was the *best* he had felt now in some time.

Things were beginning to turn around, but his father was still comatose, and the doctor still had no idea if, or when, this situation might change.

Since Dr. Rosado's return, Kayla and Elias had received blood, and the color was returning to Kayla's cheeks, although the same couldn't be said of his father.

Even so, they had gained two allies, a powerful DHS undersecretary and a caring and competent doctor. And Jalen was ensuring their safety with five special forces commandos. He was also drawing upon expensive surveillance technology only available to the upper echelon of law enforcement and American Intelligence.

Kayla had slept during her infusion, before moving to the couch, and was beginning to look much better than she had at the safe house. But while the doctor was mostly attending to Elias, he still checked on Kayla periodically.

Rosado insisted that they ignore him and speak freely. He told them he didn't *want* to know the details of what was going on, nor would he ever repeat a word of it, and Veracity confirmed that this was true.

Jalen had made small talk with Connor and Paige while Kayla slept, but was visibly relieved when Kayla was awake once again.

"How are you feeling now?" he asked her softly.

"Never better," she replied weakly, shooting him a wry smile.

The DHS undersecretary laughed. "I can see that," he said. "Then I guess I'll stop asking for a while." He raised his eyebrows. "So, would you like to see the new blocker prototypes?" he asked her.

"Absolutely."

Connor and Paige expressed enthusiastic interest as well.

"Do you have a catchy name for them yet?" asked Paige. "I mean, you can't just call them *blockers*."

Kayla smiled. "Not yet. Just blockers for now. But I can't tell you how happy I am that you're thinking in this direction. If you and Connor can get Elias on board with them, I'd love to get more creative."

Paige nodded, but didn't respond.

Jalen pulled a small velvet pouch from his pocket, which had been closed using a drawstring, and motioned Kayla over to the second examination table, which was unused. He tugged open the small bag and emptied the contents onto the table. Twenty shiny black steel balls, the size of large ball bearings, settled onto the flat blue pad on the table's surface. Thin steel pins, about a centimeter long, protruded from each, with metal clasps at their far ends.

"You did it!" said Kayla excitedly.

"I knew you'd be pleased."

"Did what?" asked Connor.

"I asked Jalen to get his tech teams to design a blocker along the lines of a black pearl earring," she explained. "But instead of sticking the pin through an earlobe, you'd affix it to your lapel. Or anywhere on your shirt, for that matter."

Paige looked intrigued. "I bet that you could eventually bake the technology into *actual* earrings. You could have an entire line. Functional *and* pretty."

Kayla grinned. "I'm going to have to hire you as our marketing manager," she said approvingly. "Yes, this should be possible. And Jalen is working on any number of other implementations. But I like this as a basic model because it's lightweight and simple, and doesn't require pierced ears."

"These are a breakthrough in terms of size and power," said Jalen excitedly. "The progress has been stunning." He paused. "Still, we need to drive the cost down further. And improve battery life. But we've taken a big step in the right direction."

"How do you charge them?" asked Paige.

"Just place them on a charger pad," replied Jalen. "Anywhere on the surface. No need to plug them in." He grinned. "Which is a good thing, since they *can't* be plugged in."

He picked up a single blocker and held it up for all to see. "Squeeze the ball and it's activated," he said. He proceeded to do just this, and a bright green dot appeared on the ball, the size of a pinhole. He made sure all three of his guests could see the green indicator light and then squeezed the ball again, turning it off, which also extinguished the light.

"Right now, all statements coming from a blocked individual will read as inconclusive," said Jalen. "Going forward, we'll improve this. We'll have the interface signal the user in some way when someone is wearing a blocker, and disable all flashes until this is no longer the case."

He encouraged each of them to pin a blocker to their shirts and activate them. When they had, he turned to Connor. "Go ahead, make some true and false statements and see if you're protected."

Connor nodded and faced the group. "My name is Connor Gibson," he said. "I'm the king of England. I have a pet unicorn."

Paige and Kayla grinned. "Works like a charm," said Paige. "All three statements read as inconclusive."

Connor made a show of deactivating his blocker and tried again. "My name is Connor Gibson. I'm the king of England. I have a pet unicorn."

"Veracity is reading you once again," said Kayla. "Outstanding!"

"Speak for yourself," said Paige. "I'm feeling betrayed that he really isn't the king of England."

Kayla laughed. "Well done, Jalen."

"Thanks," he said, scooping up the seventeen blockers that remained on the examination table and returning them to the velvet bag, which he then returned to his pocket. "I knew you'd be impressed."

Connor gestured to the blocker pinned to his shirt. "Do you need this back?" he asked.

"Keep it. The three of you can act as beta testers. Just make sure they're turned off when you aren't testing them, to preserve battery life."

"What kind of battery life do they have now?" asked Kayla. "And how much do you think this can be improved?"

Jalen was about to answer when his phone rang, in audio-only mode. He eyed it suspiciously and put it to his ear. "Hello?" he said tentatively.

"Jalen Howard," said a deep voice in perfect English, "my name is Ren Ping. I'm a Colonel in China's South China Sword. I know you're inside Dr. Rosado's examination room. I'm just outside. I need you and everyone there to put your weapons on the ground and open the door."

Jalen raised his gun, pointed it at the door, and hastily walked over to a small table on which he had set his tablet computer. It hadn't given off a warning that anyone had come anywhere near the premises, by car or foot, but he checked to confirm it wasn't muted and was operating properly. It was, and the screen continued to indicate that they were very much alone.

"What's going on?' asked Connor, as he and his two companions on the couch couldn't help but notice Jalen's raised gun and shocked expression.

The DHS undersecretary hastily waved off the question.

"I know you're lying," he barked into the phone. "So what is this all about?"

"You *think* I'm lying because you believe your surveillance technology to be infallible. Even if not, you have faith in your team of five commandos outside to protect you. But I'm afraid I used technology that trumped yours. And your men are regrettably no longer alive."

Jalen gasped loudly at this last and his eyes widened in disbelief. "Impossible!" he insisted.

"I'm sending you video footage now," said the voice.

Jalen was about to respond when he heard a chime that indicated an incoming message. He clicked on the file, which displayed video images of the five men he had brought with him sprawled out in various locations around the grounds, their faces unmistakable, even covered in blood, with gaping holes blasted into their foreheads.

He urgently motioned to Kayla and Connor on the couch, pantomiming for them to draw their own weapons, and to remain silent.

"What do you want?" he shouted into the phone as his two companions rose from the couch, now at full attention.

"I already told you," said the colonel calmly. "Disarm yourselves and open the door. I'm with three other men, and you're helpless. I'm calling only as a courtesy. Your men outside were killed with what I believe your people call *slaughterbot drones*. I have forty-five of them left."

Jalen looked ill. He was all too familiar with this theoretical weapon system, one that was all but unstoppable. And apparently no longer theoretical.

These tiny drones, fully AI capable, were the equivalent of programmable, autonomous bullets. Bullets capable of hunting a victim down, of stalking him or her for hours on end. Bullets able to navigate around corners and obstacles on the way to their target, striking with perfect accuracy every time. Tiny self-guided missiles that never missed, and could not be shot down.

Even in the unlikely event that a human target saw one coming, and had a second or two to get off a shot, he would have to hit something the size of a bullet, moving a hundred miles an hour or more, and capable of evasive action. And if more than one slaughterbot was sent to hit the same target, the chances of survival would drop from infinitesimal to *zero*.

The world had seen videos of these theoretical weapons in action many years earlier—not real, but created using advanced special effects and slick Hollywood production values—and had been horrified, insisting that they be put in the same category as chemical and biological weapons.

"Slaughterbots were *banned* in the updated Geneva Conventions six years ago," said Jalen in disgust. "If you really are from China, you know that your country was a signatory to this agreement."

"Which doesn't change the fact that I have a working swarm with me. Or that I've just used them on your men. Or that I'll use them on *you* if I have to. I can have a subset of them blow a hole in your door and have the rest follow, each with your name on them. But I'd prefer that you cooperate. Why waste them?"

There was a long pause as Ren allowed the American to digest his predicament.

"You have thirty seconds, Undersecretary Howard," said the Chinese colonel, as if he didn't have a care in the world. "Your call."

Jalen shouted a curse, and then quickly explained to those in the room with him what had happened, and that they needed to cooperate. He carefully placed his gun on the floor and motioned for Connor and Kayla to do the same, which they reluctantly did. Finally, when everyone had their hands raised, he threw open the door.

Several tiny drones zipped through the open door and hovered in mid-air. Seconds later, once the drones' cameras had confirmed the Americans had done as the colonel had asked, Ren followed them inside, his gun raised, with three comrades in tow.

"Line up against the wall," he ordered, and waited for his prisoners to comply.

The moment they did the colonel squeezed off four shots in rapid-fire succession, pumping two rounds into the chests of both Jalen Howard and Hector Rosado. Blood erupted from the gaping wounds in their torsos as they crashed to the ground, their hearts stopping instantly.

Connor heard several screams, and realized absently that one of them was his own.

Bright red blood began to pool near their feet as Paige began sobbing hysterically. She was terrified of the Chinese colonel, but also horrified by the deaths of these good men. Men who had been living, breathing, loving human beings had been snuffed from existence in an instant. Connor reached out and steadied her, preventing her from falling to the ground, while trying to push down the vomit that was rising in his throat.

Ren gestured to Yan Ling when the screaming stopped, as if nothing out of the ordinary had taken place. "Frisk them, Major!" he ordered.

Yan did as he was asked, finding a key fob for the dry cleaning van in Paige's pocket, which he didn't remove, and a cell phone in Kayla's pocket, which he held up to show the colonel.

"Let her keep it," said Ren dismissively. "Captain Long has rendered it useless."

The colonel looked Kayla up and down. "Looks like you've had a rough day," he said. "Why don't you rest on the couch," he offered pleasantly. He motioned for Major Yan to accompany her to the sectional and keep his gun on her while she remained there.

The colonel walked to the examination table Elias was on and inspected the unconscious figure, looking apprehensive for the first time. Finally, he turned back toward Paige and Connor as they stood against the now-bloody wall, studying them carefully. Paige continued sobbing, although now more softly.

Ren sighed and turned to Du Song. "Please kill these two also, Captain Du," he said in Chinese. "They're as unnecessary as the others."

The captain barked the Chinese equivalent of *roger that*, and pointed his weapon at Paige.

Then, without further delay, he calmly depressed the trigger.

40

Captain Long's hands shot out in a blur of motion and shoved Du's arm upward as the trigger hit home, deflecting the shot just enough so that it missed Paige's head by mere inches.

"Humble apologies, Colonel," said Long immediately in Chinese as Paige slid down the wall, not hit but so hysterical that her legs refused to keep her upright. "I don't mean to overstep my bounds. But I wasn't aware of your intent to kill these two."

"I just made the decision!" snapped Ren angrily. "And your *awareness* wasn't required."

"Of course not, sir," replied Long. "But I ask you to hear me out. I think they're worth keeping alive. If you disagree, I'll have delayed their deaths by only a few minutes."

"You have thirty seconds!" barked Ren.

"This is our most important mission ever," said Long quickly. "So perhaps it would be prudent to keep these two as insurance policies. Just capturing Kayla and Elias and bringing them to China doesn't ensure their cooperation. I know we have powerful persuasive techniques, but I'd feel better if we had Elias's son and daughter-in-law alive to use as leverage. There is a small chance that Elias will refuse to help us, even under threats of torture and death. But few men have the will to stand idly by and watch as their loved ones are tortured and killed."

Ren tilted his head in thought for an extended period, weighing his third-in-command's recommendation.

Paige rose to a standing position once again, having managed to partially suppress the hysteria she had felt from her near-death experience. If she was to die here, she would meet her death with as much dignity as she could muster.

Connor felt empty inside, but balled his hands into fists, determined not to die as a sheep. He prepared to launch himself at the captain if he tried to shoot again, waiting to act until the conversation among these men played itself out. He didn't understand a word of Mandarin, but sensed the man who had saved Paige's life was trying to buy them a reprieve.

"Belay my last order, Captain Du," said Ren finally. "Captain Long makes a valid point. Attend to Elias until further notice."

Du walked to Elias's side as the colonel approached the two prisoners. "That was just a demonstration," he said in English when he reached them, trying to pretend that the last-second deflection of the assassin's arm was intentional. "A warning shot across your bow. So you understand just how serious we are. Cooperate, or we'll have to turn this demonstration into reality. Understand?"

Both prisoners nodded vigorously. Connor glanced at Paige in relief and let out a breath he had been holding for too long.

"I'm not sure the DHS undersecretary had the chance to explain who I am," the leader continued. "My name is Colonel Ren Ping, with Chinese special forces," he explained, and then went on to quickly introduce the rest of his men.

"What do you want?" asked Connor.

"I'm glad you asked," said the colonel. He motioned for Paige and Connor to stand by the second examination table. Once they had moved away, he stood over Jalen Howard's lifeless body and removed his black-rimmed glasses, slipping them on his own face.

"Paige," he said, "please give your glasses to Major Yan."

Paige did as the colonel asked, and Yan was wearing them seconds later.

"That's better," said Ren. He gestured to Connor. "Now we can trade information. You'll notice I'm allowing you and Kayla to keep your contact lenses, in the interest of fairness. So you'll know if *we're* lying, and we'll know if *you* are. What better way to keep this friendly?"

"What do you want?" repeated Connor.

"We want China to have Veracity," he replied simply, "and the United States *not* to have it. We don't want your country to know it ever even existed. Which I'm afraid means that Elias and Kayla will need to come to China with us. And we'll need to destroy your Veracity supercomputer and all associated records."

Ren sighed. "We also need to eliminate anyone with any knowledge of Veracity," he continued. "Fortunately, this is a small group, consisting of just the people in this room." He gestured to the two dead bodies on the floor, lying in thickening pools of sticky red blood. "A group that's getting smaller all the time."

He paused for a moment with an uncertain expression, and then stared intently at Kayla. "That *is* correct, right?" he said. "Neither you nor Elias have shared the secret of Veracity with anyone outside of this room, correct?"

Kayla nodded miserably. "Correct," she mumbled.

The briefest flash of green shot into Ren's retinas and he grinned like a giddy schoolboy. While Connor had asked a question, this had been the first *statement* made since he had stolen the glasses. "Did you get the green flash just then?" he asked his second-in-command in Chinese.

Yan nodded. "Absolutely amazing. An elegant system."

Connor's eyes widened. A troubling thought flashed into his mind, just as surely as green had just flashed into his eyes. A hidden thread had emerged from a tangled ball of yarn, a thread he needed to pull on, but now was not the time, as unraveling this tangled skein wouldn't help him survive his current situation.

"If you need to kill everyone in America with knowledge of Veracity," said Connor, "then why am I still alive?" The last thing he wanted to do was bring this up, risk that they might change their minds, but he needed to learn why he and Paige had been spared. Besides, he doubted they would change their minds just because he asked the question, not after their heated exchange had resolved the issue.

"To keep your father cooperative," replied Ren, returning to English. "Which means that you and your wife will both be accompanying him to China."

"I see," said Connor. He paused for a moment in thought. "And when you say you want China to have this technology," he continued,

"I assume you mean the Politburo, correct? There's no way you're on a mission to give this to your people, so they can keep your government honest. You want it so your government can press their jackboots even harder against the necks of the population, don't you?"

"Individual liberty is overrated," replied the colonel in bored tones. "So tell me," he continued, changing the subject, "what is your father's condition? Will he recover?"

"He's in a coma," said Connor. "His recovery is uncertain."

A satisfied smile spread across the colonel's face as his stolen glasses delivered two more flashes of green. He turned to Kayla. "Impressive system that you helped Elias develop," he said. "Does it maintain its accuracy when assessing speakers of other languages?"

She sighed. "We think probably yes, but it's uncertain. There are too many languages, and too many cultures, for us to have tested it out with the required rigor. But there are reasons to believe that this won't be an issue."

Connor couldn't help but glare at her for giving away such key information, but he knew that this was unfair. Lying wasn't as much of an option for her as it had been only minutes earlier.

"What reasons?" asked the colonel.

"Human expressions and emotions are universal across cultures," said Kayla. "From China, to Africa, to tribes just discovered in the Amazon jungle that have never been in contact with the outside world. In all cultures, people smile and laugh when they're happy, frown when they aren't, and so on. There are differences, of course. Some cultures are more demonstrative than others, on average, when it comes to their facial expressions, tone, gesturing, and so on. On average, the Chinese culture is on the buttoned-up side. Whereas a culture like . . . well, like the Italian culture, for instance, is more on the demonstrative side. But we believe Veracity can factor this in, and perform with the same fidelity, regardless of language or culture."

"But you have no direct confirmation that this is true," said Ren.

"No. The Veracity supercomputer is 'fluent' in dozens of languages, and we can add more. So Elias did conduct some testing, but mostly on Spanish speakers, using native speakers to ask the questions. In these tests, Veracity earned a perfect score. But the tests weren't extensive enough to be definitive. We planned on doing much more comprehensive testing after launching in the States."

"And if it turns out that the current Veracity configuration doesn't do as well for some languages, or some cultures?" said the colonel. "Can I assume Elias can remedy this? That he can start at the beginning. But this time provide his computer with a database of liars and truth-tellers from an alternate language and culture. So that when it does evolve from there, it *will be* a hundred percent accurate."

"How do you know so much about the system?" said Kayla in dismay. "How do you know *anything* about it, for that matter?"

"I'll tell you. But first answer my question. Will he be able to evolve a different system for another language if this proves necessary?"

"It's not clear," said Kayla. "First, like I said, chances are it will work perfectly in every language. But if it doesn't, it's unclear if his success can be repeated. It isn't even certain that he could recreate the system already in place. There is something called the *Butterfly Effect*. From chaos theory. In chaotic systems, the tiniest variation in starting conditions can lead to a wildly different endpoint."

Ren nodded, noting that she was telling the truth. "If we thought this would be easy, we'd have no need to keep you and Elias alive, would we?" He paused. "Frankly," he added, "we don't really need *you*. But why break up a proven team?"

"Good thinking," said Kayla, having no choice but to agree with this logic. "But if you're so keen to keep Elias alive," she added in contempt, "why did you kill his *doctor*?"

"Captain Du is also a medical doctor."

Kayla blinked in disbelief. "Of course he is," she said wryly. "How could I have missed it? The man who almost shot Paige in the head. *First do no harm.* He really personifies the Hippocratic Oath, doesn't he?"

The colonel's expression didn't change. "You should know that the captain was at the top of his class in medical school," he said. "I command perhaps the most skilled team ever assembled. Each of us has multiple areas of expertise. Weapons, electronics, computers, medicine, explosives. You name it, someone on our team is a master."

"And all this to kidnap my father?" said Connor in disgust.

"All this and more," corrected the colonel. "I have the authority to activate any number of spies and mercenaries China has operating in your country. I am able to bring resources to bear to accomplish my mission that you can't even begin to fathom."

"How do you know about my father and Veracity?" asked Connor, echoing Kayla's earlier question. He was relieved to note that Paige was now steady once more, fully alert and following every word of the exchange. Not an easy thing to accomplish in a room that contained two corpses that were so fresh they were still warm.

"China has mounted its own programs to develop something like Veracity over the years," replied the colonel. "All of them failures. Recently we decided to try again. Early last month, our top people met with experts around the world under various pretexts to learn about the latest research in various related fields. Research that had yet to be published. Several of these experts commented in passing that someone had met with them and had asked similar questions a few years earlier. When pressed, it turned out that this someone was always named Elias Gibson."

Connor nodded. "So you guessed that he was after the same prize as you," he said.

"We did. My team and I were tasked with exploring this further, under the strictest confidence. We were able to draw upon entire Chinese intelligence agencies to act on our whim, without telling them why. We learned a lot about your father in a hurry. We hacked Virtuality computer archives and discovered details of his first attempt at Veracity, many years ago. We learned he had recently conducted extensive interviews, paying people to lie and tell the truth. He then followed these up with more of the same, only this time interviewing psychopaths in prisons."

Ren paused. "The fact that he was going to the trouble of interviewing violent inmates was a clear indicator that his results with normals had been stellar. And all of this was under the guise of psychology research, even though Elias Gibson was not a psychology researcher. So we scrambled some of our teams in the States to follow him. And we learned through other channels that he had gained access to a different breed of computer, which we believe was instrumental

238   *Douglas E. Richards*

to his success. And then we had our people bug his residence, only twenty-four days ago."

"Was *my* residence also bugged?" asked Kayla.

"No. We only learned of your involvement recently. About two weeks ago, my team and I arrived in the US to set up a base of operations and monitor the situation on the ground. We activated additional in-country resources in case they were needed, and began to plan a course of action. Our intelligence indicated that Elias had no immediate plans to share his discovery." He frowned. "We didn't count on what happened today. What I believe you Americans call a *shitstorm.*"

"Did you plant a bug *on* my father?" asked Connor. "Is that how you tracked us here?"

"No. We had heard rumors through our spy network of a man, Jalen Howard, whose skills at interrogation were too good to be true. He hadn't been all that special before, until suddenly, out of nowhere, he became all but infallible. We suspected he was involved with Elias's Veracity project. It was the only answer that made sense. So we bugged his office."

"You bugged the office of DHS's head of intelligence?" said Kayla incredulously. "I don't believe it. Those offices are swept for bugs as a matter of routine, using the most advanced detection technology in existence."

"Apparently not advanced *enough,*" said the colonel smugly. "This is a high-priority mission, so we've been given permission to use breakthrough technologies. So that's how we found you here. Not through Elias. Not through you. Through Jalen Howard."

Connor was struck by how all the insanity they had been through was interrelated, connected. It might all *seem* random at first blush, but it was anything but. Vader's attacks had flushed Jalen out of the brush. And these men had been monitoring Jalen, so they knew he was racing to the residence of Hector Rosado, a poor, innocent doctor who nobody even knew existed three hours earlier.

As much as Connor hated to admit it, Ren had made a smart decision. By intervening here, he had managed to catch all the principals in this drama, all those who knew of Veracity, at the same place and time.

"Okay, enough of this," said Ren to his men in Mandarin. "We need to return to our base of operations. Captain Du, get Elias Gibson into the ambulance. You'll travel in the back with him. We'll take his son, too, for leverage in case he wakes up."

"Understood," replied Du.

"Major Yan," continued the colonel. "I want you to hang back here until further notice. I'll leave Captain Long and the four lieutenants behind with you. I want you to get rid of these two bodies and scrub the scene. Why invite unwanted attention? And have some men patrol outside, just in case."

"What about Kayla and Paige?" asked Yan. "Will they be staying here?"

"Yes. I like the idea of separating them from Connor and Elias. Keeps everyone honest—and guessing. And once you've scrubbed this room, have your men search every inch of it. And the residence. The bug at Elias's home picked up mention of a briefcase they were taking with them. They may have left it off along the way, but let's make sure."

"Understood," said Yan. "Can I assume we'll be moving out before this office is open for patients tomorrow?"

"Yes. But probably not until five or six in the morning."

Ren walked over to Elias's comatose form and studied his face, turning his back to the three Americans. "We're taking Elias to a safe place," he told them, "where he'll get the best medical care. Trust me, we want him alive and well as much as you do."

"What about us?" said Kayla.

"Connor will come with us so he can keep an eye on his father. You and Paige will stay here. If Connor isn't cooperative," he continued, still turned away from them, "Paige will pay for it with her life. If *she* isn't cooperative, he'll pay with *his* life. Understood?"

They all nodded. "Can we at least say goodbye?" asked Kayla.

Ren now turned to face her, staring into her eyes, unblinking, for several seconds. "Why not?" he said finally. "But make it quick."

Paige and Connor embraced, both fighting back tears, and finally separated.

Kayla approached to within six inches of Connor and shook his hand. The back of his head was facing Ren and Long, and she made sure to stand close enough that they couldn't see her face. "Good luck, Connor," she said. "I wish I could give you hope, but I can't. I'm afraid there's no way for Paige and me to escape."

Connor stifled a gasp, glad that the Chinese commanders couldn't see him. Kayla's brilliance, her sheer audacity, was stunning. She had arranged this brief goodbye to communicate a simple message. Because her final two statements, that she couldn't offer hope, and that there was no way to escape, were both lies.

She *was* hopeful. And she *did* have an escape plan.

"That's okay, Kayla," he responded after just a short pause to recover from the shock. "I wouldn't want you to take that risk, anyway."

And this, too, was a lie, one that Veracity would instantly flag for her.

He had seized the opportunity to use the same system to send back a message of his own. If she thought she could escape, she would get no objection from him. Even though the colonel had threatened to kill him if Paige didn't cooperate, this threat had come when they couldn't see him, when Veracity couldn't verify if his statements were true.

Which meant that he was probably bluffing.

Probably, thought Connor, swallowing hard.

PART 5

"We often *want* to be misled. We collude with the lie, unwittingly, because we have a stake in not knowing the truth. It may not be in the interest of a mother with a number of very young children to catch her mate's lies that conceal his infidelity. Everyone but she may know what is happening. Or, the parents of a preadolescent using hard drugs may unwittingly strive to avoid spotting the lies that would force them to deal with a possible failure as parents, and which would bring about a terrible struggle. The targets of lies may also collusively want to believe the liar to avoid recognition of impending disaster. Which explains why the businessman who mistakenly hired an embezzler continues to miss the signs of the embezzlement. Rationally speaking, the sooner he discovers the embezzlement the better, but psychologically, this discovery will mean he must face not only his company's losses but his own mistake in having hired such a rascal."

—Paul Ekman, *Telling Lies*

41

Elias Gibson was still lifeless and still hooked up to an IV bag, but his venue had changed. Instead of being inside the expansive examination room of Dr. Hector Rosado, he was now strapped carefully to a gurney in the back of a camouflaged ambulance.

Colonel Ren Ping was in the driver's seat, and Connor was in the back of the van, securely bound to a fold-out jump seat, sharing the space with his father and Captain Du Song, who was also apparently an accomplished medical doctor.

Connor had never been inside this kind of ambulance—thankfully—and he was surprised it was so spacious and well equipped, like a hospital emergency room on wheels, complete with a ventilator at least as sophisticated as the one Dr. Rosado had gone to fetch. There were no windows in the back of the vehicle, but given that darkness had fully descended long ago, and it was a cloudy night, he wouldn't have been able to figure out where they were in any case, even if he had activated the IR feature of his contact lenses.

Connor felt numb all over, disgusted with the cruelty of the universe. Just when it looked like things were finally moving in their favor, the rug had been violently pulled out from under them. Just when he thought he had reached his limit, that nothing could shock him any more than he had already been shocked, bodies began to pile up like cordwood.

Seven dead, in the span of a few minutes. *Seven.* And he and Paige had been a single breath away from joining them.

Five commandos had been killed, snuffed out in their prime by an unseen hand, like ants crushed by a random boot. Men who had wives, children, siblings, friends.

Jalen Howard's Veracity-assisted interrogations had saved thousands of lives, but by attracting the attention of a Chinese colonel they had also, ironically, cost him his own.

And Dr. Hector Rosado, a man who had continued to help patients in and around his community long past the time when he needed the money or recognition, gunned down without a second thought.

Connor's mind's eye replayed the carnage, over and over again, like busted movie footage running in a continuous loop. Four deafening shots fired, followed by explosions of blood from two torsos, screams of horror, the onset of debilitating fear, and a look in Paige's eye he would never forget.

He shuddered, but the movie just kept coming, now joined by a jumbled montage of bizarre events that had happened just that day: the shattering of his father's slider, Paige lying helplessly on the ground, presumed dead, Kayla's arms and legs sliced up in dozens of places, Connor clubbing a man with an iron shovel. And on and on and on it went.

Every instant of the jam-packed day fought for room within his consciousness, a cyclone of events and images and words circling faster and faster. Finally, he let go of it all, and his mind collapsed in around him, driving him into a deep slumber.

When he awoke, he was unsure of how long he had been out, but guessed under an hour. Even so, the dense, pure sleep had replenished his mind a surprising amount, and he was now capable of ordered thinking.

Not that his nerves were any less on edge. He feared for his injured father on the gurney nearby, for his beautiful wife, who didn't deserve any of this, and for himself. And more broadly, for his country, and even for the people of China.

He clung to a single hope. That Kayla Keller had somehow seized on a workable plan to escape, as unlikely as this seemed.

He had given his consent to such an attempt because, in his heart, he knew that their days were numbered, no matter what. They had been a hair away from death already, and these men, and those they were working for back in China, were ruthless, and would dispose of the four Americans like spent chewing gum the moment they ceased to be useful, even if they were promised otherwise.

And the colonel's threat to kill him if Paige escaped *had* to be a bluff. What would that gain him? If Ren really did lose half of the leverage he had on Connor's father, the response to this loss wouldn't be to kill the *other half*. If anything, Connor would become even more important to him.

Could Kayla really pull it off? Seemed impossible. She was unarmed and dealing with the most highly trained men in the world. Four lieutenants, a captain, and a major. All part of a team that had taken out five trained commandos with less effort than it took to turn off a *lamp*.

But for some reason, Connor wouldn't bet against her. When she had first rushed on the scene in his father's backyard, he had been anything but impressed. But he was beginning to think there was nothing that Kayla Keller couldn't pull off.

He sat in silence for twenty more minutes, taking the time to pull on the alarming thread he had discovered earlier. The longer he pulled on it, the more disturbed he became. There was already *so much* going on when it came to the breakthrough known as Veracity, but could there really be *more*?

More than Vader, and Holloway, and assassins, and safe houses, and Homeland Security, and China? More than perfect lie detectors, perfect lie blockers, and the possible collapse of civilization?

As hard as it was to digest, he was becoming convinced that there was. A lot more.

But now it was time to start thinking about himself—and a possible escape. If Kayla could think of a way, maybe he could also. It was unlikely, but he had to try.

Right now, he could only come up with a single option—sowing discord within the enemy camp. It would just be a start, but it was the best he could do at the moment. And Veracity would help his efforts enormously.

"What was your name again?" he asked the doctor, who continued to diligently monitor Elias Gibson. Connor suspected the stakes couldn't be higher for the man. If he was the one who let China's prize die on the table, it would *not* go well for him.

"Captain Du Song," the man replied.

"In China, you say your last name first, and your first name last, right? So can I call you Song?"

"I have no interest in being friends," replied Du bluntly. "Keep talking and I'll gag you."

Connor paused. "Okay, then," he said good-naturedly. "Captain Du it is. You may not want to be friends, but I'm sure you have the normal level of curiosity. I mean, you're a man of medicine. And given the education this requires, a man of science."

"This is your last warning. Duct tape over your mouth can be very uncomfortable."

Connor took a deep breath. His time was running out. He needed to turn this around now. "Surely you have to be interested in the secrets of Veracity, right? I mean, that's your mission. So while I'm blabbing, maybe you learn something that would help you succeed. Something that might excite your bosses. Do you really want to gag me if there's even a chance I might spill something useful?"

The captain didn't respond, but neither did he root around in the ambulance to find a roll of duct tape.

"I assume you know that the glasses the colonel took from Jalen Howard's dead body are Veracity enabled, right?" continued Connor. "Doesn't that bother you? It would bother me. I mean, now you can't hide *anything* from him. If you disagree with an order. Or think he's an ass. Or maybe think his wife is hot. He'll know."

"None of these things are true," replied Du.

Connors eyes lit up. Finally, a response. The man was starting to become engaged in the topic, and had stopped talking about gagging his prisoner.

"Maybe not," said Connor, "but I'm sure you have secrets you'd like to hide. Everyone does. And the worst part is that we can't be sure the system is a hundred percent reliable in the Chinese language and culture. So maybe Colonel Ren asks you a question, and you're being honest, but it doesn't *register* that way."

Du frowned but remained silent.

"What about when you get to China? What then? You must be working for someone at the highest levels of government. Probably even your president, whose name escapes me. Are you perfectly loyal to him? Do you worship every word he says? You'd better. What about your thoughts? Ever had one that was disloyal?"

Connor paused to let this sink in. "What about your friends? Your loved ones? Are they absolutely loyal to the government? Have *they* ever had a subversive thought? You'd better hope not, or *you'll* be sent to kill them. Since you're one of the few to know about the tech, your future has limited possibilities. Either you'll end up dead very soon, so the powers that be can limit the number of people in on their secret. Or, you'll be turned into an enforcer, killing innocent men and women at their whim."

Du's expression hadn't changed, and he appeared to have no interest in responding, but Connor was sure he was scoring points. Points that could well help him at a later time.

He stared deeply into Du's eyes. "How do you feel about becoming an enforcer?" he asked him. "Kayla made a joke about the Hippocratic oath. I get that you're a soldier, and shit happens. Sometimes you need to kill. But what about when your *only* job is to be an assassin, snuffing out innocent civilians just because Veracity decided they weren't quite loyal enough?"

Connor paused. "A lot to think about," he continued. "But if I were you, I'd start with your colonel. Doesn't seem fair that he has the only pair of Veracity glasses. He should at least have the courtesy of not wearing them when he's talking to his own men, right? He should respect your right to at least keep your *thoughts* private."

Du remained unmoved. "You aren't revealing any secrets of the technology," he said firmly. "So you're now done. One more word, *a single word*, and I'll tape your mouth shut so tightly that not even a grunt will be able to escape."

The doctor paused. "You're still wearing your Veracity contact lenses. What do they tell you about the truth of what I just said?"

Connor was heartened by this reaction, the first real indication that he was getting under Du's skin.

He hadn't made much progress, but he had only just begun. Fomenting discord took time. He needed to get to know the players. Get to know their personalities, their weaknesses, their hidden fears. And he needed to continue to fan the flames.

What Du didn't know was that he planned to have a conversation with Ren. Convince the colonel that he had seen signs of disloyalty in his medical officer. Signs that Du resented his leadership, questioned his competence. Convince Ren that now that he had Veracity-enabled glasses, he had the perfect chance to learn just how loyal his people really were.

Connor would push until he generated a number of tiny embers of mistrust and suspicion. And then he would feed these embers enough oxygen to ignite them into raging bonfires.

Escape using this strategy was still a long shot, but it was the only shot he seemed to have. It would require finesse and patience.

But it wasn't as if he was doing anything else with his time.

42

Major Yan led the two prisoners and all five of his comrades to Dr. Rosado's main residence, until he found what he was looking for, a small guest room on the second floor. It was tastefully decorated in neutral colors, with a queen-sized bed and a large, shaggy area rug covering a hardwood floor. The bed was topped by a teal-green bedspread and six matching pillows, with end tables on either side of it, and a salt-oak country dresser against the wall.

The guest room had its own sizable bathroom, complete with bath and shower.

"We'll park the prisoners here," declared the major in Chinese, standing just outside the room.

"Should I bind them up?" asked one of the lieutenants.

Yan shook his head. "No. We'll want their cooperation, so let's make this as stress-free as possible. And there's no way they can escape."

The major examined the door handle on the inside of the room, which had a push button in its center, giving houseguests the option of locking the door. "Still," he added, "let's not get too overconfident."

Yan turned to another of his men and gestured at the door. "Lieutenant Quan," he said, "unscrew both handles and reverse the apparatus—so the door locks from the outside."

The lieutenant acknowledged the order and immediately went about carrying it out, using a utility tool he carried with him at all times.

"We'll also post a guard beyond the door," Yan added. "Unnecessary, I'm sure, but we should do this by the numbers, I suppose."

"I'll stand guard," said Captain Long.

Yan arched an eyebrow. "I'm surprised you'd volunteer for guard duty, Captain, when you outrank four men."

"Just trying to be helpful," said Long.

"Don't be," replied the major. "Rank has its privileges. You're with me. I want your help with the clean-up, and we have to search every inch of this place. Lieutenant Quan," he added, "you stand guard here. Lieutenants Sun, Tang, and Gao, I want you to patrol outside. Make sure one of you always keeps an eye on this room. In case they get the crazy idea of tying bedsheets together and climbing down, or some other such stupidity."

When his men had acknowledged these orders, the major switched to English. "As you've no doubt guessed," he said to the two women, "you'll be staying in here for a while—probably three to six hours. The door will be locked from the outside and a guard posted. There's a bathroom inside, so you won't have any need to leave until we're ready to move out."

The major made a show of adjusting his Veracity-enabled glasses and then stared at his prisoners. "Now tell me there is no need to tie you up," he said. "Tell me that you won't try to leave this room."

Kayla smiled icily. "Not until you and your men are all dead," she deadpanned.

Yan's eyes narrowed, uncertain of how to take this wild statement, which registered as true. "Good enough," he said awkwardly. "Although American humor escapes me."

"Will you or your men be listening in on us?" asked Paige.

The major smiled. "I'm afraid we have better things to do," he said.

Paige frowned. She had gotten used to Veracity always being there to sort truth from lies, and she missed her glasses badly, even after having used them for only a single day.

They entered the room and the door was locked behind them. Paige slumped down onto the edge of the queen-sized bed and faced Kayla. "Was he telling the truth?"

"Yes. We can talk privately."

Paige breathed a sigh of relief. This helped her feel less like a caged animal at the zoo, but not by much. She felt as if she was on the verge of melting down entirely. She wanted to roll up into a ball, close her eyes, and leave the world behind. Even so, she forced herself to stay strong. There was no point in sobbing any further, even though the chances that she would survive, that the man she loved would survive, were almost zero.

She looked at Kayla Keller, whose eyes sparkled. Elias's partner still looked remarkably upbeat, despite having just lost a highly placed ally, who was also a friend, and being at the absolute mercy of the Chinese.

"How is this happening?" said Paige softly. "Each time I think our situation is getting better, it gets worse. What's next, Russian special forces? Terrorists? The plague?"

Kayla actually smiled. "Don't count us out just yet," she said. "We're going to escape. And then we're going to find Elias and your husband."

"Have you lost your mind?" said Paige.

"Maybe," said Kayla with a wistful smile. "I guess we're about to find out."

43

"I have to pee," said Connor Gibson, risking that even these words would bring on the duct tape that Du had promised.

"Hold it," said Du simply.

"I have been," said Connor. "Hoping that we'll stop. But we haven't. And my bladder's about to burst."

"Sounds painful," said Du, unimpressed.

"You can let me pee, or I can pee on the floor. Your choice."

Du shook his head in disgust. "Hold it for a few minutes more, and I'll see what I can do."

The captain spoke aloud in Chinese into his comm, no doubt communicating with Ren in the driver's seat. After some back and forth, Du returned his attention to Connor. "Okay," he said, "the colonel is pulling over, out of sight of the road. I'll cut you loose from the jump seat, but your hands will still be bound. If you think you can pee out of the back of a van while I train a gun at your head, this is your chance."

Connor swallowed hard. Not exactly ideal conditions for urination. "Sounds fair," he said.

A short time later, Du cut the zip-ties that bound him to the chair, leaving the plastic chain joining his wrists intact, which still allowed him to spread his hands almost a foot apart.

Connor rose. "Thank you," he said, beginning to move toward the doors at the back of the van.

"Wait a minute!" said Connor excitedly. "My father just moved." He rushed over to Elias, still lying on his back, as Du studied his patient's face.

The moment Connor arrived behind his father, he threw his arms over his head and pressed his plastic shackles hard against his neck, drawing a thin line of blood, but not causing the comatose man to stir. "Drop the gun or I'll kill him!" he shouted at the captain. "Do it!"

Du shook his head. "You aren't going to kill your own father."

"Aren't I?" spat Connor. "I love my dad, but I have no other choice. I can't let you take him. So either let us both go, or kill us both."

"You're bluffing?"

"I'm not. More importantly, are you willing to take that chance?"

"Yes," said Du simply. "I am. Go ahead. Kill him. Kill your helpless father, knowing that I'll shoot you a second later."

Connor hesitated.

"Go on," repeated the captain. "Or you could wait a few minutes while I have the colonel come back here with his Veracity glasses. Then you can tell *him* just how serious you are about this. Let's see what Veracity thinks about your bluff."

Connor knew he had been beaten. He only had one choice now, and that was to follow through on his threat.

He tightened his arm muscles, preparing to choke the remaining life from his father as forcefully as he could.

* * *

Connor gasped, still bound to the jump seat, and his eyes shot open. He was no longer able to remain in the fantasy world he had been creating. Even while playing out a possible escape scenario only in his mind, he couldn't bring himself to really hurt his father. There was no way, no matter what was at stake. Even a bluff, which would fail, might aggravate his father's fragile condition.

Du studied him for a moment, but Connor ignored the Chinese captain and closed his eyes once again.

Until this brief outburst, Connor had remained silent in the back of the ambulance, not willing to test Du's threat to duct tape his mouth like a mummy. He had kept his eyes closed so he could think. And plan. And play out scenarios in his head.

He spent most of the time considering the best way to continue planting seeds of distrust among Ren and his ranks. But he had also pondered every wild idea under the sun, refusing to rule out anything right away, no matter how absurd.

But all of his ideas so far were suicidal. Or, like the one he had just played out in his mind, were bridges he wasn't prepared to ever cross, no matter what.

Still, he had to find a way. He had to channel some of the heroes from his favorite novels. These heroes were not without fear, nor did they have all the answers. What they were was smart, strategic, and resourceful. They kept their wits about them and searched for opportunity. They kept forging ahead, *despite* their fears. They were relentless in their search for a way out, even when the situation seemed utterly hopeless.

Connor would be no less relentless, no less opportunistic. He would find a way to make his own luck. He would keep his eyes and mind open.

He could give up once he was dead. But not a moment before.

44.

Paige sat on the edge of the bed in Dr. Rosado's guest room up-stairs and shook her head in disbelief. She must not have heard Kayla correctly. Escape wasn't even remotely possible. But her fellow pris-oner didn't appear to be joking, and if she were, it would be the worst joke ever.

Paige had come to like and admire this woman, which was almost as much of a surprise to her as anything else that had happened that day. "I love your spirit, Kayla," she said, "but we don't have a chance. There are two of us, and a *bunch* of them. They're trained and armed, and we aren't. And that's not even taking into account the locked door, armed guard, and the swarm of those slaughterbot things."

"I'm betting the colonel took the bot swarm with him," said Kayla. "After all, they've secured this area, so they don't need them. And they can't be worried about a couple of helpless women. We're fish in a barrel already as far as they're concerned."

"As far as *I'm* concerned, too," admitted Paige.

"We'll see about that."

"You heard the colonel," said Paige, "if we even *try* to escape, he'll take it out on Connor."

"That was a bluff," said Kayla. "They want me alive in case Elias . . . well, in case he doesn't make it. I have information they want. And they want you and Connor alive as leverage. Which means that even if our escape attempt fails, they won't touch any of us."

She paused. "Connor must think so too. He wants us to try, not even knowing what I have in mind, because he knows we're all screwed anyway if we don't."

"What do you mean?" said Paige. "When did Connor say that?"

Kayla explained how they had communicated by telling lies to each other that only their Veracity interfaces could pick up.

"So you're really serious about this?" said Paige.

"Never more."

"But I don't get it. You just told that guy that we wouldn't try to escape. And he was wearing mỳ Veracity glasses. How were you able to lie?"

The hint of a smile played across Kayla's face. "I never said I wouldn't try to escape. I said I wouldn't try to leave the room until they were all dead. Which is the truth." She shrugged. "So I guess it's time to make that happen."

"How?" said Paige simply.

"I have a few tricks up my sleeve. I told Connor earlier that my van cost twenty million dollars. There's a reason for that. I designed it so I could survive the apocalypse. I anticipated that if Veracity ever leaked before launch, a lot of bad people would be coming for Elias and me."

"Then how were you caught by surprise today?"

Kayla winced. "Fair question," she said. "Because I wasn't expecting any possible leaks until we were closer to launch. Which was stupid."

"So tell me about your van."

"It's armored and weighs nine tons, with a triple-layer battery stack that gives it great acceleration, despite its weight."

Paige nodded. "Connor was impressed with how powerful and quiet it was on the way here."

"It's also fully self-driving, and has hidden armaments. And I've bypassed the safety features on the self-driving AI."

"I thought that was impossible."

"With all due modesty, I'm not just the disgraced reincarnation of Satan. I'm one of the best programmers on the planet. And there's a lot you can do with unlimited time, money, and a really good imagination."

Paige paused in thought. "So you have the remote-controlled equivalent of a tank, more or less, parked just outside. Is that what you're telling me?"

"Yes. And while it doesn't have a weapon as powerful as the main gun of a real tank, it's faster, more maneuverable, and more lethal for close-in engagements."

"Interesting," said Paige. "But what good is a remote-controlled tank if you don't have the remote control?" Her eyes narrowed. "Unless you can control it with your phone."

"I can't. And my phone's not working anyway. They wouldn't have let me keep it if it was."

"So no matter how formidable your twenty-million-dollar doomsday device is, it might as well be a lump of clay."

Kayla shook her head. "Not at all," she said. "It may take a while, but I'll get the van awake and pointed in the right direction yet. Because they may have blocked cell phones, but they wanted to use Veracity themselves. So they didn't block signals at the frequency that Veracity uses. And it just so happens that my van is also set up to take instructions from the Veracity supercomputer."

"I see," said Paige appreciatively. "So Veracity can serve as your remote."

"Not right away, but yes. I'll need to do some fancy programming. But all I need is the proper privacy, and the proper time. And we have both. So let me tell you what I plan to do."

45

Kayla Keller sat on the bathroom floor of the guest room on six-by-eighteen-inch ceramic tiles, which were perfectly smooth. The door was closed behind her, and Paige was ready to warn her if any sudden visitors came calling. Kayla's legs were spread in front of her, leaving most of an eighteen-inch tile fully accessible to her hands.

She blinked in a pattern she had long practiced, giving an order to the Veracity supercomputer, and focused on the tile between her legs. As if by magic a perfect keyboard materialized there, its outer boundary and keys delineated by blue light, with red letters inside. Below the keys there appeared to be a large rectangular box, which she could use as a touchpad to control a cursor.

The keyboard and touchpad were virtual, of course, projected on her retina by her contacts in such a way as to maintain the illusion that they were on the floor between her legs, but the illusion was flawless. More importantly, she could type on the bathroom tile—which would still look to any observer to be nothing but tan ceramic—and the Veracity supercomputer would view her finger movements and know her intent, reading the letters as if they really existed.

Her blinks not only activated the virtual keyboard, but gave her access to all of the Veracity supercomputer's non-lie-detecting functionalities. And while her van wasn't as lethal as a swarm of slaughterbots, it could be turned into an exceptionally effective weapon.

Her fingers danced across the tile, typing instructions as quickly as she could manage given her awkward position. She could see what she had typed in one corner of her contact lenses, confirming that her virtual keystrokes were accurate.

Paige paced for twenty minutes outside the bathroom while Kayla worked, but the suspense was killing her. She decided she couldn't contain her curiosity any longer, despite the fact that Kayla had anticipated the process would take up to forty-five minutes to complete. Apparently, using the Veracity computer as a backdoor remote to control the van was possible, but it was only a third-level fail-safe option. It was one that Kayla had never expected to have to use, and as she had already indicated to Paige, would take some clever programming to implement.

Paige cracked the door ajar and stuck her head through the opening. "How's it going in there?" she whispered conspiratorially.

"A lot better than I thought it would," replied Kayla, also speaking in hushed tones. "I'm almost there. You know, even though I need you as a sentry, you have a right to be in on this. Why don't you keep the door half open. That way, you can see me and watch for unwanted guests at the same time."

"Perfect," said Paige under her breath. If anyone tried to enter the room, she could still shut the bathroom door before they could see what Kayla was up to. She could then buy Kayla time by explaining that her fellow prisoner was experiencing severe intestinal distress.

"I'm in!" whispered Kayla triumphantly four minutes later.

"And you're really seeing a keyboard down there?"

"Not anymore," replied Kayla excitedly. "Now I'm seeing a control panel. And in another field on my contacts, I can also see what the, ah . . . car sees," she explained. "Six distinct camera angles. So I basically have a three-sixty view around the van. I'm tapping into cameras that can see in both the visible and infrared spectrums."

"How good is the night vision?" asked Paige.

"More than good enough to identify targets," whispered Kayla. "I can use my virtual control panel to turn the van into my avatar, like in a video game. And I don't need perfect night vision. If it's human, and it isn't one of us," she added grimly, "it needs to be killed."

"Have you ever killed a man?"

Kayla blew out a long breath. "Not yet," she admitted uncomfortably. "But I *was* ready to kill Derek Manning," she added. "And I think I'm ready to kill now. I hope I am. It's been a very long day, and these men have every intention of killing us. Let's remember that you dodged having a hole drilled into your skull by a few inches."

"How could I forget?" replied Paige, swallowing hard. Kayla was right, of course. These men had just killed seven others in cold blood. They were ruthless and would stop at nothing.

Kayla closed her eyes as if to gather strength. "Okay," she said softly. "Enough chit-chat. I need to concentrate. Maybe it's good the van's infrared vision isn't perfect. This way, I can pretend they aren't really people. I can have an *Ender's Game* moment."

"Ender's Game?" repeated Paige, not familiar with the classic novel.

"What I mean is, I can convince myself that this isn't real. That I'm just playing a virtual video game, and the men are just pixelated targets. A game I'm calling *Dry Cleaning Van versus Chinese Special Forces*. If I pretend it's a game, it'll be easier to bring myself to do what I know I have to do."

Paige couldn't blame her. "I understand," she said.

"I've also tied the Veracity supercomputer into Homeland's system, so it can access every camera in the country. If we make it out of here alive, Veracity will start a facial recognition search for Elias and Connor. We probably won't find them right away, but I'm confident they'll appear on some camera before they leave the country. The Chinese won't expect anyone to be looking for them. We'll just have to be ready with a plan when we learn where they are."

"Then what are we waiting for?" whispered Paige, fighting to put on a brave face when she felt like trembling in fear. "Let's do this thing."

"Here we go," said Kayla, lowering both hands so they hovered just above the bathroom tile between her legs. "Don't try to talk to me until this is over," she added. "I can't let anything distract me."

"Understood," said Paige softly. "And Godspeed."

46

The major and captain completed their search of Dr. Rosado's examination room and headed to the main residence. Major Yan had found a locked briefcase hidden under gauze bandages in a large cabinet in the examination room. He intended to bring it to their base of operations as soon as possible, so experts could determine the best approach to getting it open.

Once inside the house, Yan took the front half of the first floor and assigned the back half to Long, and each began searching rooms inch by inch for anything else that Elias and his companions might have hidden.

Just outside the residence, Lieutenant Sun Shui was passing a looming oak tree, magnificent, even when only illuminated by a military flashlight. His tight route took him by three of the mammoth trees, not straying from the main residence. His two fellow lieutenants were patrolling far more territory, but both were staying in view of the road that connected Rosado's residence to the outside world.

Sun Shui's job was to stay close, keeping an eye on the inner perimeter of the property and the second-floor guest room both, to be certain the two female prisoners didn't try to escape from the window, as improbable as that might be.

Jalen Howard's black-ops borrowed helicopter sat silently, fifteen yards behind the lieutenant. Its sleek, science-fictional appearance advertised that it was a prototype the Americans had just perfected at Area 51, one that Colonel Ren had been briefed on almost two months earlier. It contained a noise-canceling system superior to anything that China had developed, but it was also carefully rigged to explode if anyone tried to learn its secrets without proper authorization.

Colonel Ren had ordered that it be left alone, but only with the greatest reluctance. He was tempted to spend the time it would take to bypass the aircraft's security features to learn what made it tick, but this wasn't their primary mission.

Lieutenant Sun turned toward the enormous aircraft once again, admiring its graceful, futuristic design.

Pop! Pop!

Sun heard two loud clicks in quick succession behind him and came to full attention. It sounded like a door lock being popped open, and then closing again, as if someone had hit a remote twice in quick succession.

He wheeled back around and tried to identify what might have caused it.

Pop! Pop!

This time he saw two flashes of light in the distance, timed precisely to the sounds.

He moved in the direction in which he had seen the brief illumination and shined his own, high-intensity flashlight in front of him. Off in the distance, near the doctor's separate office to the south of the grounds, Sun could now make out a large van. He hurried closer, his eyes trained on the vehicle, which he now remembered had been parked outside earlier. It was the dry cleaning van that had carried Elias Gibson to this site.

It hadn't moved in hours.

Pop! Pop!

The door locks on the van opened and closed, and the lights inside flickered on and off as if the vehicle were possessed. Lieutenant Sun quickly checked the second-story window he was supposed to be monitoring and continued to approach the van, wanting to determine the nature of the glitch. Captain Long was an unparalleled computer genius, but perhaps the way he had blocked signals in the area had resulted in some kind of weird feedback loop that was now affecting the van.

"Captain Long," he said into his comm, "can you confirm that all electromagnetic signals are still being jammed?"

There was a brief pause. "Confirmed," said Long. "The only bands working, beyond the outer limits of the estate, are *our* encrypted cell frequencies, and the Veracity frequency. Why do you ask?"

"Their van is experiencing some sort of electrical glitch. I thought it might be signal related. I'll check it out now."

"Understood," said Long. "Let me know what you find."

"I'm fairly close to your position, Lieutenant," said the voice of Lieutenant Tang An in Sun's ear. Tang was the team's automotive expert, and was now at the southernmost end of his route, only twenty-five yards farther away from the van than Sun. "I'll join you."

"Please do," said Sun amicably, aware that Tang was itching for a diversion as much as he was, and that investigating a phantom car fit the bill nicely.

Sun and his comrades were decorated commandos, and as such, this make-work patrol was an exercise in boredom. In the unlikely event that someone did breach their perimeter, it would probably be an elderly friend of the doctor, inching his way to the door with a walker.

As Sun approached to within twenty feet of the van, its engine purred to life, and Sun was impressed by how quiet it ran, even for an all-electric vehicle. A step later and the van's lights blinked on, obviating the need for his flashlight, and he could see there was no one inside, at least in the driver's compartment. It must be a self-driving car that had short-circuited somehow, and was now malfunctioning.

The van suddenly bolted forward as if it had been shot from a cannon, with the zero-to-sixty acceleration of a sports car, flying across the grass and closing the short distance to Sun in seconds. Sun reacted with remarkable speed, but the van ate up ground far too quickly for him to escape and tore into him at over forty miles per hour.

The lieutenant flew through the air and landed in a heap on the grass. The possessed van slammed on its brakes, quickly changed course, and ran over the broken soldier, just to be sure, killing him instantly with many times the weight of a standard car, crushing him into the soft ground.

The van accelerated again, this time going after Tang, who had also been approaching, hitting him at high speed and slamming him into a tree trunk. He was dead before he hit the ground, but the phantom van, like something out of a bad horror film, took a few seconds to grind him into the dirt, practically burying him in grass and roots.

The vehicle then drove to an area away from the bodies and began honking loudly, over and over and over again, advertising its presence, the sound blaring into the night.

Gao Lin, the third of the patrolling lieutenants, sprinted toward the sound, but stopped abruptly as his light illuminated the horribly broken body of what had once been Sun Shui. There could be no doubt how Sun was killed. The van, which continued to pierce the night with its shrieking horn, had crushed him. The force had been so great that Sun looked like a grape that had been smashed by a hammer.

Gao found refuge behind a tree so the van couldn't hit him and began firing toward the vehicle with his assault rifle, set on fully automatic.

His shots seemed unable to pierce what should have been the vehicle's flimsy shell. Instead, a turret rose up slowly from the top of the van and began firing machine gun rounds of its own, but a higher caliber than Gao was using, cutting him to ribbons, despite the protection of the trunk, which itself was almost cut in half by the savage barrage.

The honking and machine gun fire had surely been heard by the three soldiers still inside the residence. So the moment it became clear that Gao was down, the van picked up speed and raced toward the front door, bursting through it like it was cardboard and driving deep into the living room, where its monster brakes stopped it cold.

The driver's window slid down of its own accord, and a drone the size of a football exited the vehicle, its eight spinning propellers carrying the weight of two attached guns. The tiny aircraft darted up the stairs, looking for all the world like a mini version of the hunter-killer drones from various *Terminator* movies.

Lieutenant Quan, who had been guarding the door to the guest room, had long since bolted to attention after hearing the machine gun fire and the thunder the van had created as it had plowed through the front of the house. As the drone rounded the corner of the hallway, he was ready for anything, and managed to shoot it down, but he was also cut to ribbons in the process.

Major Yan had seen the drone ascend the stairs and followed behind it, crouching low. "Captain Long," he said into his comm as he moved, "I've made the colonel aware that we're under attack, and that Kayla must somehow be responsible. He's given the okay to kill her. I'm going in now."

"Wait for me," said Long.

"No time," came the curt reply.

Yan reached the top of the stairs and rushed to the guest room, but when he rounded the corner a crashed drone, sitting on the floor against the far hallway wall, opened fire, unable to maneuver but still lethal. He dived to the floor and came up firing, putting the wounded drone fully out of commission.

Yan barreled past his fallen comrade and into the guest room, his gun drawn and a fierce expression on his face.

"I'm going to kill you, you goddamned bitch!" he barked in Mandarin. "Where are you?"

He took a quick look under the bed, but after not seeing either of the two women, he came up firing at the closed bathroom door, the only other place they could be. He started high and was working his way down to chest level, turning the door into Swiss cheese in the process, when a bullet entered his head from behind, and he dropped to the ground, dead.

Captain Long Lan lowered his gun from behind the major and blew out a long breath.

"You're safe now!" he shouted at the two prisoners. "Everyone is down except me. And I'm on *your* side."

47

Long crashed through the bathroom door to find both women on the floor, uninjured, with Kayla frantically moving her fingers on a ceramic tile below her like it was a piano.

"I'm on your side!" he repeated hastily. "Look at me so Veracity can confirm it."

He waited until Kayla's eyes were on his face and then repeated this mantra. "I'm on your side. I mean you no harm."

Kayla turned her eyes back to the floor and slammed her hand down on the corner of a tile, just as a second hunter-killer drone entered the guest room behind Long. He wheeled around to shoot, but it was settling down to the floor, its weapons silent.

"That was close," said Kayla. "If I had waited another few seconds to abort, you'd be dead right now."

"If I hadn't shot the major, *you'd* be dead," countered Long.

Kayla smiled wearily. "I guess we're even then."

Paige's eyes widened. "*You're* the one who saved my life, aren't you?" she said to the captain. "The one who pushed that guy's arm so he missed me?"

Long nodded. "That's right."

"*Thank you*," said Paige.

"You're welcome," replied the captain. He turned to Kayla. "I guess we're not even, after all," he added with just the hint of a smile.

"I guess not."

"How did you *do* this?" he asked, helping the two women up off the floor.

"I'll tell you later," said Kayla. "Let's get out of here. We'll take my van."

Long was taken aback. "It just crashed through a house. Do you really think it's still drivable?"

"Oh yeah," said Kayla with a grin. "It was built to take a licking. And it's immune from surveillance."

"Why are you helping us?" Paige asked the Chinese soldier.

"I'm defecting," said Long. "I'll tell you more when I can."

"Veracity says you're telling the truth," replied Kayla. "Welcome to our side. Did you find Elias's briefcase?"

"We did. Yan left it in the examination room. Let's get it. We can collect a few assault rifles as well. I also want to retrieve a large rucksack we brought with us, filled with prototype electronics and weaponry. Then we need to get out of here."

As they passed Yan Ling, the captain took the time to recover the fallen major's glasses, which were still intact, although spattered with blood. He removed a cloth from his pocket, tried to wipe them clean, and then extended them toward Paige. "I want you to be able to trust me," he said.

Paige made a face, but still slid them on, not thrilled to wear glasses that had last been worn by a corpse, and which still had blood residue on the frames.

Long then removed a cell phone from Yan's pocket, also handing this to Paige.

"You guys use Apple phones?" she said in disbelief.

"Heavily modified ones. We've been operating in the States for weeks," he explained, "and we need to blend in. We use English in public and pose as US citizens, using US phones. But these are untraceable and unhackable."

Long took one last look at the major, surveyed the hellhole that had once been a good man's home, and shook his head unhappily. "It's very unfortunate that you did this," he said to Kayla.

"Sorry to disappoint you."

"I was going to kill all of my comrades and free you. But now you've made things more difficult."

"What's the difference?" said Kayla. "We appreciate the thought, but it turns out we didn't need a knight to rescue us from the castle, after all."

"Yes you did," said Long. "Because before I killed the major, he reported your attack to Colonel Ren. My way would have been clean and surgical, starting with the major. Once I took him out, I'd command each lieutenant in turn to meet with me inside for more orders. I'd pick them off one at a time before anyone could sound an alarm. I planned to wait until just after Yan's routine report to Colonel Ren, leaving three hours until the next one. This would give us three hours to operate without Ren knowing anything was wrong here. Three hours to catch up to him and mount a surprise attack."

Long shook his head in frustration. "Even if we weren't ready in three hours, when Yan didn't check in as scheduled, the colonel wouldn't have any idea what had happened. He'd have to investigate, thinning him out. But now, his guard will be way up."

The trio was now crossing the yard, heading into the doctor's detached clinic. Paige made it a point not to look too carefully at her surroundings, not interested in seeing any more death.

"Yeah," said Kayla, unapologetically, "well forgive me for not reading your mind. Next time slip me a Veracity-approved note that you're on our side."

"I'm not blaming you," said Long. "You did what you thought you had to do. And brilliantly. It's just unfortunate. Colonel Ren can activate dozens of in-country agents at a moment's notice, and he will now. For a mission this important, given the attack here, he'll have an *army* protecting Elias until he's recovered enough to risk moving out of the country. Freeing him and Connor will now be all but impossible. "

"We'll just have to cross that bridge when we come to it," said Kayla as they entered the examination room.

Yan had left Elias's briefcase on the nearer of the two examination tables, and Kayla picked it up, inspecting it to be sure it hadn't been opened. She put it back inside the large blue duffel bag they had left beside the couch, which had been searched through but was otherwise undisturbed.

"Come on," said Long. "That collection of prototypes I mentioned is on the backseat of one of the sedans we came in. Kayla, why don't you go back to the main house and drive your van out of the rubble. I'll get the rucksack and be back in a few minutes."

Paige pulled the van's key fob from her pocket and handed it to Kayla—not that she required it to operate the van, as she had shown.

Kayla turned to Long with a worried expression on her face. "Where are the two men that your colonel executed?" she asked.

"We cleaned the room and put their bodies in the trunk of a car. The same car I'll be visiting to retrieve the prototypes. We planned to dispose of them as soon as possible."

"You didn't remove anything from their pockets, did you?" asked Kayla.

Long shook his head no.

"Then we're going with you," she said, speaking for Paige as well as herself. "We have some prototypes of our own to collect. Prototype facial recognition blockers that Jalen Howard brought with him, and still had in his pocket when your colonel killed him."

"Then what are we waiting for?" said Captain Long Lan, gesturing toward the door. "We've already overstayed our welcome here."

48

The dry cleaning van hurtled along the highway like a guided missile. This wouldn't have been too troubling to Paige Estrella Gibson, except that the vehicle was driving *itself* while the human passengers all congregated in the back.

And it was driving without any lights.

Kayla assured them it was best for the van to become invisible in the dark night, and that the technology was up to it. In normal times, Paige would have insisted they use the headlights anyway. But compared to what she had already been through, counting on an AI to use night-vision technology to navigate in pitch-dark conditions at a hundred miles per hour was the least of her worries. And at least Kayla had lighted the compartment they were in, confident that none of the light would be visible to the outside.

Their destination was the Cloud Rock Motel, just up the base of the San Gabriel Mountains, less than an hour east of LA, and even closer to Arcadia, one of the most affluent zip-codes in America.

This motel would serve as their temporary base of operations. Twenty minutes farther east of the Cloud Rock was the Chinese team's current base of operations in the States, a seventy-acre goat ranch. Colonel Ren was even now heading there with Elias and Connor.

The Cloud Rock Motel would put the two Americans and the Chinese captain close enough to the Chinese stronghold to allow them to react quickly if Elias recovered and Ren decided to move him and his son. They could venture from their motel rooms to monitor Ren's activities, and perform recon missions, and the rooms could serve as staging areas if they ever did come up with a plan of action.

The purchase of the goat ranch a year earlier by Chinese nationals hadn't raised any eyebrows in the area, despite the property's stratospheric price tag. Chinese citizens buying up real estate in and around LA, and many other major cities, had become commonplace for some time now. The Chinese had been the top foreign purchasers of real estate in the US for more than a decade, buying up tens of thousands of homes each year, mostly in all-cash transactions totaling over thirty billion dollars annually.

The vast majority of these purchasers were legitimate Chinese citizens working and living in America, but a significant subset were working for the Chinese state, sent in for spying and other state-mandated purposes. Some were active agents, and some were sleepers. Some were actively engaged in stealing technology and intellectual property, and some were funneling tech back to the homeland in more subtle ways, as students at America's top universities, or employees in technology start-ups.

China had more agents placed in the US than almost all other countries combined. Not entirely surprising given China's burgeoning wealth, and a population four times that of America, and more than *ten* times that of other rivals of the United States, such as Russia.

Once Kayla was satisfied that the AI was working properly and would deliver them to the motel, she stared deeply into the captain's eyes. "So why are you helping us?" she asked. "And what's your end game?"

"I'm helping you because my goals and those of my team are in conflict. They want China to have Veracity and America *not* to have it."

"And what do you want?" asked Kayla.

"I want the opposite. I want to keep it out of China's hands at all cost."

"Even if this means killing every member of your team?" said Paige.

Long looked solemn. "Yes," he replied, his stoic façade melting for just a moment to reveal a surprising depth of despair. "Even though these men have become like brothers to me, I can't see any other alternative."

"Wouldn't that make you the ultimate traitor to your country?" said Paige.

"Yes. But that can't be helped. I can't let this technology fall into China's hands. This mission was ordered by Pan Shen himself."

"And he's the current president of China, right?" said Paige, not all that decisively.

"Right. Also the head of the military, and the head of the communist party. We call him our Paramount Leader. And while he seems benign on your television screens, he's a dictator, the absolute ruler of my country. The important point is that he assigned us this mission, and insisted that we not inform anyone else, including members of the Politburo. Connor was right. He doesn't intend to use Veracity so the people will know the truth. He wants to use it to consolidate his power further, and tighten his iron grip on Chinese society and the Chinese citizenry. As Connor put it, to press his jackboot even harder on innocent necks."

"But wouldn't you, personally, stand to gain from successful completion of the mission?" said Paige. "If you get in the good graces of the king, you can name your reward, right?"

"Maybe. But dictators can be fickle, and they have short memories. One can go from hero of China to enemy of the state in an instant. From naming rewards to hoping for a last meal before being executed."

"So you'd rather betray your country than be on a fickle leader's radar screen?" said Paige.

"No!" said Long adamantly. "That's not it at all. I just mentioned this to give you a better appreciation of the reality. Even if I was sure that President Pan would cater to my every whim, there comes a time when a man has to draw the line. China is one of the most oppressive and controlling regimes in the world. You may not realize just *how* oppressive, since most Americans are unaware of this. You believe Russia to be your most dangerous adversary, while my country, which is many times the threat that Russia is, largely flies under the radar. That's because Russia, Iran, North Korea, and the rest are showy and full of bluster, with leaders who feel the need to beat their chests. Whereas our leaders are more insidious. Calm, quiet, patient, and calculating. And to most, outwardly harmless. Noble even. But this hides an utter ruthlessness, and an indomitable will to spread China's might throughout the world."

Kayla nodded. "I come from the tech world, and your leaders aren't shy about expressing their plans to exert their power as much through technology as through the military."

"Very true," said Long. "China's leaders are spending incomprehensible amounts of money, and unleashing massive manpower, to become dominant in future technologies. Especially supercomputers and artificial intelligence." Long smiled wistfully. "I'm our strike team's computer expert, considered one of the best in my country. Not up to your standards, I'm sure," he said to Kayla, "but quite accomplished in my own right."

"Is that why your English is so perfect?" said Paige. "Do you read a lot of American journals to keep up with advances here?"

"I do," said Long. "But that's only part of it. Extreme proficiency in English is a requirement for our team. Anyway," he added, "to finish my point, I'm enough of a computer expert to say with conviction that it's only a matter of time before China surges ahead of the US when it comes to computers and AI."

Long sighed. "But what I've described isn't the worst of it," he continued. "What caused me to finally turn my back on my country wasn't the government's planned conquest of the world. It was their mistreatment of our populace. It's sickening to see what's happening to the hardworking people of China. Yes, the country's affluence is on the rise, but at what cost? I've read the book *1984*. While I was in the States," he added as an aside, "since the book is outlawed in China. And this is what we're becoming. A surveillance state, eliminating privacy and free will, spying on our own people."

Long paused and looked at Paige. "Any idea of how many surveillance cameras there are in my country?" he asked her.

She shrugged. Given the course the conversation had taken, she knew it had to be a huge number. "Ten million."

"*Five hundred* million," said Long. "And growing."

Paige's eyes widened. "You're right," she said. "That does have the makings of Big Brother come to life. I had no idea it was this bad.

I was aware that China had issues, but I thought they were getting more democratic all the time."

Kayla shook her head. "I didn't," she said. "I was falsely accused of selling secrets to your country, so I came to learn a lot of what you're saying. The Chinese have long been famous for ignoring patents, and for stealing technology and secrets from the West. Your country has the lowest level of Internet freedom in the world. Your government's ideological control over education has become all but absolute. Human rights abuses are rampant, and religious freedom highly constrained. China is much worse than most countries when it comes to discrimination against girls and women. And women also have it much worse there when it comes to harassment, sexual abuse, and domestic violence."

"All of this is true," said Long miserably, "and more. Freedom of the press is basically nonexistent. And Chinese authorities continue to use black jails—off-the-books detention facilities—to suppress rights activists, members of the press, and other enemies of the state, who are imprisoned without a trial."

Paige frowned deeply. She was coming to appreciate just how easy it was for large swaths of humanity to be led astray. The world was far better off than it had ever been, yet everyone thought it had never been worse. And the opposite was true of China. This country was more dangerous than ever, and more oppressive to its people, while she and many of her fellow citizens considered it harmless—despite the warnings of a handful of American talking heads. China was like the Giant Panda the country had made famous, seemingly gentle and unthreatening—until you ventured too close to its powerful claws and teeth.

"So yes," continued Long, "I decided I couldn't turn a blind eye to the oppression in my country any longer. This mission is what you might call the straw that broke the camel's back. Because Veracity would be the final nail in the coffin. If President Pan can purge the Politburo and exert even greater control—and have a technology that can tell him whenever someone lies—the fate of my people will be sealed. The most ruthless leaders will rise to the top and join Pan there, even more so than has already happened. Instead of reforms that would increase freedom, the regime will become even more oppressive. All hope will be lost. Underground dissent will be snuffed out, and citizens will have no privacy at all, not even privacy of thought."

Paige curled up her lip in disgust. Her Veracity glasses had registered every word Long had spoken as the truth, or at least what he sincerely believed to be the truth. He had truly painted a horrific picture.

"And President Pan will use Veracity to gain an overwhelming advantage in international relations," added the captain. "In negotiations, diplomacy, and the use of intimidation tactics. The technology will be huge in advancing his global ambitions. The oppression of the Chinese people will only be the beginning."

He paused while the unlit dry cleaning van continued to hurtle through the darkness.

"So I'm not betraying my country," he continued, "I'm betraying my president. There's a big difference. And while the last thing I want is to have to kill members of my own team, brothers-in-arms who I've come to admire, there is no other way. I tried to feel many of them out—very subtly—in private, to see if anyone might be on the same page as me. But they've all succumbed to the State's brainwashing."

"Why are *you* immune?" asked Kayla.

"I'm not. I was a loyal drone for more than a decade. Even after seeing atrocities committed by a smiling and seemingly benevolent Politburo that would turn the stomachs of even the most jaded man. But my missions in this country and around the world have given me a new perspective. I've read many books that have made me think in different ways. Which has caused me to be more aware of how the Chinese state has mistreated my family, and other people I love. I only wish my colleagues had experienced the same awakening."

"The most important thing is that *you* did," said Paige, not forgetting that she would be long dead right now if not for Long's intervention. "And we've had a bit of an awakening ourselves," she added. "The American vice president, Bradley Holloway, is just as much a monster as your Pan Shen. We've recently learned he's trying to kill Elias and stop Veracity from being born."

"What?"

"Long story," said Paige. "The point is that it's not all unicorns and butterflies in our country right now, either. Even if we prevail against your comrades, we aren't nearly out of the woods."

"Paige is right," said Kayla, "but let's fight one fire at a time. So ignore this for the moment," she instructed Long, "and tell me your plan, in its entirety?"

"I can tell you what my plan *was*," said Long. "It will have to be modified now. I *had* planned to kill every man on our core strike team, retrieving Elias and Connor Gibson in the process. I then planned to report back to President Pan that the mission went south. That everyone was killed, except me. Including you and Elias. And also that this happened before we were able to get the secrets to Veracity, or the location of your supercomputer."

"So Pan would think the mission was a failure and move on," said Kayla.

"He'd think it was a failure, but he would never just move on. After I reported our setback, I was counting on him to let me stay in-country to salvage the mission. To let me command a team, which I would then lead on a wild goose chase, making sure he never got Veracity."

"*Command* a team?" said Paige. "He wouldn't bring in someone over you?"

"No. I'm overdue for a promotion anyway, and I have the most knowledge of the situation. I'm confident that Pan would put me in charge. Not only because of my work on the ground here, but also because of my computer skills. He almost chose me to lead the current team, but decided he couldn't ignore the impressive track records of Colonel Ren and Major Yan."

Kayla nodded. "And after your report, he'd see how well *that* decision turned out."

"Exactly," said Long. "After I reported on our failure, I was confident he'd put me in charge. I could then become a double agent, working for America. I could provide your government with extensive intelligence on China. My value to your country would be immense, because they wouldn't have to worry that I'm a triple agent and hold back. Veracity would confirm my trustworthiness."

"Speaking of Veracity," said Paige, "even if your plan worked perfectly, even if you denied your president the technology, he'd get it soon enough. You couldn't expect Elias to wait for more than a year, maximum, to launch the technology here, after which Pan would have access. And then your cover would be blown, since he'd learn that Elias wasn't dead like you reported, and that the tech wasn't really buried, either."

"True, Pan Shen would *eventually* be able to access Veracity. But everything would have changed by then. He wanted to have the tech all to himself. And for America and the world *not* to have it. Not to even know about it. But my intent is to ensure that the world's leading democracy has it first. Upon its release, the technology will be a seismic event felt around the world. There will be no hiding it from the Chinese people, regardless of Internet censorship. So they'll be on their guard, outraged if they learn it is being used against them by their government. And the tech will become so widely available, Pan won't be able to keep other members of the Politburo, and even some of the citizenry, from using it. Which will change the dynamic dramatically. I'm unsure of how it will play out. But if it's released worldwide, I believe it will help *destabilize* the regime rather than cement its hold on power."

"Let's just hope you're right," said Paige.

"It's unlikely we'll get to find out," said Long. "After your attack, surprise is off the table. Colonel Ren will soon have Elias and Connor in his stronghold, and is fully on guard. It seems more likely than ever that this will play out exactly as President Pan had hoped, and that there's nothing we'll be able to do about it."

He shook his head. "And what you told me about Bradley Holloway makes the situation even *worse*. Because even if we manage to extract Elias and salvage my plan, we don't know who we can trust in *your* government."

"If we can stop your comrades," said Kayla, "I have no doubt we can stop Bradley Holloway."

"Speaking of stopping your comrades," Paige said to the captain, "you must have some ideas for turning this around."

"Not any good ones," said Long. "But we're all exhausted and not thinking clearly. We won't make it to the motel for another few hours. I say we sleep back here until then, refresh our minds. They won't move Elias from their base while he's in a coma, so we have some time."

Paige considered. "Why not just pretend to be injured and join your colleagues at the base as soon as you can?" she said. "You could tell your colonel a story about how you were the only survivor. How you tried to hunt us down, but finally lost us. You could do a lot of damage from the inside."

"This is the first thing I considered," said Long. "The problem is, Colonel Ren is no fool. If I'm the only survivor, he's bound to suspect that I was in on your escape."

"Let him suspect," said Paige.

Long shook his head. "You're forgetting that he's wearing a Veracity interface. Deception is a lot harder when lying isn't possible. I'm afraid this wouldn't work."

"Crap!" said Paige.

"It's a challenging problem," said Long. "So like I said, let's get some rest and tackle it when we're fresher."

"Before we do," said Paige, wincing, "and I hate to bring this up— but I could really use a bathroom. Can we find a gas station or diner that's open all night?"

Kayla manipulated her cell phone for almost a minute. "There's a 24/7 gas station six miles from here," she announced finally. "I'll redirect the van."

"Thank you," said Paige.

"Sure," said Kayla. "But let me get this right. You don't thank me for our bold escape, but you thank me for taking you to a *bathroom*?"

Paige grinned. "It's important to have priorities in life," she replied.

49

Captain Long handed Paige two twenty-dollar bills as she was exiting the van. "While you're in there, can you pick up a supply of food and water? We can't be sure when we'll have another chance."

"Of course," said Paige, taking the offered money.

The moment Paige exited the back of the van, Kayla sealed them back inside and turned to the captain. "Be realistic," she said. "What are the odds that we can defeat your colonel and retrieve Elias and Connor?"

"Very poor."

"What about your bag of prototype technology goodies?"

"There are some potentially useful gadgets, but most are for close-in conflicts, rather than for use while storming a stronghold. There are a few that might be useful, but they'd hardly be decisive. I'll walk you through them later. But there's nothing that comes close to the swarm of micro-drones the colonel has on hand."

"If they do take Elias and Connor to China," said Kayla, "would I be right in assuming that Pan Shen will kill them the moment he gets what he wants?"

"You are," said the captain.

Kayla blew out a long breath. "I think I might be in love with Elias Gibson," she said. "Which makes what I'm about to say even harder than it would otherwise be."

Long stared at her with great interest.

"If you aren't able to come up with a plan that gives us even a long-shot hope of killing your comrades and rescuing Elias and Connor, I think we're forced to consider an ugly alternative. If you're sure we're going to fail, what's the point? We'll only get ourselves killed. You'll get *yourself* killed, a man sure to be extremely valuable to American intelligence. And Elias and Connor will still end up in

China, and your country will still get the technology first. I know Elias. He'd rather die than see that happen."

"Are you saying what I think you're saying?"

A tear came to Kayla's eye. "I wish I wasn't," she whispered. "But it has to be considered."

"Which is why you waited until Paige was gone to bring it up."

Kayla nodded miserably. "If we can't find a way to free Elias, the only other option we have is to make sure that China can't use him. I assume our chances of defeating your people go way up if we're . . ." She paused for several long seconds, unable to bring herself to complete the thought. "Well, if we're willing to sacrifice Elias and Connor in the process," she finished finally.

"Yes. Way up."

Kayla took a deep breath. "If this were to happen," she said, looking sick to her stomach, "America would no longer have the man whose genius created Veracity—but neither would China. And we would still have Elias's briefcase, which would allow us to replicate the current system as many times as we wanted."

"And I could still carry out my plan," said Long. "I was going to report Elias dead, anyway. So I could still lead a new team on a wild goose chase."

Kayla wiped a tear from the corner of her eye. "This is *unthinkable*," she whispered. "Horrible beyond words." She shook her head. "But we may have no other choice."

"I agree," said Long.

"Not a specter we want to raise with Paige right now," said Kayla. "But I'm sure Connor and Elias would prefer a quick death to a few months of life as prisoners in China, where Elias will be forced to provide a tool that will cause the further oppression of over a billion people. But it's taking all of my powers of reason to even consider an idea this horrible. And I can't imagine Paige ever agreeing to give up on her husband and father-in-law. No matter what the stakes, or the odds. Even if she knew that this is what they would want."

"I understand."

"I'm counting on you to make sure this isn't necessary, Captain Long. But I'm also a realist. If we could rely on our own government right now, things would be different. Losing Jalen Howard was a major blow. I'll eventually be able to use Veracity to find others in the government we can trust, but not in the time frame we need."

"I'll do my best to come up with a plan that can save them," said Long. "But I'll also draw up a scorched-earth scenario, just in case this proves necessary."

"God help us all," said Kayla.

50

Kayla paid for two separate but adjoining rooms at the one-story motel and parked the van out of sight. It was approaching three in the morning, and the sky had become even darker as more cloud cover rolled in. The trio had all managed to get a good ninety minutes of sleep on the way there.

They congregated in the room that Kayla and Paige would share, with two queen-sized beds, a room that was larger and nicer than they had expected for a three-star motel.

They settled in and Paige began applying new dressings to Kayla's wounds, which were healing nicely. The nano-mesh spray, which had only come on the scene in 2022, was a godsend.

"My guess is that Colonel Ren is only just arriving at the goat ranch about now," said Long. "It's twenty minutes farther away than we are, and I'm sure he kept his speed down on the way there. He likes to maintain a low profile. Since we were able to accomplish this by driving without lights, we could speed here almost twice as fast."

"Yeah, let's not do that again," said Paige wryly.

"I sent a drone out to the ranch while you two were checking in," continued the captain. "It has night-vision capabilities, but this does limit its surveillance range. And I'll have to keep it farther away than I'd like to avoid detection."

"So what good is it?" said Kayla bluntly.

"I won't be able to see any individuals, but I'll be able to tell if they're moving out. Which will only happen if they're ready to transport Elias and Connor to China. Even if Elias were to come out of his coma this morning, I can't imagine they wouldn't lie low for at least another night. They'll need to plan, make sure they don't run into an ambush, and let him recover his strength before taking this step. But if I'm wrong, the drone footage will alert me."

He paused. "Even so, the faster we make our move the better. They'll get more entrenched with every passing minute. "

"Don't suppose you've had any epiphanies lately as to how to free Connor and Elias," said Paige.

"I'm working on it," said Long. "I'm trained to be able to go for extended periods on little sleep, and what I just had will hold me for a while. So why don't you two sleep until daylight. You're going to need to be at your best, and there's nothing more you can do right now, anyway."

"What will *you* be doing?" asked Paige. "Planning?"

"Yes, but also driving to LA. It's only an hour away, and there are a number of Chinese agents there. I have a no-questions-asked level of authority, so I'm sure I can get access to some powerful weapons. From experimental high-yield explosives to ground-to-air missiles."

"But it sounds as if you don't think that even these weapons will be enough," said Paige.

"No. But they'll be a good start. We all have cell phones now, so let's trade contact info. That way, you can reach me if anything comes up. I hope to be back in about five hours. Two hours round trip, and three hours rounding up what I need."

After he had entered their cell numbers, he sent a text to each woman in turn as a test. *Get some sleep,* he texted to Paige, *and I'll be back before you miss me.*

She nodded. "Got it."

His text message to Kayla was of a different order entirely. *I'll get enough explosives to turn that ranch into a crater*, he wrote. *Just in case.*

"Message received," said Kayla grimly.

"And you're *positive* calls and texts can't be intercepted?" Paige said to the captain.

"Positive. Kayla has described her phone's safeguards to me, and they're state of the art. So are the ones for the phones our team was issued. Not even Colonel Ren can use them to find us, as long as I don't actually establish a phone connection with him. He called me once after we escaped, but of course I didn't answer."

"So he thinks you died along with the rest," said Paige, "and can't track you."

"That's right."

"Thank you for everything you're doing, Captain," said Kayla, handing him the key fob for the van. "Good luck," she added. "I'd tell you to drive safely, but there's no need. If anything short of a semi hits you, it'll bounce right off."

"Very comforting," said Long with just the hint of a smile.

51

Colonel Ren arrived at his destination and threw open the back of the ambulance, which was still illuminated. He entered the vehicle and passed Du Song and Elias Gibson on his way to Connor, whom he cut loose.

"What is this place?" asked Connor, now awake after having fallen asleep in the ambulance a second time.

"Do you really think I'm going to answer?"

"Why not? Who will I tell? Or are you worried I'll escape?"

Ren snorted. "Not in this lifetime."

"Then I ask again, what is this place?"

"Okay," said Ren. "Why not? It used to be a goat farm. Seventy acres in total. But for years now it's been a base for Chinese operatives on the West Coast. We store weapons and spy technology here. We also operate advanced computer centers for hacking operations, in-country intelligence gathering, and even the creation of fake electronic identification and Internet footprints. It's also a refuge our people can use to plan operations, or to stay at between assignments."

Connor shook his head in disbelief. How could a place like this exist in the heart of America? And many more than one, since this was just the West Coast location. "So what are you telling me," he said, "that this is like your own personal Camp David?"

"If Camp David had goats," said Ren wryly.

"I thought you said it *used to be* a goat farm."

"We have a token herd on the grounds. For appearances' sake. And a large goat-milking building. We import goat milk and goat cheese, and pretend that we produced it."

The colonel gestured for Connor to exit the ambulance while four Chinese men, dressed in plain clothing but no doubt soldiers, emerged from the darkness to help the doctor usher Elias's gurney from the van.

"Where are they taking him?" said Connor.

"We have a comprehensive medical facility here. We'll do CT scans, blood work, and so on. Elias couldn't be in better hands."

Connor didn't find this reassuring, coming as it did from a man who had gunned down Jalen Howard and Hector Rosado in cold blood. But he had no doubt the Chinese would spare no effort to revive his father.

The men began to wheel Elias away, lighting the route ahead with a single flashlight beam. The night was darker than ever, and none of the many structures were illuminated. They may have been lighted on the inside, but if they were, they were windowless, and no light was escaping.

Still, the base was such a beehive of activity that Connor was able to get a snapshot sense of his surroundings. Vehicles were arriving and leaving, and at least a dozen flashlight beams moved through the night, seemingly of their own accord. The beams were widely spread out around the base's enormous perimeter, and were no doubt held by men patrolling the grounds, invisible in the darkness.

Ren produced a flashlight of his own and marched Connor away from the disguised ambulance, not bothering with a blindfold. For good reason. Despite the buzz of activity and flashlights all around, most of the facility was shrouded in total darkness. Even if it weren't, Ren had already shown he wasn't worried about his prisoner escaping and reporting the facility to American intelligence.

Connor guessed that the base was kept as dark as possible at night out of an excess of caution. If it looked like Broadway every night to American satellites, rather than a goat farm, it could well arouse suspicion.

Judging from the patrollers' flashlights, trees surrounded the far outer perimeter, with the farm carved out from a surrounding woods, much like Dr. Rosado's hideaway had been, but on a much larger scale. Connor continued to get the sense of a frenzy of activity, as if someone had kicked a hornets' nest, or perhaps a more apt metaphor given the eerie blackness, had stirred up a cave full of bats.

Connor blinked his right eye three times in a row as he walked, making sure the colonel wasn't looking at him as he did so, and as his father had promised, the night-vision feature of his contact lenses sprang to life.

Connor could hardly keep his jaw from dropping to the ground. This feature was much better than he had expected. In movies he had watched, not only were night-vision apparatuses bulky, but the images provided were green neon glows and weren't all that distinct. He had read about advances in IR technology, and even that scientists were considering it for the up-and-coming contact lens platform, but he had never imagined that it could be *this* good.

The images were still neon green, but were crisp and defined, no doubt with the aid of advanced digital algorithms taking in the raw data and improving clarity and resolution.

Connor could now see that there was only one road leading onto the grounds, protected by a guardhouse with a heavy steel gate. The periphery was protected by an eight-foot-tall fence, but one that looked laughably easy to scale, even for those without Connor's climbing skills.

Connor wondered for a moment why the facility didn't have electrified fences protecting it, or razor-wire at the very least, but realized that this was a question he had already answered. Hard to pretend a facility was a goat farm if it was surrounded by fences that were more typical of hardened military installations. Just having a guardhouse was already suspicious enough.

Still, the fence that was up would deter any innocents who stumbled upon the base, and slow hostiles down, allowing other security measures to come into play.

Connor counted at least eight buildings, but was convinced there were others he still couldn't see. The structures were of varied sizes, and all seemed to be made of dark brick, which concealed them even better in the pitch-darkness.

"Which building houses the medical facility?" asked Connor.

"Why does is it matter?" said Ren. "After you and I both get some sleep, I'll be sure to escort you there to see your father. With any luck, he'll come out of his coma by then."

As they neared the smallest building of any Connor had seen, he closed his right eye three times in a row once again, deactivating his night vision. Ren opened the door, motioned him inside, and hit a light switch, flooding the single room with bright light from two recessed bulbs spaced evenly above a large bed.

"You're in here," said the colonel. "There are ten private sleeping quarters and a number of offices in the main farmhouse. We also have several large barracks for overflow. But you get your own separate building. VIP quarters."

"Lucky me," mumbled Connor.

The building was windowless, as Connor had guessed it would be, and contained a bed, bathroom, and little else, all of it stark and utilitarian. There were two heavy bookshelves bolted into the wall on either side of the door, now completely empty, which suggested to Connor that this had once been an office for the previous owner of the property.

"What time is it?" asked Connor, turning to face the colonel.

"Just after three in the morning."

"Why so much activity? Given the importance of this base, I'm sure it's well secured. Yet it looks like you're racing to shore it up further. Like you're preparing for a war."

"Standard precautions," said Ren in bored tones, which immediately registered as a lie.

Connor's eyes widened. Could it be? Had Kayla really pulled it off?

"Paige and Kayla escaped, didn't they?" he said excitedly.

The colonel shook his head, almost as if in pity. "Of course not."

"They did!" said Connor. "You forget that I'm still Veracity enabled."

The colonel scowled, and looked as if he might reach in with his bare hands and rip Connor's contact lenses from his eyes. His demeanor quickly softened. "No matter," he said with a shrug. "We'll retrieve your wife and Kayla in due course. Not that we need them, since we still have you."

The fact that Ren hadn't even planned to tell him about their escape proved what Connor had known to be true—his threat to punish Connor for his wife's lack of cooperation had been a bluff.

"You can act unconcerned," said Connor, "but they've got you spooked. It's obvious."

"They don't have me spooked!" barked the colonel. "And now I'm glad I left you with your lenses, so you know that I mean it. They are no threat at all. They have no idea where we are, and they have no way to find out. You and your father are on your own."

"Then why the late-night frenzy?"

"Because I'm careful," said the colonel. "I always prepare for the worst. This mission is too important to do anything else." He shook his head in disgust. "But we have a better chance of being hit by a meteorite than of anyone attacking this compound."

"How did they escape?" asked Connor.

"This conversation is over. You and I—and my men—all need sleep. The newcomers that you saw outside will make sure this compound isn't disturbed."

Connor considered for several long seconds. "Okay," he said amiably. "I guess I could use some sleep at that."

Ren rolled his eyes. "You're pretending to cooperate so I'll lower my guard. That won't happen. Escape is impossible. I'm posting a guard outside this door. If you are somehow able to defeat him, the micro-drone swarm you saw earlier is helping my men patrol the area. There are forty-five of them left. Each is an AI, programmed to know who you are. And Elias, and Kayla, and Paige, for that matter. They can see just fine in the dark. They'll ignore me and my men, but *you* couldn't get ten yards from this building without one of them recognizing you and taking action."

"Action? Like what, putting a hole in my forehead?"

"No. You get special treatment. They'll take out your left kneecap. You'll never walk again. But you'll live to help keep your father on task." The colonel smiled. "Now what does Veracity tell you about what I just said? Am I bluffing?"

"And you don't think this is overkill? You do know I'm an untrained civilian, right?"

"And I'm a cautious soldier."

"Good for you," said Connor. "But I'm not your biggest problem. I had a great conversation with your man in the ambulance, Captain Du. He told me a number of lies. One of them is that he has great respect for you."

Connor paused to let this sink in. "If you think he's loyal to you, *or* the cause," he continued, "then you'd better think again. And from what I gather from his lies, he's not the only one. I'd watch my back."

Ren shook his head and smiled tiredly. "Nice try," he said. "Just because I'm not wearing my Veracity-enabled glasses at the moment, doesn't mean I don't know what you're doing. Trying to get us to mistrust each other is about your only hope. I'm sure you can spin an entertaining fantasy, but I don't have time for it now. I'll see you in the morning. Hopefully, both of your knees will be working when I do." He shrugged. "But that's entirely up to you."

The colonel spoke into his comm and a minute later a solider, heavily armed, took up a position outside the door. "Sleep well," he said.

"Drop dead," said Connor with a scowl, trying to hide the hope in his eyes as Ren shut and locked the door behind him.

Connor couldn't have asked for a more perfect situation. Escape would still be difficult, but it had suddenly become *possible*. Which was more than he had expected.

And Kayla and Paige were apparently alive, well, and free. He'd have given anything to learn how Kayla had managed it, but just knowing Paige was now free of the Chinese was the ultimate relief.

Still, even though she was free, she was far from safe. And she wouldn't be until he could escape and join her.

So now it was his turn. During any altercation, he would have the upper hand, because Ren's men wouldn't do anything that could jeopardize his life. What an embarrassment it would be for them to have to explain to the colonel why they needed lethal force to subdue an untrained civilian.

So even if his attempt failed, he would still be alive. Severely injured, even crippled, but alive.

But Connor *wouldn't* fail. He *couldn't*. And while escape would require him to leave Elias behind, he had no other choice—at least for *now*.

Still, he vowed that he'd be back. This wasn't over yet.

52

Connor Gibson left the lights on and explored every inch of the tiny building he was in. Given how this *could* have unfolded, he felt as though he had won the lottery. As sparse as the room was, there was plenty here for him to work with. His spirits soared as his plan began to come into better and better focus.

He removed a white cotton sheet from the bed and tried to tear it, but his efforts proved fruitless. Finally, after inspecting every millimeter of the heavy steel bedframe, welded together and bolted to the floor, he found a jagged imperfection in the metal, and used this to work enough of a hole in the sheet that he could now tear it into a thin strip. He repeated this exercise three more times, tying the strips together, and then retreated into the small bathroom.

Once inside he gripped the white, molded wood toilet seat with both hands, near its base, and pulled and twisted with all of his might, eventually managing to tear it away from two plastic hinges.

Five minutes later, after everything was in place, and he had rehearsed the escape in his mind several times so it would be as fluid as possible, he activated his contacts' night-vision feature and turned off the lights.

He noted with interest that the two bulbs above the bed looked like they were still on in the enhanced green glow of night vision, their residual heat making them stand out like neon torches. He waited half a minute for them to cool and then stood on the bed and unscrewed each bulb from its socket.

Satisfied, he moved to one side of the bed, faced the door, ten feet away, and began screaming for all he was worth, as if he were being boiled alive.

Connor continued screaming, even as the guard began to unlock the outer door, so the Chinese soldier would know that his prisoner was at the far end of the room and wouldn't worry about being ambushed if he entered to investigate. Not that the guard would be all that worried, anyway. What good would it do Connor to escape the room, only to have to face a swarm of AI-powered drones outside?

The guard threw open the door and hit the light switch, which did nothing. He flipped it up and down several times before conceding that it wasn't going to work, and drew his flashlight. He pointed it at Connor, who suddenly collapsed to the ground and began writhing, hoping that his acting abilities were better than his wife's.

The guard rushed toward him, completely oblivious to the taut rope of cotton strips Connor had stretched across the room's threshold, two feet in, tied to the two bookcases on both sides of the door. Connor's makeshift tripwire, about a foot off the ground, was invisible in the darkness, and the guard hit it in stride and crashed to the floor, just as Connor had hoped.

The instant the guard went down, Connor jumped up from the ground and raced to close the distance between them. He arrived in just a few seconds, but the man's recovery from the shock of the fall and his reaction speed were extraordinary, and he was already rising from the ground, his gun drawn.

If the guard wasn't now blind in the cavernous darkness of the room, while Connor was sighted, the soldier would have prevailed, but he never saw the white toilet seat coming toward him. Connor swung the unwieldy seat as hard as he could, and the meat of it hit the guard's hand, launching his gun into the far wall and breaking several of the man's fingers.

Despite the agony of broken fingers, the guard blocked Connor's next attempted blow with his forearms, showing an uncanny ability to anticipate its location, despite the darkness, but Connor held on to the seat for dear life and dealt a savage blow to the guard's head, knocking him out.

Connor blew out a long breath and closed his eyes in relief. Less than twenty-four hours earlier, he could say that he had never hit anyone in his life. But since then he had made it a habit of knocking men unconscious with ever more ridiculous bludgeons. A small fireplace shovel was ridiculous enough, but a toilet seat had to take the prize.

Connor retrieved the gun where it had flown across the room and frisked the fallen guard, not hunting for a pulse—afraid of what he might find. He located the soldier's cell phone, which looked for all the world to be an Apple model, even in the green glow of night vision, and transferred it to his pocket.

His heart was pounding wildly against his chest already, but as he contemplated leaving the building, it raced even faster. Ren had insisted the slaughterbot swarm was programmed to recognize him and take out a knee if he ventured from his prison. But he was betting that what it recognized was his face. This made sense, but if he was wrong, he would be crippled for life. Worse, his escape attempt would fail, and he would never see Paige again.

Connor squeezed the prototype Veracity-blocker Kayla had given him, still affixed to his lapel like a small pearl, and was heartened to see a pinpoint of light come to life, indicating it was operational. He closed his eyes, recited a silent prayer, and then rushed from the building, half-expecting his knee to be destroyed with every step.

But after traveling fifty yards, both knees remained intact. He allowed himself a moment of celebration before continuing on. He had been right. There was no way that one of the forty-five drones hadn't spotted him by now, so the blocker must be working like a charm, hiding his face and identity from both Veracity *and* the swarm. The night-vision contact lenses were also performing brilliantly.

He stayed low to the ground and out of any light, clinging to the edges of buildings or behind anything big enough to conceal him.

Soldiers continued to patrol the grounds, and he chose the path of least resistance, moving to the biggest gaps between men in each case on his way to the perimeter and fence.

Connor was twenty yards away from the fence when a beam of light swung toward him, sweeping across the grass, and he just managed to dive to the ground in time to avoid being seen. He felt like a convict in a bad prison-escape movie, but he had never seen one in which the convict managed to use night-vision technology during his escape attempt.

Finally, he reached the fence, elated to still be in one piece, and used his climbing skills to scale it without making a sound. He dropped to the ground on the other side of the fence and darted off through the trees, putting as much distance between himself and the Chinese stronghold as he could possibly manage.

Every second counted, because he had no idea how long it would take them to discover his absence. And once they did, all hell was sure to break loose.

53

Connor hid behind a dense clump of trees, two hundred yards from the fence line, and removed the guard's phone from his pocket, turning it on and blocking its light the best he could. It still looked for all the world like a standard-issue Apple phone, which was surprising.

He studied the alphanumeric keypad and slowly typed in the number 527-873-7678. *Last Resort*. Kayla couldn't have used a more appropriate number for her safety phone.

She had escaped, so he assumed that she still had her phone, but there was only one way to find out.

"Hello," said a groggy voice.

"Kayla, it's Connor," he whispered.

"Connor?" said Kayla in dismay, her voice coming back to life. "Are you okay?"

"I'm fine. What about you and Paige?"

"We're good," replied Kayla. "Wait a minute," she added as her full brain kicked in. "Tell Ren this is a nice try, but I won't be staying on the line long enough for him to trace me."

"Ren didn't put me up to this," whispered Connor. "I swear. I escaped."

"Impossible," whispered Kayla.

He could say the same about *her* escape, but he was well aware that he might only have seconds to make his case before she hung up. "I was lucky," he said rapidly. "They guarded me with slaughter-bots, but I used Jalen's Veracity blocker to defeat their facial recognition. And then my contacts' night-vision feature to slip through their lines."

"I'll be damned," said Kayla. "Sounds plausible."

"I'm telling you, I escaped. I'd never give them this number under any circumstances. I'm alone, and not under duress."

"And Elias?"

"I was forced to leave him behind. He's still in a coma and being cared for. But we can come back for him. You have to believe me. This isn't a trap."

"I do believe you," whispered Kayla. "I do. But you can't blame me for being cautious."

"Not at all. I applaud you for it. But I don't have much time. I'll try to get this phone to generate my current GPS coordinates and call you back, so we can get some idea of where I am."

"I know exactly where you are. At what used to be a goat farm, correct?"

"How could you possibly know that?"

"Long story. The short version is that Paige and I escaped using my van. And we were helped by one of the Chinese operatives. A man named Long Lan. The captain who saved Paige's life."

This was a man Connor would never forget. "And you vetted him with Veracity?" he whispered.

"Yes. He checked out a hundred percent. He'll do anything to prevent China from getting this tech. And he knew where they were taking you and Elias. So Paige and I are in a motel, just twenty minutes away from you."

"Awesome!" said Connor, so quietly it was almost under his breath. After nothing but bad luck, he was finally having a run of good. "And this Chinese captain is with you now?"

"No. He's driving my van to LA for supplies. But your timing is impeccable. He only left about twenty minutes ago. He'll be able to come get you in the van, and zero in on your precise location. I'm sending you his number now," she finished.

Connor acknowledged receipt of the number seconds later. "I know why *I'm* whispering," he said, "but why are you?"

"Paige is sound asleep in the next bed over," replied Kayla. "She's so beat I suspect I could scream and she wouldn't awaken. But I'll rouse her now and let her know you're okay. She'll be overjoyed."

"Thanks, Kayla, but let her sleep. She needs it, and why give her false hope? If I'm recaptured, it's better for her not to have been awakened. Let's wait until we're fairly confident that I'm in the clear."

"Understood," whispered Kayla. "Good luck, Connor. I'll call the captain first and explain what happened, and how you escaped. To minimize the amount of whispering you have to risk. Give me about three minutes."

"Will do," said Connor.

* * *

"Congratulations on your escape," said Long in perfect English a short time later. "I'll be there in forty minutes. Hopefully less."

"Thanks," whispered Connor. "But how will you know exactly where I'll be?"

"These phones can track each other, but only when connected."

Connor considered. With any luck, the colonel and his men were sleeping soundly, and none of the others had yet discovered his absence. Given their confidence in the guard and swarm, he might have many more hours until they did.

But he might not.

"I'll stay put and lie low until you arrive," whispered Connor.

"You can't," said Long. "Aren't you in the middle of a woods? This van is a tank, and can mow down small trees, but you still need to get closer to some kind of access road. Put your phone on vibrate and don't move. I'll call you back in five minutes or so."

Connor continued to scan his surroundings while waiting for Long's return call, making his night vision work overtime, but didn't see anyone coming. He was surprised to see any number of nocturnal animals scurrying about, including dozens of bats, which night vision revealed to him for the first time.

Seven minutes later, his cell phone vibrated. "I have a visual on you and your surroundings," said Long when he answered.

"How?"

"I sent a drone earlier to recon the base. It hasn't been there long. I diverted it to your coordinates. It's right above you, about fifty yards up. Do you hear it?"

Connor listened intently. "No."

"Good," said Long. "You aren't supposed to. Anyway, while you were waiting for me to call back, I used the drone to scout the area around you. There's a dirt road about a mile away that eventually connects with more significant roads. Head due east as fast as you can. The drone will watch your back."

"That's great," said Connor, "but I wouldn't know due east if it bit me in the ass."

"Understood," replied the captain. "Let's do it this way: turn to your two o'clock and go straight."

"I'm facing twelve o'clock, right?"

"Right. Six is straight behind you, and three is dead right. Find two o'clock and get moving."

"Got it," said Connor. He turned as instructed, and then rushed off through the woods once again. "Thanks."

"Hang in there," said Long. "I'll pick you up before you know it."

54

Captain Long Lan recovered Connor on the dirt road without incident. The American's escape was so improbable that no one at the compound had seen the need to confirm his continued presence. Connor could only imagine the alarm and confusion that would ensue within the stronghold when Ren came to get him in three or four hours and he was no longer there.

The moment Connor was in the seat next to him, Long reported the successful exfiltration to Kayla, who immediately awakened her roommate to tell her the good news. When the captain was a few minutes away he called Kayla again, explaining that since he was now well behind schedule, he would stop just long enough to drop Connor off on a street behind the motel before resuming his mission. He would try to make up for lost time, but couldn't imagine being back in under four and a half hours.

Kayla and Paige had the door to their room open when Connor walked the short distance from the street to the motel, and both greeted him warmly. Connor's reunion with Paige was a bit *too* warm, as neither of them had expected to ever see the other again.

"Guys, get a room," deadpanned Kayla, and then, acting as if she was seeing the two queen beds for the first time, added, "I mean, get *another* room—one that isn't this one."

Connor sat on the edge of one of the beds and motioned for Paige to join him. Kayla parked herself on the edge of the other bed, four feet away, facing them, and shot Paige a smile. "As much as I enjoyed rooming with you, I think I'll let you and Connor, um . . . bunk together from now on. I'm sure the captain won't mind if I use his room until he gets back."

"Thanks," said Connor. "But don't leave right away. We have a lot of information to share."

"Do you think you two can keep your hands off of each other for that long?"

Paige smiled. "I think we can manage."

Connor removed a phone from his pocket. "I got this from a Chinese soldier. It looks just like a regulation Apple model."

"It isn't," said Kayla. "The mimicry is remarkable, but it has a much different functionality."

"So I've gathered," said Connor. He rose and placed the phone on top of a tall dresser. "Don't let me forget it's there," he said, sitting back down. "So how in the world did you escape?" he asked.

Kayla and Paige managed to boil the entire escape into just a few-minute summary.

"Anything else I should know about?" asked Connor when they had finished.

"Plenty," said Paige, "but we should all try to get as much sleep as we can while we have the chance."

Connor pulled a gun and pointed it at Kayla across the four-foot gap that separated the two queen-sized beds.

"What are you doing?" spat Kayla in dismay, staring into the barrel of his gun.

"What's going on, Con?" said Paige anxiously beside him. "Put that down!"

"I can't do that, Paige," he replied grimly. "I'm afraid that Kayla has some explaining to do."

"What are you talking about?" said Paige.

Kayla shook her head. "You people really aren't good at thanking me for escaping from Dr. Rosado's home," she said, trying to break the tension. "Did they brainwash you, Connor? Is this some kind of *Manchurian Candidate* thing?"

"No, it's a betrayal by Kayla Keller thing."

"You're out of your mind," said Kayla.

Paige couldn't have looked more troubled. "What are you basing this on, Con?" she asked.

Connor didn't reply. His eyes never left the face of the woman sitting across from him, and his gun hand remained steady. "Come on,

Kayla. I know you're working for Holloway/Vader. Just admit it and save us all some time."

"That's ridiculous!" said Kayla emphatically, and then, turning to Paige, added, "You have to do something here. The recent trauma he's undergone has been too much for him."

Paige eyed her husband warily, deep concern written all over her face. "Hold on, Con," she said. She reached across him and opened an end-table drawer, removing a pair of black Veracity-enabled glasses that she had stored there while she slept. After awakening, she hadn't immediately put them on again, not expecting to have to confirm the truthfulness of anyone's words, at least not for the rest of the night. Connor was her husband, and she and Kayla had gone through hell together and had lived to make it to the other side.

Connor shook his head. "The glasses won't help," he said to Paige. "She can corrupt the Veracity computer. When she denies she's working for Holloway, or his alter ego, it will register as the truth. She's the one person in all the world who can lie to a Veracity interface. She could never have pulled this off if she couldn't."

"You need to explain yourself, and you need to do it quickly," said Kayla, her tone harsh. "I've made huge sacrifices for you. I saved your dad's life at his house by giving him a warning. I let myself get cut up into ribbons to protect Elias. I don't know what happened to poison your brain, but you're woefully misguided."

Paige studied Connor with a pained expression, fearful that her husband had somehow lost his mind. "You know she's right, Con," she said softly. "She did save your father. And me."

"But she *isn't* right," insisted Connor. "That's just it. She didn't save *anyone*. Right, Kayla? It was all a charade, wasn't it? No, don't answer," he added quickly. "You'll just lie again."

"You're making some pretty damning accusations," said Kayla. "But you never answered Paige's question. What do you base them on?"

"A series of coincidences and circumstantial evidence," replied Connor. "Each, alone, isn't conclusive. But taken together, they're overwhelming. We first met you when you rushed into my dad's yard to warn us of an attack. Just minutes before it began. Pretty convenient timing. Almost like you were tracking the guys who were climbing up the canyon. Almost like Holloway was telling you exactly where they were so you could look the most heroic."

"The timing wasn't *convenient*," said Kayla in disgust. "I had just been attacked myself. Almost killed. Or do you want to see the emerging scar on my arm where the bullet went through?"

"You did that to *yourself*. High marks on realism. When you play a role, you really commit to it, I'll give you that. But you were never attacked at your home. You made that up to justify your warning, and to get us all thinking we were in the same boat. To get us to think you were being hunted, a victim, rather than one of the people pulling the strings."

"I don't even know what to say to that," said Kayla. "I could have been killed at Elias's home."

"Really?" said Connor. "That's interesting, because the guys who attacked my father had strict orders not to hurt anyone but *him*. My dad got this intel from the prisoner we had in the back of his SUV. Remember?"

Kayla didn't respond.

"I seem to remember you didn't want us to take the prisoner with us," added Connor. "Something about him being able to kill us with his pinky. Now it's clear why. You didn't want us to find out that he had orders not to touch you. Because why would that be? You claimed Vader had already tried to have you killed at your home. So why would he try to kill you where *you* live, but move heaven and earth to *protect* you at my father's house?"

Connor paused, and then answered his own question. "He wouldn't, that's why. He'd have his hired killers either wait until my father was alone, or kill us all, so as not to leave any witnesses. The only way this all makes sense is if you're working for Holloway. He knew we were going to be at my father's house—and that you were going to join us. Which is why he made sure his men attacked on the day we were all there, and had strict orders not to hurt you."

"That's preposterous!" said Kayla. "I agree that it's odd. But who knows why Holloway, or his alter ego Vader, gave the orders he did. He must have changed his mind, or had other reasons. His inconsistency isn't *my* fault."

"Don't worry," said Connor, "there's more. Jalen Howard told us he learned we were on the run after finally getting wind of the attack at my dad's house. But he said *nothing* about the attack at *your* house. And you didn't mention it to *him*, either."

"It never came up," said Kayla.

"There's a *reason* it never came up. Because it never happened. You were Jalen's ally. If he was keeping watch on anyone's home, it was yours. But he was clueless. The reason he didn't pick up on the attack at your home is because there *was no* attack. You made it all up. And he complained that you wouldn't let him surveil my father's home. Why *wouldn't* you? Because you knew this attack was coming, that's why. You didn't want Jalen to see what was going on in time to stop it, or warn my father. You wanted to orchestrate things without his interference."

"I never took you for a conspiracy nut, Connor," said Kayla in disdain. "But I was wrong. I'm sure you could make a good case that *Elvis* is still alive. But that doesn't make it true."

Paige's expression had changed as Connor had begun to lay out his case. She wasn't yet convinced, but the wheels in her head were turning, and she was no longer doubting his sanity.

"We both know this is no conspiracy theory," said Connor.

"Why would I go to so much trouble?" said Kayla. "Why such a complex scheme? What would be the point?"

"Because Holloway wanted my father dead, and wanted you to bond with us. I'm an only child, and I have no doubt my father's will calls for his sixty percent ownership in Ufree Technologies to pass to Paige and me upon his death. After his death, you could manipulate us any way you wanted. We'd be innocent rubes, putty in your hands. My dad was supposed to die right away, before he told us anything, so you could tell us about Veracity in any way you wanted. Present the facts any way you wanted. You could pretend that the idea of Veracity-blockers, and your alliance with Jalen Howard, had his full support."

"If this were true," said Kayla, "Vader could have taken Elias out at any time. He wouldn't have waited until I was there. Even if his men had orders not to kill me, when bullets are flying collateral damage does happen. Why risk hitting me? I could have approached you after your father was dead and explained everything to you however I wished."

"Weren't you paying attention?" snapped Connor. "I already said, he wanted you to bond with us."

"There are better ways to bond with people."

"No, there aren't. Teaming up in a life-and-death situation is a classic trope to accelerate the creation of strong relationships. A shared crisis, a shared battle for our lives, is like bonding super-glue. You arrive on the scene and look for all the world like you're desperately trying to save my father's life. Then, when you fail, we go on the run together. We share raw emotions together. We mourn my father together. Teams of soldiers in the field become like brothers very quickly. Save someone's life a few times, pretend to risk taking a bullet for them, and you come out looking pretty heroic."

Connor shook his head. "Then you could tell us the tragic tale of Kayla Keller. A poor innocent woman framed by the evil Derek Manning. And we'd believe every word. Because we'd owe you our life, and we'd have firsthand experience of your saintliness. And Veracity would back up everything you said. As it did when you *actually* told us the Manning tale."

"Is this really all you have?" said Kayla. "Please tell me that this far-fetched conjecture isn't really enough to overcome all the trust we've built up. The trust your father has no doubt placed in me. I helped your wife escape the Chinese. And I also saved your father's life. He's only in a coma now because of *you*."

Connor cringed as this barb hit home.

"And after all of that," continued Kayla, "you're holding a gun on me because my arrival at Elias's house was too *coincidental*?" She shook her head angrily. "Again, I don't know why Vader ordered his mercs to spare us. It could be for any number of reasons. After trying to kill me, he obviously changed his mind. Maybe Holloway is a raving lunatic, and Vader is a split personality. Besides, you know from your father that Veracity *can't* be defeated. I can't tell a lie any more than you can."

"I'll get to that in a moment," said Connor. "But let me continue. My father was supposed to have been killed at his home. But I came up with a few good strategies and managed to stop that from happening. Which threw a wrench into Holloway's careful plan. We were supposed to have been knocked out. When we awoke to find my father dead, you would have rushed us off to your safe house, where we would have been attacked again. I'm sure you'd find some miraculous way to save us, and then spend a week there bonding with us. Twisting our thinking in any direction you chose."

"Paige, are you listening to this?" pleaded Kayla. "You saw the condition I was in. They tortured the shit out of me. That was real."

"It was," agreed Connor before his wife could respond, "but it looked far worse than it was. Holloway handpicked the perfect guy for the assignment, who had no idea he was torturing an ally of the man who had given him the order. Neil told me that John was highly skilled when it came to this kind of torture, and Holloway knew that too. He knew that John could make it look good, without any real danger to you. And Holloway ordered John not to touch you above the neck. Again, I know you were still hurt badly. You earn high marks for your commitment to the role. But notice again, they had strict instructions not to kill you."

Connor paused. "But I bet that wasn't true in reverse," he continued. "I bet you had a way to kill these men. Or to escape so we could continue being on the run together. So you could continue being the heroic Kayla Keller in front of us. But this time after letting yourself be brutally tortured for the cause. How could we not come to like and respect you? To develop an unbreakable bond with you?"

"That's a lot of work and deception just to look heroic," said Kayla. "Assuming Veracity would let me deceive you in the first place—which it wouldn't."

"It was worth it in the long run," said Connor. "Holloway gets Elias out of the picture. Which he wanted to do for reasons I'm not entirely clear on. And you get in tight with his heirs."

Connor sighed. "But like I said, I messed up your plan by orchestrating an escape from my dad's house. But I didn't ruin it entirely. Holloway just had to modify the instructions for his team at Borrego Springs. Have them kill Elias *there* instead of at his house. No harm, no foul. In fact, this change actually improved our bonding experience. It worked like a charm. In a short time, I found myself feeling closer to you than friends I've had for years. I went from thinking you were pure evil to thinking you were a victim, misunderstood, and amazing in every way. Which is one of the reasons it took me so long to put all of the pieces together."

Paige nodded. "I felt very close to you too," she said to Kayla. "I still do. I can't help myself."

"See?" said Connor. "Your plan was working exactly the way you hoped it would."

"And did I *hope* the Chinese would capture us?" said Kayla. "Is that what you're saying? Or am I working with *them*, also, in this sick fantasy world of yours?

"No. I think they blindsided you just as much as they did us. But you escaped to save *yourself*. Paige was just along for the ride."

"This is all just wild speculation," said Kayla. "Is that really all you've got?"

"No, there's more," he replied, his gaze and gun hand still unwavering.

"I can hardly wait to hear it," said Kayla, rolling her eyes. "What's next, you learned that I voted for Bradley Holloway when he was a senator? You found a picture of me next to a man who dressed up as Darth Vader at a Halloween party?" She shook her head. "I know you don't have a smoking gun. Or *anything* concrete, for that matter. Because I know that what you're accusing me of isn't true."

"Apparently," said Connor, "false accusations happen to you *a lot*. And you're right, there is no smoking gun. But while each of my points can be explained away, at some point their cumulative weight becomes overwhelming."

"Yeah, I keep waiting for that to happen."

"So let me continue with additional circumstantial evidence against you," said Connor. "First, it's become clear to me that Holloway has been using Veracity. And he could only get it from you."

"In what way is it *clear* that he has Veracity?" said Kayla.

"When we interrogated our prisoner in my dad's SUV, he mentioned that Vader feeds a network of mercenaries intel on powerful figures in politics, business, and the media. Embarrassing or illegal activities that he has them corroborate by any means necessary. He said that at first, Vader's intel was often wrong. But this changed to the point where it almost *never* was. This dramatic improvement in the quality of his intel must have coincided with Holloway making use of Veracity. Just like Jalen Howard suddenly became the nation's top interrogator when you gave it to *him*."

"Wow," said Kayla, "that may be the weakest argument I've ever heard. Talk about a stretch."

"It all continues to add up," said Connor. "And now we come to your safe house. You told us it was state of the art. *Could not be* breached. You overplayed your hand there, because Jalen later seconded that idea. And he was in a position to know. But not only did the men who captured us defeat your impregnable security, they defeated it with *ease*. Holloway has contacts and connections and power, but even *he* couldn't have orchestrated something like that. Not unless you two were working together. Not unless you had him tell his men exactly how to beat it, and even gave him every password he would need."

"I don't know what to say," replied Kayla. "I know I'm innocent, but I am impressed. You have quite an imagination. No wonder you want to be a novelist. It's clear that you're very good with *fiction*."

"I would have figured this out sooner," continued Connor as if Kayla hadn't spoken, "but you were *so* convincing. And you did a lot of bleeding for the cause. Most importantly, Veracity had me totally thrown off the scent. Which is what you were counting on. You counted on us believing the system was foolproof. So when it credited your lies as the truth, how could we possibly doubt you? You were like a magician."

Paige had been hanging on her husband's every word, and was now firmly in his corner. "So when did you figure it out, Con?" she asked.

"I began to suspect when we were in Dr. Rosado's examination room. Remember when Colonel Ren was bragging that he had been able to isolate everyone in America who knew about Veracity in one place? Then, just to be sure he hadn't missed anything, he asked Kayla to verify that this was correct. Verify that no one else knew about it."

"I remember," said Paige.

"That's when it clicked. It caused me to remember a discussion we had with my dad in the kitchen of Kayla's safe house. Kayla was downstairs, probably on the phone with Bradley Holloway trying to figure out how to salvage their operation. But anyway, my dad was saying that Kayla didn't want him to tell us about Veracity at first. She was worried it might leak. She told my father that she preferred *to continue* to keep the secret of Veracity *just between them.* But it had already spread *beyond* just them—and she knew it."

Paige's eyes widened. "Of course," she said. "Because she was *already* working with Jalen Howard."

"Right! So she had *lied* to my father. And he was wearing his contacts at the time. Once I realized she could beat a Veracity interface, I reexamined everything that had happened to us, and it became clear to me what was really going on.

"Not that you don't deserve credit," he said to Kayla, "because you do. You did a masterful job explaining away Jalen Howard. Explaining why my father didn't know about your alliance. I have no doubt you expected him to be dead before he could refute your story. I'm sure you still planned to finish him off the first chance you got."

Paige looked deeply hurt by Kayla's betrayal. "I was beginning to think of you as a *sister*," she said to her sadly. "I trusted you with my life."

"You can *still* trust me, Paige. Connor's arguments have seduced you, but they're still wrong. Because his eureka moment was wrong. When Elias told you what I had said at the time, he misremembered. I know exactly what I said. I've already admitted I didn't want him to know about my deal with Jalen. So I told Elias that *I wished we could keep it between the two of us. Wished.* And I didn't use the word *continue.* So my statement was true. Because even though I had already told Jalen, I did *wish* that this hadn't been necessary."

Connor's eyes narrowed. This was an argument he hadn't considered.

Kayla nodded at him hopefully. "Can you at least take that gun off me?" she asked. "You know I'm not armed."

"But hardly helpless," he said, his confidence returning. "You're a lot more than what you seem. Which is yet another indicator of your true nature. When you burst into my father's backyard, you were like a frightened bunny rabbit, about to burst into tears. Now, you're a cold-blooded killer with the skills and tech of a seasoned *commando.* You transformed in front of our eyes. So much so, that I had no doubt you'd escape from the Chinese. *Of course* you would."

"Paige was doing a lot of crying in the beginning, too," said Kayla. "But she's toughened up a lot, also. You have too, Connor. What we've been through will do that to the softest among us. So are we *all* working for Vader?"

Connor thought about this. "You're right," he said finally. "We have all toughened up. But just because I'm conceding this one point, doesn't make the others any less valid."

"So are you *finally* done?" said Kayla. "Do you have any more supposed evidence? Any more flimsy reasoning that you can stretch all out of proportion?"

"No, that's it. But I'm sure if I continue to replay events, more discrepancies will occur to me."

"So do *I* get a turn now?" said Kayla. "A chance to defend myself? To correct the record? Or are you just going to convict me without hearing from the accused?"

Connor studied her for several long seconds. "By all means," he said finally, "defend yourself. But as creative as you are, I can't see any way you can wriggle out of this one."

"I know you can't, Connor," replied Kayla. "That's what makes this so disappointing."

55

Kayla Keller looked remarkably calm for someone who had just weathered a storm of compelling accusations. She paused for a moment to gather her thoughts, and then began. "First, she said, "I need you both to focus on everything I've done for you, the sacrifices I've made. I've poured my heart out to you—and *for* you. You've known me now for less than twenty-four hours. Compared to this, Elias has known me forever. And remember how vehemently he vouched for me. How much trust he placed in me. There's a reason for that. Because I'm innocent, and you've got it all wrong."

She waited for her audience to digest these words and then gestured to Connor. "Second, and most importantly, Connor, I really need you to tell me how I'm managing to lie. I assume my denials have all registered as being true." She turned pointedly to Paige. "Right, Paige? Have I lied even once?"

Paige shook her head. "Not according to my glasses," she replied. "But everything Connor is saying has registered as true, also."

"Of course it has," said Kayla. "Because it's just conjecture. He hasn't made any *statements*. A question doesn't register, because it can't be true or false. And a conjecture is *always* true, as long as the speaker believes it. Just because Connor believes what he says, and doesn't intend to deceive, doesn't mean he's *right*."

"That makes sense," acknowledged Paige.

"It's good to know that *something* finally does," said Kayla. She stared deeply into Connor's eyes. "So are you going to explain how I can defeat Veracity, when even your father can't?"

"Because you plan ahead," said Connor. "You brought the Darwin computer to my father, and you're one of the best programmers in the world. You just told me how you were able to reprogram the Veracity computer to control your van, a truly impressive sleight-of-hand."

"I can only access the computer's peripheral functions, just like Elias. Its *non-Veracity* functions. Its inner sanctum, where truth and lies are sorted out, is untouchable. You accessed its peripheral functions yourself when you signaled it to activate the night-vision feature of your contact lenses."

"The inner sanctum is *not* untouchable," insisted Connor. "Not for you. You somehow managed to install a secret entrance into it. One that not even my father has access to."

Paige now looked confused. "But, Con," she said, "didn't your father say he locked up security long before Kayla even knew the system was working?"

"He did," replied Connor. "Because he didn't trust her. He was playing a chess game and thinking three moves ahead. The problem was that *she* was thinking six moves ahead—from the very start. She knew he'd do something like this. Like most great magicians, she completed the trick before the rubes in the audience even knew it had begun. She made sure to program the Darwin computer before she had even given it to my father. She programmed it to always keep her secret access tunnel open, no matter how many generations of evolution it went through."

Kayla shot him a look of total disdain. "You know your father is too smart to fall for something like that, right? But I suppose you don't want to ruin the brilliantly imaginative tapestry you've woven by admitting it to yourself, do you?"

"My father *is* smart. But you're smarter. And far more devious."

"Veracity *can't* be breached!" barked Kayla in frustration. "I *can't* lie to you. And deep down, you know it. The rest is just hand waving. I know you want to make sense of what we've been put through. You've just had to leave your father behind when you escaped. I can only imagine how horrible you're feeling about that. All of this would rattle anyone."

She paused and leaned in toward Connor, as if she were ready to make an irrefutable argument. "But even assuming I *could* lie. Even assuming everything you've said is true, here is my question: Why? What would I have to gain from it?"

"I already told you," said Connor. "While I'm not entirely clear on motivations, once you were able to get us on your side, you could manipulate us. Do what you want with the technology. With the added bonus that we would sing your praises in the court of public opinion. Testify to your heroism and sacrifice. Further assist you on the road to rehabilitating your reputation."

"So you're saying that this diabolical plan would allow me to dictate how Veracity is launched. Allow me to overcome Elias's resistance to launching Veracity-blocking technology. I would get to use you, and Veracity, to get my good name back. And I would get to control the company, conning you to vote your shares any way I wanted."

"Exactly," said Connor.

Kayla smiled and shook her head. "Then what does Bradley Holloway get out of it?" she asked innocently.

"What?" said Connor.

"You heard me. What would the vice president have to gain?"

"What do you mean?"

"As smart as you are, Connor, you still don't see the fatal flaw in your reasoning. The whole point is that Holloway can't let the tech get out. *Cannot.* Under any circumstances. He'd never survive it. Which is why he wants to kill Elias in the first place. To *stop* it! So why would he ally with me? Why would he send me in on a complex mission to win you over?"

Connor looked flustered for the first time. "I don't know," he said uncertainly. "I just know that you must be working with him toward some end."

"You just agreed on what *I* get out of it. I get to control the tech." Her eyes narrowed. "But let me repeat, Holloway doesn't want *anyone* to control the tech. He wants it *killed.* So what does he gain by having me bond with you? And if I helped him bury the tech, this would go directly against my own interests. If Veracity never sees the light of day, I don't control it, and I can't use it to clear my name." Kayla shook her head. "And if he *lets* me launch it, so I *can* get what you say I get out of this, he's *ruined.*"

Connor's eyes became wild and he looked like he might panic. She was right. Her goals and those of the vice president were diametrically opposed.

"And if Holloway had me on his side and just wanted to bury the tech," continued Kayla, "he would kill your father before he brought you in on this. How simple would *that* be? You'd inherit shares, sure, but I'd just explain that the company never got off the ground. You'd never be the wiser."

Kayla paused for effect. "And if I was already working with the *Vice President of the United States*, tell me why I'd need to forge an alliance with a relatively minor player like Jalen Howard. And why would I push so hard for Jalen to perfect blockers for a tech that will never see the light of day?"

Connor looked sick to his stomach and his eyes stayed wide open. He glanced at Paige, who was equally troubled by a logic that seemed unassailable.

"Seems to me," continued Kayla relentlessly, "that one of three things is true. One, that I'm on your side, and everything I've said is true. Two, I'm working with the VP to prevent Veracity's launch, in which case I don't *need* to bond with you. We'd just kill Elias and bury the tech. Easy as pie. Or three, I'm working with Holloway, working with his Vader alter ego, on a bold, complex plot. One that almost gets me killed multiple times, and gets me shot and tortured. All to build trust with you so I can launch a tech that my partner *desperately wants to stop*."

She paused and watched Connor's mind race, searching for a way to salvage his interpretation of events.

"Oh," added Kayla, "I forgot. Along the way, I make sure to out my good friend and partner, Bradley Holloway. Remember, Connor, you wouldn't have even known he was behind this if it weren't for me. So why would he and I, masterminds that we are, want him outed? How does that fit into our diabolical master plan?"

Once again, Connor didn't reply.

"You spin a nice tale, Connor, but it's just a tale until you can tell me how I could logically, *possibly* be working for Holloway. Your accusations are *pathetic*. And insulting. I've nearly fallen in love with your father. I've done more for him than you can imagine, including warning him that he was being attacked. I've saved Paige from certain imprisonment at the hands of the Chinese. And after all I've done, all the sacrifices I've made, *this* is how you choose to thank me?"

There was a long silence in the room.

"What's wrong, Connor? No good answer?"

Connor looked dizzy. "But I was so sure," he said, lowering his eyes in confusion. "I have to be missing something."

In that instant, when Connor was reeling from self-doubt, Kayla lunged forward and snatched the gun from his lifeless hand, which was already falling to the bed as his focus wavered. She had waited for this moment of maximum weakness to neatly turn the tables, and now aimed his gun right back at him across the small gulf between the beds.

Her demeanor changed just as quickly as the gun's possession. She no longer looked the hurt victim, or the raging defender of her own honor, but a ruthless demon who was totally in command. A frightening gleam came to her eyes, as if she were now possessed.

"You think you're missing something, Connor?" she barked in contempt. "Well, you're absolutely right! You *are* missing something, you imbecile! You're missing *everything*. But at least you got further than your idiot wife."

Paige shrank back in horror.

"You look confused, Connor," said Kayla with a self-satisfied smirk. "But no use wasting any more brainpower. If you haven't seen it yet, you never will. Too bad Elias's brains weren't passed down the line. Do you want me to spell it out for you, *Sherlock?*" she added derisively.

Connor nodded, a stupefied look still on his face.

"Okay, I am *not* working for Bradley Holloway. Because there *is* *no* Holloway. Yes, the man exists, but not in the context of Veracity. I framed him. I made sure the men at the safe house thought he was their boss, just to be sure he was outed. I'm sure he's guilty of many things, but trying to kill Elias and stop Veracity aren't two of them. He knows nothing about it, in fact."

"So Holloway *isn't* Vader?" said Paige in confusion.

"Wow, it's just dazzling how quickly you catch on," said Kayla cruelly. "No, the vice president is not the mysterious puppet master that everyone is calling Vader."

"So who *is?*" asked Connor.

"Amazing," said Kayla, shaking her head. "It's like I'm talking to a pair of brick walls. Even when I lead you to the dots, you still can't connect them. You really can't guess Vader's identity? Even now?"

Connor shook his head. "I only know that you're working with him."

Kayla laughed in contempt. "I'm not working with Holloway," she said, "and I'm not working with Vader, either."

She paused for effect. "Because *I am* Vader, you moron."

PART 6

"In spite of the hardness and ruthlessness I thought I saw in his face, I got the impression that here was a man [Adolf Hitler] who could be relied upon when he had given his word."

—Neville Chamberlain, Former Prime Minister of the United Kingdom, in a letter.

56

Kayla's revelation that she was behind the Vader voice ricocheted around the small motel room like a rocket-powered pinball, made even more impactful, and more surreal, by the ungodly hour and unfamiliar surroundings. It was the last in a series of earth-shattering shocks Connor and Paige had received in the past twenty-four hours, which had collectively hit them like a barrage of machine gun fire.

Both gasped at this latest bombshell, to Kayla Keller's obvious delight.

Connor couldn't remember the last time he felt this stupid. It was right there in front of him this entire time. Kayla was the man they'd been calling Vader.

Of course she was.

It was all so clear now.

"I assume this gun is loaded, right?" she asked Connor. "I wouldn't put it past you to leave it empty, having planned for me to take it in some elaborate scheme of yours."

"It's loaded," replied Connor, something he knew Veracity would confirm.

"Good," she said, and then with a grin added, "I'm more impressed with myself than usual. I actually found a way to pull a logical argument out of my ass that had you doubting yourself. Wasn't sure that even *I* could execute such a brilliant feat of mental gymnastics."

She sighed. "Alas, I've decided that even if I *could* manage to get you back on board with clever arguments, it's not worth it. Now that your suspicions are aroused, letting you live is too dangerous. You'd keep digging. You'd watch me with new eyes. So as much as I'd like to salvage our relationship, use you in the way I worked very hard to do, this is no longer possible."

She raised the gun with a clear purpose.

"Wait!" shouted Connor. "You're really going to kill us, just like that?"

"Just like that. I'm not thrilled about it. I really thought I was on the verge of salvaging this mess. I tried to keep the plan moving forward, despite the setbacks. But you had a rare moment of non-stupidity and figured me out." She shrugged. "But don't worry about me. I have a plan B to fall back on."

"How will you explain our deaths to Captain Long?" asked Connor.

"I'll figure it out. He won't be back for four hours, at minimum. Maybe I'll tell him that a few of Ren's men found us. That, tragically, you two were killed, but I managed to escape again. I'll make sure he's Veracity-enabled when I tell him, so he'll believe every word of whatever story I concoct, no matter how far-fetched."

"But what is this really about?" said Connor. "I've obviously missed something big. Some critical aspect of what you're trying to do. So why not tell us what it is? Tell us how you've managed to outsmart so many people? I'm guessing you haven't been able to tell anyone about it. So why not tell a . . . *captive* audience who can truly appreciate all the layers of this onion you've created?"

"Playing to my vanity?" said Kayla in amusement. "Using another worn-out thriller trope? Stalling for time?"

"For what reason?" he asked. "You just said the captain won't be back for four hours. Do you think I expect my father to recover, escape, and rescue us in the next twenty minutes?"

"Do you think I'll let down my guard?" snorted Kayla.

"No, I don't. But don't they let condemned men have a last request? So this is mine. In lieu of a last meal."

Kayla considered for several seconds. "Why not?" she said finally. "It might be fun for me, at that. But I might as well do it the smart way."

Saying this, she kept the gun trained on them while she removed the blue duffel bag from a dresser drawer and fished inside for plastic ties. She tossed several to the married couple, and had them tie themselves together, and then tie themselves to the bedpost.

Paige was utterly shattered, too emotionally drained to even shed a tear. She looked as though she had retreated within herself, almost as comatose as her father-in-law.

"That's better," said Kayla once they had finished. She was still holding the gun, but she had moved it to her lap now that Paige and Connor were incapacitated. "So where were we?" she said happily.

"You were telling us that you're Vader," said Connor.

She grinned. "A brilliant move, you have to admit. I used the deepest male voice I could find, one that was obviously a fraud. I knew that very few people could ever hear the voice of James Earl Jones and suspect it was coming from a woman. And I and everyone else referred to the mysterious Vader as a *he*. After that, I could *bury* most people in clues, and they'd refuse to even consider that I might be pulling the strings."

Connor couldn't help but be impressed. She was right. Even when it was staring him in the face, this had never occurred to him.

"So let me go back to the beginning," continued Kayla. "Well, almost the beginning. You were right, Connor, there is no Derek Manning. I am exactly who the world thinks I am. Some of the dirt on me truly was fabricated after the media feeding frenzy began, but most of it is true. I committed every sin in the book to get ahead. I stabbed people in the back—*and* the front—I poisoned environments, and I broke countless laws. I'm brilliant, and I'm ruthless. Morals and ethics are for idiots. We're only on Earth for a short period, and it's all just a game anyway. Turns out I'm a psychopath. I know you've studied this condition, Connor, but so have I, and it was an easy self-diagnosis to make."

Paige shook her head in horror, a sign that she was coming back to life.

"I read your article on psychopaths, in fact," continued Kayla. "And I have to say, I was disappointed. All the examples you used were of men. A little sexist, don't you think? Not that this isn't a common bias. But women can be psychopaths, too," she said with a cruel smile.

"You sound *proud*," spat Paige, having now fully recovered from her initial state of withdrawal.

"Connor will tell you that I *am* proud. Psychopaths tend to be. But I've come to believe we're in a computer simulation anyway. None of this is real. We're all inside a game, and the winner is the one who gets the most points. Who amasses the most wealth and power. Even if they have to cheat."

Connor didn't find this statement all that surprising. Boredom was a psychopath's greatest nemesis. They bored easily, yet found this state intolerable, so they often walked through life as if it were a game with no rules, desperate for stimulation. But in modern times, top scientists had come to believe that the universe actually *was* a game. In fact, many believed that the chances that the universe was a computer simulation were greater than the chances that it was not.

For good reason. Humanity had been perfecting ever more realistic computer simulations and virtual realities. Given the astonishing, ongoing improvements in computing power, did anyone doubt that within a hundred years the characters within these sims would become so sophisticated that they, themselves, would believe they were real? And given this was true, wasn't it likely that humanity, or some other species, had *already* achieved this level of technology, and that the universe as humanity knew it was just some simulation on the laptop of a technologically advanced teenager?

"You can't really believe we're in a game?" said Paige in disbelief, not knowing how mainstream this theory had become.

"Oh, I really can," said Kayla.

Paige shook her head. "This is just something you tell yourself to excuse your cruelties."

"Maybe. But it does keep me engaged. Instead of dwelling on day-to-day drudgeries, or my eventual death, I just try to have fun playing the game. I expect to win it. But if not, it at least keeps me fully occupied. So the setbacks I've been having don't trouble me. Wouldn't want it to be *too* easy. Every game avatar needs a stiff test to prove themselves."

"You are seriously screwed up in the head, lady," said Paige.

Kayla laughed. "I guess when you know nothing about psychopaths, or simulated universes, and you waste your life teaching pathetic fifth-graders, you might think so."

"So you really did kill the witnesses?" said Connor.

Kayla shot him a look of contempt. "As brilliant as I am," she said, "even *I* keep getting surprised by the magnitude of your stupidity. *Of course* I killed the witnesses. I've had the Vader thing going for many years. At first slowly. Gathering dirt on key players, expanding my reach, my power. And I had to use all of this and more to get my neck out of the noose when the shit finally did hit the fan. I had been too cocky, too arrogant. Thought I was bulletproof. So I was sloppy, made too many mistakes, and paid for them dearly. But I managed to have witnesses intimidated and killed, jurists and judges bribed, FBI agents blackmailed, evidence lockers breached, computer evidence hacked—you name it. In the end, I was able to gain my freedom and melt back into the woodwork."

"And step up your Vader activities even more," guessed Connor. "A billionaire with endless time on your hands, with nothing to do but move your mercenary chess pieces around the board and gather dirt on the powerful. And plot your big comeback."

"Exactly. Karen Preston kept busy. I pursued any number of options to rebuild my reputation."

"Including buying newspapers?" said Connor.

"Yes. I had intended to become a media mogul. But even though I didn't pursue this once Veracity came into play, it would have worked wonders. Especially since I'm very close to perfecting perfect fake video."

"What are you talking about?" said Connor.

Kayla grinned. "The mother of all fake news. You may have seen fake news before, but nothing like what I'm on the verge of perfecting. Soon, I'll be able to make videos showing sweet little Paigey here kicking puppies to death. Or screwing a roomful of tattooed bikers. Or praising Hitler. And the videos will look so real—so *perfect*—a forensic scientist will vouch for their authenticity. And seeing is believing. The potency of this tool will be astonishing."

"That's *horrible*," said Paige.

"That's horrible," repeated Kayla in mocking tones. "Can anyone really be this wide-eyed and innocent? It may be horrible, but it's been inevitable for a long time. Perfect fake videos are the goal of virtual reality companies, after all. This is just the next logical step.

"I would have perfected this already," she continued, "but I put it on temporary hold while I pursued Veracity."

"Why Veracity?" said Connor.

"I never forgot the efforts your father made while working at Virtuality. His strategy was true genius. Unfortunately for Elias, his ideas were ahead of his time, ahead of the available tech. When I got wind of the Darwin computer, I decided it was time to try again."

"You mean to have *my father* try again."

Kayla shrugged. "Same thing. I had no idea he could really do it, but it was well worth a shot. Since his first attempt so many years ago, I had often fantasized about being the only person in the world who could lie. Can you imagine? Talk about power. You know the old expression, *in the kingdom of the blind, the one-eyed man is king.* Well, in the world of no lies, the *liar* is king. The liar is all but *omnipotent.*"

"And you hit the jackpot," said Connor. "My father's creation exceeded any reasonable expectations. So how did you manage to keep yourself immune from the system?"

"You guessed it exactly. I brought the Darwin computer to the game. I knew that Elias wouldn't trust me and would block me out as soon as he could. So I made sure to program in a single private entrance before he got the computer, and program the computer to keep the entrance open no matter what. And to hide it from everyone and everything else, including itself."

"How does it work?" asked Connor.

"You mean how do I lie?"

"Exactly."

"Veracity knows who I am. By facial recognition and other means. Whenever I make a statement, it registers it as the truth. No matter what. Unless I tell it otherwise. I do this using a few quick and subtle blinks, which I've spent months learning so they're undetectable. I have several commands I can issue in this way. I don't even have to think about them anymore. Every once in a while, I order Veracity to catch me in a lie. After all, if I *always* told the truth, I wouldn't seem human."

Connor knew she was right. And using this strategy, she'd get credit for making little white lies that those wearing Veracity interfaces would know were told in the spirit of kindness, making her appear to be even more saintly. She could purposely get caught lying, but only when the lie was used to spare the feelings of another.

"Well done," said Connor. "You used this to good effect on us. Like when you said you weren't in love with my father, for example, and had Veracity call this out as a lie."

Kayla smiled. "I was really proud of that one," she said. "How could you *not* trust a woman in love with that pathetic, saccharine, *nauseating* idealist that you call your father? Especially a poor woman who's been through so much trauma she's afraid to even admit this to herself?"

Connor wanted to reach out and strangle her, to tear the self-satisfied look from her face with his bare hands. She had toyed with his father's emotions like a cat with a ball of yarn. She had felt nothing but contempt for him, so their social interactions were all a lie, nothing but cruel, cynical manipulations.

But what made this so much worse was that his father was in love with *her*. And this was *real*. It wasn't just that Kayla Keller was even more of a monster than Connor had thought, it was that she was so convincing, so brilliant, so adept at emotional manipulation.

His father would be devastated if he were to ever learn who she really was.

"Veracity was the answer to my prayers," said Kayla. "Well, if I actually believed in God, and actually prayed, it would be. It was the perfect way to get my reputation back—with a vengeance. I could go from being a villain to being a victim. And in today's America, being able to claim victimhood is priceless."

A self-satisfied smile came over her face. "Who *wouldn't* feel sorry for me? Wrongfully accused. Savagely smeared by my first love, the evil Derek Manning. Working tirelessly to help establish Veracity because of it, so I could change the world and ensure nothing like this could ever happen again. Refusing to ask for majority ownership of a company I single-handedly funded. Giving all of the proceeds to charity." She grinned. "I'd be sainted and knighted in the same year."

Connor and Paige glared at her in disgust, but said nothing.

"My tragic, inspirational story almost brings a tear to my eye," continued Kayla. "Which I can do on call, by the way, since I've perfected fake crying."

"We need to move on before I get sick to my stomach," said Connor. "Why the alliance with Jalen Howard?"

"Why, indeed. Jalen Howard was a good man. One who thought I had noble motives. But the truth is, I really do need Veracity-blockers. For the reasons I argued. If I'm eventually going to rule over a world-wide hegemony, I can't have society self-destructing around me. That wouldn't do at all."

"Ruling over a world-wide hegemony?" repeated Connor. "Really? And here I thought you were only a cruel, ruthless psychopath. Who knew that you were also insane? You'll be lucky to rule over your fellow inmates in the federal prison you'll be thrown into."

"Not that imaginative after all, are you, Connor?" said Kayla in contempt. "For someone who fancies himself a futurist, you're sorely lacking in vision. Hard to believe that you can't see how easy it will be for me accumulate massive power."

She shrugged. "But no worries. I'm happy to spell it out for you."

57

Paige looked just as skeptical as her husband. "It takes more than lies and dirt gathering to rule the world," she said.

Kayla laughed. "Does it? I guess we're about to find out. Since there isn't a world-wide government right now, I'll have to start small, of course. I'll start by becoming president of this country. Why do you think I spent so much effort making you think Bradley Holloway is Vader? Because I'm framing him. And you two were supposed to help me take him down. A few honorable sorts like you would be quite useful in the early going, before Veracity was fully accepted and my reputation restored. Like Connor said, you were there to vouch for me, sing my praises, regale the world with tales of my heroism. Tell the world what I had meant to your poor, murdered father."

She paused. "It's too bad that you'll be missing out on all the fun. I'll still be destroying the vice president, which will be quite a show."

"But it won't work," said Connor. "When he denies your allegations, Veracity will confirm that he's telling the truth."

"We've already discussed this," said Kayla. "So now you're trying my patience. The moment I'm no longer having fun telling you my plans is the moment you die. Remember that."

She sighed. "I'll repeat myself, but this will be the last time. I wouldn't get Holloway on being *Vader*. I just wanted *you* to believe he was responsible for killing your father. You'd loathe him so much you'd ignore any ethical standards to help me bring him down. And this would help us bond, as we'd be working together against a common enemy. But, like I said *before*," she added pointedly, "the plan would be to take Holloway down using a transgression he had *actually* made. One that Veracity would ferret out. Believe me, I'm well aware of the danger of making a single false accusation. If I'm ever caught in a lie, publicly, my cover will be blown. People will know I'm immune to Veracity."

Kayla paused. "The good news for me is that I have the ability to program Veracity in very sophisticated ways. The system keeps careful track of everything I say publicly, along with context. If anyone, anywhere, ever says something that contradicts what I've said previously, something that would blow my cover, Veracity knows to call them out as liars. As a default response. I can also get Veracity to indicate that a public figure is lying any time I want, even if they're telling the truth. I can program in a narrative for them, and Veracity will support this narrative when they speak. But this is also a power I'll need to use sparingly, if at all."

Connor nodded knowingly. "Because, again, if someone can prove that Veracity screwed up, this could bring down the whole house of cards?"

Kayla nodded. "Exactly. But getting back to Holloway, my plan is to take him out very soon. Why? Because, again, I'll look heroic—speaking truth to power, crusading against corruption at the highest levels—that sort of shit. But wait—there's more. If I didn't intervene at all, and there was no Veracity, Holloway would be sure to get his party's nomination. The VP of a two-term president, it's all but automatic. So when I take him out, the field for the presidential nomination will be in disarray. Are you with me so far?" she asked, quite pleased with herself.

Connor nodded. "Go on."

"With no clear front-runner, and Veracity coming on the scene, presidential hopefuls will drop like flies. No one will want to run, no matter what kind of rules we institute to protect them from past misdeeds. And then *I'll* throw my hat in the ring, the once-despised billionaire with the heart of gold. Before long, I'll have the field almost entirely to myself, and whoever runs against me won't have a chance. My story is magic. A woman nearly burned at the stake as a devil, who turns out to be an angel. And I'll be able to lie. Not about specific policy items. That would be too dangerous. But I can spout endless saccharin platitudes that will read true. I can express my love of country. Express my honest interest in bettering the poor and the middle class. I can say, 'I love all races equally' and have this be the truth."

She grinned icily. "But when my opponents say the same thing, I can have Veracity call them out as liars."

"And there's no way they can prove that they aren't secretly racists," said Paige.

"Very good. You're finally catching on. But there's still more. As Vader, I'll have my mercs continue to gather dirt on my opponents. I can use this to—"

"You won't *need* anything more," interrupted Connor in revulsion. "You'll win the nomination, and then the presidency, in the biggest landslide in the history of America."

"Ah—good to see that the futurist is beginning to show a knack for seeing the future. But I thought the bit about me becoming the most powerful person in the world was just fevered rantings of an insane mind."

"You've made your point," snapped Connor bitterly.

"Not yet, I haven't. Now that you've got me started, I might as well finish. You see, the duplicate Veracity supercomputers that will eventually spread across the globe will all have the identical configuration to the one that exists now, down to the last atom. *Identical.* Which means my backdoor entrance will continue to exist in all of them. As US president, this backdoor will make me the master of world affairs, able to lie to other leaders when they can't lie to me. By my third term—after the people unanimously demand that term limits be stricken down to keep the most honorable politician in America in office—I'll work magic to consolidate power, and move toward a global hegemony. With me at the helm, of course. Talk about winning the simulation."

"I can see your case for becoming president," said Connor, "but this global hegemony thing won't be nearly as easy as you think."

"I don't *think* it will be easy. What fun would it be if it were? I enjoy challenges. Stops life from being so deadly boring. But I'll get there, because soon I'll have another trick up my sleeve that will make me unstoppable."

"What trick is that?" said Connor.

"The fake video I mentioned earlier. I'll perfect it soon. Then I'll be able to bring fake news to the next level. I'll still have to be careful to make sure that a victim can't prove the footage is fake, but I'll manage."

"Even if your perfect fake videos fool human beings," said Connor, "they won't fool Veracity."

"Ah, but they will," said Kayla. "That's the beauty of it. My fake video is computer generated, of course. So I can have the computer change the micro and macro-expressions of the person I'm smearing, the person speaking the words I'm putting into their mouth, thousands of times each second. And other parameters as well, like speech pattern, vocal tone, and so on. I can run each iteration by an automated Veracity interface, tens of thousands of variations a second."

"Until you find a combination that Veracity will read as true," said Connor.

"Now you're catching on," said Kayla. "Not that a chimpanzee couldn't have jumped to the same conclusion. But yes, when I introduce hidden camera footage of a political opponent whispering a racial or homophobic slur to a friend in private, it will read as real."

Connor was sickened beyond words. Kayla kept coming back to racism—for good reason. It was a potent charge, and her fake video would box her opponents in. Even if they didn't have a racist bone in their bodies, when they denied it, she'd make sure Veracity indicated that they were lying.

And this was only the beginning of what she could do with technology that allowed her to deliver fake video footage that was indistinguishable from real.

"Why do this?" said Connor. "How much power do you need? Why turn the world into a nightmare of Orwellian proportions?"

"Because I *won't* be," insisted Kayla. "I'll be doing just the opposite. I'll be turning the world into a *paradise*. Remember, we're all just computer-generated avatars on some kid's laptop anyway. But as the best player, I do have some responsibilities. What you're missing is that human beings *want* fake news. They *need* it. And since I'll be the sole provider, I can't let them down."

"What are you talking about?" said Paige. "No one *wants* fake news."

Kayla laughed. "You really are one of the most painfully naive people I've ever known," she said. "But in this case, at least, you aren't alone. Pundits will tell you that we're now living in the *post-truth* age. Well, I've got news for you—we've *always* lived in the post-truth age. We're a post-truth species."

"That's preposterous," said Connor.

"Really? Fake news is the only reason our species ever got anywhere. Shared mythology, shared delusion, is the only thing that can unite huge swaths of humanity into common purpose. Untold millions of us once believed in sun gods, animal gods, and idols. Fake news, fake news, and fake news. And millions and billions more *still* believe in such things as virgin births, reincarnation, the sacredness of cows, and the existence of the underworld and heaven—with zero proof. One of these fake news stories might be completely true, but there is no way that *all of them* are."

"So you're calling religion fake news?" said Connor.

"Some might consider it heretical to say, but yes. Fake news that's lasted for thousands of years. Not that these stories all have ancient origins. No matter how sophisticated we become, we need a shared mythology to unite us. L. Ron Hubbard and Joseph Smith disseminated unprovable news stories in the recent era, and these are now believed by millions. But Joseph Smith's followers firmly believe that L. Ron Hubbard was a charlatan. And L. Ron Hubbard's followers believe the same about Joseph Smith."

Kayla shook her head. "And this isn't just the province of religions," she continued. "Governments and societies throughout history have also generated shared mythologies. In the thirteenth century, fake news began to spread that the Jews were kidnapping and murdering Christian children to use their blood in religious rituals. This was fake news believed by millions over many centuries, which led to the deaths of countless Jews."

She paused. "The Third Reich and Arian supremacy is another example of a shared fiction. So is communism. So is the long-held belief by many of the citizens of North Korea that their glorious leader is practically a god, even as much of the country wallows in extreme poverty. Every country has its own propaganda machine, and generates its own disinformation campaigns."

Kayla smiled. "In fact, fake news is much better at uniting people than the truth."

Connor was about to say that this was absurd, but stopped himself. Kayla had made other declarations that had seemed equally absurd, but had somehow come up with persuasive arguments to support them. "How can that be?" he asked instead.

"Shared belief in an absurdity is a much better indicator of loyalty than shared belief in the *truth*. And it's a much better way to create group cohesion. If a leader asks you to believe that the sky is blue, and you do, what does that prove? The truth is easy. But if he requires his followers to believe the sky is *green*, they quickly distance themselves from non-believers and become firmly united in a shared delusion."

Kayla paused to let this sink in. "And the more people who believe in a shared delusion," she continued, "the more powerful it becomes. A hundred-dollar bill is, intrinsically, entirely useless. It's nothing but a tiny green piece of paper. And yet, we're willing to give up items of actual, intrinsic value, like food and clothing, to get this silly scrap. It only has value because everyone across the globe now shares the *delusion* that it has value. But most of us don't even realize it *is* a delusion anymore. Human beings are very good at accepting shared mythology as fact."

Connor was fascinated, despite himself. Kayla Keller was truly a monster, but he found her arguments to be intellectually stimulating.

"And what is advertising if not fake news?" she continued. "The idea of proposing marriage with a diamond ring seems like a tradition so old, and so steeped in our culture, you'd think it was one of the Ten Commandments delivered to Moses on Mt. Sinai. But it's a recent, man-made creation. De Beers brilliantly fostered this shared mythology, taking a relatively abundant, relatively inexpensive item that wasn't selling, and convincing the public over decades that a diamond engagement ring was an indispensable sign of true love. This may be fake news, but try proposing to your true love without one. You'll quickly find yourself swimming against a swift social current."

"Okay!" said Connor. "Enough! You've made your point."

A slow smile spread across Kayla's face. "Good," she said. "So now that I have, why shouldn't I unite the world using a fake mythology of my own creation? Since the universe itself is fake, why not just take this another layer deeper? If you see it and believe it, then it's real. What other reality matters?"

"No clever argument can hide the fact that you don't care about anyone but yourself," said Paige.

"Very true," said Kayla. "But that doesn't change the facts. People need to be led. And even more, they need to be *mis*-led. So yes, I'll be amassing power for myself. But I'll also be uniting the world. I'll also end war and hunger."

She turned to Connor. "Your father whines about our current state of divisiveness. Well I can fix that. I *will* fix that. Because the truth is, people are nothing but sheep. Sheep who would be lost without fake news to believe in."

"You may be a wolf," said Paige, "but people are not sheep."

Kayla laughed. "You of all people—a Christian—can't really believe that. How often have you said the words, 'The Lord is My Shepherd' in church? If the Lord is your shepherd, what does that make *you*?"

Paige fumed, but didn't reply.

Kayla still had a grin on her face. "I'm so glad you convinced me not to kill you right away, Connor. I haven't been this amused in a long time."

"Glad I could help," said Connor miserably.

Kayla laughed again. "You really aren't glad, you know. Not according to Veracity. But I can't blame you for not being a fan of my work. After all, I *am* going to kill you. And then I'm going to see to it that Elias dies also. Later today, in fact."

"Good luck with that," said Connor. "I've seen the Chinese base. There's no way you're going to breach it."

"I don't need to. Because Captain Long is going to help me blow it into the stone age. Since I don't care about saving Elias, it becomes a much simpler exercise. And with the inventor of the tech gone, and you two gone, I can rewrite history to show that Elias came to me for funding *after* he perfected the tech. That will completely allay any suspicions that I tampered with the system like I did. And I can find a new Jalen Howard, who will vouch for me, and who will continue to perfect the Veracity blockers I need to hold my kingdom together."

She raised the gun from her lap and pointed it at Connor. "So now that I've honored the last request of a condemned man, I'm afraid I can't put off your execution any longer."

58

"Wait!" said Connor wildly. "There is one element you haven't touched on yet. What happened at the safe house? And what was supposed to happen?"

Kayla considered, and then lowered the gun to her lap once more. "I don't blame you for wanting to cling to life a few minutes longer," she said. "But you've already guessed the answers. Elias was supposed to die at his house, but you came up with inspired strategies that saved him. Very annoying. Then the plan was to race to my safe house, where we'd bond for several days. We'd mourn Elias together, and I'd demonstrate Veracity, tell my sad tale, and get you on my side. My two-man team—Vader's team—was standing by in Borrego Springs so they could move in when my gut told me we were ready for the next phase. The phase that would really cement the bond between us."

"Why?" said Connor. "Because you planned to let yourself be tortured?"

"Exactly. The men who called themselves Neil and John would break in and make you fear for your lives. John would torture me, not knowing that I had actually given him this very order. I made sure to plant the seed three weeks ago that Holloway was their boss. I was confident I could get them to out him in front of you. Then, when John was questioning you, I'd be heroic. I'd create a virtual keyboard on the kitchen floor and wipe them out with various remote weapons I had hidden around the place."

She sighed in disappointment. "It would have been so dramatic. You'd have thought I saved your life. Then we'd spend more time on the run together. What a deep relationship this would have forged between us. Then I'd enlist your aid in taking down the vice president, and get you to follow me to the ends of the Earth. Pretending to have been in love with your father would be icing on the cake."

"So when my father survived the attack on his home, you had to make some adjustments."

Kayla shrugged. "Only minor ones, really. I decided the plan was easily salvageable. I moved up the timetable. I had to have the attack on my safe house commence sooner rather than later, to get Elias out of the way. While you were talking with your dad in the kitchen, I was downstairs issuing new orders as Vader, using a voice changer program I downloaded from the cloud. I instructed them to torture me first, and then torture and kill Elias."

"And then you would kill *them*," said Connor.

She smiled. "Very true. But I forgot to tell them about that last part."

Kayla's smile vanished. "The torture really did suck," she added, "but it had a nice fringe benefit. I knew that if I screamed loudly enough, you could hear me upstairs. Then you'd see how much I meant to your father."

"But my father *wasn't* killed," said Connor. "And I got us out of there instead of you. So I ruined this plan also."

"Yes you did," admitted Kayla. "I underestimated you." She raised the gun once again and pointed it at his head. "Something that will never happen again."

Connor actually smiled. "Not true," he said calmly. "I'm afraid you're underestimating me this very second."

"Explain yourself!" shouted Kayla in alarm, as Veracity indicated he was telling the truth. "Quickly!"

"Thanks for sharing your plans with us, and for the reprieve. But I'm afraid I can't let you kill us. You were halfway right. I did want you to take the gun from me. I purposely let down my guard. But I knew you'd be too smart to fall for the empty gun trick."

Paige's eyes widened and she stared at her husband with her mouth open. "You planned this?"

"Sorry, Paige. I couldn't tell you about it before now."

Connor enjoyed Kayla's confusion. She had a loaded gun, and could shoot him at any time, but he knew she wouldn't. Not until she learned what she had missed.

He stared at Kayla and raised his eyebrows. "Here's the thing," he said smugly. "When I figured this out, all I could think about was confronting you. But I realized that if Captain Long was present when I did, this might present complications. You could give him a Veracity interface and make me appear to be a liar, while you registered as always telling the truth. He wouldn't know what to believe. I might end up convincing him of my case, but I might not. I couldn't take that risk."

"Which is why he isn't here," said Kayla.

"Not quite," said Connor. "Turns out the captain and I had a lively discussion in your van. His English is impressive, because I was talking a mile a minute. I was able to hit the highlights of my case against you very quickly. He wasn't sure if he could believe me, but I begged him to give me one hour to prove it."

Connor smiled. "And he agreed."

"Are you telling me you staged this to get me to confess?"

"That's exactly what I'm telling you," said Connor, knowing that Veracity would confirm it.

"Big deal," said Kayla. "So you got me to confess. So what? Because you and Paige will take my confession to the grave."

"Yeah, not quite," replied Connor. "You know that bag of high-tech prototypes that Captain Long brought with him from Dr. Rosado's house? He had a bug in there. It had some advanced features, but I thought it might be tricky to deploy in front of you. Fortunately, I didn't need it. Because there's an easy, low-tech way to place a bug." He arched an eyebrow. "Just call someone on your phone and keep the line open without anyone knowing."

Kayla's eyes widened in instant comprehension. She rose from the bed and retrieved the phone Connor had placed on top of the dresser just after he had entered the room. It showed an active call was in progress. She ended the connection and flung the phone against the wall, her face a mask of rage. "So Long has been listening in this entire time?" she said through clenched teeth.

"Very good," said Connor, like he was talking to a child. "You catch on quick."

Kayla shot him a look of utter hatred, but it vanished quickly, and her calm demeanor returned. "Well played," she said. "I have to give credit where it's due. It would have been fun to ally with Captain Long, but no matter. I can go it alone. He's in my van. So after I kill you, I'll lock him inside and drive him into a lake. And once again, there will be no one left alive who's heard my confession. I hate to lose the van, but we all have to make sacrifices."

She raised her gun and pointed it at Connor's face for what seemed like the hundredth time. "Goodbye, Connor. You were more impressive than I expected. And I guess I *did* underestimate you one last time. Thanks for letting me know about Long."

Connor shook his head sadly. "Before you pull the trigger, you should know that I haven't told you the most important part. Two things that you're really going to want to hear."

"Quickly," said Kayla. "You have twenty seconds. After that, nothing you say can get me to delay the inevitable."

"First, Long *isn't* in your van. He's in the room next door. He dropped me off on the street so he wouldn't have to see you in person. When he phoned you to explain he was still going to LA, it was an audio-only call, so Veracity couldn't tell you he was lying.

"And second," continued Connor, "a bug wasn't the only tech the captain had in that magic bag of his."

Just as he was finishing the sentence, Connor used his right thumb and forefinger to press a sugar-cube-sized electronic device attached to the inside of his left sleeve, and all three inhabitants of the motel room melted into instant oblivion.

59

Kayla Keller's eyes shot open and she found herself on the same bed she had been on earlier, but this time with her wrists bound together and tied to the bed. Connor, Paige, and the Chinese captain were standing on the opposite end of the small room, deep in conversation.

Connor noticed that she had stirred and abruptly ended the discussion. "It's about time," he said to her.

"How long have I been out?"

"Almost an hour," replied Long. "The initial effect you experienced only lasts for about ten minutes. But I gave you a little something extra, so the three of us could have a private discussion."

"How was I knocked out in the first place?"

A smile slowly spread across Connor's face. "The captain gave me a device that emits sound," he said. "At a frequency that, ah . . . promotes unconsciousness. He assured me that it wouldn't rupture any eardrums, or cause any pain. Just activate the device, and anyone in close proximity passes out instantly."

"We don't use it much," admitted Long. "Because whoever deploys it gets hit with it also. Industrial grade earplugs can block it, but that's too obvious."

"But in this case," said Connor, "I was only too happy to knock myself out, knowing that the captain would arrive just a few minutes after you ended our phone connection to relieve you of the gun."

"I see," said Kayla with a scowl. She turned to face Long. "I'm disappointed in you, Captain. I can't believe Connor got you to delay your LA mission on the basis of nothing more than circumstantial evidence."

"You, yourself, helped me to take him seriously," said Long. "You weren't shy about considering strategies that would leave Elias dead.

That surprised me, especially since you said you were in love with him. I understand that this is the rational thing to do, but most people still wouldn't be able to bring themselves to do it. But a psychopath would."

Connor was impressed with Long's knowledge, and he was absolutely right. Most people, if given the choice between saving the life of their daughter, or saving the lives of two strangers, would save their daughter every time. But not psychopaths. They had no trouble deciding this on a strictly mathematical basis, since sentimentality, compassion, and loyalty never entered the picture. They would choose to save two strangers over a loved one without hesitation.

"Also," continued Long, "why would Connor lie about this? He's Elias's son, with every reason to want to trust you."

"So now what?" said Kayla. "Are you going to kill me? Right in the middle of this motel room? Kill me in cold blood?"

"What would *you* do?" asked Connor.

Kayla laughed. "I'd kill me without a moment's thought, or a moment's regret. But then my brain is superior, free from a conscience and worthless ethical constraints. I'm sure the captain would have no problem killing me where I sit. But could you? Could Paige? In cold blood? Without a trial?"

"The answer for me is yes," said Connor, making sure she was staring at him so this would register as true. "If you had your way, my father would be dead already. Still might become that way. You committed, or ordered, multiple murders before you dropped off the grid, and God only knows how many since. Not to mention other atrocities, ordered under your Vader persona."

"So why am I still alive?" said Kayla. "Why did I even wake up? Killing me in my sleep is more humane, don't you think?"

"Because we need you," said Connor simply.

"*Really,*" said Kayla, looking intrigued. "I can't wait to hear this."

"We need your help to free my father," said Connor. "While you were still unconscious, we discussed this at length. Now that we know Holloway isn't really involved, we can get the US military behind us." He frowned. "But not as quickly as we need to."

"I see," said Kayla. "Because now that you've escaped, Colonel Ren will realize his secret base has been blown, and won't stay put for long."

"This is true," said Long. "I know the colonel well. Given what Connor has told me, Ren won't discover the escape until first daylight, which is at least two hours away. After that, he'll send search parties into the woods looking for Connor. But after about three hours, he'll give up, and institute a mass exodus from the base." He paused. "So we have no time to waste."

"But just a few hours ago, you thought a rescue was all but impossible," said Kayla. "So what changed?"

Kayla came to the answer before the captain could reply. "Oh, I get it," she continued. "A rescue was impossible when I was merely Kayla Keller. But now that you know I'm also Vader, with scores of mercs on speed dial, this is no longer true. You need me to get you expendable manpower at a moment's notice, don't you?"

"I do," said Long. "The other change was that I learned Connor used a Veracity blocker to escape, and I remembered that you have a bag full of them."

Kayla nodded thoughtfully. "How many mercenaries are you looking for?" she asked.

"Sixteen," replied Connor. "They need to meet the captain at a designated staging area within a few miles of the Chinese base in three hours. Armed to the teeth, and forewarned about what they'll be up against."

"Impossible," said Kayla. "Not within three hours."

"Possible," said Connor. "You can't tell me these men don't have access to helicopters, or can't charter one at a moment's notice. You'll wire each of them a million upfront, to capture their full attention. Four million more when the job is over, which should give them plenty of motivation. Think of it as hazard pay. Also as a way to ease the pain of having to rush here."

"That's as much as eighty million dollars," said Kayla, "assuming they all survive."

"No, that's eighty million dollars, period," corrected Connor. "You'll set things up beforehand so that all sixteen wires will be sent within seconds of the mission's completion. They get paid, even if they die, so their beneficiaries reap the reward for their sacrifice."

"You're very generous with other people's money."

"You're a billionaire," said Connor. "You'll get over it."

"I assume you won't want them to know who you are," said Kayla. "Or Paige."

"That's right," replied Connor. "They'll only ever see the captain, who will tell them that his name is Long and that he's a soldier. That's all. It's one of the most common Chinese last names. So when the op is over, they won't know who they were working with, or what the op was really all about."

"They're soldiers for hire who will be earning millions," said Kayla. "They'll know how to keep their mouths shut anyway."

"So much the better," said Connor.

"So what do *I* get out of this?" demanded Kayla.

"You get to live," answered Long. "If we're able to rescue Elias, we'll release you. If we aren't, you die. Simple as that. Is that enough incentive for you?"

"What are the chances of success?"

"Surprisingly high," said Long. "Provided we have your mercenaries and your cooperation. My plan is to first wipe out all of my former comrades, and then free Elias. I know the layout of the base like the back of my hand, and the plan is a good one."

"What if it fails despite my best efforts?" asked Kayla.

"We don't care," said Connor. "We aren't giving out trophies for effort. I loathe you. You're pure, distilled evil. But I want my father to live, so I'm willing to make a deal with the devil. But look at me closely. If my father dies, if this is unsuccessful, I guarantee I will kill you myself. I *guarantee* it. What is Veracity saying about that?"

"And if you succeed," said Kayla, "I go free? Just like that?"

"Yes," said Connor. "We'll release you and give you a twenty-four-hour head start. We won't try to find you or recapture you in this period. But after that, all bets are off."

"So after this period, you'll be pulling out all the stops to catch me again."

"Absolutely," said Connor. "And so will the US military, if I have anything to say about it. You'll be hunted down like the vermin you are."

"Sounds like fun," said Kayla dryly. "But I want *forty-eight hours.*"

"Twenty-four," replied Long. "That's the deal. Connor and I have thought this out. We knew you'd try to negotiate. So it's a take-it-or-leave-it offer. You have two minutes to decide. If you don't agree, you won't live to see minute three."

"Why *not* forty-eight hours?" said Kayla. "It's only one more day."

"What about take it or leave it are you not understanding?" snapped Connor. "You'll still have your billions, your safe houses, your minions, and dirt on scores of powerful people." He sighed. "Not to mention your ruthlessness and total lack of ethics. Keep arguing, and I'll change my mind. Unleashing you is a high price for the world to pay to save my father. Don't make me rethink it."

Kayla considered this and decided not to press her luck. "Explain my role," she said.

"You'll stay safe and sound in this room during the attack," said Long. "Paige and Connor will stay at the motel as well. They'll help monitor surveillance drones I'll be sending up, four of them. Connor will be in this room with you, and Paige will be in the room next door. We'll all have comms for communication."

"If the captain tells me he's successfully extracted my father," said Connor, "I'll let you go. "If we fail, I'll kill you."

Kayla nodded. "So you've said. But let's get back to my release. You'd have to give me a vehicle. Twenty-four hours on foot won't do me much good."

"Don't sell yourself short," said Connor. "I'm sure you'd manage to stab some driver in the back and steal a car. But Captain Long and I agreed to give you transportation. You can't have the van. And you can't keep your contact lenses either, which would allow you to control it remotely. But we'll make sure you have a car."

"How?" said Kayla. "Right now my van is our sole transportation."

"You can have one of your mercenaries rent a car under an alias and leave it at this motel," said Long. "If we succeed, Connor and Paige will drive you to the goat farm, where you'll have your pick of any number of untraceable vehicles that my comrades have driven there."

"But won't the cops be swarming the place by then?" said Kayla.

Long shook his head. "It's very isolated. And we'll make sure we aren't bothered until you get there. It's only twenty minutes away. Once you arrive, you'll just choose a car and leave—all within a few minutes."

Kayla paused in thought. "I don't know," she said. "I smell a trick. Even though I'm using Veracity, you can still pull a fast one."

"We aren't *you*," said Connor in disgust.

"Maybe not," said Kayla, "but you managed to deceive me, or I wouldn't be tied to this bed. And you did it while I was Veracity-enabled and had you at gunpoint. I guess I should have thought to ask you if I was playing into your hands. Or if you had a knockout screecher literally up your sleeve. I won't make the same mistake here."

"I assure you our offer is on the level," said Connor. "Ask whatever questions you need to ask to close any possible loopholes."

"Will you honor every aspect of the agreement you just made?" said Kayla.

"Yes," replied Connor.

"Captain?" said Kayla.

"I will honor our agreement also."

"And neither of you are planning any tricks?" said Kayla. "Like releasing me hogtied, or naked, to make things more difficult?"

Both assured her they were not.

"You are not trying to deceive me in any way, correct?"

Both Connor and the captain answered to her satisfaction once again.

"I believe that you won't kill me," said Kayla. "But I want your assurances you also won't order someone *else* to kill me, or surveil me, or hunt for me before the twenty-four hours is up. In fact, I want your assurances that you'll order everyone *not* to look for me during this period."

Once they answered properly for the last time, she finally seemed satisfied. "Okay then," she said happily. "I'm in. Let's free Elias."

"Not so fast," said Connor. "We'll need some assurances from you also. This has been an asymmetrical discussion. You know when we're lying, but we don't know when *you* are. So we have one additional, non-negotiable point. You need to help the captain destroy your little wormhole into Veracity's core. Once that's closed, you won't be able to lie, either. There's no way we'll trust you to honor the bargain we just made if you retain this ability. And no way we'll release you into the wild."

"No deal!" said Kayla.

"Really?" said Connor. "You'd prefer to die?"

"If I die, so does your father. And China gets a powerful tool. The clock is ticking, and you need me badly."

"We discussed what would happen if you refused to cooperate," said Captain Long. "The truth is, if you refuse to help, this could end up working in our favor, anyway. We'd just wait for my comrades to leave the base and follow them to their new destination. Then we'd have time to get the might of the US military on board, all but assuring our success."

"Then why not just kill me now and go with this plan?"

"Because there's also a chance we'd lose them," said Long. "And I know everything about the base they're at now, which wouldn't be the case with others. So I'd prefer to have you agree to our terms. But don't think for a moment you're our only option. You have no negotiating leverage whatsoever."

Before Kayla could respond, Paige interjected for the first time. "What's the big deal about closing your backdoor into Veracity, anyway?" she said. "What good will it do you to have it open now? The cat's out of the bag. You'll never run for president, or even show your face in public again. And everyone will be warned that Veracity is unreliable when it comes to you."

"Wow," said Kayla. "The most telling point from the dumbest, least competent person in the room. Who'd have thought it?" She shook her head. "Okay, Captain Long," she added. "I'll show you my conduit into Veracity and shut it down. And then I'll confirm our agreement again, when you can be certain I'm telling the truth."

"And you'll give your best efforts to free Elias?" said Paige.

Douglas E. Richards

"There it is again," said Kayla. "Back to stupidity. I can still lie right now, so what good does it do you to get my answer? But I'll answer, anyway. Yes, *Paigey*," she continued derisively, "I'll give my best efforts to free Elias—so I can save my own life."

"You really just might be the biggest asshole on the planet," said Connor.

Kayla smiled. "I'll take that as a compliment."

"We don't have time for this," said Long, glaring at Kayla. "You need to start making calls. Right now! We need to get your mercs in motion."

"I'll need a few minutes to download my Vader impersonation software from the cloud. After that, I'll light a fire under these men like you've never seen before. Including offering a bonus for early arrival."

"Good," said Long. "Let's make this happen."

60

Four teams of four mercenaries held their positions, two teams spread out on the east side of the Chinese stronghold, and two teams spread out on the west. Each of the sixteen men were on their bellies in the underbrush, far enough from the compound to avoid detection through the thick woods.

They had all hung well back from the most advanced Chinese soldiers until twenty minutes earlier, when Long had reported that the throngs of men searching the woods for their escaped prisoner had finally been recalled, returning to the base like moths to a flame. This was exactly what Long had predicted, although almost an hour later than he had expected.

As the Chinese line retreated, the mercs had advanced, but only in fits and starts to be sure they weren't prematurely discovered. All four teams had been ordered to halt several minutes earlier, and were maintaining their positions until further notice.

Each man in the strike force was now a million dollars richer, with much more to come. A life-changing amount of money—provided they still *had* a life when this was all over.

"Advance!" ordered Long through the general comm channel. "The search parties are back inside the compound. Six hostiles have held back on our side of the fence to form a rear-guard—three on the east, and three on the west. But they should be joining their comrades shortly."

The members of all four mercenary teams rose from the brush and carefully moved toward the fence line, striking a balance between speed and caution. They would have preferred a nighttime attack, but Long had explained why speed was of the essence. Besides, in modern times, the cover of darkness didn't confer nearly the advantage it once had.

"West Team One, get down and hold your position!" said Paige into a comm just a few minutes later. None on the team knew whose voice this was, or that she was working from a motel room eighteen miles away, but they had been told to follow her orders.

"Roger that," whispered West Team One's leader as he and his three temporary comrades fell to their stomachs once again, and slowly brought binoculars to their eyes.

"Three hostiles are now about twenty yards from your position," continued Paige. "At your seven o'clock. But they can't see you through the trees."

Alone in the small motel room that had once belonged to Captain Long, Paige allowed herself a smile. She couldn't believe she was a valuable member of a military-style operation, using terms like *hostiles*, and clock-hand metaphors to indicate directionality, but the captain had schooled her well in a very short time.

She was in control of two of Long's four recon drones, and while the sixteen mercs below these flying telescopes also had access to what they were seeing, she was in charge of moving them about to get the best visuals. The men were also hauling more equipment than Paige could ever imagine such a small force toting, like human Goliath Beetles, and they needed to keep their eyes focused on the terrain and immediate surroundings. Paige, on the other hand, never took her eyes off the feed, and rarely blinked.

Connor, in the room over, had the harder job. He controlled the two drones covering the east teams, but still had to keep one eye trained on Kayla, just in case. If she found a way to escape, the mission would be blown.

Kayla was seated in front of a cheap motel desk against one wall of the room, and her contact lenses had been temporarily returned to her. She was bound, but even so, Paige knew her husband wasn't about to underestimate her.

"Hostiles have moved away, West Team One," announced Paige. "Continue your approach."

***

Garrett Lynch, a decorated ex-marine, was becoming cautiously optimistic. They had been forced to wait for more than an hour for the thirty men patrolling the woods to halt their activities, and he was beginning to doubt the Chinese soldier running the op, introduced only as Long, knew the base's standard operating procedures as well as he thought.

Long had likened the Chinese force in the woods to a massive wave crashing onto the shore. As ferocious and intimidating as it seemed when it hit, it would soon retreat back into the ocean, leaving the sand bare once again.

And right on cue, this is exactly what had happened.

Long had assured them that reaching the fence was the most perilous part of the op. But this presupposed that Long would do his part. If not, this would turn into a massacre.

Vader had been clever, as usual. When Lynch had seen a million dollars appear in his account, he was even more motivated to see the other *four* million than he would have been if nothing had been deposited at all. This also enabled him to recruit six others in his firm for the mission in short order.

He didn't like the idea of answering to a Chinese national, but Vader had assured him that Long was highly skilled, and critical to the success of the operation. And the man's plan was inspired. If he really did have the kind of insider information that he claimed, their chances of living to spend their money were very good.

The fence was a joke, easily scalable by anyone not a hundred pounds overweight, and the six men patrolling beyond the fence wouldn't be difficult to evade until the attack began. This was especially true since Long had provided ample eyes in the sky, and two alert colleagues to man the feeds and guide them, although it was clear that both were civilians. They may have peppered their instructions with military jargon, but there was no doubt that this was their very first rodeo.

Still, there was one obstacle yet to overcome. One that would strike fear in even the bravest of soldiers. A slaughterbot swarm.

These little bastards were pure evil, and had been shunned by every civilized nation on Earth. Or at least they should have been. The

Chinese called them micro-drones, or *assassin bugs,* but a slaughter-bot by any other name was still just as lethal.

When the slaughterbots operated as they had been designed to operate, they represented an unstoppable force. But because of this, the Chinese would be too reliant on them, and wouldn't have their guard up the way they normally would.

If the bots could somehow be circumvented, their normally su-preme competence would actually work *against* the Chinese, who would be caught with their pants down.

If the bots could be circumvented. The mother of all *ifs.*

Long had assured them that this wouldn't be a problem. He had been part of the Chinese team they were attacking. Even better, he had been their slaughterbot expert, and knew firsthand that the swarm had just been beaten, before dawn that morning, providing a reassuring proof of concept. Apparently, an escaping prisoner had waltzed right through the swarm, even though the bots had been programmed to take out his knee on sight.

Lynch checked the tiny pinprick indicator light on a device Long had given him, now affixed to his lapel, which looked like a black pearl. The three men from his firm who were with him, all assigned to East Team Two, did the same. All sixteen mercenary invaders were wearing this prototype, which Long had assured them contained ad-vanced technology that would shield their faces from the slaughter-bots' cameras, effectively giving them immunity from the swarm.

The Chinese slaughterbot expert had explained that the facial recognition data of each Chinese soldier was programmed into the swarm upon entering the stronghold. Anyone who wasn't in the da-tabase would be taken out without question, brutally and efficiently.

But there was a glitch. The facial recognition blockers the merce-naries had been issued were so advanced, anyone wearing one would appear to be headless to the drones, confusing them. The slaughter-bots were programmed to eliminate any human they didn't recog-nize. But a headless human didn't register as human at all, and would be ignored as if it were a deer or rabbit.

If, for any reason during the heat of battle, the indicator light on Lynch's lapel pin were to go out, he had been told to beat a hasty retreat, fleeing from the site with his head down and covered, to give him at least a small chance of *keeping* it.

In the end, the calculus was quite simple. If these tiny devices really did give them immunity from the swarm, and if Long did *his* job, their chances of success were high.

If not, this mission would turn into an absolute *bloodbath*, over before it had even begun.

Garrett Lynch took a deep breath and motioned for his team to continue moving forward. The fence was only fifteen yards away, and there were no signs of any hostiles.

* * *

Ron Tuohy had been a Navy SEAL for eight years before his entire team was caught in an ambush, and wiped out to a man—all except him. He knew who was responsible, and even why, but the US government had been playing at international intrigue at the time, yet again, and refused to acknowledge the ambush, or do anything to retaliate.

His soul torn in two by the loss of his brothers-in-arms, feeling guilty to have survived, and disgusted at the games played by US military intelligence, Tuohy had signed on with a PMC and had never looked back.

Which had led him to this day, assigned as leader of West Team Two, and bearing down on a perimeter fence surrounding what was officially a large goat ranch, of all things. He didn't much care about his own life, but he was determined not to lose any more men, even those he had met only hours earlier.

Tuohy and his team were holding behind several close-cropped tree trunks, waiting for their eye in the sky to give the all clear. As it was, all other groups had made it to the fence and were waiting for them to catch up. It was embarrassing, but everyone knew that their tardiness wasn't competence related, it was just bad luck, as they had been forced to wait out a patrol on four separate occasions.

"West Team Two," said a pleasant female voice in his ear, "proceed to the fence. The coast is clear."

Tuohy couldn't help but grin. *The coast is clear?* The woman was cute, but not exactly a seasoned pro. So far, though, she had proven to be competent.

The team made it to the fence without any trouble, and Tuohy and his men quietly unpacked parts of a rocket launcher, which he quickly assembled and brought to his shoulder.

His men then readied grenade launchers and heavy weaponry of every kind and waited for the order to attack, which would not come from Long, but from the male civilian who had controlled the two surveillance drones on the east side.

They had been told there were twelve buildings within the fence line. Ten of these could be bombed into dust. The other two had been described to them in great detail, and couldn't be touched. Both were relatively small buildings. One, to the south of the main building, would be Long's destination. The other one, east of the main building, was a medical facility, and if this were accidentally hit, the rest of their pay would be forfeited, no matter what else happened.

Tuohy had no idea who the patient inside this facility might be, but for Vader to spend eighty million dollars on a rescue, he or she had to be pretty damn special.

61

Captain Long Lan stood next to Kayla's van, hidden a good distance away from the compound, and readied four experimental drones that had been in the rucksack he had brought with him from Dr. Rosado's home, each the size of a toddler's fist.

These drones were still being improved, but they had already come a long way. Assuming they operated properly, they would fly onto the base and create a distraction that many inside would be unable to resist. Ren knew about this technology, and would catch on quickly, but hopefully not before the damage was done.

The drones were little more than flying, coordinated, holographic projectors of the highest quality. Guided by onboard AIs, the drones could stitch together complex holographic images, and their mobility ensured they could make the images seem to move in any way that was desired. Combined with state-of-the-art audio, the drones could create compelling illusions to attract, repel, or distract an enemy, as needed.

The holograms weren't yet perfect, but they were good enough to fool an enemy for a short period of time, and that was all that was needed. The developers of the technology back in China had loaded the AIs with two hundred illusions, useful in a variety of situations and against a varied number of people, and were working to add more every day.

One of the two hundred holographic illusions was a large conventional bomb with a timer ticking down from a minute. Those seeing this hologram would flee first and ask questions later. Another was a massive tank, rolling toward an enemy. Another was a team of commandos wielding automatic weapons. This last wouldn't scare off Ren or his men, but could be quite effective against a lone target. There was even a setting that would produce holograms of a dozen enormous spiders racing across the ground, each the size of a car, a bad horror movie come to life. This illusion would do wonders dispersing political protesters, or triggering tens of thousands at a sporting event into a panic-stricken rampage.

While these settings had been designed to provoke a retreat, there were just as many settings designed to lure an enemy in. If Long wanted to entice a lone man into an alley, he could dial up an alluring female, who looked lost or in trouble, or several children, injured, and begging for help.

But for his current needs, Long had found but a single lure that he thought might work. It was time to learn if he was right.

He had programmed the drones to land near the middle of the Chinese stronghold, and he now gave the command to send them on their way.

As soon as they were off, the captain enclosed himself inside the back of Kayla's van and strapped in. He imagined her sitting at a motel desk, staring at a virtual keyboard, while Connor looked on.

"You're up, Kayla," he said into the comm. "Get me to the compound at best possible speed."

* * *

Inside the medical building, Colonel Ren Ping watched the lifeless form of Elias Gibson and willed him to come back to life. So many things had gone wrong so quickly, he could use a break about now. First he had lost Paige and Kayla, and some very good men. Then he had lost Connor.

It was *infuriating*. Ren's hands balled into fists, and if Du hadn't still been in the room, minding the patient, the colonel would have unleashed a primal scream.

Ren had recalled his search teams almost forty minutes earlier. How had the prisoner possibly escaped? How had a micro-drone not taken out his knee? Lieutenant Chang, who had been Captain Long's computer understudy for over a year, had run a complex diagnostic on the drones, but they appeared to be working perfectly.

Ren had told Connor that his face was programmed into the swarm, but this had not been technically true. The faces of the colonel and his men had all been programmed in. The drones had simply been instructed to take out the knee of anyone caught outside who wasn't on the approved list, or who tried to hide or disguise their faces.

And yet they had failed. *He* had failed.

And now it was time to abandon ship. He had stupidly revealed too much to his American prisoner, blowing the base for good. But by the time Connor convinced authorities he wasn't crazy, and that they needed to investigate a goat ranch—if he even *could* convince them—Ren would be long gone.

Six of his men were patrolling beyond the fence, and he would recall them also, in minutes. He and Du were in the medical facility, and forty-three others were instituting evacuation protocols. These procedures entailed removing key computers and papers, which would come with them, and wiring each building to explode and burn to the ground, a much quicker and more effective method of destroying documents than feeding them into a shredder.

Soon, he and Du would return Elias to the ambulance that had brought him here, and they would be on their way. They had twenty-two other vehicles on site, and each would end up driving in a different direction, so if someone out there was on to them, their attention and resources would be spread thin.

The key players, like Ren, had access to technology that would counter aerial surveillance, and they would also take evasive action to ensure that they weren't followed.

"This is Colonel Ren," he said into a comm, which would be transmitted to every man on the base. "We need to pick up the pace. Finalize extraction of vital equipment and preparations for facility sanitization now. We move out in approximately fifteen minutes."

"Colonel Ren," said an unfamiliar voice in his ear, "Lieutenant Yun here. An advanced helo has just landed in the center of the compound. No markings. Were you expecting anyone?"

"Negative," said Ren in alarm. "Have the micro-drones taken out the pilot and passengers?"

"That's just it, Colonel. There *are* no pilots or passengers. It must be self-flying, or flown by remote. No visible weapons of any kind, but it has advanced cloaking technology unlike any I've ever seen.

One moment it wasn't there, and the next it just materialized on the ground out of thin air. It has a shimmer to it, which is odd, but which we're guessing is due to the cloaking technology. Eleven of us are approaching it now to investigate. Make that twelve," corrected Quan.

The colonel gasped as he realized what the helicopter was—what it *had* to be. It was a deceptive hologram, produced by four advanced drones. He had seen this very illusion during a demonstration. But that should be impossible. Not here! Not now!

"Whoever is approaching the helicopter, retreat and disperse!" he yelled into his comm. "Immediately! I repeat, *retreat and disperse*! Get away from that thing *now*!"

* * *

Ex-Navy SEAL Ron Tuohy watched in awe as a sleek, futuristic helicopter materialized in the middle of the compound as if it had been delivered by a *Star Trek* transporter device. Long hadn't exaggerated when he described what they would see.

The activity within the Chinese compound had continued to grow with every passing minute. Like ants after a bully had kicked their anthill, men scurried this way and that in what looked like a mad frenzy, shuttling equipment between vehicles, running wires into buildings, and, in general, moving as if their feet were on fire.

But the unmanned helicopter suddenly materializing in their midst, not having made a sound, drew them in to investigate just as surely as an electromagnet drew steel. First five men, then seven, and so on, until Tuohy couldn't number them with just a glance.

As handfuls of the stronghold's inhabitants neared the illusory aircraft from all sides, the Chinese manpower in the area, which had been widely dispersed, grew decidedly more concentrated. Long was a genius. The closer they congregated around the craft, the more vulnerable they were, allowing shoulder-fired missiles and grenade launchers to catch a number of the enemy at the same time.

They had been scattered fish who were now helpfully swimming into a single barrel.

Tuohy made eye contact with each member of his four-man team, and was satisfied that each was poised and ready.

Suddenly, the handfuls of men investigating the strange holographic craft began racing back away from it as if it were about to blow. Someone had warned them off.

"Now!" shouted Tuohy, just a moment before he heard Connor's voice in his ear, shouting the exact same word.

All sixteen mercenaries fired at the center of the compound at the same time, and missiles and grenades landed with deafening thunder, shaking the ground like an earthquake and causing multiple fires to erupt.

Several of the Chinese, those who had retreated the farthest from the hologram, managed to survive the initial bombardment. But many more were well within the kill zone and were vaporized instantly, or had limbs torn from their bodies. Chunks of human flesh, viscera, and blood rained from the sky like a gruesome hailstorm, consumed by the raging fires below upon landing.

Ron Tuohy tossed the heavy rocket launcher over the fence, and he and his comrades scaled it in seconds, dropping to the other side and continuing to attack, but this time aiming at the periphery of the carnage, now forced to try to hit one man at a time.

The Chinese were well trained, and the pandemonium lasted less than a minute as they began to regroup and launch a counterattack.

The mercenary force had managed to take out roughly one-quarter of the enemy with a crushing blow. But the Chinese wouldn't fall for any further holograms, and the battle had been well and fully joined.

Still, the mercs had created temporary chaos, and were still causing a colossal distraction.

Hopefully, this would be enough to ensure that the man named Long was able to run the gauntlet, and end this battle for good.

* * *

"Lieutenant Jiang!" screamed Colonel Ren Ping into his comm, addressing the man charged with coordinating their withdrawal from the base, "Report!"

"The base has been breached by at least thirteen hostiles," replied Jiang, shouting to be heard over the raging cacophony of battle.

"They're firing grenades, missiles, and automatic weapons. At least a dozen of our men are down, but dozens more are now returning fire."

"So we still have overwhelming numbers?"

"Correct, Colonel. But the enemy is taking up entrenched positions behind natural barriers and buildings, making it difficult for us to root them out. They don't appear to want to advance after their initial attack, but simply to pick us off opportunistically. And they're well-armed and well-trained."

"US Military?" asked Ren.

"Say again," replied Jiang, as ear-numbing explosions and gunfire continued to rock the grounds.

"Are they US military?"

"Negative," said the lieutenant, just able to hear the colonel's shouted words. "No uniforms of any kind."

The colonel put Jiang on standby and contacted Lieutenant Chang. "We have hostiles on the grounds, Lieutenant!" he thundered. "Why haven't our invincible micro-drones taken them out?"

"I'm investigating that now, Colonel."

"Investigate faster, Lieutenant! This is the second time they've failed! If you can't figure it out, try a hard reboot. But find a way to get them working!"

"Roger that," said Chang, ending the connection.

* * *

Long watched the feed coming from the van's cameras as it sped along the ground. Kayla had driven the vehicle off the main road to avoid the heavy steel gate, but the van's massive weight allowed it to barrel through thick foliage and even young trees that were feebly attempting to block the dreadnought from its chosen point of ingress.

The van had used up its drones at Rosado's home, and had taken a beating, but its armor remained all but impenetrable. Hopefully, with the distraction being produced by scores of mercenaries, this would be enough.

It would have to be. Otherwise, they would all die here.

"Hit the fence at full speed," he said to Kayla.

The van burst through the fence, wearing a large section of it as a hood ornament for twenty feet before freeing itself entirely.

"Heading toward the easternmost building, as planned," said Kayla, making a slight course correction.

They only made it another fifty feet before their presence became known and the vehicle was hit with a barrage of fire of every kind, easy target practice for the Chinese.

Kayla didn't need to be told to take evasive action, but this had only limited effectiveness, and even the mighty van could only take so much. The ground shook around the van as it sped forward, and Long felt as if he were inside a milkshake machine.

The incoming fire obliterated much of the van's flimsy outer shell and its *Magic Carpet Dry Cleaning* logo, revealing its thick reinforced steel frame underneath, like a Terminator whose soft pink skin had been peeled away to reveal the indestructible monster within.

"Step up your attacks now!" Long ordered the thirteen mercenaries who were still alive. "I'm taking too many hits. If I'm stopped, we all die."

The van had lost several cameras, but the two that remained showed mercenaries to the east and west temporarily leaving their entrenched positions to dramatically increase fire, directing it at the Chinese forces trying to stop a heavily armed vehicle before it could penetrate farther into their midst, giving Long a much-needed reprieve.

Kayla activated the van's turret, which began to spin and lay down a spray of fire that instantly mowed down three nearby Chinese.

The van was no longer taking fire, but it was slowing, the cumulative effect of the fire it had taken finally beginning to bring it down, like a bull elephant hit with one too many tranquilizer darts.

But they were so close. "Come on!" Long shouted to the vehicle in Mandarin. "Don't even *think* about stopping now!"

62

Lieutenant Chang's fingers flew across the touch screen in front of him. He could find nothing wrong with the drones, even after a reboot.

But *something* was wrong, or the attackers would all be dead.

If only Captain Long were here, he'd know how to solve this. Chang was the second-best programmer on the base, but Long was in a league of his own.

Chang finally decided to extricate himself from complex algorithms and self-diagnostics and deconstruct the situation from basic principles. Forget the math, just what, exactly, were the drones seeing?

He called up this footage and gasped as it came on the screen. The drones were seeing the attackers, all right, but they all appeared to be *headless.*

It wasn't just that the cameras weren't seeing the enemies' faces clearly enough to read, it was that they couldn't even tell that the faces *existed.* Even the best tech designed to block facial recognition didn't work *this* well. At least until now.

This tech was unprecedented, and the drones' programming wasn't equipped to handle it. Apparently, these headless soldiers weren't registering as human at all, confounding the system. It was an unexpected glitch, an oversight, but not that difficult to fix. Even for Chang.

The trick was to get the drones to change their focus from defining humans—and thus targets—by their faces, and get them to define humans by their number of legs. He would reprogram the controlling computer to continue to ignore all Chinese nationals in the drone database, but to attack on sight anything else with two legs—head or no head.

When the drones did find a two-legged creature, he would program them to direct their explosive charge exactly eighteen centimeters up from the center of the shoulder blades. This should result in hits to the face or head, but since the drones would be striking blindly, misses were also possible.

Still, it was the best quick fix possible. Given that these men had tech advanced enough to confound the drones, they were sure to be wearing the latest in body armor, so attacking their torsos might fail.

Chang wasn't nearly as good as the captain, but he wasn't entirely without skills. He would have the drones reprogrammed very soon.

And once this was completed, the battle would be over in minutes.

* * *

Kayla's van limped across the finish line, crashing through the door of Long's destination and caving in some of the entrance around it before grinding to a halt. Long waited for the wreckage to finish falling and tried to get a visual on the room he had entered, but the one camera that had survived the journey was covered in debris and showed him nothing.

He exited the back of the van with his automatic rifle leading the way, his heart racing.

Relief washed over him as he realized the room was deserted.

Still, he had no time for celebration—or caution. He immediately rushed into a tight corridor leading to a second room, this one far larger. He took a deep breath and prepared to enter, knowing that anyone inside would be fully on guard. If one wanted to enter a building without attracting attention, crashing into it with an armored vehicle wasn't a great choice.

Long burst across the threshold and immediately threw himself to the ground, rolling quickly to the left, as two shots flew over his head. When he came out of his roll, his understudy had a gun trained on him and was squeezing down on the trigger, but he managed to relax his finger just in time to abort the shot. "Captain Long!" said Chang in dismay, lowering his weapon. "You're alive! What happened? How did you get here?"

Long hated to rush this reunion, but the thunderous warfare continuing outside was a constant reminder of the need for haste. "Long story, Lieutenant," he said quickly. "And sorry about the entrance. But when I arrived on site and noticed the micro-drones weren't working, I thought the enemy had taken this facility."

Chang nodded. "The drones had a problem, but I'm fixing them now," he explained, gesturing to a computer screen. "I was very close to the finish line when you, ah . . . barreled through the wall."

"Well done, Lieutenant," said Long. "I want you to know that you've been like a brother to me. I will never forget you."

Chang's eyes narrowed in confusion. "What?"

Long answered this question by jerking his weapon up and pumping several rounds into Chang's unprotected chest.

"I'm so sorry," he whispered sadly to his dead friend and comrade, "but I can't let our Paramount Leader get Veracity."

Long's eyes moistened as he rushed to the computer, but he forced himself to shake off the despair and self-disgust he was feeling. Everyone died, he reminded himself. But even someone who wasn't a psychopath could do this math. He was taking the lives of those on the base, including seven men he considered his friends, to prevent the further erosion of freedom for well over a billion citizens in his beloved China.

"I'm in the slaughterbot computer!" he announced to the ten surviving mercenaries and his three allies at the motel. "Reprogramming them now. Shouldn't take more than five minutes. Don't engage the enemy unless you have to. Hunker down and stall for time."

Long bent to his task, reprogramming the drones so that instead of *ignoring* the selected group of Chinese in their database, they would actively hunt for them, and *only* them, making sure that he excluded himself from this new enemies list. He would first have the drones take out all targets on the grounds, and then breach every building on the premises to attack any targets inside.

His fingers flew over the touch screen, even faster than Chang's had done.

But any reprogramming of this nature took time. And he was well aware that he could be interrupted at any moment.

Veracity   363

He turned the monitor around so he was now facing the open door, and tried to make his brain, and his hands, work even faster.

***

Forty-five micro-drones received their new orders simultaneously and wasted no time carrying them out. They screamed through the air as fast as diving hawks, spreading out in a search-and-destroy pattern that ensured every square inch of territory within the stronghold was rapidly covered, adjusting their pattern as necessary as individual drones drilled through target foreheads and were lost to the hunt.

In less than two minutes, every Chinese soldier who wasn't in a building was dead, twenty-six in total, and the remaining slaughterbots began searching buildings for more.

Connor watched the feeds from Long's surveillance drones with a sick feeling in his gut. The ruthless efficiency of the massacre reminded him of a scene from *Guardians of the Galaxy*, in which a whistle-controlled arrow darted through dozens of enemy chests in seconds, unerringly changing course to pick off each target. Long's attack involved forty-five drones, rather than a single arrow, but the effect was similar, and Connor had no doubt that such an arrow weapon would become reality sooner than anyone imagined.

The remaining drones completed their mission minutes later, finding and taking out an additional six targets that had been inside the various buildings.

Just like that, it was over. After the hellish barrage of automatic weapon fire, missiles, and grenades, it had become eerily quiet. The calm *after* the storm.

Only thirteen minutes earlier, the Chinese contingent within the stronghold was fifty-one members strong. Now, all fifty-one were dead, with several vaporized or in pieces. The mercenaries and Kayla's van had taken out nineteen of them, and the slaughterbots the final thirty-two.

Long took a brief pause to close his eyes and mourn the good men who had perished here. He was heartbroken by the need to take these lives, devastated, but he hadn't been able to see any other way.

Finally, he opened his eyes and returned his full attention to the mission. "West Team One," he said, "give your slaughterbot blocker pins to Ron Tuohy of West Team Two. Commander Tuohy, I need you to collect all of these, including those still worn by the fallen, at best possible speed. Then bring them to me."

"Roger that," said Tuohy.

"West Team One," continued Long, "after you've turned in your pins, drive out to the main road, hide in the woods, and be sure we didn't attract the police. If any do come this way, take out their tires and pin them down with machine gun fire—but do not hurt any of them. I repeat, *do not* hurt any of them. I think we're so isolated that we'll have an hour or so before they arrive, but if not, we need to stall them for a short while."

Long made his way to the medical facility, trying his best to ignore a dozen or so fires still raging on the grounds, which had only now begun to die out, and bodies strewn about haphazardly in every direction.

He could only imagine how surprised, and ecstatic, American intelligence would be when this base fell into their lap. It would open their eyes to the scale and scope of the operations going on right under their noses. And since none of his former comrades had survived to carry out standard evacuation self-destruct orders, the base would prove to be a treasure trove of intelligence.

Long entered the medical facility and quickly discovered the lifeless husks of Colonel Ren and Captain Du, sprawled on the floor, their heads still slowly leaking blood and brain matter.

Elias Gibson, on the other hand, was on his back on a hospital bed. And he was still alive!

The captain let out a breath he hadn't known he was holding. They had done it! Elias was still hooked up to an IV and other medical devices, but looked as good as could possibly be expected.

Long dialed up a comm channel to speak privately with Connor, Paige, and Kayla. "The enemy force has been entirely eliminated," he announced. "Elias is still in a coma, but he's alive and otherwise well. The disguised ambulance Colonel Ren used to bring him here is parked near the medical facility and wasn't hit by any fire. I'll secure Elias inside of it so that we're ready to go the moment you get here."

"Outstanding!" said Connor. "Brilliantly done, Captain. I'm forever in your debt."

"Not at all," said Long, showing the humility that was so important in the Chinese culture. "If you hadn't revealed a glitch in the slaughterbot programming, we would have had no chance."

"How many of the mercs survived?" asked Paige.

"Ten of the sixteen. Worse than I had hoped, but we all could have easily died here."

"More importantly," said Kayla coldly, "I've now fulfilled my end of our bargain."

"You have," said Long. "You've earned your freedom. Initiate the transfer of the remaining funds into the accounts of all sixteen men."

"Commencing the transfer now," replied Kayla.

"Connor and Paige," said Long, "make sure you take her contact lenses and get here as fast as you can. Break whatever traffic laws you have to. We need to get her a car, send her on her way, and get as far away from here as possible. I have a team patrolling the road, but I'll make sure they know to let you through."

"We'll be with you soon," said Connor. "I'm looking forward to thanking you and the rest of the team in person."

"I'm afraid the mercenaries will be gone before you arrive," said Long evenly. "But if it makes you feel any better, Kayla just deposited all the thanks they need into their bank accounts."

63

Connor opened the motel-room door and carefully surveyed his surroundings. No other guests were out and about, but this could change at any moment.

"Let's move," he said to Kayla, staying behind her as she made her way to a large four-door sedan parked just in front of their room, left there by one of her mercenaries. They were in broad daylight, so he did his best to conceal the gun he was pointing at her, not that her zip-tied hands wouldn't raise eyebrows if someone were to spot them.

Paige, still wearing her Veracity-enabled glasses, threw open the passenger door and stepped aside.

"Get in and seat belt yourself," Connor ordered Kayla, trying not to show just how nervous he was. Her hands were still bound, and *he* had the gun, but her odds of turning the tables at just this moment were far better than they had been at any other time since she had been captured.

Still, he took solace from the fact that he was bringing her to the Chinese stronghold to give her an untraceable car and set her free. Why would a sane person take *any* risk—of being shot or otherwise—to escape from a man intent on releasing her?

The problem was, he wasn't entirely sure she *was* sane. And even if she were, there was no telling what a psychopath might do in a given situation. He had studied the condition and knew that it came with a high level of unpredictability.

Kayla belted herself in the passenger's seat as she was told, but Connor knew the next steps would be the most dangerous, especially for Paige. Still, he had thought it through, and this was the best way forward. He had carefully inspected the car before Long had even left the motel, and knew exactly how he wanted to immobilize his temporary prisoner.

He slipped into the seat behind Kayla and pressed his gun into the leather, in line with the center of her back.

He caught Paige's eye outside of the car, and she nodded her readiness.

"Okay, Kayla," said Connor, "I need you to raise your hands and touch the handle above your right shoulder."

Kayla turned to her right and eyed the ceiling skeptically, not aware that a pull-out handhold existed there, and seemingly surprised to find one. "Is this really necessary?" she said.

"I think you know it is," replied Connor.

Kayla sighed and did as he asked. Paige slipped a zip-tie through the plastic ties already around Kayla's wrists and ratcheted her hands firmly to the handle.

"Now put your feet together and press your legs against the front of the seat," said Connor, and Paige soon had the prisoner's ankles linked and tied to the steel mechanism under the seat that controlled the power seat-adjust.

With this completed, Connor breathed an audible sigh of relief. He knew Kayla had every reason to cooperate, but it was good to see that *she* knew this also.

"Good work, Paige," he said. "Let's get out of here."

"You should drive," said Paige. "Give me the gun, and I'll watch her."

"I'd feel better sitting behind her, making sure she doesn't try anything."

"Why would she?" said Paige. "She can't move, and what would be the point?"

"I don't know," said Connor, "but she's full of surprises."

"You drive a lot more aggressively than I do, Con. And we need to get there fast. Without wiping out or attracting a cop."

He considered. "But I'm the better shot."

Paige rolled her eyes. "Are you *kidding*?" she said. "She's a stationary target six inches away. A blind man could hit her. If you're worried I'll let down my guard, I won't. I know how dangerous she is."

Connor knew she was right and handed her the gun, taking the car's key fob in return. Paige slid into the backseat behind Kayla while Connor started the car.

They drove in silence for ten minutes, each alone with their thoughts. Connor had accelerated to well past the posted speed limit, weaving through highway traffic and scanning the path ahead for any cops.

"I'm guessing we're about eight minutes out," he announced to Paige, breaking the long silence. They had just entered a narrow road, off the beaten path, and surrounded by woods. But despite the lack of traffic, Connor's focus continued to be absolute. The narrow road, and his physical and mental exhaustion, created driving challenges that required his full attention.

"Thanks," said Paige. "This gives me just enough time to have one last conversation with Kayla."

The prisoner had remained completely still throughout the journey, not that she had much choice with her hands tied above her right shoulder and her feet fixed in place, but now she shook her head. "So what do you want to chat about, *Paigey?*" she said scornfully. "Recess and boys and stuff."

Paige ignored her insulting tone. "I want to know what's going on inside that psychopathic brain of yours. What do you think about your current situation?"

"Nice to see you still care," said Kayla. "What I think is that it all turned out for the best. Yes, my original plan will have to be recast, but that's probably lucky. Because the original plan called for me to spend considerable time with you and Connor. And I'm pretty sure if I had to spend another *hour* with you two, I'd have to kill myself."

"Way to see the glass half-full," said Paige.

"It's *more* than half full. I've avoided even a hint of boredom—my Achilles' heel—for several days straight. And setbacks only make me stronger."

"Stronger?" said Paige incredulously. "You've failed completely. Your ambition of ruling over a worldwide hegemony will never come to pass."

"So what?" said Kayla. "This is all just a game, anyway. If I *had* achieved this goal, there would be nothing left for me to strive for." She shrugged. "So you might have actually done me a favor."

"I can't see your face from back here," said Paige, "but I don't need Veracity to know that you're spewing even more BS than usual."

"I guess we'll find out," said Kayla smugly.

"You're very impressed with yourself, aren't you?" said Paige. "And why not? You fooled Elias and others for a very long time. But you met your match in Connor."

Kayla snorted derisively. "Met my match?" she repeated. "Are you kidding? He got lucky. Even the best teams lose on rare occasion. Freak plays happen." She paused. "Besides, he won the battle, but I'll win the *war*."

"Not a chance!" said Paige.

"You still don't understand," said Kayla. "Not surprising. There are certain things you're good at, like helping grade schoolers learn to finger paint, and certain things you're not, like having a *clue*. I'll always win in the end. Why? Because psychopaths with high IQs and the ability to control their baser impulses *always* win. Playing fair is for losers. A conscience is just an anchor that weighs you down. Like I said earlier, you're a sheep, and I'm a wolf. The result when these two worlds collide is always the same. Predators always win. And I'm the ultimate predator."

"You do realize that Connor could have killed you back in the room, while you were still out cold."

"He *could* have, but he didn't. So pathetic, and yet so predictable. Because morals and ethics destroy rational decision-making every time. He let compassion for his father, compassion for the plight of the Chinese people, prevent him from making the right move."

Connor considered responding, but had the sense that Paige wanted to keep this between her and Kayla.

"*I* would have killed me in an instant," continued Kayla. "But Connor held back. *Of course* he did. That's what happens when you're saddled by the debilitating weakness of compassion—you make irrational choices. Like setting me free to save a man who might never recover."

"That's where you're wrong," said Paige. "You think compassion makes you weak. But it's just the opposite."

"You truly are a moron."

"I know how you feel about *me*. But do you know how I feel about *you*?"

"I can hardly wait to hear. Because your opinion means the world to me."

"I feel *sorry* for you," said Paige, ignoring Kayla's sarcasm. Fire and smoke could now be seen in the distance, an indication that their destination was now just a few minutes away. "You think your lack of soul is a blessing—that it makes you superior—but it's a *curse*. The only emotion you can ever experience is contempt. You go through life bored, impatient, and numbed. You have to take outrageous risks, destroy others, to feel even a little bit alive. And you'll never know love, or compassion, or empathy. You'll never experience the joy of doing what's right, of helping others."

"Stop!" said Kayla. "I'm about to vomit on myself."

"And caring for someone other than yourself isn't *weakness*," insisted Paige, as if Kayla hadn't spoken. "It's courageous."

Kayla rolled her eyes. "You can tell that to yourself all you want," she said. "But you *are* weak. *Pathetically* weak. I'm incapable of feeling sorry for *anyone*," she added, "but if I could, you'd be at the top of my list. Poor little Paigey, weighed down by sanctimony and an oversized conscience."

Paige sighed loudly. "Then it seems you've made another miscalculation," she said. "Because there are times when a conscience can be suppressed, even one like mine. Ethics don't always prevent decisive action. Sometimes, they demand it."

"What does that even mean?"

"It means that this is where you exit the simulation you're so convinced that you're in," said Paige. "Game over."

"Not even close," said Kayla.

"Wrong again," replied Paige. "You made Connor and Captain Long promise to honor the agreement they made with you, while Veracity looked on. You made them swear they'd let you go. Swear they wouldn't kill you, or double-cross you in any way."

Paige shook her head. "But you never thought to ask *me*, did you?" she added in utter contempt. "Because you were so sure you had nothing to fear from me. Not stupid, weak, moralistic little Paigey. You just assumed I'd be incapable of putting you down, no matter what the justification." She raised her eyebrows. "A bit sexist, don't you think?"

"Paige, what's going on?" said Connor in alarm.

"So I tried to blend into the woodwork so it wouldn't *occur* to you to question me," continued Paige, ignoring her husband. "Just to keep my options open."

"Paige, we agreed to let her go," said Connor. "She held up her part of the bargain."

"*You* agreed," replied Paige. "*I* didn't. So I'm going to kill her now. I just wanted to have a last conversation, and make sure she knew it was coming—and why."

"Don't do this, Paige," pleaded Connor. "No one deserves to die more. But I don't care about her. I care about *you*. This will haunt you for the rest of your life. She isn't worth it."

"No, Con, that's where you're wrong. If I let her go, *that* will haunt me for the rest of my life. The atrocities she's sure to commit for decades to come will haunt me. It's like not reporting a rape, knowing that the rapist will victimize scores of others because of it. You, yourself, admitted that you had made a deal with the devil. If I let her go, you'd have to live with *that* for the rest of your life. Can there be any doubt she'll kill again? She has no compassion, only appetite. She'll end or destroy countless lives, and do whatever she has to do to maximize her power, no matter what the consequences to society. And she'll do it all without a moment of regret."

"That's not true," insisted Kayla, deciding to plea for her own life now that Connor's pleas appeared to be failing. "My plans have been ruined forever. When I pretended otherwise, that was just bluster. The truth is, you'll probably capture me again within a few days. And if you don't, you'll warn the world about me. You've won. You've defanged me. I just didn't want to admit it. Besides, you know Connor made his deal with me in good faith. You can't just ignore that."

"I can, and I will," said Paige decisively. "And you claim we've *defanged* you?" she added in disbelief. "That we'll catch you in a few days. We both know that's not true. Like Connor said, you still have your money and your resources and your dirt on powerful figures. You have you brilliance and your ruthlessness. You'll manage to elude the manhunt, and you'll reinvent yourself. But I'm sure you won't just be passive about it. That's not your style. You're the self-proclaimed ultimate predator, after all. And now you'll have another motive—revenge. Connor and Captain Long promised not to hunt you for twenty-four hours. But you didn't promise not to hunt *them*, did you? And I have no doubt that's exactly what you're planning. What better way to stop a manhunt before it begins—taking out the men who plan to launch it."

Paige paused. "Besides, Connor now has a higher score than you in this simulation of yours. I'm sure you'll want to regain your spot on the leaderboard."

Kayla turned her head to Connor, pulling wildly at her restraints, but to no effect. "Paige has lost her mind," she said. "You can't let her do this. It will destroy her. Like you said, I'm not worth it. *And we have an agreement!*" she shouted.

Connor thought his head would explode. Was Paige really going to kill in cold blood? Should he try to stop her? Or should he *applaud* her?

His wife was right about Kayla. Everything she had said was true. He had made a deal with the devil, but Paige had found a loophole. She had engineered a rare instance in which the devil might get the raw end of the deal.

"Do what you have to do, Paige," he said softly. "Just be absolutely sure about it. You're the most caring person I've ever met. And you value all life. I've seen you catch spiders and gently set them free outside. So consider this very carefully. If you do this, you can never take it back."

"I *know*," said Paige as tears began streaming down her face. "That's the worst part. She's forced me to become a monster too." She shook her head sadly. "But I can't let her continue to take lives," she added in despair. "I can't let her turn the world into her plaything."

With that, two shots rang out in quick succession, and two bullets traveled through the leather seat and into Kayla Keller's back, one of them scoring a direct hit on her heart.

Paige dropped the gun in horror and slumped back against the seat, sobbing.

"It's okay, honey," said Connor, ignoring the grisly passenger beside him. "It's going to be okay. You did the right thing. You saved all the lives she would have taken."

Connor realized at that moment just how right Paige had been. Compassion *wasn't* a weakness. What she had just done, the hard choice she had found a way to make, had taken more strength than any act he had ever witnessed.

Connor glanced in the rearview mirror to find that tears were still streaking down his wife's face. They had just reached the Chinese compound, and he began to carefully steer the car across a war-ravaged field, toward the medical facility where Captain Long and his father were waiting for them. "We're almost at the ambulance," he said softly. "In just a few minutes we can begin putting all of this behind us."

Connor drew in a deep breath. "You did the right thing," he repeated. "I promise you, Paige, everything's going to be okay."

EPILOGUE

"Truth and power can travel together only so far. Sooner or later they go their separate paths. If you want power, at some point you will have to spread fictions. If you want to know the truth about the world, at some point you will have to renounce power. You have to admit things—for example, about the sources of your own power—that will anger allies, dishearten followers, or undermine social harmony.

"The most powerful scholarly establishments—whether Christian priests, Confucian mandarins, or Communist ideologues—placed unity above truth. That's why they were so powerful. As a species, humans prefer power to truth. We spend far more time and effort on trying to control the world than on trying to understand it—and even when we try to understand it, we usually do so in the hope that understanding the world will make it easier to control.

"Therefore, if you dream of a society in which truth reigns supreme and myths are ignored, you have little to expect from *Homo sapiens.*"

—Yuval Noah Harari, *21 Lessons for the 21*ˢᵗ *Century*

64

Connor Gibson gathered his thoughts and prepared to lead the brainstorming session soon to come. Although the term *brainstorming* wasn't a perfect description of what would transpire. This would really be more of a presentation of the thoughts and conclusions that he and Paige had reached, to get the group's mental juices flowing for future such sessions to come.

It was early in the morning, and he was sitting at a familiar patio table in his father's backyard in San Marcos, California. The same table he and Paige had been at when a strange woman had rushed into the backyard to warn them of an attack—a woman who had turned out to be Kayla Keller.

It was astonishing how much had changed in such a short time.

Connor soaked in his surroundings, which were magnificent. A cool breeze whispered across the mesa. The sky showed streaks of pinks and reds over the mountains, and small cloud islands floated lazily in the distance, held aloft by a strikingly clear blue sky. Dozens of massive diamonds danced and twinkled across his father's pool, reflected by tiny bits of shell that had been embedded in the pool's pebble floor.

"Captain Long," continued Connor, "thank you for coming. I know it couldn't have been easy for you to arrange."

The hint of a smile spread across Connor's face as he realized just how much of an understatement this really was. This getaway must have been *extremely* challenging for the captain to arrange. On the other hand, this was part and parcel of the life of an operative in a foreign country, even under normal circumstances.

And Long's circumstances were *anything* but normal. He had been put in charge of a new team of operatives, as he had hoped, convincing his Paramount Leader he could salvage the Veracity operation. Since Elias was supposed to be dead, he had to be sure the men who had recently arrived in-country to work with him didn't know that he was traveling to San Marcos, or what he was doing there. And soon, he would need to lead these operatives on a sustained wild goose chase.

Then, ultimately, when the four-member Veracity launch team of which Long was a part—along with Elias, Connor, and Paige—decided it was time, he would become a double agent for the US government, complete with handlers, and his life would get even *more* complex.

"I am honored to be here," replied Long. "And I'm honored to have had the chance to meet your father, a truly great man."

"Well, you did meet him before," said Paige with a grin, "he just wasn't all that talkative. Or what doctors call . . . responsive."

Long returned the smile. "I just hope I prove worthy of being part of this group."

"Since I wouldn't be alive if not for you," said Elias, sitting beside him, "you've *already* proven yourself worthy."

Although they tried to hide it under smiles and good cheer, Connor could detect a strong undercurrent of pain and melancholy in his three colleagues. And who could blame them?

Connor had been hit hard, psychologically, by the events of three weeks prior. He had nearly been killed on several occasions, and had been deeply scarred by the horrors he had lived through. He had feared for the life of his father and wife for a period of time that had seemed like forever, and had witnessed death and destruction on an unimaginable scale.

But his father, Paige, and Captain Long had each been hit so much *harder*.

It was difficult to believe they were doing as well as they were.

Captain Long had betrayed his president and slaughtered his friends and comrades. And while he had managed to hold himself together while they had fled the goat ranch, the guilt and remorse he had suppressed had soon broken free. He had thought he could handle it, but he had been wrong. For a stoic, seasoned commando, he had come very close to a total meltdown before managing to recover his equilibrium, just before they had gotten medical help for Elias.

His father had been dealt a crippling emotional blow, as well, when he finally learned all that had transpired after he had lapsed into a coma. Connor and Paige had told him just the day before.

How could his father not be reeling after learning about Kayla Keller's betrayal, and her treachery? Here was a man who had been fooled so completely by a soulless psychopath, he had actually fallen in love with her.

Just after the events at the Chinese stronghold, Long had made sure they escaped the scene without any person, or any satellite, becoming the wiser. Once he was satisfied that they were clear, they had driven straight to the Scripps Memorial Hospital in LaJolla, where they had checked Elias in—under his own name.

They had reasoned that it was now safe to come back into the light. After all, there was no one left to hunt them. Not the fictional Vader—or his real counterpart, Kayla Keller. Not the Vice President of the United States and the untold minions he might control. Not a Homeland undersecretary named Jalen Howard, or scores of Chinese commandos.

Even so, after days of unknown factions acting like overzealous children at a whack-a-mole machine, lying in wait to capture or kill them whenever their heads popped up, it had taken considerable courage for them to come out of hiding.

Elias had remained in a coma for fifteen days before miraculously coming back to life. Connor and Paige visited him immediately, overjoyed by his recovery, and had shared a watered-down version of recent events. They had assured him that they were safe and out of trouble, and had told him the tragic news that Kayla Keller had been lost.

But beyond this, they had refused to go into detail until he had regained his vigor and was released from the hospital, which had only happened two nights earlier.

At that point, they had no choice but to tell him truths they knew would be devastating.

And Connor guessed that Paige's emotional scars ran even deeper than his father's. She possessed the kindest, most gentle soul Connor had ever known, and she had also endured the terror, death, and hardship of their ordeal.

But in addition to this, she had felt forced to take it upon herself to act contrary to her every belief. To take a human life. Something that would haunt her forever, regardless of how despicable this particular human may have been, or how justified the action.

Paige had also feared that when Elias learned that she had killed Kayla in cold blood, this would damage their relationship. Fortunately, Elias had assured her that he supported her actions, despite his own heartbreak, and made it clear he would never hold this against her.

But would she ever stop holding it against *herself*?

Connor sighed, pushed all of this from his mind, and focused on the topic at hand. "So let me get started," he said to his father. "After we left you at Scripps Memorial, Paige and I weren't sure what to do. We were worried about you—to say the least. Worried about a whole host of things."

He paused for a moment, remembering. "But we finally decided we would force ourselves to be optimistic—and proactive. After all, turning pessimism into optimism was the grand vision that started you down the path toward Veracity in the first place. So we decided to assume that you'd recover, and prepare for it. We decided to analyze Veracity in light of what we'd been through, and in light of further research and brainstorming. We hoped to be able to provide you with a fresh perspective. Or, at minimum, a launching pad for further discussion and decision-making."

"A fresh perspective is just what I need," said Elias. "As I told you earlier this morning, I want this group to be Ufree Technologies' decision-making body. You've all earned it. And you've all had a crash course on Veracity and its implications—in the field rather than in the classroom—which I couldn't possibly have given you. So I can't wait to hear what you've come up with."

"We tried to be methodical in our analysis," said Connor. "We began by going back to first principles. By assuming nothing, and questioning *everything*."

Elias nodded approvingly.

"The first question we revisited," continued Connor, "was the most fundamental of all—should Veracity even be released?"

"And?" prompted Elias.

"And, after considerable thought and discussion, we decided that it should be. But more importantly, that it *had* to be. One can debate if the elimination of lying will save society, or destroy it. We're all aware of the arguments on both sides. But in our view, the situation with China seals it. We now know that a Veracity system *can* be invented. So it *will be* invented. *Inevitably.* We can bury the current version, but regardless of how difficult it might be for even *you* to recreate, someday, someone will invent it again. And that someone might not be as cautious as we are, or be as good intentioned."

"That's a great way to look at it," said Elias. "The net impact of the technology on society is unknowable before the launch. So we could debate that forever. But we can be certain that if a totalitarian regime develops it, their power will grow, at home and abroad—and this would be bad. Much worse than if *we* introduced it."

"I couldn't agree more," said Long. "As you know, this is the very reason I did what I did."

"But if this is a key factor in the launch," continued Connor, "we'll have to make some adjustments. First, we'll need to conduct further testing, to be certain Veracity works the same on members of every culture."

"I'm almost positive it does," said Elias. "But I agree, it's worth making sure."

"Then, we'll need a worldwide launch. If we roll it out slowly, starting in America, bad actors around the world can still act quickly to use it for selfish purposes. Dictators can ban it from everyone in their countries except themselves. So we need to make Veracity available to all of humanity, at approximately the same time. And we need the physical interfaces, and the Veracity software apps for TV, phone, and computer screens, to be priced so low that even the poorest can afford them. I know that you were already thinking along these lines," he said to his father.

"Yes," replied Elias, "everyone needs to be on equal footing. We can't let this create haves and have-nots, put the poor and underprivileged at an even greater disadvantage to the rest of society than they already are."

"How low-cost do you think you can get?" Paige asked him.

"Very. When you mass produce billions of something, you can drive costs down quickly. The supercomputer clones will be the expensive part. But Ufree can bear that cost if necessary. And even when the interfaces are dirt cheap, we can institute a program to give them away, free of charge, to anyone who can't afford them. All Ufree profits are going to charity anyway."

"Outstanding," said Connor. "And the concept of mass production, mass dissemination, brings us to our next point. I'll let Paige discuss this one, since it was her idea."

Paige nodded at Elias. "Your vision is to use Veracity to improve the human condition," she began. "But not just to catch lies, or prevent government corruption. You also want to promote justice in all of its facets, including the complete elimination of what has been a growing tide of false accusations, which will end the politics of personal destruction for good."

Elias grimaced at this last, almost imperceptibly, and Connor guessed the reason for it. Kayla had pretended to be on a crusade to use Veracity to prevent false accusations from ever again ruining someone's life or reputation. Ironically, the accusations against her had proven to be *true*. This didn't diminish Veracity's importance in being able to confirm the truth or untruth of an accusation, but it was a painful reminder of Kayla's treachery.

"The elimination of corruption and the enhancement of justice are lofty ideals," continued Paige. "But if I'm understanding you correctly, Elias, these weren't your initial goals. You were sickened by the pessimism and divisiveness you saw around you. You wanted to hold politicians and the media accountable for their never-ending venom. For their constant doomsaying. You wanted a system like Veracity to help reverse the current state of despair and pessimism."

Elias smiled. "You and Connor were paying closer attention than I thought," he said. "Impressive, since we were running for our lives at the time."

"We were hanging on your every word," said Paige.

"Thanks," said Elias, "but I interrupted your point."

"My point is this, why not make optimism an integral part of the Veracity launch? Of the ongoing Veracity marketing campaign?"

"I'm not sure I follow," said Elias.

"Why not present the case for optimism on the very packaging of our products?" said Paige. "We'll sell billions of interfaces and apps, which means billions of tiny billboards. Why not print our message on each? A little hokey, but a lot effective. Something like this: 'Don't despair, the world is far from perfect, but it's doing much better than you think. Go to DontDespair.com to learn more.'" Paige paused. "Or maybe 'ReasonsForOptimism.com.' I don't know. But you get the gist.

"Inside the packages, or alongside of the app, we can embed additional fun facts. Like those you shared with us. 'Worldwide poverty levels are lower than ever, yet we all believe the opposite. To learn why things are better than you think, go to our website, or read, *The Rational Optimist*, *Factfulness*, *Enlightenment Now*, or *Abundance*.'"

Elias's mouth dropped to the ground. "This is absolutely brilliant, Paige. It's a *spectacular* idea. And how did you know to cite these titles? Have you read them?"

"In the last three weeks, Connor and I have each read two of them, and discussed their content with each other."

"Well done," said Elias, beaming. "And I say again, your concept is truly brilliant. *Phenomenal*. Why just launch Veracity and hope the system will begin to weed out false pessimism, inflammatory rhetoric, and doomsaying? Why not make the point *explicitly*?"

"Exactly," said Connor. "We need to change human attitudes. This will help in a big way. On the website, we can give the references Paige just listed. And I can write a very short book that encompasses everything you've been saying, which we can also provide for free on the site. I can put my attempts at a technothriller career on hold—which was pretty much on hold, anyway," he added, rolling his eyes.

"I'll write about the history of politics and tribalism," he continued. "The case for optimism. The need to turn off the news and politically charged social media feeds, or at minimum, to not let the media manipulate emotions on such a deeply visceral level. I also think it might be eye-opening to compare the daily sky-is-falling pronouncements from politicians and the media to the actual results, which are often the opposite."

"That would be great," said Elias enthusiastically. "Then maybe the next time we hear that a politician's actions will cause the end of the world, we'll have a little perspective."

Connor nodded. "I've also considered adding in some of Paige's stories about appallingly bad predictions to further underscore how often even the experts are wrong."

"Paige's stories?" repeated Elias. "I'm not familiar."

"Well, stories and quotes, both," said Paige. "Ones I've been using in my classroom for years. For example, to encourage my students to never give up hope, to never stop believing in themselves, I tell them how many times the *Harry Potter* manuscript was rejected. I describe the many publishers who were convinced it would be a total failure. I talk about the scores of publishers who turned away the great Dr. Seuss, believing that his work couldn't possibly appeal to children."

She paused. "Then I read several quotes. Each represents an example of horrendous judgment. Like Einstein's teacher lamenting to his father that little Albert would never amount to anything. Western Union saying that the telephone had no value. A professor of military strategy commenting on the airplane, a new invention, declaring that it was useless for military applications. Or the chairman of IBM in 1943 predicting a worldwide market of only *five* computers." Paige smiled. "The kids really like this last one," she noted, "since many of them have five computers in their own *home*."

"Along with these examples," said Connor, "I'd include those that speak to the track record of political doomsaying. I've already found dozens. I can include quotes from Nobel-prize-winning economists predicting that President X's policies are sure to cause a devastating economic collapse, next to a headline a year later extolling a thriving, record-breaking economy. Whether the strong economy is *due* to President X's policies, or *despite* them, it doesn't matter. It's almost more meaningful if you *do* disagree with the policies, because this underscores the great resiliency of our country, which is able to absorb incompetence and mistakes by administrations from both parties. The bottom line I'd hope to convey is this: don't look for a tall building to jump off of when you hear doomsday prophecies, or toxic news. Instead, try to take it with a grain of salt."

"Perfect," said Elias.

"This goes toward what you told us weeks ago," said Paige. "That the endless sky-is-falling predictions almost never come true, but that they are almost never revisited, or remembered. Well, as part of Connor's short book, he can make sure they are."

"And with a revolutionary technology platform sure to reach billions of people," said Connor, "we'll have a great opportunity to change perceptions to be more in line with reality."

"I love everything about this," said Elias. "You and Paige have truly outdone yourselves."

"Ninety-nine percent Paige," said Connor, "and one percent me. But I hoped that you'd react this way."

Connor sighed. "But this brings us to a subject we know has been more contentious for you."

"Veracity-blocking technology?" guessed Elias.

"Exactly," said Connor. "As much as we hate to do it, we've come down on Kayla's side of the debate. We think this should be launched alongside Veracity. But even if you and Captain Long disagree with us," he added, "we still think it has to be done, anyway. Why? Because just like with Veracity itself, if *we* don't, someone else *will*. Every tech company in the world will be scrambling to develop a blocker. The demand by consumers looking to be able to shield themselves from Veracity will be off the charts."

Elias turned to the captain. "Have Connor and Paige filled you in on this debate?"

"Some, but I could use a more thorough grounding."

"We'll prepare a document for you that presents all sides of the issue," said Elias. "I know you have to leave soon, and it's a complex issue. We can take it up next time."

"Thank you," said Long.

"Moving on," said Connor, "we strongly recommend that you insert a fail-safe into the system—a kill switch. We know that you can't do anything to corrupt Veracity's lie detection function. But we assume you can install a method to shut it down, globally, if this becomes necessary."

Elias nodded. "It would be relatively straightforward."

"Good," said Connor. "Paige and I believe that society will be able to survive the tsunami that Veracity will bring about. That in the end it will make humanity stronger and more unified. But if we're wrong, and it becomes crystal clear that our species *can't* handle this. If this turns out to be the one disruptive technology *too* disruptive for us to survive, we want you to be able to kill it for good."

"What would be the point?" said Elias. "Didn't you just argue that others will eventually reinvent it, anyway?"

"Not if the disaster is obvious and painful enough," said Connor. "And to be clear, you wouldn't use this fail-safe on a whim. We know that things will get worse before they get better. But won't you sleep better at night knowing that a kill switch is there? Just in case the launch of this technology proves to be the most destructive mistake in history."

"Like we said, we don't expect consensus today," said Paige. "We just want to begin getting issues on the table."

"Understood," said Elias. "I'm glad you are. Do you have any more?"

"Just one," said Paige, "at least for the time being. It's a tough one. Do we bring the US military, or law enforcement, or intelligence in on this before the launch? If we agree to the steps Connor and I have recommended, there will be a significant delay before Veracity sees the light of day. So do we give carefully vetted players in the US a chance to use it to our country's advantage until then?"

Elias sighed. "I've thought a lot about this," he replied, "and I've come out against it. I'm not sure it's fair to advantage our country above all others in this way. No country is immune from corruption, or above using power for ill. Why do we deserve such a big leg up in world affairs, at the expense of all other countries?"

"With all due respect," said Captain Long, "I couldn't disagree more. I believe that too many of you Americans focus only on what's wrong with your country, while romanticizing other countries. I've gone to great lengths to ensure that America, not China, can use Veracity to its advantage. Before it becomes known to the rest of the world. You take your freedoms for granted, and assume most of the world's freedoms are equal to yours, or even exceed them."

The captain shook his head. "But I'm here to tell you that this isn't true. America is far from perfect. But you've accumulated more power than any country in history, and you mostly attempt to wield it for good rather than conquest. You help to free those in other countries, to improve their lives, rather than enslave them."

Elias nodded slowly. "A fascinating perspective, Captain Long. Thank you. It seems that I have more thinking to do on the subject."

"We all have a lot more thinking to do," said Connor. "And regardless of what we end up deciding, there's an enormous amount of work to be done."

"Which is why I've decided that I won't be returning to teaching next fall," said Paige. "Connor and I will be devoting ourselves full time to Ufree and Veracity. I consider teaching to be an important calling. But this is an even *more* important one."

"A great loss to future fifth-graders," said Elias. "But a huge gain for humanity as a whole."

Paige blushed. "That's nice of you to say, Elias. I only wish it were true."

"It *is* true," said Elias with conviction. "Your idea to market optimism along with Veracity may well be cited by future historians as a turning point in human affairs. A key factor in stemming the tide of our collective despair. A campaign that helped humanity snap out of its pessimism and get its head on straight—even one that helped it to survive the disruption caused by the death of lying."

"Anyone could have come up with it," said Paige.

"Maybe," said Elias. "But you *did*. And I'm already convinced that no one is better equipped to direct its implementation."

"I'll do my best," said Paige, clearly gratified by both the praise and the opportunity.

Connor felt a warm glow spread throughout his body. The weather was perfect, the view spectacular, and he was in the company of the two people he loved most in the entire world, along with a good man who had saved all of their lives.

Connor had always been fascinated by breakthrough technology that could extend humanity's reach. But now fate had seen to it that he become integrally involved with a breakthrough of a different order entirely, one that could change the very fabric of human behavior. One that could change society more profoundly than the most exotic futuristic technology could ever hope to do.

Humanity was extremely adaptable, and Connor believed the species would ultimately adapt to Veracity. But there was no way to know for sure. Not until the technology was unleashed.

All they could do was launch the system as carefully and thoughtfully as possible, and hope for the best. But no matter what happened, there was no question that the launch would mark a turning point in history, as profound in its own way as the inventions of fire, agriculture, and electricity had been in theirs.

Connor turned to his father. "Do you remember when I first learned of Veracity in your car?" he said. "And that I wasn't all that impressed?"

Elias laughed. "How could I forget?"

"Well, my initial reaction just *may* have been a little hasty," said Connor. "I'm beginning to think you might have come up with something pretty special, after all. I guess what I'm trying to say," he continued with a grin, "is that there might just be a tiny, *minuscule*, chance that this tech will end up being more impactful than I had first thought."

"Glad to hear it, Connor," said his father in amusement. "I had a feeling that you might come around."

AUTHOR'S NOTES

Table of Contents

1) From the Author: Thanks for reading *Veracity*. I hope that you enjoyed it. Since a large number of ratings, good or bad, can be instrumental in the success of a novel, I would be grateful if you would rate *Veracity* on its Amazon page, throwing up as many stars as you think it deserves.

Please feel free to:

• Visit my Website, www.douglaserichards.com, where you can get on a mailing list to be notified of new releases

• Friend me on Facebook at Douglas E. Richards Author, or

• Write to me at douglaserichards1@gmail.com

2) *Veracity*: What's real and what isn't (and a few personal musings)

As you may know, in addition to trying to tell the most compelling stories I possibly can, I strive to introduce concepts and accurate information that I hope will prove fascinating, thought-provoking, and even controversial. *Veracity* is a work of fiction and contains considerable speculation, so I encourage you to explore the subject matter further to arrive at your own views and conclusions.

With this said, I'll get right into the discussion of what information in the novel is real, and what isn't. I've listed the subject matter I'll be covering below, in order of its appearance. So if you aren't interested in an early topic, feel free to skip ahead to one that might interest you more.

- Why did I write Veracity (it's not because I love getting hate mail :))
- Anecdotes (killing Elias, roadrunners, and so on)
- Things really are getting better
- Is perfect fake video possible?
- Is perfect lie detection possible?
- Kayla the psychopath
- Slaughterbots (be very afraid)
- Tribalism (Social Identity Theory)
- Contact lenses as a major tech platform
- DeepMind and Alpha Zero
- Blocking facial recognition
- Self-driving cars
- China, real estate, and civil rights

Why did I write *Veracity*

You may have noticed that our current political climate is more toxic than the surface of Venus (okay, maybe this metaphor is a little *too* geeky, but you get the point). Further, you may have noticed that *Veracity* just wades right into this firestorm—on purpose!

Am I an idiot? Do I not like my career and wish to ruin it? When I see a wood chipper, do I have an irresistible compulsion to walk right into it? Do I relish getting hate mail?

The evidence from this book would suggest the answer to all four of these questions is *yes*. The country is divided. Friendships are being lost. Loving family members are no longer speaking to each other. Hatred, venom, despair, and toxicity are all around us.

No writer in his or her right mind who is trying to appeal to a broad audience, trying to entertain for entertainment's sake, would dare dip a single toe into these acid waters.

So why did I dive right into the deep end?

I blame it all on my very last novel, called *SEEKER*.

Seeker had nothing to do with politics, or our political climate. But while I was doing research for that novel, I came across several books that blew my mind. I had been pretty pessimistic about the trajectory humanity is on, but these books were packed with empirical data that couldn't be denied. The world was better than ever on practically every measure.

I couldn't resist working some of this good news into the end of *Seeker*, and into the notes that followed. So I did. And then I thought I was done with it.

For my next novel, this one, I had planned to tackle the topic of addiction. I prepared by reading book after book on the subject and began thinking up plots.

But a funny thing happened on my way to the first word of this novel. I began getting feedback on *Seeker*, and I was astonished. Readers were grateful for the section detailing reasons for optimism, and the perspective it provided. In fact, I had a more positive reaction to this content than to anything I've ever written. This passage really seemed to help a number of readers cope with the modern-day negativity factory. For many readers drowning in a sea of pessimism, it served as a much-needed life preserver.

And this made sense, actually. These surprising truths had really opened *my* eyes, which is why I made sure to include them in *Seeker* in the first place.

On the other hand, none of what I had written touched upon politics.

Still, the strength of this feedback gave me the crazy idea to try to better understand how our attitudes, our pessimism, and our divisiveness came to be. And while it may be worse now than ever, it appears that social media, twenty-four-hour news, fear-mongering, and lack of reporting on anything positive, will ensure that it stays pretty bad, no matter who comes to office.

The more I studied the topic, the more part of me wanted to write *Veracity* (the part that likes walking into wood chippers). What if politicians and the media couldn't lie? What if *I* couldn't lie when my wife asked me who ate the leftover cheesecake (are you sure you saved it? Maybe you threw it away and just don't remember :)

All in all, I found the topic irresistible. And I wanted to share the results of my research, expand upon some of the concepts in *Seeker* that had helped so many readers put our current pessimistic climate into the proper perspective. And with *Veracity*, I thought I could achieve this, while at the same time delivering a twisty, action-packed page-turner that readers would find entertaining.

Still, my fears ran deep, and I fought the compulsion. Hard! What was wrong with writing a nice addiction thriller? Or a wild time travel romp?

But I kept getting thank you emails from readers of *Seeker*.

Well, spoiler alert, I did end up writing *Veracity*. I decided to take the risk. I figured, if I did it perfectly, I could open eyes on both ends of the political spectrum, and make both sides feel better and more optimistic than they otherwise would.

On the other hand, if I did it *wrong*—well, I had images of that wood chipper again. If I did it wrong, both sides would hate me.

Then, to make matters worse, I chose to write some unflattering words about the Chinese government. I had thought China was becoming ever more benign, but the research I did suggests that this isn't the case (as I detail in the section about China). Five of my novels have been translated into Mandarin Chinese and are being sold by major Chinese publishers, but I've pretty much ensured that *Veracity* won't become the sixth. Nothing like trying to ruin my career on two different continents with one book. :)

But getting back to the subject of alienating readers on *this* continent, I can't tell you how hard I worked to write *Veracity* straight down the middle, politically, and be as non-partisan as I could possibly manage. But I do have my own views, and I feared that they might seep into the writing while I wasn't looking. So I did a test. I sent the political pages to four fans on the hard right, and four on the hard left, and pleaded with them to give me their honest opinions. Were they offended? Angered? Insulted? Did they feel the writing leaned too much to the left? To the right? Did they want to throw their Kindle against the wall?

Turns out they unanimously enjoyed it—at least that's what they said in their email messages. I wasn't wearing a Veracity interface at the time, so they may have just been trying to be kind, but I decided I might still have a few fans left when the dust settled.

If you're reading this, if you've made it this far, chances are that you've forgiven me for anything that rubbed you the wrong way. But

I'm not naive. Try to write about anything that even comes close to the realm of politics, and you can expect to tick a lot of people off. I have no doubt I'll get angry emails on this one. Which isn't as fun as you might imagine. :)

Still, it goes with the territory. One reader, offended by something in one of my books (I don't remember what), wrote that he wished he had bought the paperback version instead of the eBook. Why? So he could *burn* it.

Good one.

Yet another offended reader once wrote to tell me that one of my books was the worst book *ever written*. Now that's really saying something. Worst book *ever*? In all of human history? Out of the many millions of books written throughout the ages, not a single one was ever worse?

See, Mom and Dad, I told you I could stand out as a writer. :)

I've found that people tend to be more sensitive than they were when I was growing up, and more vocal. (And I'm sure I'll get angry letters for even writing *this*—which, in a way, will prove my point.) And nowhere is this truer than in the realm of politics.

So the only things I can be certain of are death, taxes, and that *Veracity* will anger or offend some readers, who will lash out because of it. Oh well. If I managed to stay as non-partisan as I think I have, it might not be so bad.

If not, I may have to get a new email address. :)

And while we're on the topic of hate mail, I'll give you one last example that I found particularly interesting. This is an actual email I received from a reader of my novel *BrainWeb*. I am not making this up. Here it is:

"Fuck You for naming Victor's pda Maria. I was actually enjoying the book till this point. The Mexican has a pda named Maria? Really u fucken racist prick. Couldn't have come up with anything better? Fuck you and ur shitty ass books."

Okay, just for a little context, PDA stands for personal digital assistant. These are electronic assistants, like Alexa, Cortana, or Siri.

And the character Victor in the novel was born in Mexico, worked his way up the cartels, and ended up becoming a high-tech weapons dealer.

I *love* this character. I portray him as smooth and utterly brilliant. In many ways he plays a Moriarty-like villain to my hero's Sherlock Holmes.

Second, Victor named the PDA himself. I've known women named Maria who weren't Hispanic, but even if this is the most Hispanic name in history, why would it be unusual for a Hispanic male to choose a Hispanic name for his PDA? I might expect a Russian to choose a Russian name, a Swede to choose a Swedish name, and for me to choose an American name.

In any event, I was taken aback, as you might imagine. Because the writer of this email had read a name that one of my characters had chosen, which I had selected solely for its simplicity, and seemed *sure* that he knew what I was all about. While I, on the other hand, have known me for my entire life (I can't seem to get away from me), and I have to respectfully disagree with his conclusions. I've never viewed, or treated, Hispanics any differently than anyone else. And yet just the name of this character's PDA set off this kind of rage and finger-pointing.

Just so you know how it ended, I always reply to my emails, no matter what. The overwhelming majority are amazing, by the way, from fans who couldn't be more supportive and complimentary. But I even reply to my hate mail. So I wrote back and told him I was confused. That I wasn't sure what he was talking about, and invited him to explain to me how the use of the name Maria was racist in any way.

Astonishingly, my reply must have made the emailer reconsider just how evil I am. He responded as follows:

"I'm sorry, it's a stereotypical name tho, for a while it pissed me off, like might as well put he mowed lawns and was a drunk, but now that I think about it it's no big deal, great series tho, Minds Eye was good I actually paid for BrainWeb. I left you a good review on Amazon. Sorry once again."

I almost fell out of my chair. This was as unexpected as the initial message had been. But I give him tremendous credit. He realized he had overreacted, and he wasn't too big of a man to apologize, which is a trait that I admire.

Anecdotes (killing Elias, roadrunners, and so on)

No novel comes out the way I first envision it, and *Veracity* is no exception. Originally, Elias was going to be dead before the novel even began. Connor would go to meet him, find him dead, and be propelled into action/adventure/discovery with his sister, Paige.

It would be an enigmatic beginning. What had happened to Connor and Paige's father? Whom could they trust?

But my thinking about the plot evolved, and I ended up deciding that Connor should have a wife, and not a sister, and that Elias should stay alive for a short while. Even then, I was going to kill him off just after he met with Connor and Paige. He would die in front of them, which is pretty horrible, I know.

But then I decided to let him live until they reached Kayla's safe house. I liked him. Besides, I portrayed him as idealistic, having been a part of Teach for America, and having taught third-graders in Dayton, Ohio. Turns out my *daughter* is idealistic, part of Teach for America, and *currently* teaches third-graders in Dayton, Ohio.

Go figure. Who knew that my daughter and Elias Gibson would have so much in common?

So I gave him yet another reprieve. I kept liking him more and more, and kept putting off his death. Finally, I compromised with myself by putting him into a coma, which made the rest of the novel more challenging.

I admit it, I'm a wimp. Still, I'm glad I kept him alive. What can I say?

Even after I decided to keep Elias alive at the start of the novel, Connor and Paige weren't slated to meet Kayla until much later, and there was no Kayla-owned safe house. In my original thinking, the Gibsons would discover they were about to be attacked on their own. Kayla would never rush into Elias's backyard to warn him.

And this is why I introduced the noble roadrunner into the story.

I now live in an area very similar to Elias's (although my home isn't nearly as nice as his, or as private) and I've seen any number of coyotes and scorpions and roadrunners. And roadrunners truly are the coolest animal ever, worthy of being included in any book.

My plan was that Elias would sing the roadrunner's praises while he and Connor were on the way to his house. Later, he and his son would be looking through binoculars, hoping to spot one, when they would spot a bad guy instead, and realize they were being attacked.

So I began writing the roadrunner piece one morning. That night, I was walking the dog with my wife, and had the identical conversation with her that Elias has with Connor in the book. Does the roadrunner say meep meep, or does it say beep beep? Eventually, I had to Google it to find out for sure, but my wife got a kick out of our exchange. "You're writing a novel that you hope will cheer your fans up, but might alienate them," she said during this discussion, "and all you want to talk about is whether a cartoon character says meep meep or beep beep. Really?"

I love my wife, but she doesn't always *get* me. Great artists are rarely appreciated in their own time. :)

As a tribute to her, I had Connor express the same kind of dismay in his discussion with Elias. "I can't believe you've done something that will change the world, and this is the discussion were having. Beep beep or meep meep."

In any event, when I changed my mind and decided to bring Kayla into the novel right away, and have her warn Elias, I no longer had the need for anything roadrunner related in the novel. I know I should have cut this section. But I didn't. I really do like this bird, and I got such a kick out of the conversation I had with my wife that I left it in, even though it no longer serves its original purpose.

I guess I just have a soft spot for roadrunners and Elias Gibsons.

Finally, two last items. First, motion-activated night lights are painfully real. My wife somehow learned about them, and went a little wild. I'm pretty sure I have enough motion activated night lights plugged in around my home to illuminate entire cities.

Second, one day, as I neared completion of the novel, I left my home office, passed my wife in the kitchen, and entered our garage.

When I was inside for several minutes without the garage door up, my wife came in to investigate, only to find my head on the floor of the passenger's side of my car, and my hands buried under the seat.

"Lose something?" she asked quizzically.

"Nah. I'm just trying to figure out the best way to immobilize a prisoner in the front seat of a car."

"Of course you are," she said with a bemused smile, leaving me alone once again.

By now, she's used to seeing me do unexpected things. This wasn't nearly as odd as the time she caught me with a steak knife taped to my thigh, running around the house to see if it would cut me (I began very gingerly, and it didn't cut me, by the way, so I allowed one of my characters to do the same).

But getting back to immobilizing a prisoner, the good news is that I did figure it out. I knew my wife's SUV had handholds above the doors, but I had no idea the same was true of my four-door sedan (I'd only been driving it for three years, so how could I possibly know?).

Things really are getting better

I've included a lot of information in this novel that speaks to how much better the world has become on any number of measures—and why we think it's the opposite. The books I had Paige list in the novel are the books I used as references while writing it. I'll walk through these in a moment.

The facts in these books are difficult to dispute, and really do show how so many key aspects of our lives have improved.

While I was writing *Veracity*, I cut myself hiking, and went to buy a box of Band-Aids at the drug store. Talk about *abundance*. I soon found myself lost in a maze of adhesive bandage choices. It was impossible to stare at this wall of adhesive bandages and not get a sense of how things have changed. When I was a kid, in the time of the dinosaur, you had about two choices. Reminds me of Henry Ford's famous quote about his Model T: "You can choose any color you like, as long as it's black."

But today, the choices are endless. I found adhesive bandages in dozens of sizes and shapes. Some were flexible, or fabric, or had waterproof adhesive. They came in different pigments to match skin color. Some had extra padding, or medicated padding, or who knows what else.

I decided that any society that can offer such a bewildering number of adhesive bandage choices has to be doing *something* right (and don't even get me started on the number of toothbrush options).

And after having this revelation, I came across a compelling section of the book, *Factfulness*, by Hans Rosling, which made a similar point, only much better, by looking at guitar consumption:

EXCERPT: 4.2 million babies died in 2014. But this number was 14.4 million in 1950, when the population was much less than half. It is hard to see any of this global progress by looking out your window. But if you listen carefully, you can hear a child practicing the guitar or piano. That child has not died in childbirth or early childhood, is not wallowing in poverty, and is instead experiencing the joy and freedom of making music. Culture and freedom, the goals of development, can be hard to measure, but guitars per capita is a good proxy. And boy, has that improved, from 200 per million people in 1962 to 11,000 per million in 2014, a 55-fold increase. With beautiful statistics like these, how can anyone say the world is getting worse?

For those of you who would like to read more about this subject—after you've finished all of my novels, of course :)—I can recommend the five books I read while doing research for *Seeker* and *Veracity*. All are well written, and extremely eye-opening. They are:

1. *The Rational Optimist: How Prosperity Evolves*, by Matt Ridley
2. *Factfulness: Ten Reasons We're Wrong About the World—and Why Things Are Better Than You Think*, by Hans Rosling.
3. *The Better Angels of our Nature: Why Violence Has Declined*, by Steven Pinker
4. *Enlightenment: The Case for Reason, Science, Humanism, and Progress*, also by Steven Pinker
5. *Abundance: The Future is Better Than you Think*, by Peter H. Diamandis and Steven Kotler

Of the five, if you could only choose one, I would choose *Factfulness*, and if you could only choose two, *Factfulness* and *The Rational Optimist*.

In terms of sheer amount of data, *Enlightenment* and *Factfulness* both have endless graphs showing improvements on endless dimensions, with *Factfulness* being a much easier read for the lay person. These were two new books I read just for this novel, so were not mentioned in *Seeker*.

Just to give you a sense of content, here are a few excerpts from FACTFULNESS and ENLIGHTENMENT:

FACTFULNESS EXCERPT: I have tested audiences from all around the world and from all walks of life: medical students, teachers, scientists, journalists, activists, and even senior political decision makers [on basic facts about worldwide poverty, literacy, etc.] These are highly educated people who take an interest in the world. But most of them—a stunning majority of them—get most of the answers wrong. Some of the most appalling results come from a group of Nobel laureates and medical researchers. It is not a question of intelligence. Everyone seems to get the world devastatingly wrong. [So wrong that a chimpanzee choosing answers at random will consistently outguess any group of humans.]

What's more, the chimps' errors would be random, whereas the human errors all tend to be in one direction. Every group of people I ask thinks the world is more frightening, more violent, and more hopeless—in short, more dramatic—than it really is.

This book is my very last battle in my lifelong mission to fight devastating global ignorance. It is my last attempt to make an impact on the world: to change people's ways of thinking, calm their irrational fears, and redirect their energies into constructive activities.

ENLIGHTENMENT EXCERPT: Is the world really falling apart? In this elegant assessment of the human condition in the third millennium, cognitive scientist and public intellectual Steven Pinker urges us to step back from the gory headlines and prophecies of doom, which play to our psychological biases. Instead, follow the data:

In seventy-five jaw-dropping graphs, Pinker shows that life, health, prosperity, safety, peace, knowledge, and happiness are on the rise, not just in the West, but worldwide.

I hope the information in *Veracity*, and in these notes, will help you better understand the tremendous improvements the world has seen in the past several decades, and the equally tremendous forces working to keep us pessimistic and in despair.

And if this doesn't help, I strongly encourage you to take a break from all news for a week, including social media feeds, and see how you feel. If you're like me, you'll find it difficult to let go, but will see significant improvements in your state of mind and contentment once you do.

Is perfect fake video possible?

The short answer is: not quite yet, but very soon.

The long answer is: uh-oh, we're really, really screwed (okay, maybe both of these are short answers).

In any event, it's coming, and it won't require the genius of a Kayla Keller to use, either. Here is an excerpt from an alarming piece published in 2018 by *MIT Technology Review*, entitled, "Fake America Great Again—inside the race to catch the worryingly real fakes that can be made using artificial intelligence."

EXCERPT: Guess what? I just got hold of some embarrassing video footage of Texas senator Ted Cruz singing and gyrating to Tina Turner. His political enemies will have great fun showing it during the midterms.

Okay, I'll admit it—I created the video myself. But here's the troubling thing: making it required very little video-editing skill. I downloaded and configured software that uses machine learning to perform a convincing digital face-swap. The resulting video, known as a deepfake, shows Cruz's distinctively droopy eyes stitched onto the features of actor Paul Rudd doing lip-sync karaoke. It isn't perfect—there's something a little off—but it might fool some people.

Photo fakery is far from new, but artificial intelligence will completely change the game. Until recently only a big-budget movie studio could carry out a video face-swap, and it would probably have cost millions of dollars. AI now makes it possible for anyone with a decent computer and a few hours to spare to do the same thing. Further machine-learning advances will make even more complex deception possible—and make fakery harder to spot.

These advances threaten to further blur the line between truth and fiction in politics. Already the internet accelerates and reinforces the dissemination of disinformation through fake social-media accounts. "Alternative facts" and conspiracy theories are common and widely believed. Now imagine throwing new kinds of real-looking fake videos into the mix: politicians mouthing nonsense or ethnic insults, or getting caught behaving inappropriately on video—except it never really happened.

In April, a supposed BBC news report announced the opening salvos of a nuclear conflict between Russia and NATO. The clip, which began circulating on the messaging platform WhatsApp, showed footage of missiles blasting off as a newscaster told viewers that the German city of Mainz had been destroyed along with parts of Frankfurt.

It was, of course, entirely fake, and the BBC rushed to denounce it. The video wasn't generated using AI, but it showed the power of fake video, and how it can spread rumors at warp speed. The proliferation of AI programs will make such videos far easier to make, and even more convincing.

Perhaps the greatest risk with this new technology is not that it will be misused by state hackers or political saboteurs, but that it will further undermine truth and objectivity itself. If you can't tell a fake from reality, then it becomes easy to question the authenticity of anything. This already serves as a way for politicians to evade accountability.

I'll leave this horrifying section with one last excerpt, which demonstrates just how screwed, *literally*, we really are. It's from a 2017 piece in *Artificial Intelligence* entitled, "AI creates fake celebrity porn for Redditors to fap to."

EXCERPT: AI is a game-changer. Never in the history of human existence has there existed a technology with the power to wipe out cancer and end traffic accidents. And fortunately for us, some of the smartest people in the world are working on ways to tap AI's immense power to do just that.

Others are using it to create fake videos of celebrities getting fucked.

So far the tool's creator has produced videos of Gal Gadot, Taylor Swift, Emma Watson, and Scarlett Johansson, each with varying levels of success. None are going to fool the discerning watcher, but all are close enough to hint at a terrifying future . . .

. . . all the algorithm needs to create convincing fakes is enough source material—which shouldn't be a problem considering the average millennial will snap 25,000 selfies over the course of their lifetime.

Is perfect lie detection possible?

Everything in the novel about lies and lying is as accurate as I could make it (*Veracity*, of course, is not). While I read any number of articles and books about lying and lie detection while writing *Veracity*, I relied on two books more than any others. These are:

1. *Telling Lies: Clues to Deceit in the Marketplace, Politics, and Marriage*, by Paul Ekman
2. *Spy the Lie*, by Philip Houston, Michael Floyd, and Susan Carnicero.

You may recall that Paul Ekman was referenced in the novel as the researcher who first discovered micro-expressions. Ekman, now Professor Emeritus at the University of California, San Francisco, devoted most of his career trying to understand how lying is reflected in facial expressions. He also developed the Facial Action Coding System, which categorizes thousands of subtle facial expressions, micro and macro alike.

With respect to perfect lie detection, I doubt that this can ever be achieved. On the other hand, *ever* is a long time, and there are any number of scientists working on such systems, although none are quite as elegant and hands-free as Veracity.

An article in *Salon* in 2011, entitled "The Quest to Build the Perfect Lie Detector," describes how the US Department of Defense dramatically increased its spending on perfecting lie detection after 9/11, and noted at the time that about fifty labs were working on the problem in the US alone.

Below is an excerpt from the Ekman book, suggesting that lie detection accuracy levels of up to ninety percent are already possible in certain circumstances.

EXCERPT (Page 350): All the observable behavior on more than one hundred subjects was measured: facial movements, gaze, head movements, gestures, and both the words and the sound of their voice. The statistical analysis furnished two important findings not available from our earlier studies. First, a very high level of accuracy—around 90 percent—was achieved in identifying who had lied, but only when multiple behavioral measures were considered. No one source—neither face, body, voice, speech, nor skin temperature—when considered alone yielded such high results. The second finding was the single most important behavioral source, which alone enabled better than 70 percent accuracy, was facial expression.

Below is an excerpt from a more recent article (2018) about some of the current efforts to invent machines that can better detect lies. This was in the *San Diego Union Tribune*, and is entitled, "The truth about lying: we live in a golden age of lies—and lie-detecting."

EXCERPT: About 20 years ago, UC San Diego's Michael Kalichman began studying the ethics of scientific researchers. "I had this loose idea that most scientists were good people," he said, "and a very small percentage were deceptive, lying, cheating, horrible people.

"I was pretty naive. Everybody lies. And we don't think of ourselves as bad people," said Kalichman, who founded UC San Diego's

Research Ethics Program in 1997. "To some degree, I'm just going to say this is the human condition."

While fibbing is as old as Cain, we live in a golden age of lying—and lie-detecting. Our "post-truth" society with its alternative facts is also creating new ways to uncover deceit. New high-tech tools measure everything from tell-tale eye movements to revealing patterns in the brain.

Recent developments are so intriguing, some foresee a future in which computers can detect our lies, even our unspoken emotions.

"This is something of a holy grail," said Lawrence Hinman, a University of San Diego philosophy professor emeritus, "to find a way for machines to immediately tell whether someone is lying or telling the truth."

Since 1921, though, technology has promised faster paths to the truth. By measuring blood pressure and respiration, the polygraph machine could tell when a subject was lying.

That was the theory, at least, but the lie-detector machine is still so suspect its findings are not admissible in court. Still, the search for an infallible truth-hunting device continues.

Pupil dilation; blushing; a stilted, informal tone—the stress of lying manifests itself in numerous ways.

"You look at all these things in tandem," said SDSU's Aaron Elkins, a researcher who is developing a promising new lie detector, AVATAR, the Automated Virtual Agent for Truth Assessments in Real Time. Meant for airports and border crossings, AVATAR is a kiosk whose computer screen shows a "virtual agent" who quizzes travelers.

Your reactions—changes in heart and respiratory rates, pupil dilation, blink rate, eye movement—are more revealing than your answers, and AVATAR instantly registers these.

Truthful Brain Corp. uses a functional Magnetic Resonance Imaging machine (fMRI) to photograph the brain while a subject answers questions by pushing "yes" or "no" buttons. In fMRI scans supplied by Huizenga, the brain of someone telling the truth appears in shades of black and white. Lies show up as red and yellow flares.

As sophisticated as these approaches are, some predict lie-detecting computers that have programmed themselves to sniff out truths we can't imagine.

"The computer's reasoning may no longer be transparent enough for humans to understand how it reached that conclusion," Hinman said. "We will not know why the computer thinks we are not telling the truth."

I'll leave this section with one last excerpt from the Ekman book, just to provide additional food for thought. While researching lying, I found any number of fascinating insights, but in the interest of brevity, I'll leave it with just this.

EXCERPT (page 23): Lying is such a central characteristic of life that better understanding of it is relevant to almost all human affairs. Some might shudder at that statement, because they view lying as reprehensible. I do not share that view. It is too simple to hold that no one in any relationship must ever lie: nor would I prescribe that every lie be unmasked. Advice columnist Ann Landers has a point when she advises her readers that truth can be used as a bludgeon, cruelly inflicting pain. Lies can be cruel too, but all lies aren't. Some lies are altruistic. And no lie catcher should too easily presume the right to expose every lie. Some lies are harmless, even humane. Unmasking certain lies may humiliate the victim or a third party.

Kayla the psychopath

Those of you who have read my novels know that most of my female characters are brilliant, heroic, bad assed, and competent. Many women have complimented me on these strong characters, and I haven't had any complaints from men either.

So creating a female character who is a villain—worse, who is a *psychopath*—is unusual for me, and I'm hoping that this was a twist that readers didn't see coming.

In doing research for my early novels, I became somewhat of a lay expert on psychopathy (psy-kop-uh-thee), so much so that I wrote a number of articles on the subject and was a guest on dozens of radio shows, discussing the psychopaths among us.

In September of 2013, I guested on a show called *Coast to Coast* for two hours, speaking about psychopathy and a number of other topics. Since this show is heard by almost three million listeners, I got quite a few emails afterward, including a number from psychopaths who wanted to meet with me and tell me their stories. These I very politely refused. As much fun as it would be to welcome self-proclaimed psychopaths into my life, I thought I would take a pass.

What I found most interesting were emails I received that suggested I was being sexist in my presentation. Especially since I realized they were right.

In my writings and speaking engagements, my examples of psychopaths all tended to be male. I realized I had a slight subconscious bias. When I thought of psychopaths, I thought of men. And while a very large percentage of all violent crimes are committed by males, women can be psychopaths also.

To underscore this point, here are a few of the many emails I received after the show:

EMAIL: Douglas, I was fortunate enough to hear you on Coast to Coast Thursday morning. I've been married to a perfect Psychopath for 33 years and I am living in hell. I believe she could never be diagnosed by a professional, she is way to manipulative, charming and a master of masters at deceit, endless lies and convincing twisted beliefs. These people are bullet proof when they remain on the right side of the law.

They can frame you faster than you can think when they believe they're threatened.

Never ever cross one.

They have no heart, feelings, emotions, morals and are like a robot. They cannot be reasoned with, they have no virtues or value systems through which to reach them.

She happens to be beautiful and her disease combined with physical attributes make her more deadly than any gun.

Her powerful attributes can weaken and destroy my best offenses and defenses faster than I can deploy them. She's wrecked our family. Totally brainwashed our children and put me through a living hell. I believe her father was scared to death of her until his death.

You appear to be one of the best versed experts in this field I've heard.

You seemed to lean towards men being more inclined to be Psychopaths (on the show), but women are far more gifted in this area and can hide it better than any man could ever hope to accomplish (I think) . Women possess the three most dangerous of attributes, "Beauty, Sex and better communication skills."

EMAIL: Hi, I really enjoyed last night's show with Douglas Richards. When he was talking about Psychopaths in the work place—something just clicked! I was working in a job with a woman whose traits were exactly like what Douglas was detailing. She was so bad the environment was toxic. I was eventually let go because she flat out lied to the boss (of whom she had wrapped around her finger). It was a sales position. She would brag about how she essentially talked customers into spending thousands. She was just an awful person and I feel bad for anyone that has to work with her or anyone like her!

Keep up the good work! Thanks.

EMAIL: Hi Doug, I knew someone in high school that was a psychopath. She even admitted to me, after I caught on to the game (few people did), that she saw manipulation as a game and tried to convince me that it was fun and that I should do it too. What was crazy was that even when I told friends, who agreed, they would still fall for her games. They KNEW she was a habitual liar but were still able to be manipulated. The only way to deal with these people is figure they are lying every time you talk to them, and you can kind of get in their mindset to see what their goal is.

Slaughterbots (be very afraid)

I first learned about slaughterbots from several fans, who were kind enough to alert me to this technology and send me a link to the *Slaughterbots* video, which you can easily find by conducting a simple online search.

My fans thought that this technology was terrifying, and that I might be able to use it in a novel. They were right on both counts. I encourage you to see the video, as nothing demonstrates the horrific potential of the technology as powerfully as this video.

I've also shared an excerpt below from an article in *Space.Com* that I thought was interesting, entitled. "Slaughterbots Video Depicts a Dystopian Future of Autonomous Killer Drones."

EXCERPT: A graphic new video posits a very scary future in which swarms of killer microdrones are dispatched to kill political activists and US lawmakers. Armed with explosive charges, the palm-sized quadcopters use real-time data mining and artificial intelligence to find and kill their targets.

The makers of the seven-minute film titled *Slaughterbots* are hoping the startling dramatization will draw attention to what they view as a looming crisis—the development of lethal, autonomous weapons, which can select and fire on human targets without human guidance.

The Future of Life Institute, a nonprofit organization dedicated to mitigating existential risks posed by advanced technologies, including artificial intelligence, commissioned the film. Founded by a group of scientists and business leaders, the institute is backed by AI-skeptics Elon Musk and Stephen Hawking, among others.

"This short film is more than just speculation," said Stuart Russell, professor of computer science at the University of California, Berkeley, and a pioneer in the field of artificial intelligence. "It shows the results of integrating and miniaturizing technologies we already have."

Representatives from more than 70 countries are expected to attend the Geneva meeting on lethal autonomous weapons systems this week, according to a statement from the Campaign to Stop Killer Robots. Representatives from the scientific and technical communities will be stating their case to the assembled delegates.

"Allowing machines to choose to kill humans will be devastating to our security and our freedom," Russell says in a short commentary at the end of the video. "Thousands of my fellow researchers agree.

We have an opportunity to prevent the future you just saw, but the window to act is closing fast."

Tribalism (Social Identity Theory)

This is real, as are the experiments I described in the book. Anyone interested in exploring this subject in more depth can find more by Googling Henri Tajfel, and/or Social Identity Theory (the formal name of the concepts I discuss in the book).

While I had never read of these experiments until recently, they don't surprise me. For decades now I've questioned my own sports rooting habits (not that I've changed them much). I watch a lot of tennis, and I tend to root for the American player. But I've often asked myself why. What if the American player is a jerk, and the other player is a great guy? Should I really be rooting for players based solely on their passports?

The answer I've come to, over and over again, is no, I shouldn't.

And yet it's a hard habit to break. I live in San Diego, so I root for San Diego teams. I live in America, so I root for American teams. Vigorously.

Just because you know that tribalism is working, doesn't nullify it entirely. On the other hand, this knowledge does help. There have been occasional cases when this introspection has allowed me to ignore geography and root for a competitor I believe is more deserving.

So, who knows, maybe it's possible to teach an old Doug new tricks, after all.

Contact lenses as a major tech platform

The idea of turning contact lenses into the next great technology platform is real, and being worked on now. I've used smart contact lenses now in several of my novels. So for those of you who have already read about them in previous editions of my author notes, this section won't offer anything new, and I'd recommend that you skip ahead to the next topic.

If you haven't read other novels of mine in which this tech makes an appearance, I can tell you that I'm in love with the concept of smart contact lenses (which is why I use this tech so often). If, and when, this will become a reality is unclear, but it's a very cool idea.

I have to admit, when I first used these lenses in a novel, I never would have dreamed that night vision might be a possible feature. So when I read that this capability was actually being worked on at the University of Michigan, I was blown away.

I'll leave this section with excerpts from a few articles that I found particularly interesting and relevant (but that I've used before). The first is from an article on *Trustedreviews.com* (*news*) in 2016, entitled, "Samsung's smart contact lenses turn your eye into a computer."

EXCERPT: The human eye is an incredible feat of natural engineering, but it's not smart enough for Samsung. Samsung has been granted a patent for smart contact lenses that would revolutionize the way we see.

The filing details a smart lens that would imbue a user's eye with computing capability.

The lens would come equipped with an antenna, presumably to connect to a peripheral device like a smartphone, which would likely provide the brunt of the computing heft.

Samsung says users will be able to control the lenses through gestures like blinking, which will be registered by tiny, embedded sensors that detect eye movement.

The second excerpt is from an article in *Computerworld* in 2016, entitled, "Why a Smart Contact Lens is the Ultimate Wearable."

EXCERPT: Smart contact lenses sound like science fiction. But there's already a race to develop technology for the contact lenses of the future—ones that will give you super-human vision and will offer heads-up displays, video cameras, medical sensors and much more. In fact, these products are already being developed.

Sounds unreal, right? But it turns out that eyeballs are the perfect place to put technology.

Smart contact lenses are like implants but they don't require surgery and can usually be removed or inserted by the user. They're neither on nor under the skin full time. They're exposed to both air and the body's internal chemistry.

Contact lenses sit on the eye, and so can enhance vision. They're exposed to both light and the mechanical movement of blinking, so they can harvest energy.

What you need to know is that smart contact lenses are inevitable for all these reasons.

University of Michigan scientists are building a contact lens that can give soldiers and others the ability to see in the dark using thermal imaging. The technology uses graphene, a single layer of carbon atoms, to pick up the full spectrum of light, including ultraviolet light.

Sony applied for a patent for a smart contact lens that can record video. You control it by blinking your eyes. According to Sony's patent, sensors in the lens can tell the difference between voluntary and involuntary blinks. When it detects a deliberate blink, it records a video. Sony's contact lens would be powered by piezoelectric sensors that convert eye movement into electrical power. It would involve extremely small versions of all the parts of a modern digital camera—an auto-focusing lens, a CPU, an antenna and even on-lens storage.

DeepMind and AlphaZero

I don't have much to add here in addition to what was already described in the novel, but if you have interest in learning more, a web search on the words "AlphaZero" or "DeepMind" will provide plenty of reading.

AlphaZero spent four hours learning chess and destroyed the best chess-playing computer in the world, which routinely destroys the best human beings. If you're like me, you find this awe-inspiring and wonderful, but also highly troubling. The human brain is still unmatched in its power and complexity, but it's hard to imagine that this supremacy will last forever. And on the day this is no longer true, given that computer "thought" can ultimately operate a million times faster than human thought, we could find ourselves becoming obsolete in a hurry.

Blocking facial recognition

As was presented in the novel, infrared LED light can fool or blind facial recognition cameras. But as facial recognition and camera technology improves, these blockers will have to improve also.

Here is an excerpt from an article in *Vocativ.com* that I hope you'll find interesting, entitled, "Facial Recognition Is Everywhere—But So Are Tools To Defeat It."

EXCERPT: Apart from celebrities and high-profile fugitives, most people take for granted the ability to walk around in public without being identified by strangers. But more recently, this basic concept of public anonymity has been rapidly eroding.

Thanks to the rise of social media, ubiquitous cameras, internet-connected devices, and massive police facial recognition databases, more than half the U.S. adult population can now be near-instantly identified and tracked on the street simply by revealing their face. In response, privacy-minded engineers and activists have been fighting back with tech of their own.

In 2012, Professor Isao Echizen and his colleagues unveiled a prototype of the Privacy Visor, a bizarre-looking pair of glasses that defeats face detection systems by blasting camera sensors with beams of near-infrared light, which are invisible to the human eye.

The visor worked, but it wasn't exactly subtle or flattering to wear. Now, after years of development, Echizen has unveiled an improved version of the Privacy Visor that doesn't require power or use any electronics at all. Instead, the new model uses repeating white patterns printed on a plastic transparency. The dense patterns reflect light back at the camera's sensor, causing enough noise to prevent many algorithms from successfully detecting faces.

When I got my hands on one of Echizen's Privacy Visors, I had almost no difficulty fooling the face detection schemes used by popular social media platforms. The puppy faces and other cute video filters provided by Snapchat's face-detecting Lenses quickly disappeared after lowering the visor onto the center of my face. Facebook's algorithm also didn't detect any faces in uploaded photos of people wearing the visor from various angles and distances.

Self-driving cars

Google "driverless cars" or "autonomous vehicles," and you'll see just how many companies are working on this technology, and just how far it's come. Obviously, a vehicle like Kayla's twenty-million-dollar dry cleaning van isn't possible yet, but I think it's safe to say that there will come a day when it is.

Ten years ago, I thought a self-driving car wouldn't be possible for three or four decades, if ever. Which just goes to show that even those who follow science and technology as closely as I do can be easily surprised by the pace and ingenuity of human invention.

China, real estate, and civil rights

As far as I know, everything written in the novel about China, and the poor state of its civil rights, is accurate. As I already mentioned, I had thought China was becoming ever more benign, but the research I did suggests that this isn't the case.

Before I continue, I should mention that it's true that Chinese citizens are the top foreign buyers of homes in the US, and most often buy in cash. If you're interested in learning more about this, you shouldn't have any trouble finding information online.

But getting back to civil rights, according to an article in *Time Magazine* entitled, "Five Ways China Has Become More Repressive Under President Xi Jinping," China ranked 176 out of 180 countries in 2016 on a world index of press freedom, and was "the world's worst jailer of the press" for the second year in a row.

Just to give you some additional background on the current state of affairs, I've provided excerpts from two of the many articles I read about Chinese civil rights while doing research for *Veracity*.

The first is from *Human Rights Watch, World Report 2018*, entitled, "China: events of 2017."

EXCERPT: The broad and sustained offensive on human rights that started after President Xi Jinping took power five years ago showed no sign of abating in 2017. The death of Nobel Peace Prize laureate Liu Xiaobo in a hospital under heavy guard in July highlighted the Chinese government's deepening contempt for rights. The near future for human rights appears grim, especially as Xi is expected to remain in power at least until 2022.

The Chinese government, which already oversees one of the strictest online censorship regimes in the world, limited the provision of censorship circumvention tools and strengthened ideological control over education and mass media in 2017. Schools and state media incessantly tout the supremacy of the Chinese Communist Party, and, increasingly, of President Xi Jinping as "core" leader.

Authorities subjected more human rights defenders—including foreigners—to show trials in 2017, airing excerpted forced confessions and court trials on state television and social media. Police ensured the detainees' compliance by torturing some of them, denying them access to lawyers of their choice, and holding them incommunicado for months.

In Xinjiang, a nominally autonomous region with 11 million Turkic Muslim Uyghurs, authorities stepped up mass surveillance and their security presence despite the lack of evidence demonstrating an organized threat. They also adopted new policies denying Uyghurs cultural and religious rights.

In 2017, authorities continued politically motivated prosecutions of human rights activists and lawyers who were rounded up in a nationwide crackdown that began in July 2015. The government also tried to eliminate the country's few independent human rights news websites by jailing their founders.

The government restricts religious practice to five officially recognized religions in officially approved religious premises. Authorities retain control over religious bodies' personnel appointments, publications, finances, and seminary applications. The government classifies many religious groups outside its control as "evil cults," and subjects members to police harassment, torture, arbitrary detention, and imprisonment.

According to a report by World Economic Forum, China ranked 100th out of 144 countries for gender parity in 2017, falling for the ninth consecutive year since 2008, when it ranked 57th. Women and girls in China continue to confront sexual abuse and harassment, employment discrimination, and domestic violence.

I'll leave this section with an excerpt from a 2018 article in *The Atlantic*, entitled, "China's Surveillance State Should Scare Everyone: The country is perfecting a vast network of digital espionage as a means of social control—with implications for democracies worldwide."

EXCERPT: Imagine a society in which you are rated by the government on your trustworthiness. Your "citizen score" follows you wherever you go. A high score allows you access to faster internet service or a fast-tracked visa to Europe. If you make political posts online without a permit, or question or contradict the government's official narrative on current events, however, your score decreases. To calculate the score, private companies working with your government constantly trawl through vast amounts of your social media and online shopping data.

When you step outside your door, your actions in the physical world are also swept into the dragnet: The government gathers an enormous collection of information through the video cameras placed on your street and all over your city.

This society may seem dystopian, but it isn't farfetched: It may be China in a few years. The country is racing to become the first to implement a pervasive system of algorithmic surveillance. Harnessing advances in artificial intelligence and data mining and storage to construct detailed profiles on all citizens, China's communist party-state is developing a "citizen score" to incentivize "good" behavior. A vast accompanying network of surveillance cameras will constantly monitor citizens' movements, purportedly to reduce crime and terrorism. While the expanding Orwellian eye may improve "public safety," it poses a chilling new threat to civil liberties in a country that already has one of the most oppressive and controlling governments in the world.

China's evolving algorithmic surveillance system will rely on the security organs of the communist party-state to filter, collect, and analyze staggering volumes of data flowing across the internet. Justifying controls in the name of national security and social stability, China has instituted a content-filtering Great Firewall, which prohibits foreign internet sites including Google, Facebook, and The New York Times. According to Freedom House, China's level of internet freedom is already the worst on the planet. Now, the Communist Party of China is finally building the extensive, multilevel data-gathering system it has dreamed of for decades.

While the Chinese government has long scrutinized individual citizens for evidence of disloyalty to the regime, only now is it beginning to develop comprehensive, constantly updated, and granular records on each citizen's political persuasions, comments, associations, and even consumer habits.

Well beyond the realm of online consumer purchasing, your political involvement could also heavily affect your score: Posting political opinions without prior permission or even posting true news that the Chinese government dislikes could decrease your rank.

Even more worrying is that the government will be technically capable of considering the behavior of a Chinese citizen's friends and family in determining his or her score. For example, it is possible that your friend's anti-government political post could lower your own score. Thus, the scoring system would isolate dissidents from their friends and the rest of society, rendering them complete pariahs. Your score might even determine your access to certain privileges taken for granted in the U.S., such as a visa to travel abroad or even the right to travel by train or plane within the country. One internet privacy expert warns: "What China is doing here is selectively breeding its population to select against the trait of critical, independent thinking."

This planned data-focused social credit system is only one facet of China's rapidly expanding system of algorithmic surveillance. Another is a sprawling network of technologies, especially surveillance cameras, to monitor people's physical movements. In 2015, China's national police force—the Ministry of Public Safety—called for the creation of an "omnipresent, completely connected, always on and fully controllable" national video surveillance network. One estimate puts the number of cameras in China at 176 million today, with a plan to have 450 million installed by 2020. One hundred percent of Beijing is now blanketed by surveillance cameras, according to the Beijing Public Safety Bureau.

The stated goal of this system is to capture and deter criminals. More ominous, though, are the likely punishments that will be inflicted on people who associate with dissidents or critics, who circulate a petition or hold up a protest sign, or who simply wind up in the wrong place at the wrong time. Thus, the installation of an all-seeing-eye for the government alarms civil liberties and privacy advocates worldwide. The government already constantly monitors the cell phones and social media of human-rights activists in the name of "stability maintenance." A video surveillance system would enable further pervasive and repressive surveillance.

China's experiments with digital surveillance pose a grave new threat to freedom of expression on the internet and other human rights in China. Increasingly, citizens will refrain from any kind of independent or critical expression for fear that their data will be read or their movements recorded—and penalized—by the government. And that is exactly the point of the program. Moreover, what emerges in China will not stay in China. Its repressive technologies have a pattern of diffusing to other authoritarian regimes around the world. For this reason—not to mention concern for the hundreds of millions of people in China whose meager freedom will be further diminished—democracies around the world must monitor and denounce this sinister creep toward an Orwellian world.

3) Author bio and list of books

Douglas E. Richards is the *New York Times* and *USA Today* bestselling author of *WIRED* and numerous other novels (see list below). A former biotech executive, Richards earned a BS in microbiology from the Ohio State University, a master's degree in genetic engineering from the University of Wisconsin (where he engineered mutant viruses now named after him), and an MBA from the University of Chicago.

In recognition of his work, Richards was selected to be a "special guest" at San Diego Comic-Con International, along with such icons as Stan Lee and Ray Bradbury. His essays have been featured in *National Geographic*, the *BBC*, *the Australian Broadcasting Corporation*, *Earth & Sky*, *Today's Parent*, and many others.

The author has two children and currently lives with his wife and dog in San Diego, California.

You can friend Richards on Facebook at Douglas E. Richards Author, visit his website at douglaserichards.com, and write to him at douglaserichards1@gmail.com

Near Future Science Fiction Thrillers by Douglas E. Richards
WIRED (Wired 1)
AMPED (Wired 2)
MIND'S EYE (Nick Hall 1)
BRAINWEB (Nick Hall 2)
MIND WAR (Nick Hall 3)
QUANTUM LENS
SPLIT SECOND (Split Second 1)
TIME FRAME (Split Second 2)
GAME CHANGER
INFINITY BORN
SEEKER
VERACITY

Kids Science Fiction Thrillers (9 and up, enjoyed by kids and adults alike)
TRAPPED (Prometheus Project 1)
CAPTURED (Prometheus Project 2)
STRANDED (Prometheus Project 3)
OUT OF THIS WORLD
THE DEVIL'S SWORD

34456447R00232

Made in the USA
Lexington, KY
23 March 2019